To: Guy Murphy

(signatures)

Summary

Three young women from Chicago journey to the Holy Land in search of the site of the Crucifixion. On their last day in Jerusalem, Maria, one of the young women, slips and falls while exploring a hill. As she falls, a sliver embeds itself in her finger.

Amazingly, as her friends watch, her apparently broken finger straightens itself. The area around the sliver provides a warm tingle when touched. Following their adventure, the three take a taxi back to their hotel.

A number of events ensue, including an aborted skyjacking of their plane, unexplained healings of people they encounter, plus numerous other happenings. Maria is instrumental in founding a battered women's shelter, and as the story unfolds, conflicts with drug dealers and other unscrupulous people develop.

Is the sliver a Relic of the Cross of the Crucifixion?

Are forces of evil thwarted and the miracles attributable to the sliver?

Follow the adventures of these young women in Chicagoland as they encounter good and evil.

Review of Relic of the Cross

"I'm not usually a book reader, except when I find one about Saints. The author offered me the opportunity to read this book and it was spellbinding. It kept my interest from start to finish. I could not put it down.

Although a work of fiction, it is also very realistic and a feel good book, which should motivate people to help others less fortunate. It should bring out the hero in all of us.

My congratulations and sincere admiration to Tom on his magnificent work, which will hopefully, get people thinking and acting in the right direction.

This book truly is the Triumph of Good over Evil."

With Admiration,

Sir Richard Montalbano, Sr.

Knights Grand Cross of the Holy Sepulchre of Jerusalem

P. 194

About the Author

Tom and his brother John were deposited in an orphanage at the ages of 8 and 3, after their mother passed away. Their father came to visit for a couple hours twice a month.

After graduation, Tom found a job at a bank, after passing a chilling and scary lie detector test. Have you ever stolen a piece of bubble gum? Oh, the guilt memories can create.

After a few years, Uncle Sam pointed his finger at Tom and he was drafted into the Army. He was then directed to Vietnam, with the 1st Cavalry. While in Vietnam, Tom's father passed away and he came home to raise his brother.

Evidently, the people at LaSalle Bank liked him and he was rehired, upon release from the Army. Another lie detector testing, fortunately, was not required.

Tom enjoyed a career in banking; got married and was rewarded with the most wonderful gift, when his daughter Samantha was born. She married a wonderful man, Randy, and she continues to be the joy of Tom's life.

He met Chelle a few years ago, after each had been divorced for a number of years. They enjoy a relationship in business and in life. Tom says, "Chelle does the hard work and I try to keep up with her."

Relic of the Cross is Tom's first publishing effort, classified as Religious Fiction. A sequel is in the works along with another genre of fiction.

Author's Dedication
This Book is dedicated to:
My Daughter, Samantha
My Love, Chelle
My Brother, John
My Mother, Rita & Father, John

ISBN-13:978-1497320536
ISBN-10:-1497320534

Acknowledgements

Special thanks to my daughter Samantha and my companion in business and in life, Michelle (Chelle) for their inspirations and support. Also to my brother John, who has always been there through thick and thin.

Thank you to Russell Newhouse, retired pilot, for his scintillating depiction of the landing, during a storm, of Flight 238.

Appreciation to Richard Montalbano for providing the opportunity to photograph the picture of the crucifixion that appears on the cover.

Thank you to Shania Twain for the song title: "Man! I Feel Like a Woman."

Thank you to Sarah Brightman, Jose Cura and the London Symphony Orchestra for the song title "There for Me."

I want to express gratitude, for her wonderful contribution of editing and review, to Lisa Oddo.

Thank you, to Chelle O'Connell, for her assistance throughout the process of bringing this book to fruition and for writing the Book Summary.

Contents

Chapter 1 The Pilgrimage

The Sliver

A light rain spattered the ground, turning white gravel to a murky shade of gray. Ellie Mulcahey, Sydney Anderson and Maria Esparza were close friends since grade school. They were walking up a stone path to the top of a hill. This was their last day of vacation, before returning home.

Ellie Mulcahey, the adventurous one, decided to leave the path in favor of the grass. Sydney was quick to follow, leaving Maria behind. As they walked, they noticed a bald headed man at the bottom of the hill, snapping pictures of the surrounding hillside.

"Hey Sydney, someone's taking your picture again. You'll be on the internet before we get back to the hotel," Maria teased.

Sydney shrugged and shot a testy glance at her friend. They paid little heed to the man taking pictures. Both knew that Sydney was the one who was always having her picture taken. In reality, with her slim figure, tantalizing facial features, and husky voice, she was usually the one noticed first.

Ellie and Sydney as usual, took the lead. They had climbed a distance when Maria, who was trailing, gasped loudly. The others, looking back, could see their friend's arms flailing, as she lost her footing. Maria's left knee struck the crusty ground, shooting pain up her leg. She winced at the initial contact and prepared for the worst. Instinctively, she extended her arms, reaching forward to cushion her fall.

Another stab of pain erupted, as fingers of her right hand struck a dark object, jutting from the surface. She closed her eyes. The impact was intense, leaving her face only inches from the hard surface. Overcoming their shock, Ellie and Sydney ran back down the hill.

Maria opened her eyes, taking a moment to assess her situation. As her vision cleared, she focused on a large sliver of wood that partially protruded from her forefinger. Strangely, there was no pain. She sat upright and examined her finger. It was oddly out of place and broken.

Ellie reached the spot where Maria was sitting and reached out to examine her friend's hand. They were all in their last semester prior to obtaining their RN Certifications.

"Are you alright?" Ellie questioned.

"I'm a little shaken," Maria responded.

Sydney arrived a second later at Maria's other side. The intensity in her eyes expressed fear for her friend's well being.

"What happened," Sydney shouted.

In silence, Maria's eyes remained riveted on the sliver of dark wood. She felt a tingling sensation. Both friends followed Maria's eyes to the dark object.

Maria concentrated on her hand. Her finger remained at its odd angle. She tried to review the event in her mind. At first, the contact felt like a sting; then the pain subsided. The large sliver of wood had driven itself deeply into the skin of her forefinger.

Sydney looked around and saw the man taking pictures of them again with a telephoto lens. Although the women saw him, he never approached to help and when they looked again a few seconds later, he was walking away swiftly. Each thought his behavior a little strange.

Maria's friends helped her to stand. Of the three, Sydney was the tallest; Maria was of average height, petite and appeared to be a Natalie Wood look alike. Ellie was the stalwart and reliable one. She was of average height; chose not to wear makeup, and yet possessed a wonderfully dry sense of humor and could sing like few others.

Maria was a little unsteady as she reached to remove the sliver. When she touched it, she staggered as her friends reached to hold her steady. Ellie made them stop, so that she could examine Maria's finger more closely. Turning their attention to Maria's finger, something very peculiar happened. The sliver seemed to pass through the skin and lodge itself deeper into Maria's finger. The girls looked at their friend for a sign of pain. There was none. Before their eyes, the broken finger moved to a straight position again, in alignment with her other fingers. What was broken, no longer appeared to be. They all looked at each other; expecting to find some explanation, for what they just witnessed. No one had an answer. They touched their friend's finger and felt no bump in the surface of her skin. Each felt a warm tingle, as they touched the skin over the embedded sliver. Stunned silence prevailed.

Sydney finally asked. "Where did it come from?"

Their eyes followed Maria's arm as she pointed toward the area, where her hand had struck the object. A fragment of dark wood jutted above the surface of the ground. It was discernible from the surrounding rock by its color. The girls stared, their minds beginning to race. They continued to look between themselves and back to the ground.

They noticed the man with the camera down below. He clicked a few more pictures and then got in a car and drove away.

Sydney removed a pocketknife from her jeans pocket. Opening it, she reached for the piece of wood on the ground. As the blade touched it, they heard the sound of the blade scraping rock. If it was wood, it had petrified. The knife suddenly turned freezing cold. She quickly released her grip, letting the knife fall to the ground. They watched, as the color of the wood, faded back to that of the surrounding rock and sediment. In a few moments, it was no longer discernible from the landscape.

As they continued to stare at the ground, the wind started to blow and hailstones began a staccato beat upon the ground. Ellie quickly reached down to gather her knife, as the girls collectively, stepped quickly down the path, seeking shelter. They broke into a run as the hail beat more intensely.

Upon reaching the taxi stand, one cab was miraculously sitting in wait. Without questions, they opened the doors and flung themselves into the interior, soaking the upholstery. Ellie, being more of the tomboy type, took off her sweater and wrung it out on the taxi's floor. The others laughed. That was just like her.

The return trip to the small bed and breakfast was just as interesting as the original ride. The hail was pounding on the roof and windows of the cab. The driver was yelling at other drivers. Not knowing the language, the women could only guess what the driver was saying. Upon reaching their building, Sydney put some money in the driver's hand as each of the girls ran up the stairs and began removing their soaking wet clothing. Ellie and Sydney immediately started to prepare some hot tea. Maria wanted to dry her hair; but the others chided her about it, until she relented and joined them. Each of the women sat with a towel wrapped over their hair. They all wanted to examine Maria's finger again, to see the piece of wood, buried beneath the skin. She finally pulled her hand away and jokingly stood, parading her finger in the air.

"Didn't get this much attention from the two of you for the last two years," she said teasingly.

Sydney gave way to Ellie's effort to make tea. After all, Ellie was the homemaker and Sydney could not cook at all.

They knew it was a possibility, however remote, that they witnessed something miraculous. They took turns recounting written stories and articles of miracles, associated with the timbers of the cross. All that could be determined, is that time, would be the best informant for them.

Looking up from a book, Ellie asked Maria.

"Doesn't it hurt at all?"

"Not a bit," Maria replied.

"I would think it would be painful?" Sydney added.

"No, not at all," Maria said with a shrug.

"You will have it looked at when we get home," was Elle's final response on the subject, as she rose to gather her notes from the table.

"Anyone want to eat?" Ellie queried.

"Nah," Maria responded.

"Grab an orange for me," Sydney answered in her throaty voice.

Ellie and Maria skimmed through their notes to find a mention of the cross. Unable to develop any meaningful rhetoric, they did agree that what had happened to their friend must have some crucial meaning. On the other hand, Sydney wasn't so sure and remained skeptical. As time would pass, they would find how true their thoughts would be.

"Hey!" Ellie called to Sydney, flinging the orange before her friend looked up.

Sydney looked up causally; reached up and caught the round orb, on its downward arc. She had learned to catch, throw and hit when she played high school softball. The others marveled at her athletic ability. Sydney was the only one of the three that was married. She enjoyed teasing the others about finding men. She was tall and a little heavier than she cared to be yet well within the "get looks", range whenever she was in a public place. Her husband also enjoyed the attention she received. He was handsome in his own right, and they made a beautiful couple.

The pelting rain continued well into the evening. As night fell, the rain dissipated to a light shower. It was much too late for the girls to go back to the scene, as they had an early, 4:00AM flight on El AL in the morning.

Dinnertime

After warming up with the hot tea and drying their hair, they decided to eat at the little restaurant downstairs. At the door, Penta the waiter, greeted them and immediately led the women to their favorite booth. He had deformity of his face, the result of a stroke at the age of only thirty-two. One side of his face drooped as though there was no muscle.

He was obviously highly educated, yet found speaking difficult. As if the facial deformity wasn't enough, he walked with a noticeable limp. The man's personality outshined his physical condition. Much to his delight, the three pretty women treated him with courtesy and smiles on each visit. During dinner, they shared conversation about the events of the last week amid a few glasses of wonderful tasting wines, recommended by their astute waiter.

Sydney glanced at her watch and announced it was time to go, reminding her friends of their early flight in the morning. As Maria was paying the bill, their waiter who walked with a limp approached, holding Elle's hat. Maria reached for the hat and smiled at the man, thanking him. As she took the hat, she offered her hand and the waiter graciously accepted. Their hands touched. Maria again, felt a comfortable warm tingle. He bowed to her offering a smile as much as his facial muscles would allow and returned to clear off their table.

Later in the evening, the girls relaxed in the comfortable, overstuffed chairs. Each in turn raised her head, as the sound of sirens in the distance grew closer. Sydney rose and walked to the kitchen window. The flashing blue lights of a police vehicle mixed with bright orange flames that danced on the walls, through the back window of the apartment. Heavy black smoke began to billow into the air.

"Hey, c'mere," she said aloud to the others."

The girls responded quickly. They noticed a car in a raging inferno. Firefighters arrived and began scurrying about with hoses, dousing the sides of the building with water to prevent further damage. When the fire was out, the girls ran downstairs to see what had triggered the damage to the car. Thoughts of firebombs drifted through each of the women's minds. Although they had witnessed no turmoil during their stay, the thought was in the back of their minds.

Turning the corner of the building, they saw the small crowd of men standing in conversation. They were speaking quickly, with arms flying for emphasis. The words were in a foreign tongue and not discernible. They saw their waiter, Penta, standing in the center of the conversation.

They approached. Ellie, being the most outspoken and brazen of the three, tapped the man on the shoulder and proceeded to ask, "what happened?'

The waiter eagerly tried to explain. "My car caught fire." His diction was obviously a surprise to the women who had witnessed his difficulty with speech.

"Usually, when I leave, it takes a few minutes to get in the car and position myself for the drive. I have a problem with my leg, so it is very difficult getting in and out of the car'" he said excitedly.

"How did you get out without being burned then?" Ellie queried.

"I didn't start the car tonight," Penta said, shaking his head.

"Jason wanted a ride home, because his wife couldn't pick him up tonight, so I asked him to start the car."

Another man, who must have been Jason, nodded his head in assent.

"I start car, poof, boom," he said.

"I jump out quick, no burn me."

"If Penta in car no save him, fire too fast," Jason said touching Penta's arm.

"Good for Penta, Jason start up car tonight," the man repeated.

Maria stood wondering. She looked at her finger with the sliver. No she thought. It was only coincidence. No way could it be more than that.

Time to Go

In the morning, all three were packed and ready when the green Mercedes taxi arrived at the apartment. The driver efficiently packed the luggage in the trunk. The three women no sooner closed the doors, before the driver was speeding them on the way to the airport. No one noticed the car pulling up as the taxi drove away. The door of the car opened, and Penta jumped out waving wildly. He realized he was too late to say good-bye and thank the women. He saw the taxi turn the corner, and sauntered back to the car. The limp he suffered for so many years was gone and a broad smile shone on his manly looking face.

Chapter 2 A Flight To Remember

A Dark Haired Stranger

A taxi, with a lone male passenger, approached the International terminal at Ben Gurion International Airport. The man with smartly combed dark hair was the passenger. He crouched down out of view and took a last sniff of the powdery cocaine substance. The passenger in the taxi, stuffed the inhaler into the crack behind the seat, paid the driver and grabbed the handle of the sports bag.

At the airport, the check-in lines were long. The three young women melded with the crowd, practicing patience. The line moved with agonizing slowness, while ticket agents exercised meticulous care, in checking passenger identification and baggage.

Passengers discussed with strangers around them, fulfilling the need to comment on the slowly moving line. Sydney noticed a woman with stringy blonde hair holding a small child in her arms. Looking at the child, she noticed how beautiful the baby appeared. Sydney commented to the mother and tapped her friends on the shoulder, indicating with a nod of her head, the woman with the child.

Maria looked at the woman, then at the child. Instinctively she reached out to touch the baby's small hand. As her hand touched the baby's, comforting warmth passed from her hand to the baby. The baby smiled as it grasped Maria's finger. The baby then looked to its mother with delightful dancing eyes.

Withdrawing her eyes from the baby, Sydney noticed a man standing a distance away. She garnered Maria and Ellie's attention with a finger, pointing to one man standing in an adjacent line. Something about the man made him disturbingly handsome. Perhaps it was the dark beard on his cleanly shaven face with the thick black hair, or the dark penetrating eyes and fine facial features. He shifted his weight to indicate a manner of extreme impatience as the white powder took its effect.

Ellie commented to the others. "Isn't that guy a little scary?"

Sydney responded with "Oh just let the guy alone."

It was an appropriate comment as the three women followed their friend's stare to the man.

Ellie felt the man's gaze meeting her blue eyes then travel from her face down to her feet. Unfortunately, her tight jeans accentuated her slim figure. He took in the form of her entire body. That really made her uncomfortable. When he smiled at her, it was even more disturbing. She quickly ran her fingers through her long dark hair and smoothed her blouse over her figure. She adjusted the Cardin sunglasses and looked away.

The man possessed almost childlike features on his six-foot frame. His eyes were intense. A few times he turned to look at the women, almost as if sensing them watching. Once he turned and focused a bone-chilling stare that startled Sydney. She could not remove her eyes from the man. He held her eyes for a moment, and then looked away, much to her relief. She could feel a chill remaining as though he was looking through her.

Ellie commented, "Did you see the way he looked at you?"

"Oh yes," Sydney responded. "I felt as though he could see through me. Scary," she added.

"He must be a scream in the bedroom," Sydney whispered hoarsely.

"Literally," Maria shot back to her friend with a gentle laugh.

At the aircraft, the food service vender employees were unloading and packing containers through the rear door of the plane. One of the workers opened the rear restroom door and entered. He opened the changing table drop down and placed two wrapped sandwiches behind the diaper panel. He quickly pushed the panel closed. The man quickly exited the restroom and returned to the task of bringing on the food canisters. No one made note of the man's detour.

The ticket agent beckoned Maria who was now at the front of the line to approach the ticket counter. The female agent, who was quite tall, looked down at the petite Maria. She saw the path of the three women's eyes, and followed the line of sight to the subject. Maria produced her passport identification. The ticket agent, satisfied with Maria's identification, handed her the ticket and boarding pass, while glancing again at the man in the other line. He caught her gaze and she looked back at the counter quickly.

Maria took her ticket and stood aside for Ellie, who was next in line, then Sydney. All the while, the dark haired stranger fascinated the ticket agent. After the three received their tickets, they decided they had enough of the stare routine, and busied themselves with other preparations for boarding the plane.

Time to Board

By the time, they were able to pass through customs and arrive at the gate, the giant 747's gate agents were boarding passengers. They found their row of seats and made themselves comfortable for the long flight home. Ellie was at the window, Sydney the middle and Maria in the aisle seat. For the moment, they forgot about the man that consumed their interest, while standing in line.

When the man who had become a topic of conversation reached the security portal, he was ushered into a private security area and given a thorough search that included his baggage. It seemed that he was also suspect according to security. Security performed its required tasks. The man passed. Because of the security delay, he was one of the last to board the plane.

The three friends who were chatting excitedly suddenly looked up as Ellie stopped in mid conversation with her eyes looking toward the front of the plane. As the stranger approached the row where they sat, he apparently lost his balance. Maria felt a hand grasp her shoulder rather tightly. The man's hand suddenly became icy cold against her skin. He flinched and released his grasp of Maria's shoulder. A strange look came over the man's face as he mumbled something in Arabic and quickly stepped away to find his seat, shaking his hand to get the feeling back into his fingers. On the loudspeaker, the senior flight attendant announced that it would be a full flight and requested people to find their seats so that others may board and the flight could take off on time. The announcement had little impact as aisles continued to be crowded with people storing luggage as if there was no need to hurry.

In the cockpit, the pilot was talking to the ramp agent. A few minutes later, the lumbering giant of a plane gracefully lifted itself into the air. Once the flight was airborne, most of the passengers settled into their routines for the long flight. The plane climbed to its initial cruising altitude of 31,000 feet and leveled off. The flight attendants began to roll the beverage carts down the aisle serving mostly coffee and the usual selection of fruit juices. This would happen a number of times on the long flight.

Midway through the flight, as the cart passed forward, a man rose from his seat and strode toward the rear of the cavernous interior of the plane.

A woman was waiting at the door with a small infant cradled in her arms. The hairs on the back of Sydney's neck bristled, as she looked over the seat back as the beverage cart passed their aisle. As if by tacit exchange, Maria looked at her friend.

"Something's the..." Maria quickly interrupted and cut off the Sydney's statement.

"I feel it too Sydney," Maria stated calmly, as she was already unbuckling the seat belt, rising and turning toward the rear of the aircraft as if drawn by some inexplicable force.

An Unexpected Confrontation

The dark hared man arrived at the restroom in the aft part of the plane. The door then opened as a woman exited the restroom.

"May I pass in front of you Ma'am?" I'm feeling very sick," he said, putting his hand over his mouth.

"Yes, of course," the woman with the baby in her arms said quickly, while stepping away from the door. He opened the door and seized the opportunity to leap inside, closing the door quickly. He opened the diaper changing rack and unwrapped the two "sandwich containers. With the cap, he scratched the surface of the top and immediately the magnesium ignited into a hot red torch of flame. He quickly scratched the other surface and the second flare ignited immediately.

The man held one of the flares to the inner wall of the restroom and it immediately began to burn through the thin wall of the compartment. Opening the door, he quickly exited amid the shriek of surprise from the young mother holding her baby as she saw the burning flare.

A female flight attendant was retrieving beverages in the back of the plane. She was immediately adjacent to the door as it opened. The woman felt the stiff punch to her face as she crumpled to the floor, unconscious. The man raced to the rear door on the right side of the aircraft and held the other flare until it burned through the inside of the aircraft door. He pushed it in further and stepped away.

Maria, seeing the action in front of her, continued toward the rear of the plane, passing the screaming woman with the infant. Ellie was now running to catch up. Right behind her friend followed Sydney. The passenger area was abuzz with people moving out of their seats to grab the man. A man immediately placed the woman with the child into a seat out of the way of the increasingly infuriated passengers.

Maria reached the man who was defiantly blocking the aisle and the restroom door. The man seeing Maria approaching, held out his one arm to block her path and with the other, attempted to grab hold of her. As his hand touched Maria, it was the last action that his arm would be performing for a while. His hand and arm stiffened as if frozen in place. Maria passed around the stiff arm opening the restroom door. The man sank to the floor. She saw the flare burning through the cabin wall of the aircraft. Without thinking, she placed her hand on the remaining part of the flare that was still protruding from the hole in the inner wall of the aircraft. She tried to remove it, but could not budge the cylinder that had already melted itself to the metal, but her touch had an astounding affect. As she grasped the part protruding from the wall, the flare stopped burning and became a piece of frozen cardboard. Dumbfounded, Maria looked at what was now a piece of ice, extending from the wall.

Maria heard Sydney's scream and turned to see her friend moving toward the side of the aircraft behind her. She saw the red glow of yet another flare stuck in the door of the aircraft as Sydney's hand took hold of the remaining part of the cylinder.

"What do I do with this?" Maria heard her friend's voice as she held up the hot burning torch.

Maria reached for the flare to remove it from Sydney's grasp. As she did, Sydney began to lose her grip and Maria found herself holding the white-hot flame in her bare hand, while the other end remained in her friend's hand. Maria tried to drop the flare as Sydney screamed. Ellie gasped as she saw her two friends trying to deal with the white-hot surface of the burning flare. To Ellie's astonishment, the flare extinguished as Maria's hand touched the flame. She could not believe her eyes. It suddenly became so cold, that Sydney dropped it as she felt the cold extending to her hand. For several moments, they stared at the spent flare in disbelief.

The restroom door shielded the women from the passenger's eyes. An Army Major peeked around the open door and blinked in astonishment. He proceeded to examine the areas where the man had placed the flares. The flame did not seem to have penetrated the outside skin of the aircraft. He stepped from the restroom toward the three women.

As Maria closed the door, she saw the stunned faces looking at the black haired terrorist who, other than his eyes, did not seem to be able to move. The passengers' eyes then quickly reverted to Maria. Evidently, no one other than the two friends and the woman with the baby had witnessed what Maria had done to put out the flares. With quiet assent, each looked to the other and silently understood the need for silence. The four women formed an immediate bond.

A man shouted, "I'm a doctor," and proceeded to check on the still groggy flight attendant.

"Are you in any pain, my dear?" The flight attendant slowly rose to her feet shaking her head to clear it. He then looked at Maria and Sydney who were staring blankly ahead for the moment.

Maria looked at her hand and shrugged her shoulders.

"No, no pain at all," she answered. The copilot's voice was asking everyone to return to his or her seats over the intercom. The Captain arrived on the scene amid questioning passengers. The Army Major directed him to the flares. He spoke to the Doctor and then turned to face the throng of passengers. A flight attendant addressed the Captain as Captain Newman.

"Please take your seats folks, everything is under control." He looked at the man with the black hair, his arm still frozen in position. He appeared to be in a daze.

"What about this guy, Captain?" The Captain looked at the still figure that had a gruesome grimace of pain on his face. "I really don't know Major. I have never seen anything like this before. The guy's arm can't move."

"Let's sit him down out of the way, Doc. You and the Major can keep an eye on him." The terrorist did not appear to be a threat any longer.

Captain Newman reached out to touch the man's arm.

"Wow, he sure is solid;" as he lowered the body to a seat at the back of the plane, out of sight of the passengers.

The flight attendant, who seemed to be doing better, asked if she should close the rear lavatories.

"You sit down and let the Doctor look at you a little more."

Another flight attendant was standing nearby by and asked the same question.

"Yes, said the Captain. That's a good idea. Let's ask all the passengers to move to the empty seats in the front of the aircraft. Also, ask the passengers to use the restrooms in the front."

As the three friends returned to their seats, Maria stopped at the woman with the beautiful child that they all had met standing in line at the ticket counter. "Are you ok, Maria?" asked the woman with the baby. Sydney checked the baby. She looked the infant over for any noticeable signs of trauma. The mother acknowledged that mother and baby were fine. Maria continued to her seat.

Captain Newman walked down the aisle, calming passengers while returning to the cockpit. As expected, the other flight attendants were doing their best to alleviate fear from the rest of the passengers. Once in the cockpit, he related the happenings and the situation about the stiff man who was the subject of the uproar. The flight crew listened as the Captain explained the situation to airline security. Law enforcement would be on hand in Chicago when the plane landed. None of the passengers had seen Maria extinguish the flare with her hand. Nonetheless, the topic of conversation was the two brave women who saved the flight. At least, that's what people were saying.

The trip back to Chicago proved to be one of new beginnings for the three young women. Maria was yet unaware that her life was changing and some of her friends would share a number of remarkable experiences.

Enter the FBI

When the plane landed at O'Hare Airport in Chicago, the Captain announced that there would be a delay before the passengers could leave. FBI and Chicago Police came on board the plane. FBI Agent in charge, Whitman Sharper, was the first to board the plane as the door opened to the gangway. Other agents followed, sporting FBI lettering on the back of their jackets. Sharper introduced himself to Captain Newman, who led the Agent toward the aft section of the plane.

Reaching Maria and her friends, the FBI Agent introduced himself and a few of the other agents. They ushered Maria, Sydney and Ellie toward the back of the plane where the terrorist sat stiffly, under the watchful eye of the Army Major. The doctor introduced himself to Whitman Sharper and immediately informed the Agent of the situation. The FBI agent bent to touch the man's arm. Satisfied, he turned back to the Captain, Maria and her friends. He seemed rather obnoxious as he curtly asked questions, made strange faces, and created odd sounds at the responses.

Captain Newman was getting a little tired of the process, as was the Army Major who decided to don his green beret. This immediately got the attention of the FBI agents. He got to the point of interrupting the interrogation and told the FBI Agent that the Captain was required to address some requirements in the cockpit. He began walking forward to pass the FBI Agent. The agent began to put his hand up to impede the Captain's exit, but he relented under the blazing stare of the Green Beret Major and allowed the Captain to pass.

Maria and her friends met with the FBI and then Chicago Police for over four hours, providing every detail of the event except for the fact that Maria extinguished the flare with her hand. The three women were becoming increasingly tense at the "interrogation" techniques used by the FBI people. Heck, they were the good guys. The doctor was queried but unable to explain what happened. No other explanation seemed plausible other than the flares were defective. The FBI and other officials finally allowed the three friends to leave after the interrogations. They bid each other goodbye as they met families and friends who were there to drive them home.

Chapter 3 Time For Awareness

Maria Esparza

The next day, dawn arrived much too quickly for a very tired Maria. As she looked at the alarm clock, 6:00 appeared in the blue window, followed by AM, beckoning her to start the new day. She worked at Northwestern Memorial Hospital as a nurse's assistant in the morning; attended afternoon classes into the evening, then tended bar on free days at the busy Casey's restaurant near downtown.

"Today is another Creighton day, ugh" she mouthed a couple times while shedding the covers. Mr. Creighton was a mean old patient at the hospital and she wondered what made him that way.

Throwing back the shower curtain, she gingerly stepped into the spray of warm water and let it wash over her. As she took the soap and washcloth, her eyes focused on the piece of wood embedded in her finger. Maybe she would have a doctor look at it when she arrived at work. She finished quickly, turning off the water and toweling. Before long, she was dressed and out the door.

Ellie Mulcahey

Ellie awoke suddenly to the sound of crunching metal. Startled and trying to get her bearings, Ellie quickly ran to the front window to find the source of the sound. Immediately she saw the crumpled vehicle leaning against two other cars near the corner of the street. Looking further up the street, she noticed the other automobile, its side now a concave shape. People were exiting doorways to witness the commotion. Having studied nursing for two years, Ellie rushed back to the bedroom for some clothes. Slipping on her shoes, she continued to dress as she ran out the front door to the closest car. A woman was screaming, "get a Doctor." A man standing nearby seemed to be dialing 911 on his cell phone.

Seeing all the people standing and peering into the car, the woman yelled, "Is anyone a doctor or nurse?" The group turned silently to each other without responding.

Ellie didn't wait for introductions when she arrived.

"Can I get in there? I've had nurses' training," Ellie announced.

Immediately she was ushered to the side of the car. A first glance told her that some of the people inside were seriously injured.

She proceeded to pull on the door handle to open the front passenger door. It would not budge. From the crowd, a large man stepped up to help. The overlapping metal sealed the door. He immediately broke the window with his elbow and stepped back to allow the woman to have access. As she reached inside, she tried to find a pulse on the neck of the passenger. There was none. The man's head was full of glass with a large mass of blood on the top of his head and flowing down in a stream. She was sure he was dead. The car pressed up against another parked auto. It would be impossible to get around to the driver because of the body blocking from this side, and no opportunity to get to the door on the other side.

Glancing into the back seat, she noticed a child crumpled on the floor behind the passenger seat. She immediately looked to the man who read her mind and took the door handle while reaching through the broken glass of the window to unlatch the door lock. Using his large hands, he easily pried the door open and stepped aside for Ellie.

She looked in at the body of a young boy about three to five years old. She didn't want to move the boy because of possible serious injuries. Instead, she felt his neck for a pulse. It was there, but was not very strong. She felt a warmth flow gently to the victim from her hand when she touched the boy's neck, seeking his pulse.

She looked to the big man crouching next to her as the crowd watched over her shoulder. Ellie asked the man if he thought the car might catch fire. He examined the situation and came back to her side.

"The engine's off and the gas doesn't seem to be leaking, so it's not likely, although still a possibility," he said matter-of-factly. He quickly added, "I'm a fireman, name's Jimmy Ennis."

"Ellie," the young woman replied. "Not much we can do right now. I'm afraid to move him." Let's wait for the paramedics." The firefighter nodded his assent, and then turned to the growing crowd. "Let's wait for some help to arrive. If we move anyone, we could make the situation worse. We are going over to the other car." He looked at a man standing close to him.

"Can you make sure no one touches the boy in the back?" The man nodded affirmatively.

"Let's see if we can do anything for the people in the other car."

He turned in the direction of the other car, but saw the fire department ambulance, with lights flashing coming down the street. He decided to stay with Ellie.

She looked over at the bloodied woman in the front seat. She was already dead and covered with blood. She tried again to get the front door open to reach the driver, but couldn't. Sirens wailed, announcing help approaching. The group of concerned people murmured and continued to peer inside at the accident victims.

The fire truck and ambulance arrived simultaneously. Firefighters ran up to the vehicle, followed closely by Paramedics, who advanced toward her car with bags in hand. One of the Paramedics came up past Ellie and acknowledged Jimmy Ennis with a nod of his head. A fire lieutenant was at his side.

"What do we have here sir?" Jimmy Ennis directed the Paramedic's attention toward Ellie, who quickly provided the situation, medical terms and all. The woman standing next to him impressed Jimmy Ennis by the manner in which she handled herself. The Paramedic thanked Ellie and with a "Sir," comment to Jimmy Ennis, went to help his partner. "We'll get to work getting the people out of the car," the lieutenant said as he moved away.

Two police cars also arrived and the officers began to move the growing crowd away from the heavily damaged vehicle.

Jimmy Ennis led Ellie aside from the group as they shared a few comments. Ellie looked at Jimmy Ennis and wondered who he was. She received an answer in the next second, as a police officer approached and called Jimmy Ennis, Captain. He seemed to command so much respect from the firefighters and police on the scene. They shared a few words and promised each other to get in contact again. Then they moved away to their respective residences.

Ellie glanced back over her shoulder but missed the sight of Fire Captain Jimmy Ennis looking back just before she did. The crowd remained to watch the firefighters and paramedics remove the bodies from the vehicle. Down the street at the intersection, another ambulance and fire truck were tending to the other vehicle. It must have continued some distance after the collision, before rolling up on lawn, where the engine obviously died.

Ellie climbed the stairs shaking. She thought of the passenger whose head had forcefully hit the windshield and the child who had lain unconscious and unmoving in the back seat. Ellie rethought the situation and wondered if she should have tried to remove the young boy from the car or attempted more forcefully to get to the driver. Her nursing instincts told her that she might have done more damage to the young boy if she had.

There never would be a right answer, she thought, while pouring water into the coffeepot. Her morning started with a bang and she wondered what the rest of the day would be like. Her first class was at 9:00a.m, so she had a little time to relax with a cup of coffee.

Sydney Anderson

Bailey, her trusty Terrier, awakened Sydney. Her husband Damon had risen early to prepare breakfast.

"He is such a sweetheart," she was thinking. Her thoughts drifted to the scene at the airport when Damon had swept her off her feet and twirled her around providing abundant kisses to confirm he was happy to have her back.

She sat at the table opening the morning Tribune to catch up on current news. The local Polish weekly paper sat on the table near her coffee. Curiosity forced her to look for information on the rains that she experienced in Jerusalem. On the International pages, the paper listed two stories on the uncommon events and told of the resulting damage. She read the articles with interest as her mind floated to the event experienced with Maria just before the second heavy rainfall had begun. Her husband was into the sports section and as usual, blanked her out. As she spoke to her husband, the responses were limited to "ahums" and "hmmms." It was not a two-sided conversation in the least. She finally reached over and closed the paper around his head. That got a reaction.

When she finally had her husband's attention, Sydney recounted the events of the previous day on the mount in Jerusalem. He felt the story was quite incredulous and made a few flip comments about the "Second Coming" and the new "miracle worker", as he referred to Maria's episode with the sliver of wood. She spoke in her somewhat clipped accent that had become common. It was a habit formed since childhood. He had learned to pay attention to that accent when she used it.

He did not want to take the story seriously, but having known his wife's penchant for fact finding and honesty, he was interested in knowing more about what took place. They finished breakfast with an intense conversation about the history of the cross and how after some three-hundred years, someone could have found it and made the claims that were so abundant in Church history.

Sydney thought of calling her friends. She reached for the phone; then decided to wait until later. She might be awakening one of her friends who probably needed sleep and made a mental note to call in the evening. Pulling back a chair, she seated herself at the kitchen table and gazed at the man seated in front of her.

Dr. Alhandro Pedroza

Maria sat on the examining table as the doctor studied the object under the skin of her finger. He was talking to himself, and Maria could not discern what his muttering meant. Doctor Pedroza was a tall man. The staff liked him for his cheery smile and demeanor. His ancestry was evident in his lightly colored skin and slight accent when he spoke. Doctor Pedroza finally looked to Maria's face.

"How did you get this big sliver in your finger?"

Maria shrugged and responded, "I was just walking with friends. I reached out to cushion my fall and suddenly this piece of wood was stuck in my finger."

The Doctor looked at her quizzically. "How did it become so deeply embedded? He asked.

"That's the strange part Doctor," Maria continued.

"It just seemed to seal itself into my skin."

The Doctor furrowed his brow. "It is very, very deep."

"I know," Maria responded.

"Let's take an X-ray and decide what we can do, OK?"

Maria shrugged in agreement.

Maria walked over to Radiology for the X-ray of her finger. The technician looked at her finger for the longest time.

Maria finally asked, "Do you want to take a picture?"

The technician apologized and quickly proceeded with the X-ray preparation.

"I've never seen something embedded that deeply," the tech stated.

"I'm sure it's very uncommon," Maria responded.

The technician took the X-rays from the top and sides of Maria's finger.

As Maria was leaving the X-ray section, she noticed the familiar face of the woman that was on the plane with the small child. The women noticed each other at the same moment. The woman approached Maria wearing a huge smile.

"How are you?" Maria said to the woman before they reached each other.

The woman's smile told the answer clearly. She was almost breathless.

"I came to bring my baby to this hospital because he had a hole in his heart and the only hope was to have a very delicate surgery to repair the heart. I was told it was only a 50% chance that my baby would survive."

"Well what happened?" Maria said excitedly.

"Oh my goodness," the woman continued.

"The Doctors took Cat Scans and X-rays and were astounded," she replied.

"There's no evidence of any problem with my baby's heart." The Doctors said it was a miracle. My baby's heart is perfectly normal."

Maria smiled a broad smile at the woman. "Miracles do happen, I guess."

"I saw the X-rays before," the woman said excitedly and there was a hole in his heart, now it's not there."

A nurse approached the two women and asked the woman talking with Maria, to come with her to clear up some paperwork.

"I have to go," the woman said to Maria.

"I'm so glad that everything worked out," Maria said to the woman as the woman turned to follow the nurse. Their eyes met and Maria could feel the happiness in the woman. It shone like a glow around her.

Upon returning to Dr. Pedroza, Maria sat quietly as the doctor reviewed the X-rays with a look of dismay on his face.

"We will have to perform surgery to remove this," he told the girl.

"Oh, I don't know?" Maria countered.

"There isn't any other way to remove this," the doctor noted with a serious tone. "It could also cause a serious infection if we don't remove it.

"I was afraid of that," Maria responded.

"We can use a local anesthetic," he offered with his clipped accent.

"OK," Maria responded, as fear crept into her head.

The doctor administered the xylocaine at three different locations in Maria's finger. After waiting a few minutes, he tested the area. When Maria acknowledged that there was no pain from the needle, the doctor reached for the scalpel. Maria turned away to avoid the sight. He cut deeply into the fleshy area of her finger until touching the sliver with the surgical knife. The Doctor felt a sudden jolt of freezing cold pass through the scalpel and into his hand. He quickly let the instrument fall to the floor. He could not move his fingers or his hand. It was as if it was frozen. The feeling subsided quickly as he felt normal again. He flexed the fingers of his hand. All seemed normal again. Slightly spreading the incision, he inserted a small tweezers again and attempted to grasp the piece of wood. The same thing happened but was more intense this time as he dropped the tweezers and fell to his knees. As far as he could tell, the sliver seemed to have molded itself to the bone of the girl's finger.

Becoming exasperated, he abandoned the attempt. Taking the magnifying glass, he again examined the incision and the piece of material. He decided to stop the procedure rather than create a problem for the girl using her finger, as well as avoiding another shock.

Maria was breathing heavily all during the procedure. Finally, the doctor spoke to her.

"I can't easily remove this object," he admitted with a tone of resignation.

"For some reason I'm not surprised," Maria responded.

"I knew something was unusual from the way it happened," she admitted.

"I will give you a tetanus shot, an antibiotic and a couple stitches," the doctor stated.

They both stared at the dark area beneath the Maria's skin. As they watched, the wound made by the scalpel fused together. The skin on the woman's finger showed no evidence of the invasion of the scalpel. Their eyes met as the realization hit them both simultaneously. The doctor spoke first.

"Ah, I guess we can forget the stitches. You will check back with me to make sure there is no infection, Okay?"

"Of course doctor"

"Are you in any pain?"

"No, none at all," Maria responded.

"OK," the doctor intoned, shaking his head.

Maria jumped down from the examining table and looked at the doctor.

"You don't think this thing will bother me or become infected, do you doctor?"

"You take the antibiotics and check back for the next week," he said.

She took the prescription to the pharmacy and went to resume her duties.

Doctor Pedroza stood in pensive thought. He felt embarrassment at being unable to help the nice young woman. Never had he seen something like this before. In his native Brazil, he had seen many people with deep slivers under the skin, but never anything like this. This piece of wood seemed to have sealed itself to the skin and bone of the girl's finger. He made a mental note to ask a few colleagues for their thoughts. He left the room to perform his rounds.

As Dr. Pedroza took the chart of his first patient on rounds, he read and asked the patient a few questions about how she was feeling. He put down the chart and walked over to the nurse's station where he asked the nurse a few questions. Satisfied, he turned to leave. As the Doctor left to continue his rounds, the nurses huddled and spoke in hushed tones.

Maria

As Maria moved through the Emergency Room, she noticed the area was a flurry of activity. She stopped for a moment to ask one of the nurses what happened.

The nurse told her there had been a bad accident on the near West Side and the trauma team was working feverishly to save the surviving three of the six victims of the accident. One was a young boy and they were not sure he was going to make it. "The others were DOA," she said with sadness. Maria thanked her for the information and continued to the elevator.

Chapter 4 Cruel Men

Marshall Creighton

Maria gathered her medical cart and proceeded to the patient rooms for her daily routine. During her two years at the hospital, she traversed through a myriad of people and unique personalities. Recently, one of her dreaded tasks became assisting Marshall Creighton. The man was extremely rich and apparently ruthless. He seemed to think everyone was below him, especially the hospital workers.

Creighton was dying of liver and pancreatic cancer. He was a fighter though and was able to hang on longer than most people who had been stricken with the dread disease.

As Maria entered the room, Creighton looked up. As he spotted her, a look of disdain flooded the features of his face.

"Why are you here again?" He growled at Maria, his voice dripping with sarcasm.

Maria cheerfully announced "Just here to check on you, Mr. Creighton."

"Aren't you Spanish?" He growled out at the girl.

"Yes I am," Maria responded in a level tone.

"You people are all alike. You come up here illegally and take jobs away from poor people here."

"I am here legally Mr. Creighton, I was born here."

Her mind was unable to comprehend why the eccentric old geezer was so unable to accept Hispanic heritage. She let the thought drift off attributing the strangeness to eccentricity.

Maria noticed a paper lying on the floor and reached to retrieve it under his bed. She bent to pick it up. Rising, she offered the paper to the grumpy man. He looked at her hand and pushed the paper away causing it to fall again to the floor. Maria picked it up again and placed it on the tray near his bed. He obviously did not want a mere nurse's assistant to touch or help him.

"Yeah, well you're all the same," she heard his ranting mumble begin again.

"What a piece of work," Maria whispered to herself. "How did he ever become so successful?"

At that moment, his wife entered the room. Pacey Creighton was a duplicate of the old man in many ways, except she wore a skirt sometimes. She was discourteous to the staff and most demanding of anyone who was in the area, including the doctors. Maria pictured her with a baton in hand, chastising the band for the least mistake. She looked at Maria with the same disdain the husband showed.

"Aren't you through yet?" Her tone was condescending.

Maria looked at the woman with flawless facial features and nary a hair out of place. The woman was beautiful even as an older woman. In her case though, the beauty was truly only skin deep. Her heart had to be made of stone.

A doctor entered the room as Maria gathered her materials to leave, thankful to be finished and away from the crotchety old man. Maria always looked for the good in a person. With this Marshall Creighton, she could only come up with a one-word description. Hopeless!

She started toward the doorway, slowed and turned to Marshall Creighton.

"Good bye Mr. and Mrs. Creighton," she managed with a smile on her face. "See you tomorrow," she added, swiftly taking her exit.

Maria heard the old man commenting to the doctor about Spanish something. She was out of earshot quickly and moved to the next patient's room, which would be the last one of the day.

Maria packed up, put away her supplies, and changed to get ready for classes. The painkiller in her finger had worn off. She knew because she could touch things and her feeling returned, yet there was no pain. She thought this a little odd as she looked at her finger in disbelief. There was no evidence of the deep cut made with the scalpel. Her skin was perfect. Beneath, she could see the wood sliver still solidly embedded. Something very unusual was taking place. She would call her Ellie and Sydney tonight to tell them.

She walked toward the door to leave for her other job at the restaurant, before attending classes. She noticed Vera Creighton, the daughter of the distastefully garrulous old man upstairs. Vera noticed Maria and approached her with her hand extended. Both women smiled genuinely as they shook hands. Vera Creighton felt a warm tingle from contact with Maria's hand. It was not painful though, just a quick warm feeling. Maria felt it too.

"How's my grumpy father doing today?"

Maria shrugged her shoulders in response. "He's still the same, only more ornery."

"Not surprising," the woman responded. "Sorry!"

"Have a nice day Maria," the younger Creighton woman said with a convincing tone.

"You too," Maria replied as she continued out the door.

As Vera Creighton neared the elevator, she also looked at her hand. When shaking hands with the Spanish woman, she felt a sudden warm feeling. She thought about it again and pressed the button that would take her to her father's floor.

The elevator door opened at the third floor. As the door opened, Vera Creighton was startled as she found herself staring into her mother's eyes. Her mother spoke first.

"They've taken your father for a treatment," her mother stated.

"Oh, we can sit in the waiting room then," the daughter said.

"I don't like that place," her mother responded quickly.

"They're just people mother," Vera replied.

"Well OK," her mother stated," as they walked in the direction of the large open room.

Two shabbily dressed young boys about 10 years old were the only occupants.

Pacey shot a disdainful look at her daughter.

As she caught the look, Vera rolled her eyes. Mixing with the riff raff, she guessed to be her mother's feeling about being in the room with the two boys.

The boys were sitting, reading a magazine and pointing to pictures. In general, they were just having fun.

One of the boys asked the other, "What would you do with a hundred dollars?"

The second boy laughed. "A hundred dollars?"

He sat looking at his friend; wheels whirring inside his head as he pictured all the things they could buy.

"I'd give it to my mom to get her medication and fix the car," the boy finally said.

"I'd go and buy all the candy I could eat," the first boy responded.

"The car is always breaking down and my mom can't get a better job because of it," the second boy told his friend.

"We don't even have a car," said the first boy.

"Well maybe one day you will"

"Yeah, maybe one day," the friend said with a shrug.

"When you buy it for us," he added.

The two boys laughed and high-fived.

Vera Creighton
Vera Creighton listened intently to the conversation as her mother just sat continuing to make under the breath comments. Vera suddenly

pulled her purse onto her lap. She reached inside and removed five $20.00 bills. Upon noticing, what her daughter was doing, Pacey Creighton asked, "What are you doing my dear?"

"Don't faint mother, but I am going to do something I should have begun a long time ago. We have more money that we will ever be able to spend. Why not share some of it."

Pacey Creighton sat ramrod straight in shock as her daughter began to rise holding the money in her hand.

"Vera Creighton, you come back here," she said in controlled anger.

"Sorry mom," was the only answer given. Vera Creighton patted her mother's perfectly manicured hand gently as if to console her. Pacey Creighton abruptly rose and headed in the other direction for the elevator.

As Vera Creighton began to walk toward the two boys, the mother of the one who wished for the money to fix the car came around the corner.

Not seeing Vera approaching, she said to the boys, "OK you two, let's get our act moving"

She felt the gentleness emanating from the young boy's mother. It was in her voice as well as her demeanor.

She approached the black woman and introduced herself. The woman's face broke into her usual smile as she acknowledged the introduction from the stranger.

"Hi, I'm Vera Creighton," she said to the woman.

"Hello Vera Creighton, I'm Jennifer Mayberry"

Vera explained the conversation she overheard between the woman's son and his friend.

Immediately, Jennifer Mayberry felt the embarrassment rise in her throat.

"The boys think differently than we do," she said.

"We never know what will come out of those young mouths."

Quickly, folding the money, Vera Creighton took the other woman's hand and placed the money in her palm, gently wrapping her fingers around the bills.

The woman looked up and tried to refuse but Vera Creighton had already moved away in haste toward the elevator to catch up with her furious and upset mother. Jennifer Mayberry just stood and stared at the money in her hand. The boys echoed at the same time. "What did she give you?"

As tears appeared in the woman's eyes, she replied.

"Just a kindness," she said. "Yes, just a kindness." The surprised woman looked upward and mouthed a quiet "Thank You God."

Jennifer Mayberry put the money in her purse and gathered the boys with their coats to leave. She thought to herself, wondering if that woman would have only known her situation. Jennifer Mayberry's diagnosis was pneumonia and she would require new medications. Her doctor wanted to put her in the hospital, but that was something Jennifer Mayberry couldn't think of and certainly wasn't going to leave her young son to fend for himself. The money would be a big help in the right direction. As they reached the outside air, the woman raised her eyes again and mouthed "Thank you."

They left the hospital in the old car as Jennifer Mayberry headed for the second hand store. Her hair was turning prematurely gray and she had allowed herself to gain a little too much weight as she often hid her anxiety by eating too much fatty food. One could tell by looking at her however, that her soul was good. They parked and she went through the aisles looking for a couple of pant and shirt outfits for her son and his friend.

The young boy's sister, who had quit school to find work, was raising her son's young friend. The father had passed away shortly after the young boy was born and the mother was in jail for drug dealing. Jennifer Mayberry decided to try helping whenever she could.

Finding the outfits, she ushered the two boys toward the checkout counter. They were elated looking at the almost new clothing Mrs. Mayberry was buying for them.

The next stop was the food store, where she looked for the absolute best prices on sale items, and BOGOs. She went to the pharmacy where her prescription was ready, as the predictable efficiency of the doctor's office was again apparent. They had called in her prescription for Furosemide and an anti-biotic, to reduce the buildup of liquid in her lungs. Finding the few other articles she required, the next stop was the checkout line. The boys were getting rambunctious and she wanted to get out of the store quickly.

They only traveled a few stores down, when her son asked, "Can I have a dollar mama?"

The woman replied, "What do you want with a dollar, young man?"

"I just need to get something and it only costs a dollar," was the boy's excited response.

"Here then son, and make it quick!"

He ran into the grocery store. The owner waved to the woman who smiled and waved back. Occasionally she would stop in and they would talk. He loved the smile she always wore. It made him feel good to know her.

The boy ran into the store and was out in a flash, holding a lotto ticket.

His mother at first felt irritated that he would waste the money so frivolously.

Then she caught herself. She had done the same thing every once in a great while in the hope that they might someday win. They never did.

The boys ran toward the car and they climbed in for the ride home.

Bertrand Cooper

The restaurant lunch crowd was thinning. Maria set tables in preparation for the evening rush, which she would thankfully avoid in lieu of her studies. She was waiting tables today, because one of the servers had called in sick.

The afternoon had gone reasonably well with only a few problems. She earned a nice tip from four men who were having a business lunch to celebrate the signing of a new client. They were upbeat and in good spirits.

Some of the other patrons habitually complained about the food or service. It was expected and dealt with in good management fashion. Maria had a wealth of experience dealing with the complainers and was usually able to satisfy them without giving away free meals or drinks. Her smile was always heartwarming and engaging.

One situation created tension during the afternoon. An obnoxious customer relentlessly complained about the service, food and drinks. Unfortunately, he came in a couple times a week and complained constantly. His name was Bertrand Cooper and he was not a very nice man. Cooper was one of the higher ups at his company. The staff suspected that he was a drug user. They often referred to Cooper, with the nickname "High beams". A term used to define the wide-open eyes of some drug users.

Today, he made a point of being nasty to a co-worker of his, by the name of Carl Sarna. Sarna used a wheelchair, but that never stopped Bertrand Cooper's tirade, whenever he had a few drinks. Carl Sarna seemed almost angelic in comparison and never returned a nasty word toward the drunk.

When it came to drinks, Bertrand Cooper was a pain. There wasn't enough ice, or not enough alcohol. It really didn't matter. He would complain anyway. The obnoxious attitude even made his tablemates uneasy. Maria watched the man as he displayed his animosity toward everyone. She felt a deep empathy for Carl Sarna, who became the object of the drunk's fury. She could feel the poor man, sitting in the wheelchair, fighting to maintain control of something that was very much out of his hands. The feeling made her uneasy and sad. She wished ole "High beams" would stop his verbal harassment, but he continued.

As Maria observed him lifting yet another drink, she secretly wished that he would drop the glass and embarrass himself, when the server left the table. As if in response to her wish, the man not only dropped the glass, he spilled the contents on one of his co-workers, a middle-aged woman seated to his right. Abby Tisdale shot straight out of the chair as the liquid flooded off the table toward her dress. She was fast enough to be out of the way before it got to her. The look she gave the man was scalding to say the least as he lowered his head under her gaze. Abby was the peacekeeper of the group. Her experience with Bertrand Cooper's acid comments, allowed her to maintain a calm atmosphere, regardless of the situation. She had been with the company quite a while. This helped allay the effects of Cooper's comments to others.

Maria smiled to herself. If solutions were always that easy, she thought. The man sat quietly during the rest of the meal seething and staring at the man in the wheelchair. At one point, he looked at the other man and with a grimace hoarsely whispered.

"It's your fault you inept cripple."

A noticeable gasp erupted from the others at the table. Maria decided to handle the receipt of the payment directly. Mr. Sarna was usually the one who paid the check, so she walked toward him with the check. Mr. Sarna, in the wheelchair, stared at the man with a look of disdain then turned away. Ms. Tisdale, who scarcely avoided the spilled drink, motioned for the check and handed the check to Carl Sarna. Mr. Sarna glanced fleetingly at the check and provided Ms. Tisdale with his American Express card. The woman handed the card and the check back to Maria. She quickly returned with the approved billing for a signature. Carl Sarna was embarrassed for himself and the others. He included a thirty- percent tip, signed the check and handed Maria the slip with a slight rolling of his eyes. Their hands met and each felt a sudden warmth as they touched. Maria understood the gesture as the man in the wheelchair mouthed, "I'm sorry." The woman at his side rose and everyone at the table did the same. Carl Sarna, in the wheelchair refused help and wheeled himself as they all moved toward the door. They left quietly.

Maria's shift was over. She performed her last minute duties that included making sure that the setups were in place for the next meal. She punched out and waved good-bye to the others as she effortlessly pushed open the door and entered the now quiet street.

Frank Wilson Bellini

Frank Wilson, as no one knew him in particular, had become a bum. His friends were street people who longed for the shelter of a good night's sleep without fear of someone taking their few valuables. About a year ago, Frank Wilson was on top of the world. That is, until he became the target of a federal probe into felony theft for stealing money from clients of his own Investment firm. He had been set up well. By the time he tried to gather information to defend himself, it was destroyed or conveniently missing. Having no chance at freedom, while looking at a serious jail sentence, Frank Bellini went on the lam and changed his name to Frank Wilson. He was Frank Wilson of the street people, who hung around lower Wacker Drive, in Chicago.

Frank's past included quite a list of accomplishments. He was a decorated fighter pilot, flying F4 fighters in Vietnam and F14s in the Gulf. At forty, he left the Navy and began his own Investment firm. For a while, he missed the head and body jarring "traps", landing on the carrier's deck. Then his body acclimated to walking again and he became more of a regular person than a fighter jock.

His family was wealthy. They sold a meat packing business that was under his family's last name and made quite a hefty sum of millions. Shortly after the sale, his mom and dad passed away, leaving him and his sister to deal with the family fortune.

Now he had nothing. It had all been confiscated or stolen. While walking, he heard a commotion down the street. He quickened his pace and as he turned the corner, he saw and heard the commotion.

Maria

She had not walked more than a couple feet before she heard a voice coming from behind her. It was the tipsy customer, Bertrand Cooper, who immediately began making snide comments while pointing to Maria. She tried to ignore the man's words, but he moved toward her with his voice increasing in volume. Maria looked around and decided to head back inside until the man left. She was almost at the door when she felt a tug at her arm, spinning her around. Without warning, she felt her body pushed against the hard brick wall. The man was holding her and screaming obscenities in her face.

Maria spoke softly.

"Don't do this."

He tightened his grip on her arm. As he did, he felt a sudden cold shock and tried to release his grip. He couldn't, and he felt his hand becoming cold, hard and heavy. He was no longer able to move his fingers. The tightness began to move to his wrist as he suddenly became scared at what was happening.

From the corner of her eye, she noticed another man approaching from around the corner. He heard the commotion and began walking quickly toward Maria and the man. The new stranger's appearance was very unkempt. In a flash, he arrived beside Maria, dwarfing the man who was holding her. He didn't hear the brief exchange as he was approaching. Maria looked at the face of her would be rescuer. With a quick movement, he removed the man's hold on Maria's arm and pushed Bertrand Cooper up against the building, holding Cooper's free arm twisted and high up against the man's back. His hand hit the bricks hard close to the other man's head and he noticed a cut on his hand. Bertrand Cooper's face was hard against the bricks and there was no struggle.

"Do you want to call the police," the stranger asked.

Maria shook her head.

"Just let him go," she responded quietly.

"He's had too much to drink."

Her rescuer looked at the man. The assailant's face continued to exhibit a look of bewilderment.

"Are you going to leave the woman alone?"

The man nodded affirmatively.

"You ever show up here again and I'll find you and break your hand. Do you understand?"

The man nodded. He glanced at Maria and turned to walk quickly down the street. He looked back a couple times, his head unsure of what had taken place. He had no idea of the forthcoming result of his actions against Maria. His hand remained stiff and cold.

"Are you hurt Miss?"

Maria responded with a shake of her head, still too surprised to speak. The stranger put his hand on her shoulder and looked into Maria's face for a sign that she truly was in control of herself.

"I'm OK, thanks," but you cut your hand." Let me see?"

Maria studied the man's finger and in doing so, rubbed her finger against the cut. They both experienced a strange sensation as part of the sliver attached itself to the cut on the man's finger. A warm comforting feeling passed between the skins of their hands. Then the skin on both their hands immediately sealed. She looked into the gaunt looking face, with the scraggly beard and soiled clothes. The man bore noticeably Italian facial features. She felt there was a handsome face beneath all the covering and wondered what his situation was, but decided not to ask. She did not need to. Somehow, she felt their paths would cross again soon.

"Are you sure you're ok?" Maria asked the man.

"You look like a wreck."

"I'm ok," he said.

"Thank you so much." She touched the hand on her shoulder.

"I'll be just fine," the man answered.

"It was only a customer who needed to vent his frustrations about the way he acted with the others he was lunching with," Maria said with uncomfortable laughter.

"Whatever you say," the man responded, allowing a small smile to show on his lips.

"You take care of yourself," he added as he began walking away.

"Hey! You're going to be someone's White Knight." Maria called to the man. He turned to look back at her.

"Don't say that too loud, someone might believe you."

"What's your name?" Maria asked. As soon as she asked, the name Frank Bellini was on her lips.

"I'm Frank Wilson, at your service."

"Thank you Frank Wilson, .ah… Bellini, you're a good man." The words slipped from her lips before she could catch them.

Frank Wilson froze in his steps at hearing the name no one had spoken in over a year. The look of surprise was on his face as he looked back at the woman. He quickly decided since he would not be seeing her again, that it didn't matter.

The comment brought a smile to Maria's face.

"I'm Maria and thanks again Frank Bellini." Frank Bellini smiled. He raised his hand to wave an acknowledgement as he continued with a spirited gait down the street.

As she stood alone, Maria examined her finger. Curious she thought, very curious. She glanced again at the man's shape growing smaller in the distance. A White Knight? Hmmm! She wondered what that would mean.

Frank Bellini's Memories

Frank Bellini felt something unusual happened when he was with the woman who called herself Maria. He looked at his hand. There definitely was a sliver in his hand, but it wasn't irritable and it didn't hurt. He just wondered why he had it. It definitely came from the encounter with the man assaulting the Maria woman.

In the cool afternoon breeze, he walked along the busy sidewalk of Michigan Avenue. While passing the high priced stores, he reflected on the times he shopped there for girlfriends and then for his wife. He allowed himself to flashback to another place and time. The pain from deep within returned as it did whenever he thought about the woman he married and adored.

They did everything together except have children, although they tried.

When the financial scandal hit the fan, she distanced herself from him with amazing alacrity. She also secured as many of the assets as she was able. Frank never knew what she got away with. He was too busy fighting the accusations alone to pay attention.

He remembered the painful thoughts of the empty house when he opened the door. Everything of value was gone, as was Meredith, his wife. Of the three cars usually parked in the garage, all were gone but the one he was driving.

Looking around the vacant rooms, he arrived at the decision to quit fighting and disappear. He knew someone rich and powerful set him up as the scapegoat. His accounts were "hacked" with transactions transferring money all over the world. By the time, he found out, the Security and Exchange Commission was filing charges of fraud and more. It all happened surprisingly face. Too fast, he thought.

At least by going into hiding, he would be able to live and fight another day. It would be difficult, as all of his resources were no longer available. It just didn't matter anymore. Raising his head, he allowed himself one last look around the house.

Tears welled in his eyes with the fleeting thoughts of the past. His hand grasped the brass doorknob, pulling the door closed behind him. "I need your help now Mom," he said silently. He wiped the moisture from his eyes, wishing that his mother who had always made things alright was still alive." She passed away years before yet her son held his belief that she was still aware of what was happening and he continued to allow her in his thoughts.

His memory brought back the last walk down the driveway to the Lexus coupe. Getting in, he started the car and headed for the City.

He drove down Western Avenue south to the area with many car dealers. He knew some of them from his business. They were cash customers. They were careful only to bring in less than $10,000 cash to avoid the required filing with the IRS of cash deposits of that account or more.

He pulled into one of the lots and saw the owner extolling the virtues of a car to a potential buyer. He waited until the conversation was over and the owner came over. He was greeted warmly and escorted inside to the owner's private office. Frank told him that he needed to sell the Lexus and asked how much he could get. They agreed on a price in Cash. It wasn't near the real value, but beggars can't be choosy. He took the money and left.

That was it for Frank Bellini's plan. From now on, it would be on foot.

They days passed, and the heavy beard continued to grow. At times, he looked like a wild man. It was a safety feature that probably scared would be muggers away.

He bought a fake id under the name Frank Wilson and deposited the money at different financial institutions. When he found someone truly in need of help, he gave him or her what they needed. Money was running out quickly, but he didn't care. It rather brought him peace of mind to help others.

At least he would be more difficult to spot for the time being. He went by the name of Frank Wilson and gave that name to anyone who asked. One could say Frank was now a homeless statistic.

Chapter 5 The Unexplained

Baffled Doctors

A few days later, at the hospital, doctors were holding a review conference. The topic of conversation drifted to the boy from a car crash the other day. His mother was dead on arrival, the driver arrived in critical condition and passed away soon thereafter and the young boy looked like a crumpled shirt. Each of the doctors studied the x-rays taken at the time of boy's arrival.

The orthopedic surgeon kept studying the X-ray of the neck and back. He continued to shake his head as he studied what appeared to be a fusion of vertebrae. The attending physician indicated that there was no scar from surgery on the boy's neck. He wondered how a boy so young could have been through surgery to fuse the area together. Baffled, he put down the X-ray and studied another.

"Are we sure, these are the right X-rays?" He asked.

The Radiologist looked over the lenses of his glasses.

"Yes, I'm sure those are the correct X-rays," the Radiologist spat.

The other doctors looked at the picture of the fusion and wondered too. Each of them knew that if that bone had been broken removing the boy from the vehicle, he would be either dead or facing a life of total paralysis.

As it was, the other injuries would heal in time and the boy should be able to lead a very normal life. That was the prognosis of the attending physician and his peers.

Ellie Mulcahey

Ellie finished her classes for the day and boarded the L train for the short ride home. She exited the train and walked down the stairs to begin the two-block walk. The wind had calmed considerably so the coolness of the temperature was not as penetrating as it was during the morning. She noticed the colorful signs in the windows of the small shops along North Avenue. The area was moving toward upscale at a fast clip. As she reached her street, she glided around the corner and ran smack into Jimmy Ennis, her new firefighter friend from other morning's events.

As her arms automatically wrapped around his arm for balance, the big man enfolded her against him. She looked up into his face. He immediately released her as they both began to apologize. A second later, laughter replaced uneasiness. They exchanged pleasantries about the day's events and the weather. Jimmy mentioned that he had talked to the paramedics and found that the passenger and driver had succumbed while the young boy survived but was in critical condition.

They talked a bit more about the accident, until Jimmy Ennis looked at his watch. He mentioned that he had an important appointment at the station. Ellie stepped back as if to tell him she understood. As they parted, they agreed to contact each other sometime in the next couple of days. With a wave, they continued on their separate paths.

Maria had set up a conference call with Ellie and Sydney for 8:00 that evening. They were buzzing with excitement about the trip. During the call, they agreed to meet the next night at a small watering hole near school.

Maria, Ellie and Sydney

Ellie and Sydney arrived at Jilly's bar simultaneously. They greeted each other excitedly and found a booth at the far wall where they would be able to talk without the din of the other customers and music inhibiting their conversation. Maria walked in and as her eyes adjusted to the dimly lit interior. She glanced at the faded pictures of famous Chicagoans covering the walls and noticed her friends across the room

They ordered a pitcher of beer and began their conversation in earnest. Each in turn recounted the happenings since they returned. As Ellie told the others of her experience at the accident, Maria seemed to look at her friend with curiosity. They expected to hear something that Ellie did because of her nursing training.

Maria was at the hospital and knew about the situation of the people from the accident. Maria decided to allow Ellie to provide a full description of the events before telling the girls of what she had found out at the hospital.

As Ellie finished, Sydney asked a few questions for clarification of what Ellie experienced. Maria could contain herself no longer and touched each of the girls' hands in excitement. The feeling of two warm shocks as their hands touched interrupted her. Each of the women looked at the other.

"You said you touched the passenger and the boy from the back seat," she directed the question to Ellie.

"That's right," was Ellie's quick reply.

"Why do you ask," Sydney interjected.

"Listen to this," Maria responded.

Maria went on to tell her friends of the situation with the passengers from the cars at the emergency room. The girls listened intently, trying to piece together a connection.

Maria told them about the fusion of the boy's vertebrae. Sydney looked quizzically at Ellie.

Ellie shrugged her shoulders as if to indicate she did not understand the importance of what Maria was telling them. Maria explained further about the unlikely survival of the boy without the vertebrae healed.

Suddenly, Ellie sat frozen in place, a stunned look on her face.

"Here, here, here," she exclaimed excitedly.

"Does this make any sense? I touched the passenger whose head had gone through the window. She had already died and I couldn't reach the driver. Then I felt the boy's neck for a pulse. It was very weak, but he was still alive. This huge fireman who lives across the street was there with me. The decision not to move the boy was a joint one. We knew the paramedics were on the way. The other bystanders had then stepped back and just looked inside the car at the victims."

Sydney couldn't resist the question and asked.

"And what is the fireman's name?"

"Oh shush," her friend exclaimed with a push of the air with her hand.

Ellie smiled as they all laughed.

Sydney then asked seriously of her friend Maria, "What do you think happened?"

Maria shrugged. "I don't know really, but something is very strange about all this"

Ellie nodded in assent, as Sydney's face remained frozen with a quizzical expression.

Maria looked at her friends as the silence continued.

"Well I have something to tell you that is also unusual," she said.

"I went to see a doctor at the hospital a couple days ago," she continued.

"I showed him the sliver in my finger and he suggested removing it"

"So what happened?" Sydney asked.

"He tried to remove it" "Using a local anesthetic so it wouldn't hurt, he cut deeply into my finger,"

The two friends looked at Maria's hand. She held it up and they saw the sliver still deeply embedded under the skin of her finger.

"You say he cut into your finger?" Sydney asked.

"Yes", Maria replied.

"But there's no cut or mark," Ellie exclaimed.

"That's right!"

"He couldn't remove it. He tried like crazy and it would not budge with the tweezers."

"He was baffled just as I was."

The three girls looked at each other in utter silence.

Sydney examined Maria's hand again. There was no mark whatsoever.

Ellie was the first to speak.

"I felt a warm tingle when I felt for the boy's pulse this morning," she said. But I felt nothing when I touched the dead passenger. It only happened when touching the boy"

"How strange," Maria remarked.

"Very," said Ellie in reply.

"And your finger healing so quickly," Sydney commented.

"There is something very unusual going on," Maria said. "The boy that you touched?" Maria said looking at Ellie.

"His vertebrae were fused back together without any sign of a surgical incision.

"The passenger, whom you also touched however, was dead."

"So do you think I had anything to do with healing the boy by touching him?" "What makes a healing take place?" Sydney asked. No one answered.

"That's something that has to be figured out," Maria stated in earnest.

All three agreed that there has to be some unique power at work. Maria considered telling them about the woman passenger on the plane with the baby. She weighed the decision, and then decided to tell them.

"You remember the woman on the plane with the baby that needed surgery for a heart defect?" Each shook their heads in affirmation.

"Well, I saw the woman at the hospital. She was going home, because the doctor's had found no hole in the infant's heart as first indicated." There were certainly more questions than answers.

"I'm going to talk to a priest friend at my church. Maybe he will shed some light on this," Maria told her friends.

"You'll let us know if you find out anything, won't you?" Ellie asked.

"Of course I will," Maria replied.

Maria considered telling her friends about the customer at the restaurant and her "White Knight", but thought she had said enough for now.

Ellie looked to Sydney.

"You know folks, I've analyzed this thing that's happening, given a measure of room for anomalies, and come to the conclusion that I have no idea what the heck is happening to all of us here. Let's wait to see what my Priest tells me and I'll apprise both of you when I know more." They all agreed to table the subject until then.

Sydney looked at her friend. "You are right Ellie; things do not make sense."

"How is everything with Damon?" Maria asked with interest.

Sydney looked again at her two friends.

"Well things seem to be at low ebb," was her clipped accent reply.

"What's the matter?" Maria asked.

"I'm not sure, we just don't seem to have the flair for each other we once did," Sydney replied honestly.

"That happens sometimes," Ellie shot back to her friend.

"Ever think of spicing things up a little," Maria asked.

A quizzical look appeared on Sydney's face.

Both women looked to Maria for further comment.

"Try a little role play is what I mean," Maria responded gaily.

Sydney raised her eyebrows at the mention of the role-play.

"Yeah, that might be good," Ellie added.

Shaking her head, Sydney asked her friend. "Like how?"

"Well sometimes, a couple can create a scene to act out with each other that can be exciting and have the effect of drawing them together. Of course, the entire idea is based on the trust each has in the other. That is essential."

Maria continued by explaining an example of a scene where both meet somewhere as strangers and wind up together. The idea immediately intrigued Sydney, as she became interested in the thought. Ellie jumped on the idea first with telling about a scene she had been told. It was about an older couple that was looking for ways to increase the interest in their marriage.

She talked with the couple, as part of her research for a psychology class.

"They loved it, and have continued to use different ideas," she added

Ellie continued to describe what the couple had told her about their first role-play experience.

Sydney sat intrigued and felt excitement build, as she pictured Damon playing out the scene with her.

"I'm gonna talk with Damon about that," Sydney exclaimed excitedly.

"Yeah you should Syd; maybe Damon will get a "chubby" over the idea." Sydney punched Ellie lightly in the arm at the use of the "chubby" term. They always used it to talk about some who they thought they turned on. All three girls laughed as they added quick ideas about the thought for their friend.

Some loud mouth at the bar interrupted the conversations at times. For sure, he had drunk enough to make anyone slur and be obnoxious. The girls ignored him even as he made an occasional comment in their direction.

The girls continued their conversation well into the night. As it approached midnight, they decided it was time to head for their respective homes. They decided to pay close attention to the situations that developed around them and keep mental notes, and they would meet again later in the week.

As they neared the door, the loud mouth at the bar hopped off the stool and reached for Sydney's arm. That was a mistake. Sydney had the man's arm held behind his back before he understood what happened.

"Sorry, my goodness, you'd think I was going to maul you."

"Then you shouldn't act like that mister." Sydney shot back and released the man's arm. Without warning, he suddenly grabbed Maria's arm. He began to turn her toward him with some force. Maria quickly put her arm up to defend herself, remembering how defenseless she had felt with the man outside the restaurant. Sydney stepped toward the man with a look of disbelief on her face. The man recoiled suddenly as he felt the shock of coldness in his hand. It proceeded up the man's arm to his shoulder. He quickly released his grip on Maria's arm, his chest muscles tightening from an invisible grip. Sydney reached them and touched the man's hand. It was cold as ice. All could tell that he was also in serious pain as they watched the grimace on his face. He stood still with his hand still extended but holding air. He looked at Maria in fear as he backed up toward the bar and slumped onto the stool. He turned back to the bar and dropped his head in silence, looking at the curled and cold flesh of his hand.

Without another word, the women left the bar. Each holding onto their own thoughts of what they witnessed. The message to each however was abundantly clear. Do not mess with them. That was now obvious.

As they left, Maria shook her head trying to find some logical reason for what happened. She had not had time to think of anything other than the man was a jerk. She had felt threatened though. Perhaps some unconscious thought or fear had precipitated the effect on the stranger. They bid each other adieu.

Some higher power was at work protecting her for sure. She just could not figure out how or when it could develop. At the restaurant, nothing bad happened prior to their leaving, Then Bertrand Cooper attempted to accost her. Perhaps she would not have met Frank Bellini were it not for that situation. She wondered what role Frank Bellini was going to play in the future. It was all very confusing. Time would tell.

Sydney

On the way home, Sydney wondered aloud about the chain of events in Jerusalem and Maria and Ellie's account of what happened since they returned from the trip. There wasn't anything in Sydney's life that was different.

As she drove home, the memories of her wedding returned. It seemed that since, her husband's interest in her was waning. The excitement diminished and she didn't look at him with the same feelings. They weren't mean to each other and rarely even argued. It just seemed that the luster was diminished and their life together just became common and ordinary, lacking in excitement. She reached the parking lot below their condominium and parked in her assigned place. All was quiet within the expanse as she walked to the doorway of the small lot.

Sydney inserted her key and turned the lock on the front door. She heard the familiar sound as the tumbler clicked to grant her entry. She saw Damon sitting at the desk on the computer.

Her thoughts ran to their recent visit to the birdcage at the zoo. Damon held her hand as they gazed upon a pair of loons. He looked at her.

"You know loons mate for life, unlike other bird species," he said. She giggled and asked him if he was comparing them to a pair of loons. "Yes, maybe I am," he replied. They both laughed and hugged when he said it.

"Anything exciting going on?" she asked

"Just all these women after me here online," Damon responded with a laugh.

"Well that's not news," she added.

She walked over to him and slowly surrounded his neck with her arms, placing a gentle kiss on his cheek.

Damon was not strikingly handsome. By most standards, he was average looking. To the woman standing above him, he was once the most handsome man in the world. He was able to touch her mind in ways that no one else alive could do. He took her hands in his and turning his head slightly touched her lips with his in a gently soft manner that sent electricity through her. That feeling hadn't happened in quite a while. She felt a sudden arousal developing.

Sydney looked at her husband quizzically, surprised by the sudden surge of feeling that coursed through her. He noticed the reaction too. Turning toward his pretty wife, he gently pulled her into his lap. She stared up into the handsome face of the man she loved. Feeling his hands touch the top button of her blouse, her body arched as anticipation began to surge through her.

Father Martin Ruby

Maria attended ten o'clock Mass, and it was uneventful with the usual pleading for funds for some new project. During the customary Peace ceremony, Maria turned around to shake hands with the others near her. She looked behind her and saw a familiar black woman, Mrs. Mayberry with her sister and group of children. The Mayberry woman always brought a number of neighborhood kids to Mass. Maria wondered what she was like, as she always had a big smile and air of comfort in spite of her old and worn clothing. There was an empty row between them, so she wasn't able to reach and shake hands with the children, but she did make eye contact with the Mayberry woman who extended her hand and echoed the common "Peace be to you," to Maria.

As their hands touched, Maria felt the warm tingle. Jennifer Mayberry felt it too. "You're spreading warmth today," she said to Maria with a smile. Maria smiled back.

"Maybe you are," Maria commented in return. They both looked to each other's eyes and returned their attention to the front of the church.

After Mass, Father Martin Ruby as usual, was outside bidding good wishes to the parishioners. His presence was sartorial. A short gray beard with matching colored hair outlined a studious looking face on his portly frame. Father Ruby noticed Maria and walked forward to greet her. She smiled at the kindly priest.

"How was your vacation to the Holy Land Maria?"

"It was wonderful Father."

"I even picked up a souvenir," she said holding up her finger.

Jennifer Mayberry walked by with a smile and nodded to Maria.

Father Ruby nodded to her and turned to examine Maria's finger with interest.

He touched the skin over the impression. It was warm. Father Ruby looked at Maria in surprise. He took her aside by the arm so that they could talk further. Maria continued talking as they walked toward the Rectory where Father Ruby lived. Father Ruby invited Maria in to continue their conversation. That sat on the sun porch and enjoyed the gentle breeze.

As Father Ruby sat listening to the interesting story Maria conveyed, his mind wandered to the days of his research and development of opinions formed and delivered about a similar set of circumstances.

Father Martin Ruby invited Maria to tell him as much as she could about what she knew and thought about the connection to the sliver in her hand. She told him of the happenings at the hospital and of what her friends had told her.

He listened without interruption as Maria told him of events that took place since leaving Jerusalem.

After listening to Maria's recounting of the incidents, Father Ruby decided to confide in her regarding research and studies he had done. One of the parishioners, who helped at the rectory, brought iced-tea to them as they talked.

Fr. Ruby told Maria of his thoughts on the crucifixion, the cross, possible miracles associated with the time of Christ's life and more. It was Maria's turn to listen.

"While I was studying for the priesthood, I chose to review the Crucifixion and the collateral happenings leading up to the event as well as what took place afterwards. My thesis was written on miracles attributed to artifacts associated with the cross and people involved with the associations."

"My findings became known within the hierarchy of the Catholic Church. Then, I offered an opinion on events that took place. I found a man with a wooden artifact. They say it was part of the Cross. "

He continued. "The only problem was that I couldn't be sure of anything. All the man could offer was that he could make good things happen for people he touched."

Maria interrupted him. "How can you keep this secret and not tell others," she wanted to know.

"I know of no one whose life was miraculously saved or died because of the man's touch. That man logically assumed it was the passing of good. In some cases, I was able to verify the facts. The man also noted that at times, he was able to wish things to happen. The man did not remember any incident when someone attempted to hurt or strike him."

How strange Father Ruby thought that out of nowhere; this woman called and was now providing the bewitching series of events that tied in so perfectly to his own findings as well as the similarities to the other man's story.

In the man's case, Father Ruby investigated further and although unable to confirm his theory, he was satisfied that the man was speaking the truth.

"Tell me more about this feeling of warmth Maria."

"When I touch someone with my hand, I have this warm feeling and the other person feels it too. What does it mean Father?"

"The man I interviewed also mentioned the unusual event that you describe. Father Ruby noted."

"Do you think I should talk with someone else in the Church about this Father?"

Father Ruby looked at Maria intently.

"Maria, I believe you should keep your gift to yourself for now. The Church has what I call a "Stained Glass Curtain" regarding miraculous happenings. You may come under scrutiny and lose some of your freedom, if the Church became involved. It might be a matter of control and deep scrutiny."

"Thus the term Stained Glass Curtain," Maria finished the Priest's sentence.

"I understand Father; I think I'll keep it to myself."

"Maria, you aren't God, but an agent for good. Know this, as a very holy man told it to me. All that is good already resides within everyone. You have been chosen to bring that out for others to experience. Relish that, and be thankful that you are able to make a difference that others only wish they could. Do the best you can with the gift."

Maria looked intently at Father Ruby.

"I will Father, I most definitely will."

With that, Father Ruby gave Maria his blessing and she walked to the door, with a feeling of confidence wrapped in the unknown mystery that she would be living.

"Would you mind checking your papers to see if there is anything else that might help me deal with this gift, Father?"

"Of course Maria," he replied smiling.

"Thank you Father."

"Ah, Maria? You should know something else. The person that told me about a similar gift also said that warmth could pass on the good and a feeling of coldness should serve as a warning. Keep that in mind for the future."

She stood open mouthed at the door.

"Take care of yourself and God bless, Maria"

He opened the door for her and watched as she descended the stairs.

He closed the door as his mind drifted to earlier days. Maria looked back for a moment and saw the vision of the crucifixion in her mind's eye.

The Three Friends

Maria, Ellie and Sydney continued to meet when they could. Maria told them of her conversation with Fr. Ruby. Nothing of note happened between times they met, so they talked about other things. After each get-together, they would share their community hugs and noticed that the feeling of warmth always happened. They felt this to be a good sign.

Chapter 6 A Game And Karaoke

Ellie

A few days passed since the accident where Ellie and Jimmy first met. Ellie decided to call her firefighter friend, ostensibly to discuss more about the accident. During the conversation, as she hoped, he asked her out.

"How would you like to see a Bear's game," he asked suddenly.

"Wow, I'm not much of a sports fan, but it sounds like fun. Sure I'll go," she responded. After a few brief pleasantries, he said he had to go, but he would call with the details. As she put down the phone, she twirled and felt a delightful flutter.

Ellie's and Jimmy Ennis's busy lifestyles and commitments to others, kept Ellie from seeing or speaking with Jimmy for a couple weeks. At last, they were able to work out the date and decided to attend a Bear's game.

Jimmy and Ellie Shine

Pink and orange clouds to the West, lit the sky with reflections from the setting sun. Ellie felt very special, as Jimmy Ennis pulled the Explorer into one of the private, reserved, parking areas. They were just outside the renovated Soldier Field, home of the Chicago Bears.

The Bears would be playing the Rams, on Monday night and a rush of excitement filled the evening air.

She met his smile with one of her own, as they continued toward the gate. When they entered, it was obvious that Jimmy was well known. Men and women alike, greeted him as they climbed to the executive boxes, high atop the stadium. Ellie was even more impressed when she learned of the seating arrangements. People who stopped by to shake hands and exchange banter with her date surprised her. He seemed to take it all in stride.

Curiosity getting the best of her, after a popular reporter had stopped for a few words, she asked.

"How have you come to know all these people Jimmy?"

"My family is well connected," he replied. "Blame it on my father. He's the one who really knows everyone."

Jimmy obviously knew a number of influential people on this own. He gave Ellie a little information about himself and his family. His father was a Chief in the Chicago fire department for a number of years. Through his dad, Jimmy met an array of notable men and women. He followed his father into the fire department. He was also becoming popular within the department and through meeting some of the influential people who were friends of his family.

The game was one of the Bears usual three yards and a cloud of dust games, with the defense unable to stop the Rams passing attack. There were a few times that the Bears scored and the crowd got involved, but mainly it was more ho hum than exciting. If there was a highlight, it was the Bear's middle linebacker, Urban Knacker, who was all over the field, as usual, making plays to the cheers of the crowd.

By the end of the game, she was glad she attended. The Bears won for a change and the crowd was in good spirits. As the game ended, the throng of fans began to exit quickly.

After meeting a few more people, Jimmy led Ellie to an empty stairway. They proceeded down the stairs that led to a single doorway. As they approached one of the doorway guards, Ellie was shocked to see the guard greet them and open the door, inviting them into some place of inner sanctuary.

There were people milling about in the room, and a few came over to Jimmy. He introduced Ellie to them. Ellie was referred to as, his special friend. The term of endearment evoked smiles and a few raised eyebrows and winks. Ellie knew enough to understand the meaning. She smiled up at the man by her side and he returned a genuine smile of his own.

As they stood exchanging pleasantries with others, the doors opened and players began to emerge. All had changed to street clothes. Some were in suits, while others wore outfits that were more comfortable. Some of the folks, whom Jimmy had introduced as press people, moved toward the players with recorders. Others just sauntered up and began conversations. Everyone seemed to be in good spirits. Of course, Ellie couldn't tell a Bear from a Ram, the way they were dressed. She of course, knew some of the players' numbers but not their faces. Without uniforms, it was impossible to identify them. Jimmy pointed out a few of the more popular players. A couple came over to shake hands and share a few words. She looked at her friend in admiration. He seemed so comfortable with everyone and that made her at ease as well.

Finally, the player all were waiting for came out from behind the doors. It was middle linebacker, Urban Knacker. Ellie recognized him from seeing his picture often on television. On the scene, he became the immediate focus of attention. He was very cordial to everyone and shared his notable wide smile without hesitation.

Questions were coming at him from everywhere and he calmly retained his composure with short word and phrase answers. Then, with a wave of his hand, he was able to convey, that the question period was over.

Most of the people in the room withdrew with respect for the expression. As the athlete walked toward the outer door, he noticed Jimmy standing with Ellie. Immediately, a smile broadened on the popular athlete's face. He turned from his trail toward the door and approached Jimmy standing with the red haired woman. Jimmy extended his hand and Urban Knacker grasped it, in a friendly exchange of manly acceptance. After a few words, Urban Knacker looked at Ellie and asked Jimmy.

"Is the pretty lady a secret Jimmy, or do I get an introduction?"

Ellie was mortified. She felt her face flush the color of watermelon.

"Sorry, this is Ellie Mulcahey, a special friend."

"Glad to meet you Ellie, you also have a very special man here."

Ellie was too flabbergasted to respond.

She was only able to spurt, "I know, thanks".

He looked back at Jimmy and slapped him on the arm with a "Take care Jimmy, I'll see you around."

"You too Urban" Jimmy responded with a large smile.

Ellie looked at Jimmy Ennis. She had many questions. Her friend looked at her with a grin and took her arm, to lead her toward the exit.

She reached for his arm and held it tightly, as they walked out into the cool evening air. In the car on the way home, Ellie noticed an envelope, addressed to Captain James Ennis. So, Jimmy was more than a just a firefighter. He was a Captain in the Chicago fire department. She wondered if there was more to his popularity.

Ellie didn't feel like going home yet. She looked at the handsome man sitting behind the wheel.

"How would you like a little Karaoke before heading home?"

"What?" Jimmy Ennis replied in surprise."

"Karaoke," Ellie said again with a laugh.

"Are you serious?"

"Sure, why not." Ellie continued.

"I don't sing," he stated with an apologetic tone to his voice.

"Cool. Turn left when we get to Halsted Street," Ellie said providing direction.

Maria

Maria sat at "Speakers Restaurant" in the company of her brother Torreo. She always liked the atmosphere and the karaoke singing.

It was one of those rare times, when Maria was able to spend time with her always-busy brother.

My, she thought to herself, how quickly he's growing and maturing." They were celebrating his 21st birthday before he set out to join his friends in celebration, later in the evening.

Maria decided to tell her brother a little of what was happening to her. She usually didn't see much of him because he was always busy. Her brother stared at his sister in disbelief at some of the information Maria was telling him.

"Can I see the sliver?" he asked.

Maria lifted her hand for her brother to see.

Immediately, he took her hand for a closer look and felt the warm glow emanating from her hand to his.

"What the heck is that," he asked when he felt the warmness.

"That's what I was talking about silly."

"Hey, that's a little quirky isn't it Sis?

Maria sat and shrugged, waiting for her brother to return to the real world.

Torreo was asking questions like a machine gun. He wasn't even allowing his Sister to respond before asking another question.

"Can I do anything to help you Sis?" He finally blurted out.

"You can keep our secret, my dear Brother. I will need you to do that for me, at least until I can get a better handle on this thing."

Torreo smiled and took his Sister's hand in his.

"I will Sis, you can count on me. It's a little hard to believe anyway. I don't think anyone would believe me anyway."

Ellie and Jimmy

Within minutes, Ellie and her friend were at "*Speakers*", the popular Karaoke bar. "*Speakers*", an upscale restaurant and bar on the near West Side, was fast becoming a new "Hot Spot" for Chicago nightlife.

Ellie explained to Jimmy,

"The clientele consist of very upper class wannabes as well as up and coming talents. Some rich and well to do, often come to receive the adulation of their friends. Not all however, were considered to be as talented as they believed themselves to be." "Should I be surprised?" he shot back.

"Nonetheless, all are welcome and the *Crystal* champagne is served as well as the more plentiful orders for beer by the bottle or tap," she added.

As they made their entrance, a man greeted Ellie at the door. She responded easily and pulled her date further forward and toward the stage where manager Billy Banners stood. The sounds coming from the stage drew the attention of the crowd.

Jimmy felt the beat with Ellie swaying against his side.

As Jimmy and Ellie waited, a song ended. Billy Banner's attention drifted from the stage to the crowd. He turned and a broad smile broke onto his face as he saw Ellie. He waved and came over to greet them.

"Hi Billy."

"Hello Ellie." I saw Maria sitting in the back with a very handsome young man. They seemed to be deep in conversation, so I didn't bother to say hello."

Ellie nodded in acknowledgement.

"Billy, this is my dear friend Jimmy Ennis."

Jimmy offered a hand to the smiling man. He felt the limp handshake. They were led to a table in the center of the room. The location was a fine vantage point for view and sound, Jimmy thought to himself.

The server appeared and they ordered two Miller Lite beers. Each looked at the other and smiled. As the next singer ended the song, they applauded and were able to converse. Another couple came to the table and introduced themselves. They exchanged small chat. The couple could tell that Ellie was not in the mood to share her date. She told them they were waiting for friends. The others moved on.

Torreo's Exit

Torreo decided it was time to join his friends for a little birthday celebration. Maria rose and walked her brother to the door. She decided to go home rather than stay. She envisioned a full day tomorrow. Maria exchanged kisses on the cheeks with her brother, as they headed in different directions at the door. Looking back at the other each waved.

Fun and More Songs

As the evening continued, more people came by the table to share a joke or comment as the crowd grew. Jimmy Ennis enjoyed his somewhat celeb status with Ellie whom most of the people seemed to know. A few offered suggestions to Ellie for songs that she should sing. She laughed and thanked them for their input.

Jimmy finally couldn't take it anymore and asked Ellie if she would please get up and offer a platitude to those who kept asking her to sing. She laughed.

"You want to hear me sing, Mr. Ennis?"

"Yes, Ms. Mulcahey, I would like that."

Without another word, Ellie rose and strode quickly over to the DJ. They shared a few words and the man smiled broadly at the pretty and vivacious woman.

Ellie returned and took her seat. As she did, she raised her arm to the server and made that usual circle that meant another round. The server saw her and nodded.

Within a minute, two more Miller Lites were on the table.

As the singer on the stage finished to serious applause, the DJ announced the next vocalist. Jimmy heard Ellie's name and he reached over and patted her on the arm.

"Go get em Ellie," he remarked.

With that, she rose to cheers and clapping. She walked toward the stage, accepting the microphone from the DJ.

She nodded and the music began.

Jimmy immediately recognized Shania Twain's *Man I Feel Like a Woman,* and wow, did the lady with the mike do something with that song.

The throng recognized the beat too and conversation ebbed as eyes focused on the red haired talent on the stage. The beat was pulsing and Ellie Mulcahey took the beat and wrapped herself in it. In a few moments, she had the entire room rocking. The crowd was dancing wherever they could find room. The whole room was alive and jumping.

Jimmy Ennis sat in awe. This woman is good, he thought to himself. Looking around, he noticed that his thoughts were not his alone. Those that were not dancing sat silently watching. Ellie's voice and movements on the stage became a magnet. She had just taken over the place.

As he watched her move and listened to her voice, he could feel the sensuality, within the woman, belting out the song in the most enticing voice, he could remember hearing. God, he wanted to jump up and stand next to her. She was amazing.

As the song ended, the crowd erupted in tumultuous applause.

"Encore, encore" could be heard above the yelling and clapping.

Ellie knew how to handle a crowd too. She bowed and smiled with hands waving in each direction. She gently handed the microphone back to the DJ, with a smile and a kiss on the cheek.

Jimmy Ennis rose to greet her, as she neared the table. He reached out and offered a hug that she gratefully accepted, by simply smothering herself in his arms. She stepped back and looked up at him as he kissed her on the cheek and whispered "pretty and talented too, what a mix." At hearing it, she tossed her head back and smiled broadly with a gleam in her eyes.

After her performance, the DJ decided it was time for some canned music and announced a twenty-minute break. It was a fortuitous thought on his part as no one was willing to get up on the stage after that performance. Ellie had set the standard and everyone sat back to share conversations for a while.

As the place filled, Ellie waved to a few friends standing nearby to join them. She winked at Jimmy and his generous return smile, told her it would be fine. The entire place was abuzz waiting for more Karaoke to start again.

As they talked with the others at the table, there soon rose a growing chorus for a song. The DJ happily responded with the next person on the list. As each presented their vocal renditions, it seemed that the talent continued to grow. The crowd roared after each singer concluded their rendition.

Then a name could be heard. It began in the back of the room and spread.

"Jose Jose Jose' the crowd began to chant. Jose Santiago must be here," Ellie said.

Jimmy Ennis's face showed a question mark.

"Jose's a friend of Maria's who stops in now and then. He is well known locally, because of his great voice."

"He's a Christian crossover singer who enjoys singing opera."

Jimmy Ennis nodded in recognition. "He and I occasionally team up," Ellie told Jimmy.

"Go ahead," he urged her with his biggest smile.

Ellie rose to see if she could find Jose in the crowd. She saw him waving from the bar. With a flick of her arm, she motioned toward their table. Jose responded with a wave and spoke to the woman next to him as he took her by the arm, leading them to Ellie's table.

Ellie remembered a couple years back when Jose first began to sing at "Speakers". The crowd wasn't into what was termed, "long haired music" at the time. Jose suffered through a number of nights where the crowd actually booed his singing. It was very different now. As the crowd became more refined, he found a following that enjoyed his style and choice of music. When the male opera tenors became popular, his stock rose, as the crowd became more familiar with his songs and phenomenal voice.

"He's coming up Jimmy." "You'll love this."

Jimmy Ennis looked up just as Jose Santiago and his date reached their table. Jimmy rose to shake hands with the man.

Jose Santiago introduced Alexi Davidoff, the woman at his side, as Ellie motioned them to seats at the table. As they were about to sit, the crowd began its chant. "Jose, Jose, Jose." He shrugged his shoulders and took his date's arm, while rising walking toward the stage. It appeared that Jose's date feigned bewilderment as if part of the act. She smiled coyly regardless.

"Do you know her Ellie?" Jimmy Ennis asked. "No. Doesn't she seem Eastern European," was the response. Jimmy nodded in agreement.

The two approached the stage. The DJ met them handing them both microphones. Jose Santiago said something to the DJ and the man turned and inserted a new flash drive and in a moment, the music started.

The introduction lilted in the air. The crowd's noise diminished as if on signal as the woman with Jose began the words of the song. *There For Me*, the hit by Sarah Brightman and Jose Cura. Silence filled the room as he sang. The DJ turned off the equalizer as the enchanting woman and Jose's voices began to build in volume. As the song went on, the strains built in volume and emotion, one could see tears forming in many of the patrons' eyes. The music and the voices of the two singers were so moving they created an emotional reaction from the audience.

As the song gently concluded, there was a moment of hushed silence. Then the tumult of the crowds, cheering and clapping took over and shook the room. The two were hailed as they were congratulated coming down from the stage and returning to Ellie at the table.

Returning to the table, Jimmy Ennis rose, shook Jose's hand, and kissed the woman's cheek in a sign of admiration. He escorted her to the chair.

Jimmy Ennis looked at the smiling face before him listening to the well wishes and congratulations from those nearby. He could feel his heart pounding in pride.

Ellie moved closer to Jose's partner Alexi, and they exchanged a few comments and laughs with each other. Ellie and Jimmy Ennis stayed to talk and listen to a few of the other singers and finally decided it was time to go. They waited for an intermission and tried to be as unobtrusive as possible leaving the table. They made their good-byes to Jose and Alexi. They were only partially successful, but did manage to work their way to the door within a reasonable timeframe. Handshakes and good wishes were accepted and acknowledged. Smiles were everywhere as they reached the exit.

Meeting still night air had an immediate effect on Ellie, as she felt suddenly drained from the events of the evening. Looking over at Jimmy, she noticed he was stifling a yawn. Quite a night, she thought. Quite a night, he thought. They wrapped arms and strolled comfortably together toward the car for the ride home.

They kissed as they exited the car with smiles on their faces and proceeded to their respective houses. It had been quite a day for both.

Chapter 7 Endings And Beginnings

Maria

It was early in the morning. Maria climbed onto the bus followed by a man. She dropped her token into the slot and proceeded to an empty seat. A man followed and took a seat further back in the bus.

As the bus neared the hospital stop, Maria rose for her exit. She climbed down the two steps to the street and entered the hospital through the main doors greeting some of the workers as she walked to the elevator bank. Maria walked to the elevators for a ride to the third floor where she would empty the patient wastebaskets and perform general clean up duties. The soft ding of the bell announced the elevator's arrival. Maria stepped in

Maria continued her rounds and finally could no longer avoid the room of Marshall Creighton.

She entered the room and found the crotchety old man asleep, much to her delight. The joy was short-lived however as his eyes opened at the noise of Maria checking his water. She felt his hand grasp her wrist in a viselike grip.

"What are you doing," Maria exclaimed in surprise. She immediately reached for his hand with her free hand to try to disengage from his hold on her. He looked at her with cold, penetrating steel gray eyes.

Marshall Creighton was not prepared for what happened next. As she placed her hand over his in her attempt to gain freedom, he felt a frightening cold feeling flow though his arm. The shock was surprising and severe to the old man. She felt him quickly let go of her arm wringing his hand as if to relieve it of something. He felt the sharp pain and clutched his chest. She had felt nothing other than his hand on her arm. His face wore a stunned look. His eyes that had appeared so cold turned to look away from her in fear. She was awaiting another outburst of swearing and indignity from the man, but it never came. Instead, there was silence.

Now that she was free again, she decided to ignore whatever he was going to spew and walked toward the door. Just as she reached the doorway, he let out his stream of curt remarks about Maria's nationality. She had grown accustomed to his antics, but it still made her furious that she could not and would not return the hurtful comments to the mean old man. Maria checked the vital signs monitor once more. His blood pressure was up a bit, but it was not a concern. She also knew why the reading was up. She emptied the water container and returned with a fresh one. She was subjected to more unkind words.

At one point, she turned her head to stare at the old man. His words froze in mid sentence, almost as if, like before, in fear of the look from the young woman's eyes. He looked at her. She returned the look. Marshall Creighton felt the girl's eyes piercing him. He turned away, unable to continue the stare. The man felt as though someone had just seen into his soul, and had sent him a message of displeasure. He felt remorse. He was suddenly sorry for subjecting the young woman to his vicious tirades. It was a feeling he had never before experienced.

What kind of power did this girl have that was so overwhelming that it shook him so deeply?

Marshall Creighton quickly pulled the sheets over his head and took several deep breaths. He reached for the morphine button that would inject a dose into the IV attached to his arm. He decided it wasn't necessary. The ugly feeling subsided. The feeling of the awesome power the girl possessed lingered as his eyes closed in sleep.

When his wife arrived, she awakened him. This was something she rarely did. Usually, he was awake and in pain. He told her of the strange experience. Pacey Creighton was surprised to hear her husband explain the feeling.

She looked at him questioningly. There was a change. She wondered about this strange effect and if the Spanish girl caused it in her usually mean and venomous husband. She would soon know.

Marshall Creighton tapped his hand on the bed as an invitation for his wife to sit next to him. Here was another first for Pacey Creighton. They had not been close together in sharing a moment of conversation in years. She had just decided to put up with his ranting and not allow herself to become anxious or upset any longer. It worked for her.

There was an obvious change in the face of her husband. His countenance no longer bore the fury of his discontent. It seemed to have softened. The look in his eyes was more lenient and accepting. She didn't quite know what to make of it at first.

It didn't take her long to find out. Marshall Creighton, it seemed had found his reality and he wanted to talk with her about it. She simply stared in amazement as the man in the bed began to tell her of his feelings.

Maria came by the door as she was wrapping up for the day. Marshall Creighton noticed her and tugged at his wife's sleeve to get the young woman to come back to the room.

"Young lady, please come over here?"

"I promise not to do anything to upset you."

Maria approached the bed. Pacey Creighton didn't know what would happen.

The man's voice spoke in a new tone she had not heard before.

"I'm sorry for how I've treated you."

He raised his hand with his palm open to fortify his honest feeling.

Maria reached over and touched the man's hand.

"It's alright, Mr. Creighton, you're having a difficult time. I understand. Their hands touched again as he felt a comforting warmth flow from the young woman's hand. It was nothing like the shock he received a few moments ago. "You rest now, Mr. Creighton."

"I'm sure you'll be feeling better soon."

Pacey Creighton was mesmerized at the tone of the -conversation.

Maria glanced at Pacey Creighton, turned and quietly walked out of the room without looking back.

After the scene, the Creightons had a long discussion that lasted for hours. Numerous times, she had tried to rise but he insisted she stay. He talked and she listened. The man who was dying seemed to want to make peace with himself and certainly with her. He discussed the happenings of the years that had past in ways that amazed her. He related minute details of their relationship. He told of how he did things and said things that hurt her. He apologized many times. She could see he was becoming weaker as he shifted position in the bed to gain some relief from the awful pain. He pressed the button for the morphine. A few times during the conversation, she took his hand and held it gently. He allowed that. In the past, he would always pull away as if saying, don't touch me. Now he seemed to want her close to him.

He told his wife of the daily torments he had unleashed at the Spanish girl, who had never done anything to harm him or invite the ridicule.

Pacey Creighton felt sadness for the girl and a relief for the man lying in front of her, as he told her what he had done. At one point he stopped and simply looked at the woman sitting next to him and said,

"I'll never be able to make it up to her or ask her to forgive me."

Pacey Creighton felt the tears forming in her eyes as she was listening to her husband.

"I believe she will forgive you, Marshall." In fact, I would bet she has already considered your condition, and granted you her forgiveness.

"There is a kindness about her Marshall, which I feel is very real. She understands."

Taking his hand gently, she added. "She does Marshall, and I will also have to ask her forgiveness for how I've treated her too."

With that, Marshall Creighton surprised his wife once more.

"Get a Rabbi for me?"

"Of course," she responded.

"Now?"

The obvious intent surprised her.

"Right now?" she asked.

"Yes." Was the man's response.

She removed her hand from his, stood and walked to the nurse's station.

As the nurse looked up, she saw the tears in the other woman's eyes.

"Can you contact a Rabbi here at the hospital?" She asked.

"I can certainly try," the nurse responded reaching for the phone.

As the nurse pressed the buttons on the phone, her feelings of dislike for the woman and her husband abated. Something good ``was happening now and she wanted to help.

Pacey Creighton listened as the nurse communicated her request. She waited in earnest.

"He'll be here shortly, Mrs. Creighton," the nurse informed her.

"Thank you, I'll be in his room."

The nurse nodded her assent.

As Pacey Creighton turned to return to her husband's room, she saw her daughter walking toward her. Moving toward her, she wrapped her arms around her tightly. Vera Creighton was surprised at the emotional display. Her mother was not one to show any emotion.

Vera Creighton

Vera Creighton's face bore a look of surprise as her mother provided a capsule commentary of the last few hours. A few times, the daughter shook her head to be sure, she was hearing correctly. They began to walk toward the room, arm in arm. Upon entering, they both viewed the fragile looking man in a different light. It was still hard to believe; yet something had changed and it was for the better.

The father motioned his daughter to sit on the bed. He took her hand and looked at her. His eyes taking in the features he had long ago forgotten to notice. She was a woman of her own now. In a few sentences, Vera Creighton felt more for her father than she had in many years. She felt sadness and relief.

There was a knock on the door. The Rabbi arrived. Both of the women stood to greet him. Marshall Creighton asked to be alone with the man. The women nodded in understanding and walked toward the door, eyes riveted on the man lying so helplessly now in the bed.

They walked toward the waiting area to sit and wait. As they reached the area, the alarm went off. A patient was in need of immediate treatment. They saw people in green and white moving quickly by them.

The Rabbi approached. Without a word passing between them, they knew what the Rabbi would be saying. The patient alarm sounded on the monitoring machine. They knew the alarm was for their father and husband. Seeing the look on the Rabbi's face, they knew it was a fruitless endeavor. Marshall Creighton had passed on. While they talked, the Creighton women knew that the sickly man had made his peace with God and with them. Pacey Creighton also knew that she had to find some way to abate the suffering of one person who her husband's cruelty had caused to suffer severely during the last few weeks. She would contact the Spanish woman to make things right for them all.

Maria

Maria entered her apartment and shed her coat, flinging it onto the coat rack near the door. Before she was able to close the door behind her, the phone rang. She decided to let the answering machine respond.

The day was a trying one and she wasn't yet ready to have a discussion with anyone. She walked to the bathroom and looked at her tired face in the mirror. Her ears heard a female voice talking faintly on the answering machine. She would listen to the message in good time. For the present, she turned on the faucet, cupped her hands and splashed the warm water on her face. She patted her face with the hunter green towel and walked toward her bedroom fully intent on getting into some comfortable clothing again.

The phone rang again. She looked at the number and lifted the cordless phone from its cradle. It was Chelle Leriget from the employment agency that provided her with the hospital and waitress jobs.

"Maria? This is Chelle Leriget," the voice questioned pleasantly.

"Yes," she responded as she recognized the woman's voice.

"I wanted to call and tell you that we have a new opportunity that you may be interested in, if you'd like to stop by soon to discuss it?"

"Oh, how wonderful, Mrs. Leriget. Sure, would tomorrow morning be OK?"

"That would be wonderful Maria, about ten o'clock then?"

Maria thought for a moment.

"That would be fine, Mrs. Leriget"

"See you then, thank you."

Maria let the phone fall gently on the bed as she began to shed the work clothes and put on the comfy fleece sweat suit.

Looking at the clock on her dresser, she felt like talking to Ellie. She promised to call, and it seemed like now was the right time. Picking up the phone, she pressed Ellie's number.

Ellie was out, so she left a quick message and hung up. She flopped on the bed and was fast asleep immediately.

Carl Sarna

For Carl Sarna, the days passed slowly. The feeling of dread he was harboring lessened, yet still remained. Occasionally, his thoughts drifted to the embarrassing event at the restaurant and the disturbing happening with the waitress outside afterward. He was unable to help, being too far away and in his wheel chair. When he had observed the man coming to the rescue of Maria from Bertrand Cooper's assault, he turned and made his way to the waiting car that his friend Abby had parked close to the curb.

Another workweek began as usual. Monday morning presented its dull self. He wheeled himself into the office as usual. Abby Tisdale walked by and greeted him cheerfully. She was the administrative assistant to Bertrand Cooper. Cooper was the dominating force within his section of the company. The man was overbearing and downright mean, yet the company heaped praise on him for the resulting profits attributed to his unit.

Carl Sarna knew better. The profits were a conjured jumble of non-existent transactions; that eventually, would be found by the accountants and the company would be thrown into financial disarray. He just wasn't able to get close enough to produce proof, as Bertrand Cooper shielded everything with his overbearing attitude and ridicule of anyone that questioned him. He truly ruled from a pulpit of fear. He also controlled all the delivery companies that served as vendors for the company.

Carl Sarna thought Cooper must be receiving kickbacks, and they must be sizable. No other shipper was allowed to gain entry to the company's list of vendors for a number of years. Shipway Freight and its ghost subsidiaries got all the business. Cooper made sure of that, and Sarna felt they paid him well for the business.

He couldn't figure how Abby Tisdale could be a willing accomplice. That part just didn't make sense.

Abby walked by him in her navy blue business suit with stylish pumps and gave him a wink. He wondered what that was all about. Stopping at his cubicle, he checked his emails and the notes from fellow workers on his desk. Nothing required his immediate attention. He opened a file and reviewed his notes for the morning meeting. As he shuffled the papers, a stapled set fell to the floor. He reached down to pick it up and as he looked at it, he laughed. It was a warehousing analysis he had undertaken as a cost saving measure.

A Meeting of Meetings

Under the plan he proposed, the company should save 31% of its freight shipping costs after expenses. Considering the amount the firm spent each year to adjust production because of a lack of warehouse space, the benefits could likely be even greater than his estimate. He glanced at the clock and knew it was time for the meeting. Gathering his papers, he cleared his computer screen and headed toward the bank of elevators.

Carl Sarna wheeled his chair into the room and took a place near the middle of the table. He noticed a few new faces, and introduced himself as a friendly gesture. Bertrand Cooper made his grand entrance, speaking into the cell phone as if he was making another significant decision. Those in the room were on to the Cooper gimmick and silently chuckled, as they knew Abby Tisdale was on the other end of the line. Cooper took his customary seat at the head of the table and announced the start of the meeting.

He was only able to mutter the word "Let's," when the door opened and the Company President, Eldredge Connelly with a few other high-ranking officers of the company, entered the room. Without saying a word, they took up empty seats at the far end of the table. Cooper interrupted to introduce the newly arrived men. They acknowledged the recognition. Eldredge Connelly told Bertrand Cooper to continue.

For fifteen minutes, the group studied monthly budget projections to actual and held minor discussions regarding small anomalies. Bertrand Cooper then announced the new report on warehousing that would cost the company a "ton of money," or be a waste to implement. He passed copies to everyone.

Carl Sarna received his copy. His eyes widened in stunned disbelief at what he saw. He quickly glanced through the pages. There were different figures from the one's he had drawn, but the analysis part of the report was nearly identical, with a few significant exceptions to the one he had submitted almost three months previously to Bertrand Cooper. He studied the figures with more intensity, and noticed some irregularities that hadn't been in his original. Two particular areas were the cost containment in production and the proposed savings in warehousing costs. The figures were far less that he estimated, making the analysis look like a waste of time. He stared at one page in particular, on which the columns didn't foot correctly.

Eldredge Connelly was watching Carl Sarna's reaction. The error was glaring. Sarna continued through ach of the other pages and noticed the error was continued through the other sets of figures, providing an amount much different from what it should have been under the scenarios involved. Abby Tisdale would never have let that happen on something she worked on. She was a perfectionist. Carl Sarna wondered who worked the revisions into the report if it wasn't Abby. He let the thought drift away.

Cooper continued through the analysis and report, smiling as he went. Upon reaching the last page of analysis, he sat back in his chair and voiced aloud, "What do you think, gentlemen?"

The room was silent. Many of the meeting participants had no idea what the content of the report meant. It was pretty far out of their league.

Carl Sarna continued to stare at the report. It was his report, with major paragraph revisions and bore some major financial misstatements. Only his name was missing and in its place stood the name of Bertrand Cooper, but the report summary was totally different and contrary to his.

This report indicated that the entire effort would result in very little savings and more likely, additional expenditures. However, his analysis previously indicated a sizeable amount of savings, worthy of immediate consideration.

As if on cue, one of the senior company officers began to ask Bertrand Cooper a few questions concerning the content and projections. At first, Cooper responded comfortably as if the questions were meaningless. Then the questions became more direct, focusing on specific pages of the analysis.

The official directed everyone to page four of the report.

"Why this figure and how did you arrive at that scenario," Bertrand Cooper was asked. Everyone could sense Bertrand Cooper's uneasiness. He was shifting in his chair uneasily now as his responses were disputed and new questions asked.

Without warning, Victor Connelly slammed his fist on the table. The president stood and walked around behind his chair with the report in hand.

"Carl, do you feel this analysis is sufficient for the company to scrap the project?"

Sarna looked in disbelief, first at the president, then at Bertrand Cooper.

"There seem to be a few errors in the projections sir."

"What errors Carl?"

"Well, ah,"…Carl Sarna fought to find the right words.

He was cut off as he again began to speak.

"Whose report is this, Bertrand?" The president spoke in a commanding tone.

There was a long pause in the conversation.

"Well Sarna did the preliminary and I corrected the assumptions in the analysis," Bertrand Cooper offered quietly.

"I see," Eldredge Connelly, responded.

"What figures did you decide to change, Bertrand?"

"Well, some of the savings estimates were way off, sir."

"So you adjusted them Bertrand?"

"Yes sir."

"Did you consult with Sarna?"

"Well ah … No sir, I didn't"

Eldredge Connelly held out his hand to one of the senior officers. The man handed the President a bound report. As Carl Sarna watched, he saw that it looked just like the original one he submitted to Bertrand Cooper. Eldredge Connelly approached Bertrand Cooper who continued to shift uneasily in his chair.

Connelly flung the binder onto the table. It landed a few inches from Bertrand Cooper's hand.

"Ever see this before, Bertrand?"

Cooper grasped the binder and fanned the pages.

"I think that looks like Carl's preliminary report, though I can't be sure," he responded.

"OK, this meeting's over," Eldredge Connelly informed everyone.

"Carl, I would like to see you and Mr. Cooper in my office right now."

Without another word, Eldredge Connelly left the room.

Carl Sarna directed his wheelchair around the room and made a beeline for the washroom, leaving the other participants with their mouths open. He wanted to be sick as he bent over the sink throwing water on his face. He had no idea what was going to happen next, but he didn't like the feeling in the pit of his stomach. After raising himself to look in the mirror, he opened the door and wheeled himself toward the paneled executive offices. He felt Bertrand Cooper would find a way to cover things up and he would be looking for a job. He didn't see it any other way.

Carl Sarna entered the executive suite and saw Bertrand Cooper with a look of dejection emblazoned on his pudgy face. Two hefty security personnel were leading him, toward another exit. Sarna broke out in a cold sweat.

The secretary motioned him to enter, as she strode behind him to wheel his chair into the burled oak-paneled office. He noticed Eldridge Connelly standing at the window. The president turned as he heard Carl Sarna enter. He reached for the binder on his desk. Lifting it, he handed the neatly bound papers to Carl Sarna. At the same time, he nodded to his administrative assistant to leave them in privacy. The neatly clad woman smiled and closed the door as she left.

"The company is excited about your project, Senior Vice President Carl Sarna. You run with this just as outlined and save us all a lot of money. You are in complete control. If you have any needs, tell me. Otherwise, get some changes made around here that we can be proud of."

"Brief me with your plan Friday. Can you make lunch at Butterfield?"

"Yes sir," was Carl Sarna's response as he felt the conversation was over.

"I'll send a car for you. Is 12:00 agreeable?

"And thank you Carl. See you then."

He left the office as Eldredge Connelly was picking up the phone. A slight smile tugged his lips apart. Butterfield is the prestigious country club whose members included many, very well connected individuals. Lunch would be just fine he thought, as he directed his rolling chair back into his cubicle to find Abby Tisdale sitting in one of his reception chairs.

"Feeling better, Carl Sarna?" The woman in the blue suit asked. He looked at the woman for a long moment and nodded.

"Yes, I feel a lot better, thank you."

"Well what would you like me to start with, sir?"

"Let's make a few copies of this and get out a notice for a meeting tomorrow morning."

"I think I'm going to need an assistant for this, but if you could make the copies and get the meeting memo prepared that would be a great help."

Abby Tisdale rose and stepped away from the chair.

"You already have your assistant Mr. Sarna, and she will most definitely get the memo out and take care of anything else you'll need for the meeting."

"Will that be all for now?"

"Yes, Ms. Tisdale, for now." He sat in his chair, smiled for a moment and closed his eyes, offering a silent prayer of thanks.

Abby Tisdale stopped at the cubicle entrance and turned around.

"I have begun arrangements for your new office, as directed by Mr. Connelly." With that said, she was out of sight in a few seconds, leaving Carl Sarna with a question formed on his lips, but no one there to answer.

Chapter 8 Changing Times

Alhandro Pedroza

The steel gray fog covered the water like a glove. The air was heavy with the moisture of dawn, as Doctor Pedroza gazed out upon the gently lapping waves. He was relaxed, dressed in comfortable jeans and a T-shirt. He turned around on the pier to return up the hill to the cozy log cottage.

He loved the feeling the cottage brought to his being. It was his getaway, where he was able to shed the worries and trials of daily life at the hospital. His family had bought the small place on the lake many years ago when he was younger. As time passed, he learned more and more to appreciate the privacy and comfort of the place away from the hectic city life. The waves gently lapped at the boat moored to the pier, as he smiled and gazed at the wonderful sounds of nature around him.

Birds with their chatter gently interrupted the morning silence. He felt secure in this place. There was a growing longing for a companion to share the pleasures of life. His thoughts drifted to the pretty Hispanic woman, Maria Esparza, who always made him feel excited when she was around at the hospital. He guessed she was a few years younger than he, but not too young for them to enjoy many of the good things that life could provide.

As he prepared to shave for the day, he noticed the smile that greeted him in the mirror as he thought of the woman. Reaching for the washcloth, he turned on the faucet. Having a second thought, he turned off the running water and decided to fix some coffee. He opened the refrigerator door.

Maria

As she opened her refrigerator door, the phone rang. Maria decided to couch potato the night before and rose early to catch up on the new day. She answered the phone from her bedroom. "Maria Esparza?" the voice asked pleasantly.

"This is she." Maria responded lightly.

"This is Pacey Creighton, Miss Esparza."

Maria removed the phone from her ear and stared for a brief moment at the white plastic in her hand. Her mind raced with a sense of questioning awareness.

"Why on earth would this woman be calling?"

More so, how did she get my number? Letting the questions rest, she caught herself and put the phone back to her ear again.

"Yes, Mrs. Creighton, is there some problem?"

"I just want to call and thank you, Miss Esparza, for taking care of my husband and putting up with all the terrible things he did to you. I want to apologize for the way I treated you also. Please accept my apologies for both of our actions and words."

Maria looked at the phone incredulously.

"What?" she blurted unable to contain her reaction.

"I said I wanted to..." Maria cut the woman off with her response.

"Mrs. Creighton, I don't feel it necessary for you to apologize for your husband."

The Creighton woman cut Maria off in turn.

"He passed away yesterday Miss Esparza."

The young woman felt relief and a sense of sadness at the same time.

"I'm sorry Mrs. Creighton," was all she could say in reply.

"Thank you."

"I felt it necessary to tell you."

Why, is all Maria could wonder?

"My daughter and I would like to talk with you after the funeral, if that would be possible."

"Would sometime next week be alright?"

"Yes, sure," was all Maria could find to say in response.

"Oh, that's wonderful, Miss Esparza," Pacey Creighton said with a feeling of relief.

"I'll call you so we can set an appropriate time, Okay?"

"That will be fine," Maria responded.

"Good, that's set then," as Maria heard the phone click.

Still looking at the receiver, Maria shook her head, wondering what prompted that woman to call. Not sensing an answer, she let the thought drift away.

Jennifer Mayberry

Jennifer Mayberry stood sorting the clothes in front of the dryer at the local Laundromat. It was a ritual she performed twice a week. She had to, in order to keep clean clothes on her son and his friends. Usually her young son was there to help, but today, he disappeared as soon as she stuffed the first load washing machine. She knew he would not drift too far away, yet she looked around for the comfort of knowing he was all right.

A commotion at the door drew her attention. She could hear her son's excited voice. He was waving his hand and yelling unintelligible comments about winning something. As they drew near to each other, she could see the tears on the boy's face. He didn't seem to be hurt and he was smiling broadly, yet in tears. Jennifer Mayberry reached out for him and he grasped her hand tightly. She could see the item he was waving. All she could hear him saying was, "Mama, Mama, we won." It warmed her to see him so excited. Figuring that perhaps one of those drawing tickets she always filled out at the stores had selected her for a shopping spree or something of the sort, she smiled fondly at her young son.

"Please calm down Anthony," she said to him, but the boy continued to jump up and down. She noticed some paper in his hand and took it to study. At first glance, it appeared to be a crumpled piece of paper. Then she recognized it as she bent back the corners. It was a Lottery Ticket. At first, she was confused. Then she remembered the stop last week after the kindly woman at the hospital had given her the money.

"We won Mama," the young boy said in a more understandable, yet excited tone.

"Won what?" The woman responded.

"This is a winning ticket Mama." I just checked it. "We won," he exclaimed.

The woman stopped holding her son's hand and let it drop.

Standing there looking at each other, the boy finally said.

"Mama, there is one winning ticket for the lottery and this is it." He pointed to the still somewhat crumpled ticket in his mother's hand. It will pay 12 million dollars. She looked at her son in disbelief.

Just then, four boys from the neighborhood entered the front door. Looking around, the tall one asked.

"Who has that winning lottery ticket?"

Jennifer Mayberry's feelings suddenly turned to fear as she looked at the boys.

The boy in front saw her holding the ticket. As if on cue, the four young thugs began to walk hurriedly toward her. The Mayberry woman suddenly felt fear building. Those boys are going to take the ticket, she thought, yet she stood motionless, unable to move. Her son also knew what they were after. He knew them from the neighborhood. They preyed on anyone and freely stole things from people too afraid to fight back or call the police. These four were the worst.

Young Mayberry reached for his Mama's hand and grabbed the ticket from her. With the ticket firmly in his grasp, he quickly ran around the machines to the back door. The thug group followed on his heels; the leader, felt a quick cold shock as he pushed the woman's hand away. Anthony continued to the metal door and pushed on the release, opening the gray steel door. He could feel his pursuers. They were gaining on him. As the door flew open, the Mayberry boy turned quickly to his right, avoiding the electric pole in front of the door.

A tall thug, who was closest, followed. He lacked the adroitness of Anthony, although he was gaining closure. He followed the young boy through the door opening at full speed. His eyes riveted on the fleeing target.

Suddenly, before he could react, the steel pole was in his path. His face smashed into the hard surface with critical force, crushing his mouth against the cold unyielding steel. Teeth disengaged from gums as the force of impact crushed his face against the metal. His nose disintegrated immediately, the bone becoming a dagger as it thrust into his brain. The other boys running at full speed piled into him. The bone in his forehead cracked with a loud, sickening sound, as the additional weight of their bodies magnified the impact. As they regained their footing, they backed away from their leader. His body began to slide down the pole. His arms fell limply to his sides. The three dazed companions looked in horror at their leader as the lifeless body crumpled to the ground; blood flowing freely, from his mangled face.

The three boys gathered themselves and moved away quickly glancing back at the body that now lay motionless. As the reality sunk in, they ran, fearful of the former association. The neighborhood would not be suffering from the antics of this group any time soon. That time was now past.

Anthony Mayberry came around to the front entrance. He glanced back to see what happened to his pursuers and saw the boy run into the pole but kept running. He was out of breath and scared now.

Another woman who followed the boy's path through the aisle came out shrieking, "Call the paramedics, call the paramedics".

Everyone ran to see what was causing the woman's reaction. As he came slowly around to the entrance, Anthony rushed to his mother, who wrapped her arms around him. Jennifer Mayberry was still unaware of the quick turn of events that had taken place outside. She was just thankful that her son had returned.

Gathering the clothes quickly, she stuffed them into the laundry bags and made a quick exit with her son, vowing never to return to that place. She didn't know that in a short time, her life would be changing. For now, however, she was happy that her son was safe by her side. The winning lottery ticket in her son's hand would be her chance to make life better for a number of people. That reality was yet to sink in.

Doctor Pedroza
Dr. Pedroza returned to the hospital for his shift on Monday morning. The usual number of patients required his services. He thought of the experience with Maria Esparza and couldn't get the picture of the sliver out of his head. One of the nurses interrupted his thoughts and he turned his attention to her.

Maria
The following week, true to her word, Pacey Creighton called and they agreed on a time and location for the meeting. Maria was still wondering what was going on. She decided to leave her car and take public transportation downtown. An L ride and short bus trip to Sears Tower took only a short time.

The Creighton Women
At 7:00 in the evening, Maria entered the doors of the Sears Tower and took the elevator to the 67th floor. She entered through the heavy wooden door and walked into the Metropolis Club. She heard of the place and was interested in seeing what all the fuss was.

As she removed her coat, she was aware of the two Creighton women approaching. The attendant took her coat, giving her a check ticket. They had obviously been awaiting her arrival. She was glad she was punctual. It just seemed appropriate.

Vera Creighton was, as usual smiling. She exhibited excitement. The woman was slightly older than Maria. Pacey Creighton, on the other hand, seemed like a totally changed person. The first thing that Maria realized was that the woman could smile. The smile seemed genuine, which made her feel much more at ease than the apprehension she usually felt from the woman.

They made small talk about the weather. A waiter approached to ask about cocktails. Feeling more comfortable, Maria ordered a glass of Chardonnay wine. The two women ordered martinis. They sat in the bar area for a while as Pacey Creighton apologized again and tried to explain her deceased husband's mindset and way of life. Maria sat more amused than curious. She sensed that the women placed some importance to the meeting. They were both doing well at making her feel more at ease. The difference in the demeanor of Pacey Creighton continued to be a wonder to Maria.

The elder Creighton stood, suggesting they move to the dining room for dinner. Maria allowed the women to lead the way. As she took in the surroundings, she could feel the opulence of the wood paneled rooms and comfortable décor. She laughed to herself with the thought that she could get accustomed to this type of setting. The thought quickly dissipated, as reality came back in the form of the uniformed waiter. He waited for the women to sit. Standing there suddenly was a wait staff woman. She introduced herself.

"Welcome ladies, my name is Lori and I will be serving you this evening."

Everything was perfect. Lori attended to their every need and request. She was a delight.

Maria selected the Fresh Sea Bass with a cilantro sauce and vegetable. The conversation ensued as the women ordered another cocktail.

During a lull in the conversation, the two Creighton women looked to each other and Maria noticed an almost imperceptible nod by Vera Creighton to her mother.

Maria felt the bombshell was about to fall and prepared herself for the unexpected. Pacey Creighton moved closer to the table as she began to speak.

"Miss Esparza, my daughter and I would like you to consider an opportunity."

Still awaiting something, Maria listened intently.

She was very unprepared for the words that followed.

"We are willing to expend a sizable amount of money to fund a charity in support of abused women."

Without hesitation, she continued.

"We would like you to manage and run it, Miss Esparza."

Maria sat in shock. No preparation would have been sufficient for what she was hearing. Pacey Creighton continued speaking but Maria never heard the words following. The look of astonishment finally became evident to Pacey Creighton.

She stopped talking and watched the look on Maria's face.

Vera Creighton broke the silence.

"Maria, we're really serious." She directed the words toward Maria.

"I don't know what to say," was the only comment she could make. Maria Esparza simply sat shaking her head.

The rest of the conversation continued throughout dinner as the women explained their ideas and thoughts, but Maria couldn't fathom the conversation and allow it to make any sense. She was confused, elated and mesmerized. She didn't even remember eating.

Her mind began to return to some sense of normalcy, after a few sips of coffee. Maria began to ask a few questions, to which both women excitedly responded. They told Maria finally, that they expected her to think it over and talk to them when she felt ready to decide.

Both women gave Maria business cards with their phone numbers.

The dinner ended on a good note with all smiling and sharing some laughter and camaraderie.

The waitperson Lori Boby helped each of the women out of their chairs. Maria reached out to thank her by touching her hand. Immediately, Maria sensed the warmth passing from her hand to the woman. They both looked quizzically at each other and smiled.

Lori Boby had no idea what just happened, but she was surprised.

As they were leaving, Pacey Creighton asked Maria where she parked. Maria felt somewhat taken aback when she replied that, she was using public transportation. The elder Creighton would have none of it. She told Maria that their chauffeur would drop them off, and then take Maria home. Maria decided not to argue. At this point, she had so much to think about; she simply agreed and joined them in their elegant black limousine, parked just outside.

Chapter 9 New Friends

Lori Boby

Lori Boby finished the last of her clean up chores at the Metropolis Club in Sears' Tower and gathered her purse as she moved toward the door. She said her good byes to the remaining employees and proceeded to the escalator for the one floor ride to the elevator bank.

She exited the building and proceeded across the street to the public parking garage. The lot had been unusually crowded with cars when she arrived so she was forced to park near the roof. The elevator was not working, so she climbed the stairs humming softly "*No Matter What,*" the hit by Boyzone. She loved the tune as it brought memories of her meeting with her current beau. At the fourth floor exit door, she pulled the handle and walked into the garage and the night air. She was happy as she thought of the drive home and spending time with Maurice. She loved him dearly and they were planning to set their wedding date in the near future.

Frank Bellini walked with an idle gait down Wabash Street. Going nowhere in particular, his thoughts drifted. He needed money to help his Vera, another homeless friend. She made everyone who met her feel like they were the most important person in the world. Maybe she was right. Her heart was failing and she needed serious medical care, but couldn't afford it. He didn't really care very much how he would get the money. He also felt desperate. He let his thoughts travel back to the woman called Maria, whom he befriended outside the restaurant. That situation made him feel good; after all, he'd been though. Who knows, some good might still come of it.

Lori Boby walked the short distance to her car and searched for the keys in her purse. She always liked to dress well, as she felt it set her apart from the others. How she looked going to work was always important to her. Since she made her own clothes, she was able to copy the best original fashions and clothe herself accordingly. Upon seeing her, one would think she was anything but a waitress. More likely, someone of upper class was the look she presented herself to be. She reached in and felt the key ring in her purse. As she grasped it, she heard a sound behind her and turned to find the source.

Lori Boby wasn't able to complete the turn as she felt herself grabbed around the neck by a strong arm. She felt another arm encircle her waist pulling on the straps of her purse. The intruder dragged her away from the car. The car keys dropped to the floor with a jingle as they hit the cement. She began to struggle against her antagonist. The grip was unrelenting. She could feel pressure against her neck, choking off her ability to breathe. As she gasped for air, she flung her arms wildly, reaching for the attacker's hand around her neck.

The man felt a sudden freezing coldness in his hand that quickly ran up his arm. He released his hold on the woman quickly. She was in deep panic. Suddenly without warning, she heard a gasp as the hand and arms around her let go. She sprung free of her assailant and began to run back toward her car.

Picking up the keys, still laying on the cement, she quickly inserted the key and opened the door. Pulling the door closed, she started the car. Without looking, she backed the car from the parking place and turned the wheel. As she looked forward again, she saw the man's arm waiving in the air. The man seemed to be gasping for air just as an asthmatic would do. He was immediately in her path. There was no way to get around him.

She stopped the car watching the man who grabbed her so violently, writhing on his knees for breath. She knew how he must feel as the way he had grabbed her throat gave her the feeling of a lack of air. She stared at the form in front of her car. Her mind told her to step hard on the gas and remove the creep from ever attacking anyone again. It would be easy. No one was around, he was incapacitated, and it would make her feel whole again. Her mind raced. She debated getting out of the car, to kick and beat him senseless. The thought of getting out of the car was quickly negated. She thought he might try to grab her again.

She was about to step on the gas when her eyes caught the flicker of a yellow flashing light. It was the security cart making its way up the incline toward her floor. She honked the horn a number of times hoping to catch the attention of the security guard. The horn echoed through the structure. The flashing light became visible as the cart neared the top of the incline. It stopped for a moment. She honked again. The driver turned the cart toward her and accelerated toward the man on the ground. She could hear the driver talking into the radio speaker on his shoulder. He was calling for assistance. As he neared the figure on the ground, her former assailant turned toward the security guard waving his arms again. The driver stepped from the cart and rushed over to the man. The man tried to rise from his knees with his arm around the security guard. The guard hefted the man up and led him over to lean against a car. With the way now cleared, Lori Boby stepped on the gas and drove past the security cart toward the downhill exit.

She didn't look back as she turned and proceeded down the ramp to street level. Inserting her credit card into the machine, the gate opened and she hit the gas pedal as the car jumped ahead toward the exit.

A man, walking down the street was startled, as the car roared toward him. Hearing the screech of tires, he jumped to the side as the car sped onto the street narrowly missing him.

Lori Boby turned onto Wabash and toward home. She looked back to see the man rising from the ground. He seemed to be OK. She didn't remember any bump, as she saw him jump at the last minute to avoid her car.

Nonetheless, she turned at the corner and made successive right turns until she was at the place that the man jumped out of the way to avoid her.

She saw a man standing. Pulling over she rolled down the window and asked.

"I'm so sorry, I almost ran you over. Are you all right?

Frank Belini looked into the eyes of the pretty woman.

"I'm fine, but that was a little close."

"Do you need a ride somewhere," she asked.

"Oh no thanks. I feel safer walking," he added with a chuckle.

"You take care of yourself, promise?"

"Yes sir, I promise." They smiled at each other. She closed the window and stepped on the gas, with less urgency this time.

Something strange happened to the man who grabbed her, but she was way beyond caring about the outcome. She viewed her hand on the steering wheel, remembering the small jolt of warmth that passed between her and Maria at the club. Then, she thought about the sudden coldness of the attacking man's hand. Looking out the front window at the dark sky, she quietly said the words "Thank You God," as if in response to a question.

The Boby woman put a note in her mind to call Chelle Leriget at the first opportunity to see if she could shed any light on the night's happenings.

The Attacker

The security guard helped the man who seemed to be regaining his ability to breathe once more, but his arm felt frightfully cold. The guard asked him for the location of his car and the man tried to motion the guard away. Suspicions aroused, the guard wondered what the man had been doing. Remembering the woman in the car sitting there honking the horn, he wondered what had taken place. Perhaps she was honking for help for the man. He was sure this man, still trying to regain his breath, would not be a willing communicator. The guard led the man to his cart and drove down to street level, where the now almost fully recovered man climbed out and walked away. He continued walking toward the subway entrance, his mind in a daze. The security guard turned back to the station to complete his report. It wouldn't say much, other than "man with almost frozen hand needed assistance and walked away." Oh well, the security many thought.

Frank Bellini

After he dodged the car and picked himself up, he continued walking. He didn't go far when he looked ahead to the corner and found himself staring at the largest black Labrador retriever he had ever seen. It had a barrel chest and tan muzzle. The animal looked all business. Frank Bellini wanted no part of some big canine taking a bite out of one of his limbs. He looked for some avenue of escape. The animal continued to approach, its head erect watching him as he came closer. Frank Bellini thought of changing sides of the street and began to walk toward the curb. The dog, as if sensing the intention, moved toward the curb to cut off that route of escape. He stopped, waiting to see what the animal would do next. The animal began a faster gait as he approached.

Suddenly, while a few feet away, the dog stopped and barked. It wasn't a vicious sound, but one that immediately got the listener's attention. Turning, the dog began to walk away. Frank Bellini decided to remain rooted in his steps. He watched. The animal stopped, turned its head and looked back in his direction.

It seemed that the animal was inviting him to follow. Frank Bellini thought he must have experienced more unusual things, but none came to mind. The dog began to walk back toward him and barked loudly again. It turned away again. Frank Bellini got the impression that he should follow. He noticed the dog had on a collar with a green colored tag, which should mean that at least someone owned the animal.

The entire happening was strange. He could feel his own sense of danger at the sight of the large animal, yet it seemed that the dog simply wanted him to follow. Frank Bellini took a step forward. The dog's gait increased as the man took additional steps in the direction of the animal. The dog looked back a few times and barked what seemed to be acknowledgment that the man was doing the right thing in following. He had to increase his pace to keep up with the dog. The dog kept looking back and Frank Bellini didn't want to make an enemy after all this.

An Injured Stranger

Man and animal reached State Street and crossed without incident, as the traffic at this time of morning was thin. Across State Street, the dog led Frank to the first alley near the Palmer House hotel. The dog turned down the alley and the man followed, looking carefully for signs of anything that may endanger him. He watched the dog run a short distance and stopped near a figure propped up against the building.

Frank Bellini was unable to discern the figure, other than to note it seemed like a crumpled form. His ears picked up a moaning sound. The dog barked twice in quick succession. Frank Bellini ran forward to find a woman lying in a heap against the wall. He couldn't make out the face in the poor light, yet knew instinctively that she was in pain.

The massive canine led him to a woman who seemed in dire need of help, by a dog he just happened upon. He knelt next to the woman with an eye on the dog. The dog barked once and fell silent observing the man and the woman. It sat waiting. He raised the woman's head and noticed she was bleeding from a cut near her right eye. The blood was beginning to cake on her face so she must have been there for some time. He was still very afraid that the animal might attack if he did something to the woman. Even touching her was a question in his mind. He tried to get information from her. She could only moan and place her hands on her stomach. He put his hand at the cut on her face to examine it more closely.

As he touched her skin, he felt a sudden warm feeling emit from his hand. Then he looked down. She was largely pregnant. He knew that help was going to be required and quickly. He looked at the dog, his mind beginning to dictate his actions.

"You stay," he said to the animal.

With that, he turned and ran toward the street. Reaching the street, he looked quickly one way and then the next. He decided to try the hotel for help. He entered the door and made a hasty entry to the nearest hotel employee stand. He gushed aloud to the woman behind the counter, that he needed help for the pregnant woman in the alley. The employee was cautious but listened to his story. She reached for the phone to call 911 and handed the phone to him.

The operator was on the line immediately and he quickly explained the situation and location. The operator insisted he give his name. He did, Frank Wilson. He then also mentioned the large dog, in case the arriving help might be concerned. Totally out of his usual personality, he thanked the woman at the desk and headed quickly for the door. Out the door, he turned the corner and focused his sight on the limp figure near the wall.

As he approached the woman again, he heard the sirens. He looked for the dog. It was nowhere to be seen.

Two police cars followed the fire department ambulance. They entered the alley. The paramedics immediately jumped out and began to administer to the woman. The police officer came around and began inquiring about the woman and the situation.

Frank Bellini recounted the story to the police officers. He mentioned the dog leading him to the woman. The police officer cocked his head when Frank Bellini said that. The police officers looked around in search of the missing animal. Nope, no dog. The paramedics placed the woman on the gurney and into the ambulance. The police assessed the man. He was reasonably good looking, with an unshaven appearance and dark black hair. His eyes were intense, giving the feeling of a man very much in control of himself. The look was almost scary to the police officer asking the questions, yet there was no feeling the man was lying. They asked him for identification. He produced his State ID card in the name of Frank Wilson, as he had no driver's license.

The police officers finished their questions, deciding the man committed no crime and didn't seem to be a problem. They decided to leave with the ambulance. As the ambulance hobbled against the brick surface of the alley, its siren began to wail. The man followed it toward the exit of the alley. The police cars passed him with a wave from the driver of one of the units. As the cars turned the corner, he was again alone. Alternatively, so he thought.

He took a few steps and froze at hearing a growl. He glanced around to find the source. He knew that sound. The dog was standing there, its tail wagging. Frank Bellini took a step to see if the animal would come to him. To his surprise, it did and stood by his side, looking up at him. He reached down to place a hand on the immense head of the animal. The dog leaned against his leg at the touch. Relieved, Frank Bellini began to walk again toward the end of the alley with the dog by his side.

He was going to find a place to sleep. It would be outside again and the weather wasn't too bad. This was his ritual, as he rarely had any money. The dog walked with him as he headed for lower Wacker Drive, where some of his other street friends hung out.

Carl Sarna

He was enjoying his newly found freedom and authority at the firm. Changed were already in the work to increase productivity and profitability. Abby Tisdale was a major contributor to getting this done.

One morning, he awakened and began his laborious effort to get out of bed. His arms were so strong that he relied on them to lift himself into his wheelchair to begin his daily routine.

On this morning, when he lifted himself, one of his arms slipped and he began to fall. Strangely, he didn't fall but landed on his feet. They supported his weight. Carl Sarna looked around in wonder. He took one-step and then another, waiting for his legs to buckle. They didn't.

Chelle Leriget

Chelle Leriget owned the employment agency for which Maria worked. The time arrived that she would be required to make a few changes and add staff because of the company's growth. They were getting too big for the space they now occupied. People were sharing desks and that had to stop. The company was also experiencing a demand for more blue-collar jobs. Chelle Leriget needed to expand to meet the increasing employment requests. One afternoon, she decided to let the work pile up, while she reviewed who could help her.

She called a dear friend from her church, Mazie Shepard. She was a commercial real estate agent. Mazie was a no nonsense, tireless worker who became extremely successful at meeting the requirements of clients. Chelle talked to Mazie about her situation. She had six months to run on her present lease, but needed at least three more offices and additional space for the staff.

Mazie Shepard immediately thought of a property, not too far from Chelle's present location that would fit the needs of her friend. Mazie arranged for Chelle to view the property right away.

A few days later, Chelle Leriget met Mazie at the property. It would need a little build-out, but the space and layout were just what she envisioned. Mazie told her the tenant was experiencing some financial problems and needed a smaller workplace. Mazie said the tenant still had a number of months on the lease and perhaps they could work out a deal.

When Chelle Leriget returned to the office, Maria was waiting to meet with her. Chelle Leriget told her of the changes that would be taking place at the agency and offered her a new position, as a manager with the company. She asked Maria to think about it and get back to her. Maria decided to wait for things to settle and included a new prayer every day for help in making her decision.

Maria and Pacey Creighton met several times over the next few days. She could more fully understand why she was chosen to develop the battered women's charity shelter. She wanted to know much more about the expectation and responsibilities that would be on her shoulders. The scope of the project was immense; in that, she would be responsible for organizing the operation and all of the financial matters required to run the company. The amount of money available also made her feel uncomfortable.

To start, there would be funds to purchase everything that Maria felt would be required. There would also be a significant funding for her in order to continue the effort. She was thankful for this.

Setting up an office and hiring a staff were also included in the plan set out by Mrs. Creighton. Maria soon learned from the elder woman that the Creighton's needed to feel included, but not wanting to be involved in the day-to-day operation of the charity. Maria was also surprised to find that Pacey Creighton had performed an in depth background check before talking with her about the offer. It just made sense but still was a little unnerving to the young Spanish woman. She wondered what the Creighton woman might do in the future that she would not be aware of, as she certainly didn't give Pacey Creighton permission for the background check.

This also became a point of discussion between the two women. Vera Creighton remained on the sidelines throughout the discussions. Maria learned that the daughter Vera, had come up with the idea, and as expected, Pacey Creighton took over from there. So as not to be a third wheel, the younger Creighton bowed out of the process almost completely. Therefore, it would ostensibly be Maria's opportunity to make the venture successful.

As the time passed and the structure became more easily understood, Maria became more comfortable with the thoughts and requirements necessary to make the venture work. She knew of friends she would be able to talk with for help and ideas. Through her Church connections, she knew that there would be a continuous stream of women seeking help. They would also need understanding; as they fought to survive the physical abuses, they endured.

Maria

Maria called Chelle Leriget and asked to meet. She told the older woman about the offer from the Creightons. Maria also stopped at the employment office to visit with Chelle Leriget. She informed Chelle of the decision and thanked her for the consideration she had shown. Chelle Leriget frowned a bit, knowing that she would like Maria to stay with the company, but clearly understood Maria's desire to delve into something that she truly looked forward too. She told Mrs. Leriget, she would continue working for a short while, until a suitable replacement was found. Chelle Leriget already had someone in mind. She told Maria she would call within a week to let her know and thanked her for her commitment.

Mrs. Leriget told Maria that they would be moving a few blocks away to larger office space. Maria's comment was, "Chelle, I don't know how you've been able to work in these cramped quarters at all." Chelle Leriget smiled back at Maria. "I know," she said. "I know."

Although unaware at the time, Chelle Leriget and her agency would also become an integral part of Maria's future. As both began to draw their new plans, they decided to let their friends in on the new opportunities. As Maria and Mrs. Leriget said their good-byes, they hugged and their eyes met with a keen understanding that they would be in contact again. Their hands touched and the warm feeling extended to both. Maria noted it and Chelle Leriget didn't know what to make of it. Time would tell.

After Maria left, Chelle Leriget immediately returned to her desk and picked up the phone. She dialed the number and waited. Zeneta Michaels answered. An excited older woman became thrilled at the prospect of having a new job. Zeneta would be at the office in the morning to find out the details. Chelle Leriget hung up with her knowing smile in evidence. Chelle made a few more calls after that, and before long was in meetings for hours on end, interviewing people to hire. It was an adventure to be sure.

When Maria arrived home, she called her friends Sydney and Ellie to inform them of the quest she was about to undertake. They agreed to meet at the same eatery where they were going for months to discuss classes and their personal lives. Each of the young women was forthcoming in telling the others what their life was like. The friendships that developed were real and comforting to each of them.

The night of the get together arrived. Maria had simply told her friends that she had something to talk to them about and wanted some time to ask their thoughts about a new opportunity that was available.

Girls Night Out

Each of the girls arrived and happily greeted their friends. They quickly decided on the usual fare of hamburgers and a pitcher of Miller Light Draft. The beer was their unanimous favorite. As the sharing of experiences was underway, Ellie looked at the other two and asked Maria to break the suspense and tell them what was happening. As Maria explained some of the happenings, the focus of all the interest became the hospital where Maria worked.

Maria related her account of the dealings with Marshall Creighton at the hospital. She complained before to her friends about the treatment and they were very helpful in providing support. Therefore, when she told them of the happenings of the final day, the conversations and questions stopped, as a look of genuine surprise took over each of the women. Silence reigned for a moment as each absorbed Maria's account of the happenings.

They looked at each other with a question on their lips. Finally, Sydney brought up the subject they all wanted to discuss, above even Maria's news. That being the effect each experienced with others, due to some strange and so far unexplainable reason.

Ellie asked Maria about the young boy from the accident near her place and the unexplained healing of the young boy. Maria told them of the doctor's comments. Ellie produced a noticeable shrug of her shoulders and asked if the girls would like to know of a couple events that she experienced that might, not have anything to do with the subject, but were worth noting.

As usual, the girls gathered closer to hear Ellie's recounting of what took place. She was always an interesting storyteller. She told of meeting Jimmy Ennis at the accident scene and the ensuing date and introductions at the football game as well as the evening's Karaoke fun. At that, the women laughed and high fived each other.

"Well I have some interesting news too," said Maria.

Remember the old jerk that I mentioned who was making life miserable whenever I walked into his room?" He passed away."

Her friends remained silent.

"And that's not all," Maria continued.

"His wife and daughter have offered me the directorship of a battered woman's shelter for which they will be willing to put up the capital and finance."

Ellie and Sydney looked at Maria in shock. Maria told her friends a few additional events about Marshall Creighton and the Creighton family episode. She also mentioned Jennifer Mayberry, the woman the younger Creighton woman befriended at the hospital. She won the lottery and ran into some trouble as a result.

Sydney interrupted. "I remember the gang was trying to steal the ticket from the boy and his mother. I read in the paper, one of the gang wound up dead."

The more the women talked, it became evident that something was taking place that had serious consequences for good and bad. Ellie, the fact finder of the group, asked about maintaining a diary to keep the facts straight so they might be able to piece together the hows and whys of happenings that were taking place. Each agreed this was a very good idea. Of course, they chose Ellie to maintain the record. As they agreed, an eerie feeling descended upon them. It wasn't a bad feeling, but more of a discovery of something unusual and a little surreal in its tendencies.

The women felt a serious need to keep the information confidential. They all did agree on what seemed to be a source of the events. Maria held her hand outstretched on the table as each looked at the sliver of wood buried deeply within her finger. Instinctively they knew it had something to do with what was taking place. Each said they would be mindful of the happenings around them and share them with each other when they met.

In an attempt to lighten the conversation, Ellie told her friends of seeing Jimmy Ennis a couple times since. Everyone leaned closer hoping to hear the lurid details of the budding relationship.

Maria told Ellie she could use a little help to pass inspections for the business license and perhaps she might be able to stop by with her new friend. Ellie jumped at the opportunity and they agreed to meet tomorrow afternoon.

Maria excitedly asked each of the women if they would be interested in taking a role in the creation of the new venture. She asked them to think about it and let her know soon of their decision. Since school would be ending and graduation loomed nearby, the excitement was noticeable. Maria told them of the commitment that would be required and each nodded in assent and understanding. As it approached time to leave, each of the women could feel a meaningful attachment to the other. A bonding had formed, much closer than the friendships of days past.

Something was bothering Maria. She couldn't put a finger on it, but the thought lingered and started to become perplexing.

As the women said good bye, Ellie and Sydney walked down the street together to their cars. As they each went their separate ways, Maria glanced back at the door and saw the man putting on his hat. Something struck a chord with Maria at the sight.

Chapter 10 A Roll Of The Dice

Pacey Creighton

Pacey Creighton enjoyed her trips to a Casino, in the Far West suburbs. She enjoyed playing the slot machines and a little craps. She was always looking to win big. Sometimes she did and it exhilarated her. She lost too, yet that never bothered her, as the supply of money seemed endless. She did this for the plain thrill of winning. The amounts really didn't matter. She would dress very ordinary and wore a wig, so as not to be noticed. She saw many of them over the years and became familiar with their gambling habits. Some she knew could ill afford to be there, while others acted just as she did, for the thrill. Her husband never knew of her penchant for playing with money. The thought intrigued her, as she knew he would have been wildly perturbed if he knew.

She also made a habit of dropping off part of what she won to unsuspecting people. She would look around for someone whom she felt was in need and find a way to give him or her some money. When finished, she would always dine in the plush surroundings of the restaurant upstairs. The service was always wonderful and she would enjoy people waiting on her as a plain ordinary looking woman. She felt it exciting.

Today, she had put on a very plain brown wig with no makeup and very plain black sweater over baggy slacks with well-worn boots. Her look was at best, described as ordinary.

The Pacey Creighton arrived at the casino in her black Lexus sedan accepted the parking ticket from the attendant and proceeded to the gambling area. While walking through the crowd to the craps tables, she remembered the odd sensation that she had felt on her hand when Maria had touched her the night before when saying good-bye. She looked at her hand and could see nothing. The thought passed as she heard the whooping cry from the nearest table as someone hit a winning combination on their roll of the dice.

Excitement began to build as she approached the table of excited people. She noticed the pile of chips pushed toward the person throwing the dice. She recognized him as one of the frequent visitors. In her mind, he was a player and a real bastard.

He gloated at winning and seriously showed his frustration when he didn't win. The man seemed to treat everyone with disdain, as if he was the only one playing at the table. Everyone knew someone like that. She didn't care for the man at all, but when he was hot, he won a lot of money.

Pacey Creighton decided to watch for a while before joining and placing bets on the board table. The man was on a roll, as the pile of chips in his slots above the table grew quickly. She watched as a middle aged, black woman approached the table and stood beside the man as she placed a five-dollar bet on the Pass line. The man looked at her and with a shrug, moved to establish some distance from the woman. He couldn't move far, but he was able to create room.

The woman looked at the man standing there. She felt him noticeably distance himself from her. Pacey Creighton watched in surprise. How he must have made her feel. Putting herself in the woman's shoes, she would have felt very small.

The feeling was a bit strange for her. Previously, she knew it wouldn't have mattered to her, yet now she seemed to feel more about what was happening to people around her. Since her husband passed away, she felt a new awareness of people. How interesting she thought as her eyes returned to the player at the table.

The man was winning big time. Everything he seemed to play was in his favor, as the chips count mounted. Interestingly, Pacey Creighton watched the black woman next to him with interest. The woman began to accumulate a small amount of winnings. As Pacey Creighton watched, she noticed the woman mirroring the player's bets. She walked over to stand next to the woman as someone left the table who had been standing next to her. The Creighton woman threw five one hundred-dollar bills on the table. As the croupier took the bills, he slid them into the slot and pushed them out of sight. He provided a pile of chips in return.

Pacey Creighton chose to play with twenty five-dollar chips. The croupier recognized her. He couldn't place her, but knew her only by the type of garb she was wearing. He smiled in acknowledgment as he placed the chips in front of her. She placed a chip on the pass line and as she did, her hand touched the black woman's hand, as the woman placed her five-dollar chip there also. Both felt a slight, warm shock. They looked at each other, amused more than anything. The woman apologized immediately, as Pacey Creighton smiled and shook her head to indicate no apology was necessary. The player continued to roll the dice and win. Each time, the woman at Pacey Creighton's side also won.

The player was beginning to get more daring with each roll accumulating larger winnings as he continued to beat the odds. The table players watched as the player suddenly lifted a roll of the hundred dollar chips and placed a thousand dollar bet. The gasps were noticeable. The table boss held out his hand to stop play as he reached for the phone. The conversation was brief with someone in charge of approving large bets. He hung up the phone and motioned for play to continue. This time, the woman didn't follow suit, choosing instead to place a five-dollar bet on the 12. She won. She was now up by over a thousand dollars. As he reached for the dice, the player's hand touched the hand of the woman. He pulled his hand back immediately, but not before, he felt the slight pulse of feeling as their hands touched. The woman repeated her bet with $100.00. The player stared at her as she did. Pacey Creighton could feel the tension from the man as he threw the dice. As they bounced against the opposite end of the table, everyone watched as they settled. He lost.

The player's face turned bright red. He was furious. God knows what was running through his head, but it wasn't something very nice. The man was so noticeably upset it scared some of the people at the table. He stood watching; saying nothing aloud, yet his lips were moving. He mouthed silent expletives. The roll passed to the woman next to him. As she gathered the few hundred dollars in chips from her winnings, she placed them in her slots above the table. The table boss came around the table to say something in her ear. She nodded her assent and handed him her driver's license.

Pacey Creighton felt exhilaration for the woman. She watched her with intent.

The woman took a one hundred-dollar chip this time and again placed them on the 30 to 1 box on the table.

The man who had been rolling the dice stood and watched without placing a bet. The dice bounced once and careened off the far facing of the table. As she threw the dice, everyone watched intently. Against all odds, double sixes showed up again on the dice. The table went wild. People jumped in excited response to the winning bet. The man at the end of the table just glared at the dice. Anyone who looked could see his noticeable discomfort. The woman collected her winnings again and moved them to the slot on the top of the table. The man next to her looked at the mushrooming winnings of the woman. She looked up at him this time. Her eyes caught his without expression. It was just a look.

She gathered her chips.

"Are you leaving ma'am," questioned the table boss.

"Yes I am," she replied with a smile.

A roll box was handed across the table to the woman. She smiled and worded "thank you", with her lips.

She proceeded to place her chips in the rolls. When done, she lofted three hundred dollar chips to the employees at the table.

She heard thank you when she turned to leave. Pacey Creighton touched her arm and smiled. The Creighton woman felt her knees buckle in excitement for the other woman. She had never felt this way before about someone.

This time, she just allowed the wonderful feeling to wash over her.

The man who bet was now silent. His face was beet red. Inside he felt as if the lowly black woman moving away from him at the table had shown him up. He felt those winnings should have been his and that she caused his luck to change. He watched her walk away as he seethed his feelings of vile discontent for her.

The woman approached the cashier's cage with an inner feeling of thankfulness. She looked toward the ceiling and mouthed.

"Thank you God," as she placed the chips on the cashier's table.

"Can I have a check please," she asked in a kindly voice.

"Of course Ma'am."

The table boss came to her side at the cashier's window and congratulated her on her good fortune. He handed a sheet of paper to the cashier who nodded in acknowledgment. The woman smiled at both men.

In just a few moments, she had her check. She felt fantastic. The money would now be available for her niece to attend college. The girl lived with her since her mother's death. She was a bright girl who deserved a chance to make it in this world. A wish the woman had since her sister died. Yet for two years, she had come to the casino every couple of months with one hundred dollars that she would save and try to win "big" so that her niece would have a chance. Now that chance was a reality.

The man at the end of the table continued to exhibit his anxiety and frustration. He took a handful of hundred dollar chips and spread them around the table, making a variety of bets. Pacey Creighton placed her own wager on the pass line. One hundred dollars. She threw the dice. As the square objects bounced against the backboard and settled, normalcy returned to the people at the table. The upturned faces of the dice showed a four and a three staring back at her.

The man at the end of the table threw up his hands in frustration and picked up what remained of his chips. Ninety-five dollars. He threw them on the table toward the table workers and quickly made his exit from the casino. Whispered expletives continued to flow from his lips as he pushed his way, without caring who he jostled, toward the restroom. Upon arriving, he went to a stall and opened the small bag with the white powder, inserted his finger, and took a sniff. He then headed for the Casino exit. He felt, the black woman made him look like a fool to his way of thinking. She'll get hers someday, he thought to himself.

The man turned in his parking ticket to the attendant and waited for his car. Before long, the beige Cadillac STS arrived. He handed his ticket to the driver and pushed his way into the car, stiffing the attendant in the process.

"No tip, your Casino has all my money."

The attendant just shrugged his shoulders and turned away. The Cadillac pulled away with a squeal of tires. As he hit the brakes at the exit looking into the street, the engine died. He turned the ignition key to restart the car. Silence. The car wouldn't start. He pushed on the shift lever. Nothing, the engine was dead. He got out, slamming the door as he trekked back to the attendant area. The person who brought the car was coming out the door. The man reached for the attendant's arm as he approached.

"My car is dead, you must have done something to it," he stated with rancor in his voice.

The attendant stared back at the man with a questioning look.

"Well can't you do something for me?" The loser was now irate, as his voice began to increase in volume

"I can call a tow truck for you," was the calm reply.

The others waiting for their cars heard "Fine, do that."

The attendant returned inside.

Within minutes, a tow truck arrived on the scene. The driver listened to the man as he explained the problem of the car just dying on him for no reason. The tow truck fellow proceeded to check the car and popped the hood.

"You want me to try to give the battery a jump?" He asked the man.

"Yeah, sure, jump it," was the curt reply.

The driver attached the cables. Giving an up sign to the man, he turned the key and the engine sprang to life again.

The driver removed the cables from the battery and replaced them on the truck.

"That'll be fifty bucks", was the laconic statement from the tow truck driver.

"Fifty bucks?" The man screamed at the driver.

"Yes sir, that's the charge for coming out to jump a battery."

The man reached into his pocket and took out a wad of bills. Peeling off two twenties and a ten, he flung them at the tow truck driver's hand. The driver had to catch the bills as they floated toward the ground.

The car owner yanked the shift lever into drive.

Pressing hard on the gas pedal, he again squealed the tires as he exited right in front of an approaching police car.

The police officer braked to avoid the careening Cadillac and watched as the driver sped down the street trying to keep the car under control. At the stoplight, the Cadillac just proceeded to continue although the light was red. The police officer had seen enough of the erratic driving and turned on the blue and red strobe lights. He followed the car for a full block before it finally pulled over.

As the police officer exited his vehicle, he wondered if the subject had been drinking. He approached the car. He could see the driver visibly upset inside the car and took it as a warning sign. He anticipated a confrontation. There was none. The man offered his license and insurance card immediately. He even offered an apology stating that he had lost money at the Casino, and was upset.

The police officer decided to just issue the ticket and let the man go on his way. He took the license back to his car and called it in. He wasn't surprised to hear the radio dispatcher inform him that there was an outstanding warrant for parking violations. He called for a backup, feeling that the confrontation was about to begin with the driver of the Cadillac. The backup Sergeant arrived. The driver must have known, because he offered no resistance when told of the outstanding warrant. There was no scene as the handcuffs were placed on his hands as he was escorted to the back seat of the patrol car. In a few hours, the driver would be free on bond again and able to proceed with whatever his life held for him. The police car drove toward the station.

As Pacey Creighton decided to leave, she noticed the woman who had been standing at the craps table nearby. The woman's face was beaming.

Walking over to her, Pacey Creighton met her eyes with a smile.

"Well you certainly did yourself some good at gambling today," she said to the woman.

"My niece is going to college now," she said. The reply made, as tears began to form in the woman's eyes.

She could feel the intense joy that covered the woman like an aura.

"How wonderful," she said to the woman.

"Thank you."

"God must love me today"

"Good luck in your future." Pacey Creighton said smiling.

She turned back and looked at the craps table again. She won several thousand dollars herself today, yet there was no thrill like the feeling of happiness she had for the other woman, who had done so well.

Pacey Creighton turned in her parking ticket. She waited for her black Lexus. She had no way of knowing that the man bringing her car was the same one that the previous fellow stiffed and left no tip. She handled the cash in her pocket. As the attendant brought her car, she looked around. No one was paying much attention to anything. The attendant opened the door and began to step from the car.

She blocked him from getting out of the car and reached for his pocket to slide what was in her hand into it. The man looked surprised.

"Zip your pocket and don't touch that until you get home," she admonished the attendant.

"You got it lady, whatever you want." was his cheery reply.

"Thanks," she said in turn.

Pacey Creighton smiled and stepped into the car. Adjusting the seat, she drove away.

The attendant walked toward the office to pick up another car key for retrieval. He decided to honor the woman's request for some strange reason, figuring it wouldn't make any difference anyway.

When the parking attendant left work, he made his way home quickly to see his wife. She greeted him with her customary kiss and hug. It had been another long day and his legs were hurting from the constant in and out of cars.

"How did today go," she asked.

"Well things were a little weird tonight," he said.

"One guy stiffed me on the tip and next, a woman stuffed something into my pocket and told me to zip it and not look until I got home."

""Well did you look," his wife asked smiling.

"Not yet," he laughed.

"Let's see," she said excitedly. "Maybe its a hundred dollars," as she reached into his deep pocket laughing at her comment.

"Yeah, right," he laughed.

She reached inside and felt wads of paper. Extracting the paper, she laid it on the table.

They both stared in amazement at a pile of hundred dollar bills that lay before them.

They were stunned to immobility. Each looked at the other with incredulous eyes.

"Well count it," he gasped excitedly to his wife."

She collected the pile of bills. There were thirty-two of the one hundred dollar bills sitting in a pile now on the table. Ironically, she would be thirty-two years old tomorrow. What a birthday present, she thought.

His wife jumped and placed her arms around his neck. He held her close as a sense of relief flooded through him. They would finally be able to pay the bills for a change and even have some money left over. They hugged and did a jump step around the table.

Chapter 11 Becoming Reality

A New Property

In the weeks following, Maria spent time and energy to develop the shelter. The Creighton women were wonderful. They gave Maria complete control and any financial assistance required to get the project off the ground.

The Creightons through a Trust purchased a property to their liking, on Division Street in Chicago. The two-story walkup would make an ideal choice and location for the shelter. Maria set to work creating the layout and called Chelle Leriget to help with the employees. Chelle wanted Maria to meet Samantha Marsten, who would be able to help with the purchase of construction materials and design. Maria thought that was a great idea. She called to ask Samantha to stop over as soon as possible. Samantha said she was free and could come right over. Maria responded that would be great. An hour later, Samantha rang the doorbell.

Samantha was taken aback with Maria's light heartedness. Usually, Samantha would find people stressed out when she met them, regarding building details. When they shook hands, she felt a sudden warm glow come from Maria's hand. Maria didn't make anything of it, so the Marsten woman didn't either. Samantha took measurements and chatted with Maria Esparza about a myriad of subjects that were interesting to both. After an hour and a half, Samantha Marsten had taken all the measurements needed and promised to get back with Maria shortly.

Maria swore everyone to secrecy regarding the location. Everyone agreed.

As the building of the shelter came close to fruition, Maria sought the help of her friends to make other necessary requirements to inhabit the building.

The hiring process was long and arduous. She interviewed over fifty applicants for the few employee positions at the Shelter. One of the most difficult situations that arose was dealing with the referrals from well wishing friends and contributors. It seemed the list was endless and troubled her because she didn't want to offend anyone trying to help.

Maria finally settled on the employees she would hire. All were capable and educated to provide the best care and comfort for the transient residents. A few were battered women survivors that knew of the experiences they would be facing with their new clients.

Maria already gave notice at her jobs, so they were no longer a distraction. On a few occasions, the restaurant asked her to work an extra shift and she complied, telling them that she wouldn't be able to continue this for long. Everyone understood.

The shelter became pivotal in the needs of women. It was a fast learning experience to be sure.

Ellie and Jimmy Ennis stopped by to visit with Maria, as promised. The firefighter was in a uniform white shirt, looking a bit more formal than usual. Ellie decided not to comment as they drove to the Shelter in the Fire Department SUV.

Jimmy Ennis provided some helpful information to Maria regarding fire inspections of inhabited buildings. Maria was grateful for the help. As they were about to leave, Maria leaned up and kissed Ellie's friend on the cheek. Jimmy Ennis's face gushed and Ellie laughed. The Jimmy took Maria's hand to wish her well and was a little surprised at the sudden feeling of warmth he felt. Maria looked at Ellie with a look of *darn it* on her face. Ellie knew immediately what had taken place. She took Jimmy Ennis by the arm and whisked him toward the door.

"That's enough electricity between you two," she said with a lilt of laughter. Jimmy Ennis shrugged and Maria put on her biggest smile as the two headed down the stairs.

Ellie thought about mentioning something about the possible effect, but let silence reign, as she thought better about it. They had agreed to keep their secret and that was what she was going to do.

Maria

The days passed as life settled back to normal for all except Maria. She took time to think about the amazing opportunity the Creighton family offered her.

She called Samantha Marsten from time to time, usually after Jimmy Ennis or a building inspector came. The two women were fast becoming friends. Samantha was also wondering about the meaning of the warm touches that happened when they greeted and left each other.

Chance Encounter

As Maria walked down the street toward her apartment, three men approached her at a fast pace. They were jabbering in some foreign language, carrying bags of food from the local market. Not paying attention to their direction, Maria saw them directly in her path. She tried to get out of the way, but they didn't see her. One of the men walked into her knocking her to the ground and dropping a bag of food. A loaf of bread landed in her lap. The man exhibited a look of surprise as he also fell. The other two men stopped to survey the woman as she began to get up. They were involved in conversation and didn't see her approach.

The two men looked at her and reached to help their friend to his feet, leaving her to rise by herself. She heard the name Amhudy used in the foreign tongue as the men spoke to him. She felt no malice toward the men, yet she felt an unusual rejection from them. The contents of the bag had spilled and they rushed to gather the articles. As Amhudy noticed her holding the loaf of bread, he wordlessly reached to snatch it from her grasp.

Their hands touched. Maria felt a sudden coldness again, as she had a couple times, before when she had touched others. The man felt a slight tinge similar to a light carpet shock, but his skin immediately felt very cold. Their eyes met for the briefest moment. The man shuddered. Fear ran through him as he saw the woman's eyes look into his. He broke the eye contact. Maria on the other hand witnessed the brief vision of Jesus on the Cross. The vision was so fleeting, she wondered if she had really seen it. Deep within she knew though. It was real. The feeling of being there at the crucifixion was so strong, if only for the briefest moment.

As the men gathered and continued down the street jabbering, they cast glances back at Maria. She wondered why the encounter took place. Somehow, she knew she would eventually find out.

Adele Dozier

The tall authoritative looking woman left the Mayor's office with a wave to those remaining. Adele Dozier's hair was golden, yet she preferred to present a gruff exterior, which came in handy when dealing with politicians.

It was 5:30 and she decided to head home. She felt in good form for the time spent on the phone and meeting with important members of the city council. It seemed that she would be successful getting the battered women's bill passed in the council. She felt very involved in the proceedings, as she also suffered as a battered woman, early in her marriage. Fortunately, her faith led her to a counselor, who helped her end the ordeal, and pick herself up again.

The sun was bright but lacked the wind's cooling effect downtown near the lake. The drive home was quick with nothing extraordinary to hold her up in traffic. It was a little unusual for the time of day, yet much appreciated.

She opened the door of the condo that looked out over the lake. It was a beautiful sight and Adele thrilled at the opportunity to pour herself a Bombay gin martini. Her usual practice would be to sit on the balcony looking out over the blue waters of the lake along the North Shore. The scenic view was spectacular.

Just as she found a comfortable position, the phone rang. She neglected to take the phone with her onto the balcony so she quickly rose to catch the call. It was a wrong number after all the effort and Adele Dozier looked at the phone with mock disgust. She turned to return to the balcony. As she did, her foot caught against the leg of the couch table and her motion carried her forward. Her knee hit the floor hard even through the plush carpeting. She felt the stab of pain shoot up her leg as she landed forcefully. Looking to her right hand, she almost laughed as she noticed the martini glass with its contents undisturbed in her hand.

Placing a hand on the couch, she tried to pull herself up. As she put weight on her knee, she felt an enormous pain and she fell to the floor again. It was immediately apparent she would need help. Not wanting to call 911 and suffer the embarrassment, she decided to call Doctor Martin Bartleson who lived on the same floor. Hoping he was home, she entered his number and waited. Doctor Bartleson, in his masterfully controlled tone answered.

"This is Adele Dozier, Martin. Can you come over to my place right away?"

"Is everything all right Adele," she heard his surprised reply.

"No, it's not. I need your professional help Martin."

"Be right there," came the swift reply.

Within a minute, there was the knocking at the door. Adele Dozier crawled to the door and was able to reach up to the handle to open the door slightly. Dr. Martin Bartleson saw the woman on the floor and waited for her to clear out of the way before pushing the door further open to enter.

In the next few moments, Doctor Bartleson helped Adele Dozier to the closest chair as she explained what had happened. The doctor immediately turned professional and with skilled hands, he felt the woman's leg, moving it slightly. As the leg moved, Adele Dozier grimaced in pain. A sign not lost on the Doctor.

"This seems pretty serious Adele," Doctor Bartleson told her.

"I was afraid of that," was the quick response.

"Let's get you to a hospital for some X-rays and a look see from a specialist."

"I'll make the arrangements," he said without waiting for the woman's reply.

Within minutes, an ambulance parked in the horseshoe drive downstairs. The paramedics knew exactly what to do as the Doctor told them of Adele Dozier's condition. As the paramedics entered the room and saw the injured person, they knew right away, who she was and a manner of respect was evident from both of the men. It was only a short time and they had a mobile cast around her leg and lifted her onto the gurney for the elevator ride down to the ambulance. Doctor Bartleson didn't have to do much as the men were very professional and he could tell they knew their business. In less than ten minutes, Adele Dozier was on her way to the hospital with the siren screaming the presence of the ambulance to traffic.

Upon arrival, she was immediately scheduled for knee surgery. The staff whisked her from the Emergency Room to the waiting surgical team.

The surgery was a non-event for the doctors. She would be required to remain a week or so in the hospital before getting out of bed to move her leg around.

During that time, she was able to help the city of Chicago continue services to the citizenry. She remembered the phone call from Pacey Creighton, telling her of the plans for a new-battered women's shelter, on the West side. The Creighton woman asked Ms. Dozier to keep any roadblocks from getting in the way. Adele Dozier replied.

"Don't you worry dearie, I'm all over it."

Anyone could bet that would be true.

To no one's surprise, Mayor Richard Dalby stopped by unexpectedly. Adele told the Mayor of the new women's shelter that was opening on the West side. She asked him to keep his eye on the progress. Mayor Dalby knew exactly what his employee meant. In the hospital room, he picked up the phone and got the office of the building inspector of Cook County on the line. After a brief exchange, the Mayor hung up and smiled. "All taken care of. Now you get better and out of here. I need you at City Hall."

Jennifer Mayberry

Jennifer Mayberry collected her lottery winnings and placed the money safely in a few banks for the time being. Knowing nothing of investing, she decided to sit still for a little while and let the banks pay her some interest. She thought that in due time, she would be able to ask someone she could trust, for some investment advice. She did want to talk to the woman who had been so kind in helping her at the hospital, by giving her the money.

Through a few friends, she was able to get Vera Creighton's phone number. She called the Creighton woman, wanting to simply to thank her for her generosity and to tell her what had happened as a result. It was Jennifer Mayberry's way to give thanks for the good deed. Since no one answered, Jennifer Mayberry left a message on the recorder. She would try again to reach Ms. Creighton woman in the future.

Planning the Charity Ball
Pacey Creighton made all the arrangements for the grand affair. The opening of the women's shelter for battered women was about to become a reality. Invitations were sent to everyone who was anyone in the Chicago area. Usually these Charity events were an opportunity for a little press and all the up and coming were sure to attend. The who's who list included many that had their own foundations that may decide to grace a charity event with their presence and funds.

Pacey Creighton asked one of her many contacts for the use of Navy Pier for the event and the contact came through. Not surprising, considering the vital political contributions the Creighton family annually contributed to support political allies. The contributions usually paid off during the year tenfold. It was a game the rich played and enjoyed.

St. Rita's Harmony Place (The Shelter)
The building for housing the women encompassed almost an entire block of second floor apartments above stores on Division Street on the West Side of Chicago. Counseling and other services would be offered on the first floor of buildings and the second floor for apartments to house any battered woman and their children.

Surprisingly, Maria was staying within the prescribed budget for everything. She and her wonderfully supportive friends found and scrounged furniture and all types of fixtures from all around the city and suburbs. One family in Winnetka donated a huge dining set that would have been impossible to fit in any of the apartments. Maria accepted the gift and found a willing buyer through the efforts of her special friend Mrs. Leriget at the Employment Agency. Samantha Marsten continued to provide assistance with everything from woodwork and door installations to planning the décor.

Pacey Creighton called one day out of the blue and asked Maria to lunch. Maria gladly accepted and they agreed to meet at a quiet neighborhood restaurant on the near North Side, Bigsbys. When Maria arrived, she was surprised to see both Pacey and Vera Creighton awaiting her arrival. Maria sat at the table. The Creightons suggested that Maria order and then they would talk. Maria ordered her food, placed the menu on the table and looked at both women.

"Is everything alright?" There was silence

"We want to know about a name for the Shelter Maria, Pacey Creighton said rather seriously." We've heard a number of names bandied about and were wondering what you are thinking regarding a name."

Maria sat with a frown and surprise on her face.

"Are you concerned about something," she asked again.

"Absolutely not," they both said in unison.

"We just thought it would be time for the Shelter to have a name.

"I was thinking St. Rita's Harmony Place Shelter for battered women," Maria suggested.

"Doesn't that speak of religious overtones?" Vera Creighton added.

"I hadn't thought about it that way," Maria weighed in.

"But now that you say it, perhaps it may give that thought."

Pacey Creighton continued. "I know this is important to you Maria, but we want to let everyone know that the Shelter is available to all battered and abused women, not just those with a religious background."

"I agree with you wholeheartedly, however, it is up to us to spread the word. First we need to get the word out about the existence of the shelter, then the fact that it is available for any battered or abused women regardless of race, ethnicity or religious affiliation."

Vera and Pacey Creighton looked at each other. They nodded in agreement.

Vera Creighton spoke.

"Ok, Maria. The name of the Company will be St. Rita's Harmony Place Shelter for Women."

"We want to stress the Harmony Place name though, so that everyone gets the right idea.

It was decided that the public name of the Shelter would be Harmony Place. The Corporate Holding Company would be St. Rita's

Harmony Place. This provided for expansion and provided a path to the offering of other services not necessarily associated with Harmony Place.

"Sold," Maria, stated emphatically.

Adele Dozier

Doctor Pedroza continued his rounds visiting the other patients. Fleetingly, he thought of Maria, but the lateness of his rounds, prohibited him from trying to make contact. He would certainly call her when he found a free moment.

The alarm bell sounded for the "Code Blue". A crash cart with two nurses passed him as he stepped to the side. His eyes followed the cart. The nurses steered the cart into the room of a patient by the name of Adele Dozier, another knee surgery case. It seemed odd that she would be in cardiac arrest however. He followed the nurses to the room. Sure enough, the line on the electroencephalograph was flat with the dull monotonous single tone filling the air. He saw the doctor place the paddles on the woman's chest and call for the amp reading from the nurse.

One of the nurses began CPR.

Another placed the breathing bag over the woman's face, trying to draw breath.

"Clear." All stood back.

The woman's body jumped. No reaction.

The nurse returned to CPR.

The airbag was pulsed.

Again, the doctor calmly voiced, "clear". The woman's body raised again from the shock.

No reaction.

A third time. Nothing.

The nurse called off the body readings again.

No sign of life.

The doctor called for a needle to inject epinephrine, the stimulant, directly into the heart.

He plunged the needle in and waited.

No reaction.

He called for the paddles again. No reaction.

He looked at the nurses. All faces were grim.

A look of resignation covered all of those attending.

Once more, the doctor said quietly, futility in his voice.

"Clear". The jolt again brought no response.

The doctor looked up to see Doctor Pedroza standing in the doorway.

"This your patient doctor," he asked?

"Yes, I'm the attending" was the only reply.

"Sorry", the emergency doctor replied sadly.

"Thanks," was all Doctor Pedroza could say with a shake of his head.

The other doctor called out the time. This would be the time of the patient's passing.

Dr. Pedroza stepped into the room to look at the woman's face. He thought of the laughter and joy she brought when he came to the room before surgery. She was a vital and caring woman. He knew she loved life. He wasn't aware of her background in childcare. However, he was aware of her reputation as an advocate for advancement in caring for needy children. She worked as an administrator in the Mayor's office. He knew her as a very alive and motivated woman who worked tirelessly behind the scenes to improve living conditions for the unfortunate. She also had the Mayor's ear on many important issues for the poor and needy. He trusted her judgment. She was very ordinary in looks, yet seemed to project a wonderful sense of perpetual enjoyment. Now it was gone.

A tear formed in Doctor Pedroza's eye as he reached to touch the woman's hand in a final good bye. Touching her now lifeless skin, he felt a slight pulse of electricity. He attributed the feeling to the defibrillator's energy. Sometimes after being shocked, the body holds an electrical charge.

The nurses gathered the gear to replace on the crash cart. The emergency doctor walked slowly toward the door. The nurses began detaching the probes from the machine that monitored the woman. Doctor Pedroza patted the woman's hand one more time, and lifting his hand from hers, turned away.

In mid stride, he was frozen by a shriek from one of the nurses. He turned quickly to see the woman's eyes open and looking around as if in a daze. The nurse quickly reattached the probes and turned on the monitor. The emergency doctor returned to the room, to find the reason for the commotion.

The woman's searching eyes found Doctor Pedroza's face. She stared into his eyes with a deeply hypnotic look. He was unable to discern the message other than to feel an attachment to the woman as her eyes looked deeply into his. Although he knew this happened before, he was never a witness. Someone returning from wherever it is they go when life is over was a miracle and a mystery. This time he experienced it firsthand. It was both shocking and rewarding.

The mystery would stay with him for the rest of his life. He felt he had just witnessed the unbelievable, were it not for the woman looking at him. He smiled at her. There was something about the awesome display of power, he had just witnessed. The feeling was very rewarding. The nurses packed up the cart and left, noticeably bewildered, as was the emergency doctor. There was neither rhyme nor reason for it. It just happened.

One of the nurses remarked to her co-worker a studied question.

"Do you think God is here today?" she asked.

"Why not," was the reply?

"I was just wondering"

"Well, I think God could be in anyone we meet at any time."

"We never know."

"That's something I never thought about," her co-worker replied.

"Something for ya ta think about then."

With that, the nurse turned the corner and began to unload the crash cart.

Maria

Things became more hectic for Maria and her friends. The tests for the RN Certification were completed and they all passed. Now that the tests were out of the way, Maria was able to concentrate on the more hectic happenings that developed with the Shelter.

She found herself very busy fielding new phone calls and finishing the hundreds of little to-do's that required attention at The Shelter. The Office of the State's Attorney General had also been in contact with Maria as well as the Department of Children and Family Services. She knew that it would be impossible for her to continue doing everything herself and that she would require assistance very soon in order to maintain the contact with women who were in need.

Presently, she had the help of three part time volunteer nurses with psychological license credentials. The rooms were beginning to fill up, as the Shelter achieved recognition within the Chicago community.

As fortune would shine, Chelle Leriget called one afternoon for a check up on how Maria was doing. Maria decided to let her newly acquired friend know of the growing need she had for some help. Chelle

Leriget was saving some information for the correct time to inform Maria of some opportunities. It seemed the time had arrived. They arranged for a lunch meeting that Friday and said their good byes.

Maria Esparza was about to find out just how versatile Chelle Leriget was going to be in providing help to her. She began receiving phone calls from professionals that offered their services on an as needed basis. All were highly qualified people with a genuine interest in providing help and support.

Mrs. Leriget also spoke with Lori Boby, the waitress from the Metropolis Club about the attacker and surprising conclusion to the attack. Lori described the entire event, even to the point of almost running over the man at the exit. Chelle Leriget informed Maria of that happening during their conversation, and was very inquisitive of Maria's thoughts, about the feeling of warmth exchanges. Maria feigned lack of knowledge about it for the time being. Mrs. Leriget didn't pursue the matter further.

Mrs. Leriget called Lori to inform her that there was another opportunity, as an administrative assistant, to a female lawyer at a downtown law firm. She asked her if she would be interested. Lori said she would and they agreed to talk about the opportunity in the coming week.

St. Rita's Harmony Place Shelter
Walls were removed and rooms redesigned, to make the housing comfortable for the women. It was not a long-term solution for them; but at least a place to rest, away from the torment they had endured.

During the time of preparations, her friends Ellie and Sydney contributed vital hours. Ellie would arrive with Jimmy Ennis to help with everything from addressing envelopes to moving furniture. Ellie and Jimmy had definitely become a twosome. Sydney and her husband were there constantly to help with whatever was necessary. Maria's biggest surprises were from those who made contact and sometimes delivered entire rooms of furniture. The items that could be used were retained, while some of the other larger pieces and period works of significant value were kept and stored. They would be sold at auction during the gala kickoff ball. Everything was falling into shape with almost miraculous precision.

Overall, there would be small apartment type quarters for twenty-two women. St. Rita's Harmony Place Shelter was completely furnished; with essentials including five bath facilities. Beds, sheets, towels and most essential amenities were on hand. There were nice furnishings with matching colors, to make the inhabitants feel as comfortable as possible, were in each room. Each of the girls took the responsibility of furnishing the apartments and the competition turned out to be surprisingly fulfilling for them all.

A larger apartment was set up as an office and sleeping quarters for whoever needed to stay there during the improvement time. Maria often found herself on the couch in the morning after falling asleep while working at the computer, late into the night. All of the licensing requirements were met thanks to her friends and their contacts with lawyers and state authorities. Applicants for positions were interviewed and screened for the jobs. Chelle Leriget was extremely helpful. Employees were given start dates.

One night at around one in the morning, the phone rang. It was a juvenile officer from the nearby police precinct. He met Maria at one of the many preparatory meetings and remembered her shelter. Maria answered the call and before she could take a deep breath, a police car arrived with a woman and two young children. Her husband threatened her. He developed a habit of beating her whenever he lost a job, which became more frequent due to his drinking habit. The unfortunate woman never knew what to expect when he walked in the door and finally decided she had been through enough.

Maria met the new arrival with the accompanying police officers, and led her to one of the apartments that would accommodate the two small children. The woman was mentally exhausted from her ordeal and was extremely grateful for the opportunity to hide from the malicious habits of her husband. As they shook hands, Maria felt the very warm feeling and her mind was flooded with the vision again. She knew right away that the woman would be Okay now and in the future. Maria introduced the woman to the nurse who led them away to their new temporary abode. Another worker took the children to get food in the kitchen.

Suddenly, the shelter was in operation. Maria was excited and fearful. This was still all a new experience for her and she began to doubt her ability to hold things together. Soon she would find more about support. For the present, she put her head on the pillow and sank into a deep and comfortable sleep.

Amhudy

The man, who ran into Maria on the street a few days before, sat in the top floor of the abandoned apartment building. He was looking for some solace from the constant jabbering of his friends. He rolled and lit a joint. Sitting on the floor and leaning against the walls stripped of wall covering, he looked at the large vat containing fertilizer. He went to take a drag and the ash fell off onto his pants. He quickly jumped up and pushed it away. Not seeing where it went, he lit and smoked what was left of the joint and headed downstairs to the basement, where his friends were most likely talking about him.

Chapter 12 A Fiery Twist

Captain Jimmy Ennis

Crimson tongues of flame licked the darkness of the night sky, above a four flat apartment building. The entire block was in danger, as the wind blew the flames toward the adjoining structures. Air brakes on the fire trucks hissed as they rolled to a stop, their red and white strobes creating a psychedelic effect on the surrounding buildings. Firefighters quickly emerged and connected hoses and equipment, as they took orders from their command personnel. There were already two engine companies from the Chicago Fire Department's second District on the scene. Lieutenants were barking orders as the men and women in yellow coats prepared to do battle with the already raging inferno.

The site was just adjacent to the I-290 expressway near a major connecting artery for downtown, as well as the north and south sides of Chicago and suburbs, known as the Dan Ryan and Edens expressways. Captain Jimmy Ennis arrived on the scene in the specially equipped SUV. He noticed an oil delivery, tank truck parked in the small lot next to the expressway, at the end of the block. Two of his inspectors from the Investigations unit were with him. The call had come in to 911 and whenever the department thought there might be a cause, that needed investigation, Ennis's unit would be involved. As the firefighters trudged in their heavy gear, Ennis told his investigators Lindsay Ballenger and Bill Gaines, where to situate themselves to locate the area where the fire may have started.

Ennis could feel the heat filling the cold night air as the fire raged just a short distance away. Smoke was already beginning to appear in the building next-door. As he looked skyward, he could see the intensity of the flames creating an almost surreal picture against the blackness of the sky. As he stood watching his inspectors proceeding toward other areas, he looked up again. The ground shook beneath his feet at the tremendous force of an explosion that literally blew off the entire top of a building. The force knocked him to the ground. Immediately he was on his feet again and moving forward to where the pumpers and ladder trucks were parked.

Debris was raining on the equipment and those below. Ennis took shelter in a doorway to avoid being hit by the wood, steel and roofing. As he waited, he saw the debris hitting men and their equipment. There was some crucial damage already, and deep in the recesses of his mind, something told him this was just the beginning. He stepped from the doorway and ran forward to the staging area. The scene was unbelievable.

Heavy pumper trucks were sitting under tons of material. He reached down to help one of his comrades in a heavy yellow jacket. The man's face was bloodied and his arm hung at an unusual angle. Ennis knew the man was not going to be able to do much. He helped the wounded firefighter to a sheltered area, where recently arrived paramedics had set up station. There were already a number of firefighters under the care of the medics.

He tapped the call button on his radio, to ask for a check in of the engine companies on site. Each lieutenant checked in as required. It seemed like Ennis was the ranking officer on site. He issued a command to all companies to vacate the residents from both sides of the block. Firefighters all over the area, executed the command to get the residents out of the buildings on the block.

His mind blurred as he tried to estimate what was happening. Nothing like what had already taken place should happen with a residential building fire. This one already began to spread fear among the men in yellow. Looking to the right, he noticed Chief Tom Carlisle approaching. On recognizing Capt. Ennis, the Chief made a beeline for him, leaving his escort behind. They scurried to follow their boss. Carlisle nodded to Ennis with a questioning look on his face. "I don't know sir," Ennis offered immediately. There was no time for the usual small talk amenities between high-ranking officers. Get to the point is the order of the day at the site of a fire.

Ennis took the Chief's arm and led him to the scene of the wrecked equipment. While walking, he explained the force of the explosion and the unusual violence it created.

"Blew the entire roof up into the air and then it scattered the wood, metal and other materials all over the place."

"Injuries?" questioned Chief Carlisle.

"Afraid so, a bunch," Jimmy Ennis responded.

"I ordered an evacuation of the entire block."

"Good idea Jimmy."

The Chief surveyed the scene.

"Jimmy, this entire area might catch before this is over. You better detach some men to the next street to survey the scene and evacuate there too."

"Already done sir," Captain Ennis responded. The Chief smiled at the answer.

"Stick with me Jimmy; let's find out what's going on here."

"You bet sir."

As they walked, Tom Carlisle pointed to the building south of the burning structure. The fire was flicking its flames out the broken window of the top floor. They knew it would only be a matter of time before the entire building would be engulfed. They looked to the next building and noticed the flames on the roof of the third structure. Flaming debris from the explosion were starting fires on the adjacent buildings.

The two officers walked around the damaged vehicles toward the area where the Site Chiefs were standing. As they neared the other group huddled in conversation, another enormous explosion rocked another building, bracketing the entire area in more flaming debris. Everyone found himself or herself on the ground from the enormous force.

Ennis could hear the expletives from the others as he picked himself up for the second time. He reached out to the Chief, lying in a heap next to him. A piece of debris hit Chief Carlisle. He fell instantly. He wasn't moving. The other officers noticed the limp body of the Chief as they picked themselves up and ran over to help. Carlisle's eyes suddenly flew open and a stream of obscenities spewed forth from the mouth of the swarthy Irishman. As he rose to his feet, he brushed away the helping hands of others. Ennis watched the intense man, thinking he was more embarrassed than hurt. The truth was that a brick had struck Carlisle a glancing blow that his helmet deflected. It was fortunate for the Chief or he might have been history.

Ellie Mulcahey

Ellie Mulcahey was walking under the streetlights. A little girl, about three years old, was skipping in front of her mother, smiling and having a good time. Suddenly she tripped on a piece of cement and landed hard on her face. Ellie ran to the little girl to help and saw that she lost a couple teeth in the fall. Ellie knew that they were the young girl's permanent teeth and tried to think of some way to reset them. Perhaps a good dentist would be able to help. The little girl reached out to grab the two teeth from Ellie's hand. The mother arrived at the same time. Both women saw the girl put the teeth back into her mouth, and unbelievably, they stayed in the places from which they had come. The women looked at each other in surprise. Ellie looked at the woman and smiled as she said, "someone must be smiling on your daughter today.

The mother just looked in disbelief. Ellie patted the little girl on the head and turned to continue down the street with mischievous smile on her face.

The Dangerous Blaze

Men gathered, exchanging opinions on how to deal with the quickly spreading blaze. The wind was blowing flames across the small parking areas next to the buildings. The roof of the structure to the south was already afire with flames shooting from the roof into the night. Each wondered about the explosions and wondered if there might be more. The radio waves lit up as the command group asked for information from the other unit chiefs on the scene. The fire designation changed to a three eleven, meaning that more equipment would be on the scene shortly. The fear of more explosions however was high on everyone's mind.

"Let's get that expressway closed." Tom Carlisle said to no one in particular.

Heeding the Chief, who was never to be taken lightly, one of officers immediately got on the radio to the command center with the message to close the expressway near the fire site.

Within minutes, the ramps of ingress and egress to the area closed.

Reports began to filter in. Something was very wrong with this fire. Nothing seemed to fit the usual circumstances experienced before in residential housing areas. By the time an hour passed, the firefighters' efforts to fight the flames, was becoming futile. Tom Carlisle had rung an escalating alarm making it a five-eleven fire. That was the first code for a really large and dangerous fire.

Some of the firefighters risked their lives going to the entrance of the building. They hoped to find a source or reason for the enormity of the explosions. There were casualties. Some of the firefighters had died already from the ferocious explosions. Helicopters were called in. They provided a wider scope of information to analyze. This would provide help from an overhead view.

The area was teeming now with residents attracted by the fire. This always happened at fires. Chicago police were continuing to rush men to the scene to establish control and to let the firefighters have the freedom needed to attack the fierce blaze.

One of the helicopter pilots was heard on the speaker of the Area Chief's car. The pilot told of a large drum sitting inside the building adjoining the initial fire point. It was visible because most of the roof was blown away. As the pilot conveyed the information, the command group began to look to each other. The sign of fear building as each felt the thoughts of the others. The pilot reported that fires had broken out on the street behind the building. The fire jumped the alley and the roofs on the other side were not burning. Flaming debris was everywhere igniting new fires on roofs and in rooms where the windows were blown away. The chopper pilot reported fires in five of the buildings behind the initial blaze.

One of Jimmy Ennis's Inspectors came running toward the group. It was Lindsay Ballenger. As the woman inspector gasped for breath, she told Capt. Ennis what she had found. Ennis took the woman's arm, facing her toward the group so all could hear. The men stood silently listening to the information the fire inspector was telling them between breaths.

As the woman investigator spoke, the men who were listening to broadcasts from the area, turned toward her with fervent interest. Most of the buildings were abandoned the inspector explained. According to some residents of the area, trucks were coming to unload large crates and packages at three of the buildings in the center of the block. The other buildings had also received packages, but they were smaller deliveries by vans and cars. All of the activity had taken place within the last few weeks, so said the residents.

According to the story, a number of men and women seemed to be living in the buildings. They were seen moving about outside during the night. Chief Carlisle thanked the inspector. As he did, he turned to Jimmy Ennis.

"You best stay on top of this Jimmy." Ennis nodded.

"Keep us posted. I'm going to get some units on the next block before something else goes wrong.

"Yes sir." Ennis responded and led his inspector back toward the scene.

As they walked, Lindsay Ballenger told her boss more about what the people told her.

"They say that there were some very large pieces of sheet metal delivered. The doors and doorways were removed to provide entry.

"Some of those doorways are ten feet tall Captain," Lindsay Ballenger said with a start.

"Holy sh......." Jimmy Ennis began. Lindsey Ballenger added.

"Isn't the President coming by this way tomorrow?" Ennis did a quick about face and began running back to the area where he left Chief Carlisle and the other chiefs.

He reached the other officers quickly. Taking Tom Carlisle by the arm, Ennis told him what Inspector Ballenger had relayed, adding his take on the matter.

"Remember the chopper pilot mentioning the large drum?" Ennis quickly asked his superior.

"Sure, we're trying to figure that out Jimmy."

"Chief listen," Ennis interrupted.

"What if they have been building one or more of those large fertilizer type bombs in there?"

"That's what could have caused the other explosions."

"What if this one and others are still gonna blow sir?"

"The President is coming this way early tomorrow morning."

Carlisle froze. He quickly remembered the briefing of the schedule for President Bush's visit to Chicago in the morning.

Jimmy Ennis continued looking at the man he admired so much.

"My God man, what if it is?"

Ennis quickly related the conversation Lindsay Ballenger had with the residents. Three buildings received these large shipments of sheet metal. At present, in spite of the fierceness of the fire, only the two buildings were involved. The others were afire, but not consumed as the others.

Amhudy

The three men huddled in a basement of the building three buildings from the fire area, arguing feverishly in a foreign language. Two of the men were asking the one named Amhudy what he had done when he went to check on the other buildings. The thought of running into the woman on the street flooded his mind briefly.

He continued to repeat he had done nothing wrong. In the recesses of his mind, he remembered lighting the reefer. He bumped his arm and lost the ash. He lit it again, while he glanced at the floor, strewn with newspapers and other materials. The effect of the marijuana started taking its intended effect. This he would keep as his secret.

The others were trying to determine how a fire began. Now the whole area filled with police and fire units. The arguing continued as they realized their entire three months of carefully laid plans were exposed. One of the men stood shaking his arms for emphasis as he spoke quickly to the other two. The seated men stood and reached for their jackets.

Chief Carlisle

Chief Thomas Carlisle quickly went to the nearest command vehicle. He reached for the department phone.

"Who's in charge at this location he asked the operator. The fire operator always knew where the officials were and who had responsibility. It was this way for years and worked well.

"Commissioner Jerry Groton sir," the operator responded. Carlisle recognized the voice of Sizzle Macrie.

"Get him on the line, Sizzle"

"Yes sir"

Tom Carlisle lifted his head with a slight chuckle. Sizzle got his name from his reputation as a woman's man. Always made em sizzle, was what the people said about him.

A minute passed.

"Sir, Commissioner Groton doesn't respond."

Tom Carlisle wasn't surprised as his eyes surveyed the wrecked vehicles and debris from the explosions.

He reached for the phone inside the nearby command car.

Immediately the department phone operator responded.

"This is Chief Thomas Carlisle."

"Get me Jim Jarrell," was all he said.

Carlisle realized the call was unusual, but he wasn't going to spend time trying to find the senior chief on the scene. He immediately decided to tell Jim Jarrell, the Chief of the Chicago Fire Department what he had found and thought.

Within seconds, he heard the voice.

"Yes Tom, this is Jim Jarrell."

Another enormous explosion rocked the area, flattening Tom Carlisle to the seat of the car. The phone went flying from his hand. Bricks, glass and metal were flying everywhere past the car that sheltered him. He hugged the seat as he felt the blast of hot air enveloping the area around him. He shook his head to regain focus and didn't bother to look around this time.

He picked up the phone again.

"Chief, we may have a serious problem and if I'm right, we need to take some drastic measures, right now."

"What the hell is going on there Tom? Was that another explosion I heard? Are you all right?"

"Another explosion sir, yes, "was all Carlisle could say.

"Go on Tom, I'm listening," he heard the calm voice of Jim Jarrell.

Tom Carlisle recounted his conversation with Captain Jimmy Ennis and told the Chief how he felt about his high level of confidence in Captain Ennis.

Jarrell listened while Tom Carlisle explained the suspicion of lurking danger.

"Ok Tom, you inform the unit chiefs at the site and find Jerry Groton. He's the senior there right now. I'm making the necessary arrangements from here. I'll find Jerry and tell him. Just make sure he's aware of the situation. We'll address any questions afterwards."

Jim Jarrell had known Tom Carlisle for years. There was no doubt about his knowledge as a firefighter and his decision-making ability as a person. Jarrell ended the conversation with a click.

Carlisle called the department operator again.

"This is Tom Carlisle again."

"Keep trying to reach Chief Groton, Sizzle."

"Tell him to call the Chief."

"You mean Chief Jarrell," the voice replied.

"That's right Sizzle"

"Got it sir," call the Chief, Yes sir."

Tom Carlisle walked back to Jimmy Ennis and informed the Captain of what was going to happen. He patted him on the shoulder.

"Good work Jimmy"

"Go and find Jerry Groton for me, I've got to take care of a few things right away.

"Ok, sir." Jimmy Ennis turned without another word and set off in the direction of the staging area.

Chief Jim Jarrell picked up the phone to convey an unprecedented decision resulting from the conversation with Tom Carlisle. He based his decision on the trust in his men. He was immediately connected with the Special Operations unit for the Chicago Fire Department, at the O'Hare Airport Fire Control Center. He issued an unusual order to the Officer on Duty there.

"I need three of your foamers, right away on the near west side of the city. Can you spare them?" The operator asked Chief Jarrell to wait for one second. The O'Hare Battalion Commander came on the phone quickly.

"Sure Chief, where do you want them?" Jarrell gave the location. Equipment motors started and men were quickly moving to act in response to the command. Everyone knew that O'Hare had three foamers in reserve and when called, they knew the situation was hazardous. There followed many comments, yet no one questioned what they were about to do.

Tom Carlisle hung up the phone and stepped away from the shelter of the car. He looked to where Jimmy Ennis was standing. Someone was lying on the ground. Carlisle rushed over to help his fellow firefighter. Lindsay Ballenger, Ennis' inspector, was shielded from the blast by the wrecked pumper vehicle, now lying on its side. Jimmy Ennis was nowhere to be seen. As Carlisle reached the figure lying on the ground, he noticed movement. Feeling relieved he quickly helped her to her feet.

"Where's Captain Ennis," Carlisle asked.

Ballenger shook her shoulders.

"He was right here just before the blast," was all she could say.

They both looked around. Sounds came from a pile of debris behind them. They turned to find the source of the noise. A large piece of plywood moved as Captain Ennis emerged. The plywood was splintered with glass and metal. Jimmy Ennis stood there feeling himself, pleased to find he was still intact. As he reflected for a moment, he felt that someone or something was watching over him.

News reporters were on the scene from every local and network station. Ennis could hear them yelling to the chiefs for an interview. Hands went up in refusal. Tom Carlisle in particular, wanted no one speaking to the press before he was somewhat sure of the gravity of the situation. He walked toward a police sergeant and asked him to start moving the people back another whole block. The sergeant began to ask for the reason, but the fire Chief simply told him,

"It's bad Sarge, and it's spreading. Move em back."

The sergeant respected the Chief by the tone of voice and look on his face.

He immediately gave the order and radioed for his Lieutenant to tell him of the Fire Chief's order. Within minutes, the police were moving the citizens, news people and area residents back further from the scene.

Frank Bellini

Frank Bellini was in the downtown area scrounging. He saw the fire first erupt and heard the explosion before the fire department and police arrived on the scene. He decided to stand around and watch while the fire department did their usual fantastic job. Before long, he was amongst a number of firefighters pulling hoses and connecting them to the fire hydrants. A young firefighter was running by and tripped over one of the hoses. He seemed to have a little difficulty getting up again. It was obvious, he hurt his leg and he tried to stand and put weight on the limb. Frank Bellini rushed over to help the injured firefighter who acknowledged the help with a smile and a grimace at the same time. Frank Bellini knew the reaction. He had seen it many times before. They looked at the man's leg and it was already beginning to swell. It must be broken or at least a bad sprain. He reached for the firefighter's helmet that had skipped away when the man fell. As he put the helmet on the firefighter's head, he asked. "What's your name?"

"Tommy Kennedy," the firefighter said.

As Frank Bellini placed the helmet on the man's head, he felt a quick warmth where his finger touched the man's face. The firefighter felt it too.

"Well, see ya', the firefighter smiled as he went on his way.

"You take care," Frank Bellini replied.

He turned to go, but looked back and saw that the firefighter no longer had a limp. He was walking just fine.

Jimmy Ennis

Jimmy Ennis heard the familiar sound of a diesel truck engine. His ears told him it wasn't a Fire Department vehicle. The sound was foreign to him. He looked around. As he did, Lindsay Ballenger saw him gaze toward the end of the block where the oil truck he noticed on their arrival, began to move. He yelled to the investigator to follow it, get the license number and get that truck stopped. Lindsay Ballenger was a sprinter in college and kept herself in top shape. She took off in a dead run without even acknowledging her boss's order. Her only hope was that the truck would have to slow or stop at the police line a block down the street.

The two passengers in the truck urged the driver to drive faster. As the truck began to pick up speed, they looked ahead for an opening between all the vehicles parked ahead. It was the only route available and they hoped to get out of the area quickly. The truck reached the end of the block where a Channel 5 news van blocked its way.

One of the men jumped out waving his arms and yelling at the van to move out of the way. He was speaking in English. When no one responded, he began swearing at the crew near the van. The driver thought about trying to move the van from their path. Sweat began to break out on the man's forehead as the other passenger stuck his hands out the window waving for the news crew to move.

Lindsay Ballenger watched the scene ahead of her and turned on the speed to reach a group of police officers standing near their police car with its lights flashing their eerie glow on the buildings. She reached the first officer and wearing only her Inspector's badge quickly pulled the department ID from her pocket and showed it to the officer.

"I want that truck stopped and those people held so we can ask them some questions about this fire," she voiced between breaths.

The young officer took one look at the petite woman's ID and yelled to his fellow officers.

"Hey men, Fire Department Inspector wants to talk to those guys", as he pointed toward the truck. Without a word, all three officers drew their weapons and ran toward the unmoving oil truck. As the police officers approached the truck, the driver of the Channel 5 van got in and started the motor. The closest police officer waved his arms to the news crew to stop.

"Don't move that van," he yelled to the cameraman whom he approached.

The cameraman heard the order and yelled to the driver while signaling with his arm to stop. The van driver shut off the engine as he saw the police approaching on the run. Lindsay Ballenger followed, allowing some distance between the officers and herself. She had a feeling something might happen and she did not want to be in the middle of a confrontation until the police had the situation under control.

She wasn't aware that one of the officers already called for a backup. Suddenly there were police coming from all directions. Some had guns drawn as they approached the oil truck. The man, who was trying to get the van to move, stopped and became silent. The police ordered the other two out of the truck with guns pointed. The two men complied quickly, speaking in their foreign tongue as if they didn't understand. A sergeant took charge of the situation, motioning the men to place their hands against the truck. He spoke into the shoulder radio. "This is Sergeant Buckman. I need a mid east translator. Is Sergeant Rashid on the scene?" The response was immediate.

"This is Rashid, Bucky."

"Come on down by the expressway Rashid, I need your tongue and ears."

"On the way Sarge."

Tommy Kennedy

Feeling they had the men under control, the police and surrounding firefighters relaxed. That was a mistake. One of the men turned quickly, taking a knife from his pocket and plunged the knife into the closest firefighter. The others immediately took the man to the ground. The firefighter simply crumpled and lay still. His companions found the wound in his upper chest and began applying pressure, trying to stop the bleeding. Someone came up with a gauze bandage pad and the paramedic on the scene, slapped the pad on the wound. The blood stopped much too quickly for the paramedic that came to the firefighters aid when the stabbing happened. The paramedic turned over the firefighter to check his back for a puncture wound. There was none. He opened the man's shirt to examine the wound again and found the bloody bandage, but underneath the bandage, the wound was gone. The paramedic stared in disbelief. The firefighter came to consciousness again. He was a bit hazy, but seemed alert. The paramedic asked the firefighter his name.

"Tommy Kennedy," the man replied.

"You sure are a lucky man," the firefighter responded. "I thought you weren't going to make it.

"Huh, what happened? The firefighter replied.

Orash Rashid

Orash Rashid came to the scene in a flash. He witnessed the last conversation between the paramedic and the firefighter and dismissed it as something that didn't concern him. He turned his attention to the Sergeant to find out the situation.

Lindsay Ballenger

By this time, Lindsay Ballenger told Sergeant Buckman about the situation. Noticing the commotion, a fire lieutenant ran over to find out what was going on. He saw Lindsay Ballenger and approached her.

"Hello Lindsay."

"Hi sir," she responded noticing his department shoulder radio.

"Sir, would you try to get Captain Ennis on the radio for me?"

Without hesitation, the Lieutenant complied with the Inspector's request.

"Captain Ennis please," he said into the radio.

In a second, Jimmy Ennis responded.

"Hold one sir, one of your people wants to talk to you."

He peeled off the Velcro and handed the radio to Lindsay Ballenger.

"Lindsay here sir."

"Yes Lindsay, did you get the truck stopped?"

"With a little help from our friends in blue sir," she responded looking at the closest officer.

"I'll be there in a short Lindsay, have the police hold those people."

"Already under control sir"

"I think they're Mideastern sir and we have Orash here too."

"Nothing like taking control, Lindsay."

"Nice work, be right there."

Jimmy Ennis went over to Tom Carlisle and told him of the situation on the next block.

Carlisle decided to join him in talking to the people in the truck. They walked down the block in the direction of the Channel 5 news van.

Flames shot high into the night sky from another building. The heat created additional ripples of hot air that appeared as a visual floating sensation. Firefighters had hoses on the fronts and backs of the buildings. Snorkels reached high into the air showering the flames with a more intense spray of water. Still the flames surged southward in the wind touching off a fire on the roof of another building. The tar of the flat roofed building soon added additional fuel to the inferno now developing.

Police moved crowds back, for fear of additional explosions. The expressway was closed to traffic. Surrounding streets of Halsted and everything east/west for a mile were also blocked. An evacuation of the blocks around the fire was also successfully addressed. Police and firefighters moved from building to building, ordering residents to leave until the danger was over.

The newscasters from each of the major networks were on the scene. Channel 5 of course had been witness to the holding of the suspects for questioning, so the word was out on the airwaves with the so called "terror experts" providing senseless points of view on what was taking place.

Orash Rashid

Police Sergeant Orash Rashid listened to the captives talking among themselves. A smile broadened on his face. They were speaking in Farsi, an Islamic dialect that he understood and spoke fluently. Before long, he was standing and listening to the suspect trio from the oil truck. As he was sifting through the jabber, one of the firefighters decided to check the truck's contents. With some help from members of the same Engine Company, he opened the valve. The air was immediately inundated with the smell of kerosene and something that created the most pungent sickly odor he had known. He quickly closed the valve. The firefighting team looked to each other with a sign of recognition. They knew the smell. It was a deadly mixture. Similar to that used in the well-known Oklahoma City bombing of the Federal Building there. Quickly one of the firefighters with a radio called for their chief.

Just as the call went out, Chief Carlisle, Captain Ennis and Lindsay Ballenger arrived on the scene. The whooping of a helicopter drowned out the noise of the fire. The figures jumped from the door and quickly moved toward the police command center. The police officers knew immediately who the new arrivals were. Two men and a woman in dark blue jackets with yellow FBI markings smartly tailored onto the coats approached. The FBI received word of the chase and holding of the oil truck passengers, from the police radio and decided there was a jurisdictional situation. They decided that they should take command. It was their usual method of operation.

Walking up flashing their badge IDs, the lead agent, a man by the name of Whitman Sharper spoke to the Police Captain on the scene. He was not satisfied with the information provided. He looked toward the Firefighter's command area and beeline for the most senior member there. It wasn't long before the location of the three foreign speaking men was determined. The FBI group approached Chief Tom Carlisle, with their usual air of authority. Flashing badges with the customary

"We'll take things from here."

The only problem this time, was that Tom Carlisle needed information from these guys, right now. His decision was immediate.

"No way. Not till we get some information from these guys," he said with a wave of his hand to the lead FBI agent. As everyone around knew there was going to be an authority issue right then, as tension mounted quickly. The lead FBI person told Carlisle he was relieved of authority. Carlisle simply shook his head and began to walk away from the group in the direction of the truck.

The FBI trio became furious at the insult, of being left standing by some mere Firefighter in a yellow jacket. One of the men grabbed Chief Carlisle by the arm, turning him around in mid stride.

"We are taking over, and you are going to tell us what's going on, or you'll be in jail," the man shouted right in Carlisle's face.

Firefighters in yellow gear had begun to filter toward the scene. The loudness of the FBI leader's voice and what he was yelling at the Fire Chief meant nothing to them. Their concern was for their fellow firefighter who although seeming to be handling the situation well, might still require some assistance. For sure, they would be willing and most capable of providing it, if and when necessary.

Tom Carlisle looked around at the men under his command. He wanted nothing to do with a confrontation with the FBI. He simply wanted information and the only way to get it was to continue questioning the suspects.

Looking at the FBI Agent's ID hanging from his coat, The Fire Chief said to him.

"We have a grave situation here Sharper," Carlisle pointedly stated. He used the last name of the agent purposely.

"I want those suspects," Whitman Sharper shouted back.

By now their stride led them to the van where Police Sergeant Rashid was inside, talking to the men in their native tongue. He was there with three other police officers. A captain and two lieutenants. A couple patrol officers standing nearby stood with firearms drawn. Jimmy Ennis was also inside listening intently to the questioning.

A firefighter approached and rushed by the FBI man and Chief Carlisle, straight to the door of the van. He knocked vigorously until a police lieutenant opened the door. Sergeant Rashid recognized the firefighter and motioned at him with his hand to wait.

"Excuse me a second," Rashid said to no one in particular. He jumped off the back of the van and quickly huddled with the excited firefighter. He patted the man on the back and returned to the van.

At seeing a police sergeant moving toward the door, Whitman Sharper made a quick move to follow through the door. He looked in surprise as two large firefighters in their bulky yellow coats grabbed his arms pulling him back and forbidding entry.

Sharper was furious. The veins in his neck bulged as his entire head turned red from the fury he was holding inside. Once the door closed, he was released. He wasn't used to being physically overpowered. The feeling of intimidation and humiliation began to set in.

Sharper stared at Carlisle.

"I want in there," he yelled at Carlisle.

Carlisle reached out and put his arm around the FBI agent, pulling him next to him.

"Look Sharper, we have a police interpreter in there getting us any information he can."

"We need to know what those guys have been up to."

"Heck Whitman," he said in a quiet tone, trying to befriend the frustrated agent.

"We wouldn't even know what they are saying"

"I'll get a real interpreter down here," Sharper shot back.

"When Whitman, in an hour or two? This whole area could be gone by then." The Chief stated matter-of-factly.

Finally, the reality sunk in. Sharper knew the firefighter was correct. He just couldn't take being outside the circle. He shrugged in quiet agreement.

"I want custody of those guys before they leave here." he turned and exploded at Carlisle.

"That you will have Whitman, you will."

Tom Carlisle walked back toward the van and the escort of Firefighters standing near the door.

"Fellas, you guys do what Captain Ennis asks of you," he said with authority.

"Nobody gets in there till the Captain says Ok."

"This is a fire and the fire department overrides any other authority. Got that?"

To a man, the men in yellow coats and the police officers standing with them nodded in tacit agreement. The showdown was over and whatever ramifications would result; would be on Tom Carlisle's career and shoulders.

Orash Rashid

The questioning continued inside. When Sergeant Rashid returned from outside the van, he had a menacing look on his face and moved right to the face of the man who previously was outside yelling at the Channel5 van to move. He spoke something unintelligible to the others standing there. The other two suspects suddenly were at rapt attention when they heard the words.

The man responded with a rash of apparent refusal. Rashid repeated the words. Only this time, slowly and very distinctly, pointing to the other two. The man began to speak again and stopped. Whatever was said had a profound effect. Amhudy suddenly spoke in English. The words were simple and straightforward. The other two sat in shock as their associate told of the entire plan.

They jumped forward but the gun of the police lieutenant spoke first. His shot rifled the air in front of the two men as they started to step toward Amhudy. They froze, ending the threat.

"Explosive drums in each of the buildings. Large ones. "

Amhudy was yelling, his arms waving in excited confirmation.

"They are filled and ready to be triggered tomorrow. A timer is in place for them."

Rashid asked another question quickly in the native tongue.

The man responded in the same language.

Rashid jumped immediately.

"Keep these guys here," he said to the police officers.

Rashid opened the door followed by Jimmy Ennis.

As their feet touched the ground, Sergeant Rashid looked at Jimmy Ennis.

"That was so strange," he remarked.

"What was?" Ennis replied.

"The guy just suddenly started telling us everything" "That is so unusual for a person like that. They usually sit silent or are extremely defiant and yell obscenities instead of giving information."

"It's like someone just forced him to talk."

"I don't really care why he talked," Captain Jimmy Ennis replied.

"What on earth did you whisper to that guy?"

"Oh a little phrase that got his attention."

"It certainly seemed to work."

"Thanks buddy," he said with appreciation to the police Sergeant.

"I've got a lotta work to do."

"Good luck," the Sergeant said in return with a hefty pat on the back, as he returned to the truck.

As he started to move away, another explosion rocked the air. This one wasn't the magnitude of the others, but that was probably because it was more distant.

The men inside the van mumbled unpleasant words to each other, as the incredible turn of events was unfolding. It was unbelievable to the two that Amhudy would tell the American police officer of their plans.

Jimmy Ennis set out to find Tom Carlisle. He didn't have to go far. Approaching him, he quickly relayed the information about the explosives. As he talked, he heard the heavy sounds of more diesel engines arriving on the scene. They both looked up the block to see the source of the noise.

Chief Jarrell had followed through on his promise. The foam trucks from the airport were arriving on the scene. It was the fastest way they could think of to get the massive fire under control before all hell broke loose. The radios came alive with commands. Through years of practice, the unwritten words of understanding came before the orders.

It would be dangerous for a short while as the foam trucks moved into position. The hoses would be turned off at precisely the moment the foam would begin to spew from the nozzles of the truck hoses.

Like a grotesque ballet, the scene changed as vehicles moved and repositioned themselves, for what was hoped to be the final act. All knew what to do and they executed the scene precisely as it was written.

With sudden precision, the water hoses shut down with a deafening silence following. Within seconds, the foam trucks began to bathe the scene in a sea of white. The wind even died down as the foam began to blanket the buildings. The flames, once roaring, dwindled, as the oxygen smothering foam covered the buildings, suppressing the fire. As the flames yielded to the foam, additional arson and bomb units began to arrive on the scene. The department had practiced this situation many times. Like a well-orchestrated play, it just seemed like everyone knew his and her parts. Massive searchlights were rolled into place, bathing the scene in white light.

Night became day as the powerful beams lit the entire area. The water hoses, which had been silent, began to spout anew as each geyser of water from the powerful generators again saturated the buildings. Now the intent was to cool the hot timbers and steel as quickly as possible to allow the bomb teams to find and disarm the devices that had been placed in the buildings. They feared that some of the devices were attached to timers, and did not want any additional time to pass before disconnecting the explosive potential of the bombs.

The three men, were turned over to the FBI, but kept at the scene. There was not going to be an opportunity for them to become martyrs, with the devices they had built. Orash learned from the one man, where the devices had been planted and the man knew if anything went wrong from there, the penalty Orash had so definitely imprinted on the man's mind would be effected. At least the police sergeant thought that. Maria Esparza would soon find however that she knew the real reason.

The suspect continued talking to the FBI agents telling them of the planned explosions and resulting confusion they would have created. He explained the planned explosion at the Halsted Street Bridge over the expressway that would effectively trap the Presidential motorcade between exits. The agents were stunned however when the man explained the role of the oil truck.

The truck was prepared with fertilizer and kerosene explosives to be set off in the morning. The truck would drive through the chain link fence and down the hill to the expressway. It would meet the President's car that would be sitting, waiting for debris from the Halsted Street explosion to be cleared. The truck would simply ram into the presidential limousine triggering the explosion. The FBI agent's thoughts were frozen at the audacity, complexity and simplicity of the plan. Whitman Sharper made a mental note to find Tom Carlyle and let him know the rest of the now thwarted plan. He also notified the District Chief at the site about the Halsted Street bridge explosives that had to be removed.

One by one, the ignition devices were located and disarmed. The fire hoses continued for another hour on the houses across the street and behind the source of origin. Before long, all the flames were tamed and white smoke filled the air as the burnt materials began to cool.

The next day, tank trucks arrived to drain the remaining makeshift drums of their deadly content. The buildings were boarded and scheduled for demolition. Chicago city crews arrived on the scene, but were intercepted by FBI officials. The Mayor was called to settle the dispute, because no one in a lower position, was willing to address the issue. Mayor Dalby told the demolition crews to leave everything to the FBI. The Mayor said the FBI would be in charge now. The last thing the Mayor wanted was a squabble between the city and the FBI. Mayor Dalby turned to an aide after hanging up the phone.

"They can build a swimming pool out there if that's what Washington wants. They can also haul the water from the Atlantic too if they choose.

Chapter 13 A Night To Remember

A Resplendent Affair

The day of the Gala arrived. The evening weather was just right for summer or fall dress. The sky was clear and the stars shone brightly.

Although it was to be a fund raising event, which was usually drudgery for the people involved in preparation, this one seemed to flow together with a life of its own. All the carefully laid plans and preparations led to this event. Samantha Marsten and her husband Randy did some of the work and also provided contacts for creating the inviting scene that created oohs and aahs from the throng. At the Creighton household, everyone there was in preparation mode. Hairdressers and beauticians were addressing hair, faces, hands, nails and, oh well, other things.

At the shelter, Maria was fidgeting with her hair and trying to find the right look for herself. The handsome Doctor from the hospital called her for a date and she took the opportunity to turn the tables, and ask him for the date. His surprise was genuine when she heard him sputter, in response to her invitation to the charity gala. Upon regaining his exposure, they laughed hilariously. She knew they would have a wonderful time. She thought about him many times while she worked at the hospital. They even took the time to chat a few times too. He was truly one of those tall dark and handsome men that women describe as the ideal looking person. In truth, he was a "hottie".

The late summer's night at the lakefront was breathtaking. Navy Pier crowds of sightseeing guests from around the world made a storybook type scene. The cruise boats, for those who loved to party on the lake, were taking on passengers, while the gentle waters of the harbor became the evening playground for boats of all shapes and sizes.

The news people were there with cameras and microphones. Chauffeured limousines waited in a long line to deposit their special guests. The Ballroom was resplendent in its décor of shimmering silver and blue for the evening. Joe Kelly and his blues group greeted guests with their version of some upbeat blues as some of the guests stopped to chat with the talented, gray haired music master.

Inside, a harpist with raven hair, deftly caressed the long strings of the golden harp. Glissandos rang throughout the grand entrance as the dulcet chords reverberated from the walls and ceiling. In the ballroom, the Joe Brady orchestra provided soothing background music. They would continue during dinner. Guests were greeted by a bevy of handsome men in tuxedos and women graced in gowns of satin, velvet and lace. Blue, violet, black and burgundy materials glittered against the shining overhead lights. Greeters took orders for drinks and escorted attendees to tables and places of interest in the room. Uniformed and plain clothed security, with watchful eyes, mixed with the expanding crowd. Their obvious presence served as a reminder for the persistent need to guard against the unexpected.

Two of the first to arrive were Samantha and Randy Marsten. They were making sure that all the decorating arrangements were according to plan. Maria ran up to greet them and thank them for all their help. They smiled in return as Maria complimented Samantha on her dress. The plain black full length formal was just the right touch with Samantha Marsten's blonde hair and pretty features. With a pat on the hand, exchanging that warm glow again, Maria was off to greet other guests.

The guests gathered in groups as others moved directly toward the grand ballroom. Bright balloons graced the walls as streamers hung and danced gaily with the breeze from the lake as the doors opened to allow guests a look at the calm waters and beautiful array of boats dancing across the gray green waters.

Dignitaries from the political arena as well as Presidents, Captains and Matrons of industry were viewed wafting through the throngs, greeting friends and vying for the attention of the more noted of the groups and personalities on hand. The customary grouping of sports figures was obvious in their presence. Notable players from the Bears football team, tall members from the Bulls basketball team contrasted with the muscular smaller in stature Black Hawk hockey stars. Members of the Cubs and White Sox baseball teams were conversing with the many beautiful women as the women awaited the return of their escorts from places of viewing or speaking interest.

No one was to be left alone, on this evening of splendor. That had been the order of Pacey Creighton who appeared regal in her burgundy gown with glittering gold braids that crisscrossed the bodice, accenting her tall and very distinctive figure. Vera Creighton was radiant in her gown of diagonally contrasting colors of blue and black angling across her well-formed figure. At her side stood Steven Carter whose handsome chiseled features and six foot four inch frame made him extremely noticeable. He drew the immediate attention of the women as they watched the couple's comfortable interaction with everyone who approached. Carter owned one of the largest and most successful private investment firms in Chicagoland.

Maria Esparza looked spectacular. Her formal gown with red black lace accents coordinated splendidly with her jet-black hair and high cheek boned face. She would have made any male wish to be a matador to gain her attention and favor. Maria's friends were also bedecked in sumptuous dresses of silk and organza. Ellie in a peach colored Bill Blass number that made her red hair appear vibrant with just the right touch of understated elegance. Jimmy Ennis stood next to her, dashing in his black tuxedo. Sydney stood in her usual statuesque splendor in solid black satin with shimmering diagonals of interwoven silk. Her husband appeared very interested in her as he watched her greeting people who came by the group.

Maria noticed Chelle Leriget entering with an extremely handsome man at her side. The man held the arm of Chelle, who looked beautiful in a cranberry colored dress, with silver lining around the neck and wrists. Doctor Pedroza smiled as their eyes met. Maria studied her mother on the doctor's arm. She had not seen her looking so happy in a long time. Maria remembered the gentleman's face so well as the three approached. Maria's eyes surveyed the man from head to toe, as she remembered the doctor whom she had only seen in hospital green. Doctor Alhandro Pedroza's darkly handsome features created a striking contrast to Chelle's white-gray, finely coifed hair and very white skin. As a couple they didn't match, yet for two people, who were striking in their looks, some of the attendees found them a feast for the eyes. Maria felt a tinge of jealousy.

As the distance lessened between them, Maria felt the intensity of the doctor's gaze. Her face flushed as Chelle Leriget and the handsome man reached her. The Leriget woman took Maria's arm as her eyes conveyed a mischievous look. She whispered into Maria's ear.

"I brought your date my dear."

Maria's eyes looked at the woman with a mock surprised flavor.

Doctor Pedroza had an emergency and told Maria he would be late. Maria had no idea that Chelle Leriget knew the man, yet she was so very thankful that her new friends knew each other.

"He told me of the happenings at the hospital just before you took on this fabulous new venture." Maria winked at the Doctor who smiled broadly in response."

"I see Steven Carter is attending. I must say hi to him." "Catch you both later."

With a wink, Chelle Leriget flicked her wrist and was off leading Maria's smiling mother toward the people milling about the ballroom.

The Doctor smiled and began to apologize.

Maria took his arm and began to walk toward the doorway where the fresh night air awaited. As they walked, she looked into the handsome face of the man at her arm and smiled.

"Thank you for being here Doctor, let's enjoy the evening."

With that, Alhandro Pedroza returned the smile and felt a warm surge of enjoyment, being with the beautiful and intelligent woman at his side.

"Please call me Handro," he asked her with a gentle tone.

"It's the name my mother would always use."

With a smile, Maria looked up at the doctor.

"Thank you Handro," she said softly and tightened her hold on his arm.

Local Chicago celebrities, from all walks of life also came to the event. Opia Winston, the well-known celebrity was seen talking quietly with Maria Esparza and Vera Creighton. Jerry Spartan and other on air personalities were milling with the crowd.

Maria's brother Torreo looked dashing in a tuxedo. He was turning into quite the handsome magnet for women. His date for the evening was a beautiful young woman, who Maria had not met before. Maria wasn't sure she was right for him, but thought well of the look they exhibited.

Before long however, Torreo noticed his date was spending a little too much time sipping the champagne. Exhibiting his take-charge mentality, he drew the woman away from the crowd and told her clearly that he wouldn't accept her drinking to excess and becoming a potential embarrassment for his sister. The woman noted the importance of the comments immediately and apologized. Torreo led her back to the room as they both displayed wide smiles. Even under the circumstances, the woman's smile was genuine. A euphoric feeling of being on the arm of her handsome date made everything worthwhile tonight.

The lights dimmed, indicating that dinner would be starting soon. Groups dispersed and guests were directed to their assigned seating.

Joe Kelly, who provided the musical greeting with his group, took the microphone as Master of Ceremonies.

The evening continued after dinner with a variety of speakers providing support for and monetary donations to the new shelter Harmony Place Shelter for battered women. Speakers extolled the virtues of the Creighton Family Foundation and the crowd applauded the Creighton women for their generosity in providing the seed money for the shelter. Maria spoke of the dream to help women to improve their situations and begin a new and better life through the efforts of the shelter.

Maria's friends stood in the wings as their wonderful friend kept the audience in rapt attention with her words. Some members of the crowd who knew the Creighton family wondered aloud what miracle had taken place that lent itself to the family's apparent devotion to helping other people. Some thought it was perhaps, the "ole bastard" Marshall Creighton's way of making peace with God; that made the newly found devotion possible.

Tonight however, it was the beginning of a dream and the focus of many that would provide a future benefit for the Chicagoland area.

Joe Kelly later took the microphone to introduce the renowned Arthur Murray dancers amid oohs and aahs from the crowd. As the band began, Musetta's Waltz from the opera la Boheme, dancers in resplendent costumes began to flood the floor with graceful twirling movements as they glided effortlessly to the music. The band broke into "In The Mood," the old Glenn Miller tune and the dancers quickly shifted to swing dancing as the partners performed a variety of swing moves, thrilling the attentive audience. The tempo slowed as the MC invited all of the guests to

"Hold that special someone close and share in the joy of the night's event."

Dancing went on throughout the night. Couples who were swept up in the exuberance, kept the dance floor filled.

The event was scheduled into the early hours of the morning and after dinner; many of the guests remained to take part in the partly like atmosphere. On such a beautiful evening, many of the attendees walked outside to enjoy the lovely clear air at the select site on the lake. Music played by a stringed quartet, from Elmhurst College, wafted through the air.

Ellie and her date Jimmy Ennis were kept busy all evening with inquiries as to what happened at the fire a couple weeks back. The news of the trio of terrorists became known recently and the subject was a popular query topic.

Jimmy Ennis noticed the Marsten woman with her husband coming from the dance floor and greeted her with a smile and a hug. They worked together well making sure that Harmony Place met all the building and fire code requirements. Samantha and her husband Randy also contributed much of the carpentry and miscellaneous work that was required.

The two couples exchanged pleasantries for a while and were about to part when a woman suddenly flew up against Ellie, knocking her down. Jimmy Ennis was quick to help Ellie up and Samantha with the help of her husband returned the woman to her feet. While raising the woman, Samantha felt a sudden warmth similar to what she noticed coming from Maria's hand when they touched. She wondered what that was all about. The woman, while not intoxicated, was enjoying herself to the fullest on the dance from and did one too many twists with her partner. She apologized profusely to Ellie and thanked the Marstens for their help.

The Mayor of Chicago, Richard Dalby and his wife joined the reception after dinner. Whispers were heard among the guests, "the Mayor's here", as Mayor and Mrs. Dalby joined in conversation with some of the guests. Maria was introduced to the Dalby's and the Mayor was seen whispering something to her as they shared a moment together. Mrs. Dalby also leaned closely to Maria and mentioned something only for her ears. Anyone watching could tell from the look on Maria Esparza's face, that whatever she was told by the Dalby's, was something treasured and good. They all beamed as Maria responded to the attention. Quickly the moment of togetherness with the Mayor was shortened, as other guests approached with outstretched hands to exchange pleasantries. After a few minutes, Maria made a small hand wave gesture to them and moved off to find her friends.

At 10 o'clock, Joe Kelly returned to announce a fireworks exhibition that would take place shortly at the east end of the pier. Each time Joe took the microphone on stage, his presence was known before the words were spoken. He was a visually powerful man. The gray white hair set him apart and the eloquence of his voice almost demanded attention as the crowd fell silent waiting for him to speak.

Joe also had the distinction of having been the noted trumpet player at Arlington Park Race Track. In the past, he thoroughly enjoyed creating excitement at seeing the long trumpet that announced the races. Joe usually presented an amusing anecdote about something taking place at the event, and the crowd seemed to love the opportunity to laugh and appreciate the humor. As Joe walked off stage after the announcements, the crowd began to saunter toward that end of the pier with anticipation of witnessing the spectacular upcoming event.

Fireworks lit the sky with colorful displays and shapes. One of the most awesome sights was the display of the waterfall effect created by the layers of vibrant color exploding in a cascade as it fell to the water. At the end of the fireworks, the wait staff appeared to offer guests glasses of champagne.

Steven Carter remained at Vera Creighton's side throughout. Standing together, the two were a veritable treat for the eyes. They danced a few times and he could feel the excitement as she molded herself to him at times while they danced. The hint of Lauren perfume sent just the right message as they shared their time together. He marveled at her virtuosity during a swing dance as she tapped her feet and sashayed in tune to the beat. Being a smart dancer himself, he joined her as they created new steps and performed like a well-rehearsed team.

Their dancing attracted the crowd's attention as people nearby stopped to marvel at the two putting on their own exhibition. Steven Carter remembered the old saying during one of the band's breaks and repeated it to his date.

"Dance like nobody's watching," he said smiling.

"Really!" Vera Creighton replied, returning his smile.

"Live like there's no tomorrow," was her quick response.

"Work like you don't need the money," he added with a laugh.

"Love like you've never been hurt," Vera Creighton finished the prosaic statement, leaning herself against Steven Carter and looking up into his eyes, batting her eyelids in jest.

"Whew, you think we might have something in common here?" The question dangled.

"Could be."

"Let's dance."

They headed for the dance floor again. Only this time, they were looking at each other with wide smiles and longing eyes.

One of the special opportunities of the evening was the appearance of horse drawn carriages. Guests took the opportunity to ride around the Navy Pier area and view the lake from other places as the tuxedoed carriage drivers gave commentary on the different sights that riders would visit and view. Many of the younger couples lined the waiting area to enjoy the ride in the calm night air. Photographers were everywhere, shooting flash bulbs at the throng.

The fund raising auction was another of the highlights. Bidders overbid on every item; creating an unexpected, but greatly appreciated, source of funding windfall. Maria was overwhelmed at the generosity and almost broke into tears. One of the surprise high bids for the evening was received on a painting contributed by Maria's brother Torreo. It was a street scene of Greek Town painted by a local artist, who was of course, yet unknown. Maria ran over to her brother when the bid was accepted and planted a big kiss on his cheek, thoroughly embarrassing him. His return smile warmed her heart. She knew his art collection was growing and that her younger brother was becoming a true connoisseur of the arts.

Doctor Pedroza waited for the sister and brother to have their moment, and then offered his hand to Torreo in respect and admiration for the young man. Torreo smiled broadly, as he shook the Doctor's hand.

Samantha and Randy

Many of the guests were watching the fireworks and taking rides on the luxurious boats. The view of the Chicago night skyline was breathtaking. Samantha and Randy Marsten were among those enjoying the remaining events of the evening. Randy excused himself, for a restroom break. Samantha walked along the end of the pier watching the awe-inspiring fireworks.

Out of nowhere, a woman crashed against her, spun around and headed for the edge at the end of the pier. Samantha watched in shock as the woman who seemed to be moving in slow motion, fell over the end of the pier. A number of people saw the incident, but remained frozen in place.

Randy Marsten was walking back to his wife when suddenly, in disbelief, he saw her run to the end of the pier and jump in. The action seemed incredulous to him and he raced forward to the end of the pier.

The cries of "Help, I can't swim," began shortly after the woman disappeared. Samantha watched a group of people gather at the end of the pier. They were watching the woman flail in the water, but no one seemed to want to help.

"Damn it anyway," Samantha Marsten exclaimed, as she ran to the end of the pier. She got a fix on the flailing woman, kicked off her heels, and jumped in. Within a few strokes, she reached the woman, who immediately grabbed her and pulled her under.

Randy reached the end of the pier. He looked into the water and saw his wife holding this struggling woman afloat.

This was not supposed to be the way it works, Samantha thought as she surfaced and gasped for air. The woman was reaching to grab her again. This time, she hit the woman with a slap across the face. Samantha yelled at her to stop or she would swim away and let her drown. The woman stopped thrashing.

At that moment, a man came over with a life preserver. Randy Marsten grabbed it and threw it into the water, trying to make it land near his wife. It did.

Samantha helped the woman hold onto the preserver, as she treaded water, waiting for additional help. Randy looked around for something to help the women up from the cold water. He noticed a small rowboat about twenty yards down and attached to the pier with a rope. He ran to the end of the pier. Looking for a way down to the boat, he didn't see any. Removing his tuxedo coat, he decided to jump in the water and swim for the boat. Within a few seconds, he was climbing aboard the boat. He rowed it to where his wife and the woman were trying to stay afloat in the water. His wife told him to help the woman into the boat first. When she was aboard, he took Samantha's arm and helped her aboard.

Torreo Esparza had been looking for his date, who was nowhere to be seen. He noticed the commotion near the water and walked quickly over. As he arrived, he saw his date being hauled into the rowboat.

Samantha first checked to see that the woman was ok. Looking closer, she noticed it was the same woman, who crashed into them earlier on the dance floor. The woman recognized Samantha and offered a weak acknowledgement.

In a few minutes, the fire patrol boat came alongside, and helped them from the rowboat. They and their woman friend were taken back to the firehouse boat dock at the other end of the pier. The paramedics checked everyone over and gave them the okay to leave.

Samantha and Randy witnessed how each of them looked, and it was pretty bad. Let's go home, we've had enough excitement for the night," Samantha looked at her husband and said.

"Yeah, I think so. But what about my shoes"

"Oh yeah, and my tux coat is at the end of the pier too."

"Maybe a good Samaritan will return them," he responded.

As they walked away to their car, Samantha's husband stopped and looked at her.

"What's the matter Randy, you don't like my hairdo?"

"That's not it," he said. "I really liked that dress and you ruined it."

They looked at each other and burst into laughter. Randy hugged his wife and they continued to the car, arm in arm and soaked.

Torreo Esparza
As the crowd thinned at the end of the pier, he noticed a tuxedo jacket at one end and a pair of shoes at the other. He quickly gathered them and walked hurriedly to meet the fireboat at the dockside of the pier.

Let's Call It a Night
As the night drew toward its conclusion, Maria and the Creightons found themselves in close proximity. Horse drawn carriages carried some of the guests to the waiting limousines of every shape and color. The guests stopped by each to wish them well on the upcoming venture, thank them for their invitation and shower praise for the event.

Special hugs were shared when Ellie and Sydney came by to say goodnight. As they left, each waved to the other in that special acknowledgment of the future.

As Maria and the doctor walked toward the limousine, she took his hand to thank him for being there with her. He echoed the comment, and they hugged each other. Dr. Pedroza shrugged and told Maria that he was scheduled for early surgery in the morning, and wouldn't be able to continue the night's festivities. Maria insisted on taking the doctor home as their friend Chelle had left long before. He smiled and shrugged his shoulders in acceptance.

When the limo arrived at Dr Pedroza's house, he leaned over to give Maria a gentle kiss on her cheek. She touched his hand with a special tenderness. The gentle warmth was felt by both as Maria laid her hand over his. At that, he was out the door and walking to his place. Maria noticed as he looked at and felt his hand. She wondered what miraculous event might happen. She hadn't intended it to happen, she just touched his hand and suddenly it took place again. Maria smiled as the limo proceeded to take her home. Upon arriving, she thanked the driver who refused her gratuity, telling her that the Doctor had taken care of him. She slowly dragged her suddenly tired body up the stairs. She fell onto her bed and sleep took over immediately.

Ellie and Jimmy
Ellie invited Jimmy Ennis up to her condo for a nightcap. Neither really needed one, as they were feeling so powerfully attached to each

other already. Ellie poured the Metaxa 7Star brandy into two crystal snifters. Jimmy Ennis stood by her side. Taking his hand in hers, she led him to the deeply tufted and comfortable burgundy couch. They sat together. Each kicked off their shoes at the same time and raised legs and feet to the coffee table. It brought an immediate bout of laughter for each of them.

They weren't able to talk about recent events during the gala. This was their wind down time, and Jimmy recounted to Ellie some of the unannounced events at the fire that never reached the news. Ellie sat attentively listening to the unusual events that took place. At times, she failed to hear his words as she studied the features of his face. She awoke from her reverie, when he mentioned how the terrorist suddenly began to tell them of the bombs and triggering mechanisms. She thought that very odd as she watched his facial expressions exhibit the same curiosity.

Her thoughts flew to Maria, but she quickly dismissed them and there was little likelihood that she would have encountered a terrorist. Still the thought intrigued her and she made a mental note to mention it at their next get together. Putting that thought aside, she adjusted her attention to Jimmy sitting closely by her side.

Without pre thought, she reached her hand to his face and moved her head closer to him. She proceeded to place a gentle kiss on his cheek. As he turned his head, her lips found his as their lips touched for the first time. The feeling was exhilarating. He could also feel himself wanting to reach out to the pretty woman seated beside him. He did as he took her shoulder and gently pulled her closer to him. Ellie broke the kiss gently and continued to hold her hand on his cheek. As she did, gentle warmth flowed to his face where her hand touched his cheek. She noticed it, but he didn't seem to feel anything unusual. They looked into each other's eyes.

Ellie took Jimmy's hand, as she lifted herself from the couch, pulling him toward her.

Sydney and Damon
Sydney and her husband set out for home in the limousine. It had been a while since they were driven anywhere. It was enjoyable to be absorbed by sights of the city on their way home. Sydney asked the driver to take them to the Magnificent Mile a one-mile section of Michigan Avenue where all the glitter and glitz of expensive shops filled every nook and cranny of the buildings. They smiled as they

passed the Old Water Tower, its small turrets standing against the skyline of the city. The sight bore the distinction of being one of the few buildings to survive the Chicago fire. They even held hands as they pointed out different points of interest to each other.

Vera and Steven

The Carter-Creighton duo said their good-byes to friends and proceeded toward the exit. Carter's limo was waiting as they reached the staging area. Once inside the luxuriously appointed limo, Vera Creighton asked if they could just drive around the downtown area for a little bit. Steven Carter smiled at the thought of being able to spend a little more time with the enchanting woman. He asked the driver to take a tour.

"You bet sir," was the instant reply.

The limo pulled out into the streets of Chicago's near north side and they took in the sights and sounds of the city.

Vera Creighton lived up on the north shore, far from Steven Carter's downtown digs. He decided to enjoy her company and share their time together. The thought crossed the Creighton woman's mind as they visited the early morning nightlife of the near north side. "I think I'd better get home," she said as one of the revelers from the street drunkenly lurched against the car's side. We can do this another time if that's alright."

"Not a problem," was Steven Carter's response.

The driver headed for Lake Shore Drive and the trip up to the North Shore.

The two talked about the fun and events of the evening. Vera was interested in telling Steven Carter of the dresses and looks of the women and he responded with comments about the fireworks and their dancing.

They laughed at the memory of some of their high stepping antics on the dance floor.

The limousine arrived at the Winnetka residence of Vera Creighton. It was a small house in comparison to others in the neighborhood. However, the old Georgian provided plenty of living space and it fit her needs perfectly. The guesthouse in back had become useful to her as a studio where she spent time painting and drawing. Always a budding artist within, she began to exhibit some talent and wanted to make the most of her ability to create scenes that she felt interesting.

"Why don't you come in for a little while Steven," she said.

As he remembered, it was the first time she had used his name.

"I'm kind of tired," was his naturally expected reply.

"Let the driver go home and get his rest."

"You can sleep here. I have a very nice guestroom."

"Ok, you win," he responded with a smile.

"Pick me up at ten in the morning, Johnson."

The chauffeur opened the doors and offered good nights to both.

Steven Carter took her arm and led Vera Creighton to her door.

As the door opened, they stepped inside to the sweet scent of berries.

She stood aside to let the tall gentleman enter and closed the door.

Steven Carter heard the click of the door, just before he felt the arms move up his lapels and around his neck.

In the dimly lit entrance, he felt soft lips touch his cheek.

They moved, as he felt them touch his lips in the most gentle and yearning kiss, he had ever felt before.

He returned the kiss as he wrapped the woman in his arms. The phone rang.

"Who on earth is calling at this time?" They both spewed at the same time.

"It'll just take a moment Steven."

She sped off to the nearest phone and lifted the receiver.

"Hello dear."

Geez, it was mother.

"Is everything alright Mother?"

"Oh sure, I'm just calling to tell you what a nice time I had tonight."

"Oh, that's great Mother, I'll talk to you tomorrow if that's okay."

It was as if Pacey Creighton knew she was interrupting something. After a few minutes, Vera interrupted.

"Okay, mother let's talk about this in the morning. I have an early appointment and need to get some sleep."

"Oh alright my dear. You call me when you get up."

"Okay mother, I will."

Vera Creighton hung up the phone and took a drink of water from the sink, before re-entering the front room.

When she got to the room, she became immediately dismayed. There half sitting half lying on the couch was Steven Carter. She shook her head and went to the closet for a blanket to put over the sleeping form. "Gosh darn it mother," she said as she went to the stairway."

Chapter 14 How Can That Be?

Vera Creighton

Steven Carter awoke in a manner that was unusual for him. As his senses became aware of where he was, he heard a voice say softly,

"Relax Steven, would you like some coffee?"

He nodded his head in affirmation. He could feel his neck hurting from the position he slept in. Afterwards, he wanted to say something to the woman, who gave him the cup of coffee and sat beside him. She placed a finger gently against his lips to silence him. She produced a beguiling smile that said everything he needed to know.

Harmony Place Shelter

For the next few weeks, Maria was so busy that she would simply flop into bed at the end of the day. It was becoming a common occurrence, as she was out making arrangements and dealing with City Officials as well as forming The Shelter.

She continuously talked with Samantha Marsten about woodwork, doors, windows, associated requirements and of course, decor. When Samantha told her about the happenings at Navy Pier, Maria couldn't help but smile. She knew the meaning of the warm touch with Samantha. She thought about telling her new friend about it, but decided to do that at another time.

She talked with Grant writers and laid plans to obtain funding from Federal as well as State sources to help with the running of the shelter. Fortunately, the first few years of the St. Rita's Harmony Place Shelter funding, would be taken care of by the generosity of the Creightons and the Charity Fundraiser.

Maria also knew of other shelters in the city and suburbs and contributed funding for some special project for each. Chelle Leriget became a major source of help to the recovering women.

Labor Skills Employment Agency was constantly finding employment opportunities for the residents of the Shelter. Ms. Leriget spoke with her friend Steven Carter, the Investment guru and together they designed a program to place several of the women in part time, secretarial and even executive jobs. If there was a woman with a skill, Chelle Leriget tried to fit the skill with some type of meaningful employment. In time, she employed Janitorial Workers to Vice Presidents on a consulting basis.

One of the advantages that the agency offered was their in-house schooling program provided by Harriet Maynard a local teacher. Ms.

Maynard was on hand to improve language skills and other essential learning ingredients for the Employment Agency. Mrs. Maynard was a battered woman herself, so she knew the ropes and was able to do a lot to help the women.

Fortunately, Maria's employees were experienced in the care required by residents. Some women who came were addicted to drugs or alcohol. Others were abused. The treatment process was an arduous one, yet necessary.

At times, the requirements taxed the patience of the workers. Nursing people through withdrawal was something new to Maria. She was happy that the staff was experienced in dealing with the drug and alcohol maladies that affected so many. The psychological help came from dedicated professionals, many of whom donated time to the benefit of the women. Truly, the dedication of the employees was a joy to behold. They never faltered.

Her workers exhibited their dedication in so many situations. The effect on the temporary residents of the shelter was truly amazing. Of course, not everyone was able to stay off the drugs, shake the drinking habit or adjust their minds to what had happened to them. Through it all, a small group was forming that consisted of former patients who were bonding together to help newcomers. It was truly wonderful to witness the formation of friendships.

Women came and went. Some brought their young children to be cared for during the time they sought shelter while others came alone with seemingly no other source of help available to them. Maria refused to turn anyone away. She even took in some women who had been in jail for a variety of crimes. Her belief was that she and the staff would be able to make a difference. Through a variety of methods of intervention, she and the staff were achieving success.

Through her established friendships, she was able to provide lawyers who would work pro-bono, from some of the most respected law firms in the city. Many independent lawyers also offered their services.

Father Martin Ruby was great to the women. He listened to their stories and offered help by contacting people who offered jobs to the shelter inhabitants. He also counseled many of the women to overcome the drawbacks present in their lives.

Dr. Pedroza also made himself available as time permitted. Some of the other doctors from the hospital offered time also. At times, a specialty was needed and there always seemed to be one of the doctors who found the time to offer the professional assistance required.

Cook County Hospital provided the more meaningful required health care when surgery or special needs help was required.

Within a few months, Harmony Place was a thriving enterprise that provided assistance for many women in getting through difficult times. Teaching volunteers offered time to instruct and care for the schooling needs of the children of residents. The teachers contributed time and patience with the variety of child students.

Maria loved her Grant writers. They performed miracles with the pen and keyboard, obtaining funding from a variety of sources.

As she had time to reflect on the success of the Shelter, she thought about her gifts and the possibility of divine intervention. Surely, someone was watching out for the women who were coming to the shelter for assistance.

The Creighton women also contributed from behind the scenes, when something special was necessary.

In a few cases, husbands or boyfriends of the women would show up at the shelter to reclaim their "property". Several of the women, turned to or were forced into prostitution, by pimps or in some cases, financial need. Some of the pimps were extremely possessive and exhibited their proclivity for ownership of the women. Most of these men showed no fear in reclaiming what they felt was their "property", and source of income.

One of the numerous pimps, who fought for control of the women, showed up at the Shelter one evening dressed as a woman. He talked his way into a meeting with Maria who dropped her guard and let the apparently needy woman into the Shelter without a referral. Once there of course, the man let his real intentions become known. With a quick tug of his hand, he whisked away the flimsy dress covering his clothes and threw it to the floor.

He cornered Maria and began a verbal assault, berating her in a loud vicious voice. At first, Maria moved back from the approaching stranger. The hands of the man continued making threatening gestures as he swatted the air in front of her face and stressed his views by pointing his fingers downward toward Maria's face. He reached inside his belt and drew a gun, immediately pointing it at Maria. He raised the gun and lowered it as if to convey a message of its danger. The commotion caused the residents to gather in witness. Most felt afraid for Maria, as the man moved closer and closer with intimidation in his voice. He was adamant about walking out with his "woman". The alarm to the police station was set off as soon as the commotion began. Employees were well aware of what could happen without the assistance of the police. They hoped the police would be coming soon. In the meantime, all had to witness what was happening until help arrived.

As the initial fear wore off, Maria regained her mental control. As the man's voice got louder, she felt calmer. Maria began to look directly into the man's eyes. The effect began slowly, but soon the man's speech became disjointed. She continued a penetrating look into his eyes. The man became more furious as she maintained eye contact. Sensing an uncommon feeling, he began to look away, unable to continue glaring into the woman's eyes. This made him even more frustrated and perturbed at the woman standing defiantly before him. She stood her ground as he drew to within inches from her face screaming obscenities. She didn't waver, but stood unyielding.

With the man's frustration reaching a peak, he raised his hand. "Don't you dare touch that woman," one of the women behind him, who was witnessing the situation, declared stepping forward.

The man turned and glared at the woman making the statement pointing the gun at the group. He mouthed obscenities at her and turned back to Maria, his hand continuing to wield the gun, again raised in a striking position. The women residents moved closer to the man. He could feel the sets of eyes upon him as he stood and glared at Maria who stood only inches from him. He quickly turned and pointed the gun at the women again. They immediately put some distance between themselves and the man.

When he turned back to Maria, the women again moved closer to the back of the man. Maria held out her hand as if to stop their forward movement. She looked again into the man's eyes. She saw the blackness of his soul in his eyes.

The man's hand wavered in the air about to strike this brazen woman, having the nerve to stand up to his verbal assault. "Don't do this," Maria said to the man in a calm voice. The words had the effect of making the man even more unbalanced. She felt the movement before the man's hand began its downward travel toward her face. Maria also felt the acrimony from the women behind the man. She stared at the man's face. The man's eyes met hers. In that fleeting moment, Maria absorbed the look and reflected the feelings back to the man. The result was instantaneous. The entire scene switched to slow motion as the channeled hatred from the man was countered by the feelings from the women standing behind him, focused by Maria's eyes back to the man. As the hand with the gun neared her, the pimp's face began to form a grimace of distortion. His lips moved to one side as his mouth in a grotesque form, froze open. His words stilled within his larynx. The man's tongue remained curled in the form of the words he was speaking. His facial distortion became a terrifying mask as the features of his face, became as if glued in place. His arm stilled in mid air only inches from Maria's face. Maria watched the assailant's facial horror as she stood defiantly before him. Maria heard the collective sigh from the women as they watched in disbelief at the scene unfolding before them.

The doorbell sounded. Immediately, the open door switch was pressed by one of the workers. Police were in the room in seconds. As they saw the man standing over Maria, guns were drawn in haste. All were pointed at the man. Maria spoke calmly to the man who just seconds before was her threatening tormentor.

"Turn around," was her icy comment.

The man turned as if a puppet on a string. As he did, the sounds of women gasping filled the air. Some covered their eyes while others raised a hand to their mouths in shock. The police officers with guns drawn, stared in disbelief. The face they saw bore a horribly distorted look. A few of the woman ran back to their rooms, unable to continue as witnesses to the situation. The sight of the man's face was almost impossible to look at. The discontent he had caused so many, was now apparent for all to see. It manifested itself in his countenance, frozen in place. Two of the police overcame their shock and approached the man to arrest him and place the handcuffs on his hands.

One began to remove the gun from the hand but had to peel away the fingers from their viselike grip on the weapon. The arm was frozen in the moment tried to strike the brazen young woman. That, along with his face, was a jail the man had created for himself. It may have been a fitting reward for the actions of his life. The hideous reflection was there for all to see. A police officer slowly took the intruder's arm and lowered it to place the handcuffs on the man's wrist. The man's arm was very cold. The police led the man away. One of the detectives, Manny DeLeon remained to talk with Maria about what happened. He could not take his eyes off the man's face as he was led away in the arms of the other police officers.

Maria placed her hand on the chair for stability. She felt she was going to be sick. Detective Manny DeLeon put his arm around Maria's shoulder in consolation and positioned her to sit in the closest chair. Another detective gathered the women together in an effort to allay fears of an event like they had just witnessed ever happening again.

Chapter 15 Drugs Here Drugs There

School's Out

It was three o'clock in the afternoon. All over the city, schoolchildren were finishing classes for the day. As school doors swung open, children of all ages shuffled off in every direction. At Berry school on the near West Side, a small group of children headed for an alley two blocks away from the school.

Waiting there was a boy about sixteen years old with black work out pants and a lightweight puffy jacket. The boy stood shuffling his feet and walking back and forth tracing a path on the dusty cement of the alley. As he heard other kids approaching, he turned to the space between the back porch stairs of the apartment building above.

One at a time, kids walked toward the place where the boy was standing. Each had dollar bills in their hand. The exchange took place quickly. The approaching child held up fingers to indicate the selected drug for purchase and the boy waiting reached inside the puffy jacket. As the child walked by, the kid took the money and handed over a small zip lock bag. The bag contained either pills, or powder, or in some instances, crack cocaine. As the buys took place, the purchasers quickened their step to exit the alley at the other end. Within fifteen minutes, the sixteen-year-old was on his way to another location.

The same scene took place at just about every school in the city. Age didn't matter as long as the money was available. Kids from ten to eighteen were buying the drugs on their way home and in some cases, before meeting friends.

Johnny Lemtick was a twelve year old. He made his buy of the little pills on the way home. As he got to his room, he felt a need for a little extra rush after a hard day with one teacher in particular, who was on his case for a missing assignment. He hated the woman because she was always telling him he could do better. He did better, only he had to be out of school for that to happen. His two little sisters were playing in the front room and had the television blaring as usual. Today, it was particularly bothersome to Johnny for some reason. He put the pills in his mouth and threw his head back to help them down his throat. In a few minutes, he would be feeling better. He always did. Today, he took an extra one just to be sure he would be able to shut out that irritating teacher from his head.

He laid himself on the bed and closed his eyes. It didn't take long before the feeling of euphoria began. It was like being in a dream this time. Everything seemed to float, but something was disrupting the peaceful setting. The television that his sisters were watching and that goofy Simpson's show was one. It was so loud.

Johnny decided to fix the problem. He walked into his parent's bedroom, took the chair and reached up to the shelf for the gun his dad kept there. He wanted peace today, and he was going to have it. The television had to go. He jumped down from the chair and walked into the front room with the gun. His sisters must have heard him coming because they were looking up when he entered the room. They saw the gun in his hand and froze. The younger sister started crying. Johnny pointed the gun at her and yelled.

"Shut up."

His other sister put her hands on the younger sister. As she did, Johnny turned the gun toward the television.

"No Johnny," she cried aloud.

Johnny squeezed the trigger. Bart Simpson's face exploded and the noise stopped coming from the television.

"You shut up too," he screamed at his other sister, leveling the gun in her direction.

The younger sister, seeing the gun pointing, reached out for her brother's leg in a futile effort to gain his attention. As she did, Johnny lost his balance for a second and in reflex, his finger involuntarily squeezed the trigger of the gun. The bullet hit the older girl in the forehead, knocking her backward against the wall. Her lifeless eyes staring straight at him as her body slid to the floor.

Johnny looked at his sister's body against the wall, and then looked back to his other sister lying at his feet. She was getting up to go over to her sister. Johnny watched the scene, now playing in slow motion. As his young sister reached the body against the wall, she turned to Johnny.

"What did you do?" She shrieked at him.

Johnny looked at his sister's eyes and ran out the door, just as neighbors were coming to see what happened. He ran past them into the street and kept running.

The neighbors from next door rushed into the room to find the two sisters. Both were not moving. The man reached down to touch the girl who was holding her sister's head in her arms. She moved. The man sighed with relief. At least there was a survivor.

The evening newscast told the stories of three separate incidents of children dying in different areas of the city. The anchorperson stated that in each case, drugs were suspected as a major motive for the incidents. Above in the sky, the clouds turned an ugly gray with shards of lightning passing from cloud to cloud. It lasted for only a few moments and the clouds quickly dispersed.

Doctor Pedroza

At the hospital, Doctor Pedroza was making his rounds in the customary manner. A smile broadened on his face as he entered the patient rooms. Always presenting himself in good spirits was important to him as well as the patients under his care. He truly believed that he made a positive difference in their lives. For those who would be returning home, he was bright and lively, presenting good words to their ears. For the long-suffering, he offered compassion and the hope that their situation would soon become better. Some of the other doctors felt he spent too much time listening to patients, but that was just the way Doctor Pedroza tended to his trade.

Torreo Esparza

Maria's younger brother pursued his ability to make money wherever he went. Some of his dealings may have been shady at times, but never against the law or hurtful to anyone. He could engineer the sale of someone's car or furniture or arrange bartering services, always finding a way to receive payment for his services. The young man already accumulated a collection of "junk art", that consisted of paintings and sculptures from relatively unknown artists for which he performed some type of service.

The moving business was also one of Torreo's interests. Whenever help was needed by someone locals, he would be on hand to work. He looked at the physical work as his exercise.

In spite of his quest to be paid for his services, Torreo Esparza was painfully honest and possessed a big heart.

One of the older women in the neighborhood was in need of help because she was being evicted. He found her a place to stay, paid two months' rent and put the move together with the help of friends. He paid some of them with his artwork to maintain a balance of trade. The woman paid nothing for the help from him and his friends. Torreo felt that it was just the right thing to do. For others who were capable of payment for a service, he was demanding. He received some type of fair exchange for the service. Torreo was quickly making a name for himself as a broker and dealmaker.

Torreo loved his mother and relied on his sister for guidance in many situations. She was so smart and her awareness of business transactions proved valuable to him through his young learning times.

Possessing dashing good looks, many of the women in the area vied for his attention. While he seemed to have his pick of the field, he always treated any woman he dated with the utmost respect and courtesy He was a role model that others envied. Inevitably, he made a few enemies among the other young men who were trying to eke out a living for themselves, but lacked his talent. He would learn to deal with those as time passed.

A few of his friends told him of the new drug pusher near the school. Torreo assured them he would address the situation soon. Torreo made a point of finding the drug pusher and speaking with him about avoiding the kids in the neighborhood and at school. The man laughed in Torreo's face as the group of druggies gathered around. "Let him go," exclaimed the drug pusher.

"He can't hurt us."

In reality, fear arose from the stare from the guy named Torreo.

Torreo walked away; maddened at the treatment and the reluctance, of the man to listen to him. Torreo knew this would not be their last confrontation, even if the police wouldn't help.

Chelle Leriget

Chelle Leriget awoke to the ringing phone.

She lifted the transparent receiver.

"Hello," she said lightly into the mouthpiece.

"Hi, Mrs. Leriget. I hope I didn't wake you,"

Chelle Leriget looked at the clock. It was 8:00AM. She thought for a moment.

"Well you did," she said letting a hint of irritation show in her voice.

"Oh, I'm so sorry," the woman's voice replied meekly.

Chelle Leriget laughed freely.

"I should have been up my dear. I'm glad you called."

"I just wanted to thank you for bringing Dr. Pedroza to the event," Maria said excitedly.

"Oh that was my pleasure dear."

"I figured if you didn't care for him, I would have a splendid companion for the evening," she replied with a laugh.

They continued the conversation and said their good byes, each wishing good things for the other.

Chelle had no sooner hung up the phone, before its tone filled the air again. My goodness I am popular, she thought to herself.

"Hello." She answered.

"Is this Chelle Leriget?" was the response.

"Who's calling?" she asked idly.

"This is Carl Bateman, from Bateman's Furniture."

Chelle thought for a moment.

"Oh, hi there Mr. Bateman," she replied, remembering the kindly man who helped pick out the furniture for the company offices.

"What can I do for you?" She asked.

"I was wondering if you would like to go out for dinner some evening Mrs. Leriget?"

Chelle removed her earring, removed the receiver from her ear and looked at the phone in mock surprise.

She thought for a moment.

"Hello?" Came the questioning comment from the other end of the line.

"I'm here Mr. Bateman," she replied.

"I'm just a bit surprised to be honest."

"Well, I've wanted to ask you for some time now Mrs. Leriget, and today finally got up the nerve."

She knew the man as a kind and gentle person.

"At this time of the morning," she replied.

Deciding to take the initiative, she did.

"How about this evening Mr. Bateman?"

She could hear the stutter on the other end of the line.

"That would be wonderful Mrs. Leriget," he belatedly replied.

"Well that will be fun then Mr. Bateman," she replied with legitimate excitement.

She gave her address to Carl Bateman, who was fumbling furiously for a pen.

"Could your repeat that again, Mrs. Leriget?"

She gave her address again with a chuckle. They agreed on 7:00PM.

"We'll have a cocktail here if that's alright Carl," using his first name for the very first time.

"Will be there at 7:00" was the reply.

"And Carl, please call me Chelle," she said lightly.

148

"Deal Chelle. See you at 7:00PM.

The line clicked as Carl Bateman hung up and danced about his bedroom. He was very happy.

Chelle Leriget felt a shiver of excitement as she pictured the well-manicured, distinctive and slightly overweight furniture storeowner.

Chapter 16 A Sense Of Understanding

Sydney and Damon

Sydney and her husband Damon sat at the table having breakfast. Damon was reading the paper as Sydney recounted the fun they had the previous evening at Navy Pier. A preacher could be heard offering bible verse from the radio in the background. She smiled as she thought of the two dancing around the floor as if no one was watching. Her husband intently devoured the sports section of the daily paper. She could feel the embers of love rekindling within her. What her husband was thinking, she wasn't sure, but he seemed receptive to her advances recently and appeared to enjoy the moments they shared. Sydney remembered the conversation with her friends about role-playing. She also remembered that Damon brought up that very subject once and she passed on it without much interest or even a comment. At first, she put the thought on hold. Her husband looked over from the paper. She looked up immediately sensing his eyes on her.

"Say Honey," she began.

"Remember when you wanted to act out a scene about us meeting in some fantasy thing."

Her husband thought for a moment.

"Yeah," he said questioningly.

"I remember that you thought it was a pretty lame idea," was his quick reply.

"I know that's the impression I gave, I'm sorry Hon."

"I've been thinking about that more and more", she responded.

"Really, why?" He asked with genuine interest in his voice.

"Oh, I don't know."

"It's just a thought that you might like to try something like that."

"Why now," was her husband's reply.

"Well, we haven't exactly been love birds in the last year or so."

"Tell me about it," she heard him respond.

"I know with my schoolwork and all, you must have been feeling left out."

"You got that right, my dear," he shot back.

"I know," she responded again.

"I'm sorry."

"Did you have something in mind?"

Sydney decided it was time to broach the subject again and took the opportunity to lay out her thoughts about enacting a scene that might be interesting and exciting for both of them.

Her husband listened with interest, adding a comment here and there for clarification.

"It all has to be based on absolute trust though," he added as she concluded the fantasy thoughts.

"I agree Honey, otherwise it would never work."

Smiling at each other, they agreed on a time and place to try out their opportunity.

Damon returned to his sports section and Sydney began to clear the table.

Doctor Pedroza

Doctor Pedroza walked out of the doctors meeting and headed for the locker room. He was upset at the razzing that took place regarding the woman Adele Dozier, who recuperated after the code blue incident. Doctor "Magic" was what one of the staff doctors had called him when he walked into the room, bowing almost as if in ridicule.

The doctors at the hospital morbidity meeting were in heated discussion about the happenings this week with Dr. Pedroza's patient Adele Dozier. Each offered a differing opinion on the possibilities and likelihood of this type of event. Like rising from the dead was the term frequently bantered about in explanation. In a case like this, there was always a question of whether the attending physician had missed some stagnant form of life. In this case, however, all the attending nurses were experienced and witnessed the expiration of many patients before. When questioned, each agreed that there was no sign of life and no likely possibility of their having missed something.

The woman when declared expired was definitely without any vital life signs and had been that way for a time. For her to awaken again as she did was something that was thought inconceivable by all those that attended. It was as if Dr. Pedroza had somehow caused the woman to return from the dead by touching her. That was the only consensus agreement available within the group. Nothing else short of a miracle could be the explanation and few of the doctors present believed in miracles. They had all seen some miraculous recoveries, yet reality of death had become a thoroughly understood subject to all of them.

The head of the committee, Dr. Fortenzi looked over at Dr. Pedroza and jokingly commented to the group.

"All the patients in the hospital will be requesting our Dr. Pedroza to touch them to ensure that they will live through their experience here at the hospital."

"You will be known as the angel of life doctor," Fortenzi commented with a slight sense of humor.

"Dr. Pedroza just sighed with a nod in understanding of what the chief Doctor had just said.

The Chief raised his hands and looking at his peers, stated somewhat reluctantly.

"With these hands."

Dr. Pedroza did not find the situation funny at all. He just wanted to get out of the hospital. Then he shrugged his shoulders trying to understand what happened when he touched Adele Dozier. He would relive that moment many times. Especially, he thought of feeling that sudden warmth when he touched her. He wondered what that meant, if anything, and if it would ever happen again. In any case, he was certainly not going to mention it to his colleagues.

As he left the room, Dr. Pedroza froze; his mind suddenly focused on that feeling conveyed with Adele Dozier. It was the same feeling he received from Maria, when they touched hands the evening before. He continued walking quickly toward the doctor's lounge. He needed to talk to Maria to tell her of the happening. Maybe she could make some sense of it. He doubted it, but was anxious to find some kind of answer.

Chapter 17 The Perfect Strangers

A Trial Run

The rest of the week went by uneventfully. Each day reinforced Maria's thought of how the unique power she now possessed was designed to work. By the end of the week, she was sufficiently convinced to test her theory further.

She decided that Chelle Leriget was adequately distant for the trial. The woman was a lovely person in looks and soul. Maria decided to proceed without letting her subject know but still try to find out if there would be any result. It would be an interesting trial, but worth the effort and the test. She just had to get an understanding of how the potential miracle opportunities would work. She decided that trusting Chelle Leriget would be worthwhile, as the woman seemed to be a genuinely good person.

Maria called Chelle at the office and arranged to stop by to see her for a few moments. When she arrived, she was happy to see her lovely smile of greeting. They shook hands immediately and did the cheek kiss thing that women often do when greeting. Maria felt the warm feeling flow, as did Chelle who passed it off to static without remark.

They talked about the gala and Maria took the opportunity to thank the woman again for bringing Dr. Pedroza to serve as her companion for the evening. Chelle blushed at the compliment. She took it as just part of her interest in what Maria had done, to prepare for helping needy and abused women.

Chelle told Maria of her pending date with Carl Bateman, whom Maria vaguely remembered from the past as a furniture store owner. They made plans but others things kept getting in the way for both of them. They decided that enough is enough, and this Saturday they would get together regardless.

"Thanks Chelle," that means a lot to me.

"Not a problem at all Maria," was the quick reply.

Maria rose to leave and asked her friend to keep in touch. Chelle agreed and walked Maria to the door and bade her farewell.

A Date with Carl Bateman

Carl Bateman arrived at her house as Chelle Leriget was taking out the garbage. He quickly exited the car and offered to help which she gratefully accepted. Bateman always seemed like a nice man and Chelle Leriget felt a thrill of excitement at the thought of a date with the handsome man. He was somewhat tight with his purse strings as she remembered, but that didn't seem to be a crucial fault. After all, he was a business owner who had become very successful. She would have the opportunity to learn more she figured as time passed.

She gathered her purse and they climbed into the big Lincoln automobile for the drive to the restaurant. Carl Bateman enjoyed the finer things in life. He decided to take Chelle Leriget downtown to the Metropolis Club in the Sears Tower. Chelle was a member herself; and enjoyed the plush woodwork surroundings, the wonderful food and the attentive wait staff.

Upon arrival at the club, they were greeted at the door and led to the lounge area. Chelle always enjoyed the look of the city from high above on the 67th floor. Carl Bateman felt the scene was a romantic beginning to a nice evening with the fine looking woman at his side.

They sat for dinner and the wait staff served their every need. They ordered a Shiraz wine recommended by the sommelier and it was wonderful. The woman that waited their table was a delight as she recommended the fresh fish for an Epicurean delight. Her name was Lori Boby and Chelle Leriget remembered her from the Agency. Chelle was instrumental in her hiring at the club, and the woman always made a point of thanking her whenever she was there.

Lori Boby was one of those hidden talents that we rarely come across. Born in Zagreb, Croatia, she obtained a degree in journalism and studied how the well-to-do acted in given situations. Fluent in Spanish, English, Russian, and Polish, in addition to her native tongue, she was able to speak easily with a range of people. She was average looking with a barely discernible blonde streak that flowed through her dark hair. Lori took the job at the Metropolis Club because the tips were fantastic, and she was able to meet many influential people. Some of those acquaintances would come in handy later on.

The atmosphere provided both Carl and Chelle with a wonderful setting for their meal. As dessert of crème brulée was served, Lori Boby inadvertently tipped over the wineglass that sat in front of Chelle. Both reached immediately to save the glass from spilling. As they did, their hands touched and Chelle felt the gentle surge of warmth, similar to that shared when Maria Esparza had touched her hand. The waitress felt it too, yet thought nothing of it as they collectively set the glass in place on the table.

After dinner, the couple rode down the escalator as the lights of the city appeared through the large windows. Carl remarked about the "breathtaking" sights. Chelle squeezed his arm as her eyes took in the scenic panorama.

Carl Bateman opened the car door for his guest. Chelle Leriget was enjoying a wonderful evening with the handsome and debonair man. Bateman handled the driving flawlessly as he negotiated the turns of the parking garage and approached the exit to Wabash Street for the return trip home to Chelle's place.

As the light turned green granting access to the Eisenhower expressway, Carl clutched his chest suddenly and gasped in pain. Chelle heard the sudden exclamation and turned quickly to see the man at the wheel holding his chest in serious discomfort.

"Pills in my pocket," she heard him say hoarsely.

She reached into his coat pocket to find a vial of pills.

"How many," she asked quickly?"

"One," was the whispered response.

She took a pill and placed it in Carl Bateman's mouth watching the man closely for a reaction. She felt sudden warmth, just as with Lori Boby, when their hands touched.

Almost immediately, he began to relax. The hand clutching his chest slid away and he was able to breathe normally again.

Chelle had seen this type of reaction before with victims of heart attacks. She felt this one was a narrow escape for the man seated next to her. Little did she know at the time how serious the situation really was.

"Are you all right, Carl?"

"Yes, much better thank you," he responded with a sigh.

"Let's go to a hospital Carl, you should be looked at."

"It's all right now," he said calmly.

"I have these attacks occasionally that are the reason for the nitroglycerin tablets."

"Still, you should have yourself examined, Chelle Leriget insisted."

"I'll call my doctor in the morning," he responded.

"You'll call him right now," she ordered in a take-charge voice. With a chuckle, he reached for the cell phone and autodialed a number. Chelle heard the person at the other end answer.

"Yes Carl, what's happening," was the question from the other end of the line.

"I just had one of my episodes," Carl Bateman responded.

"I see. How are you feeling now?"

"Much better, after taking my pill."

"No chest pain or shortness of breath?"

"No, I'm feeling fine now."

"Be at the hospital at 9:00 in the morning," the demanding tone replied.

"OK," was the simple response.

"I'll do that doctor."

"Good night then Carl."

"Good Night Doc:"

They continued the drive home in silence. As they arrived at Chelle's home, she let herself out of the car and came around to the driver's side.

"You make sure you're at that hospital in the morning Carl," she told the man as she placed a kiss on his cheek.

"I will Chelle, I promise," was the reply.

She stood watching as he pulled out of the drive and turned down the street.

Torreo

Torreo abhorred drugs; so when he got wind of a new kid in the neighborhood, who was thought to be dealing, he put a plan into action.

He had sufficient connections with the police at the district station, to be put through to the Sergeant of the Watch, right away. He told the Sergeant of his findings and found that the police were already alerted to this new kid. In Torreo's unassuming manner, he asked what would happen with the kid. The Sergeant told him that nothing was planned for the immediate future, but he would keep Torreo informed about what would be happening. Torreo thanked the Sergeant and said good-bye.

As soon as the Sergeant clicked off, Torreo dialed his sister. He was pleasant at first, but became more demanding as the conversation continued.

"Sis, I know you can do something about this without anyone being harmed. At least none of the good people.

"So can you help me with this new kid with the drugs?"

"I'm not sure," Maria shot back.

"What do you want me to do?"

"Well, stop it from happening," he said.

"How?" She asked.

"You tell me. You're the one who can make things happen."

"I can't just will things to happen Torreo," Maria stated.

"Okay Sis, I don't want to put you in an uncomfortable position. I'll handle it my own way."

"I'm sure you'll do the right thing for all concerned."

"I will sis, don't worry. Everything will be fine."

Damon Anderson

The doorbell rang. It was Damon.

"Sydney forgot her glasses," he said as he climbed the stairs.

Maria let him in as she quickly went to the kitchen drawer and found the pouch containing her glasses. She admitted sheepishly that she forgot to call her friend. Damon was non-plussed.

Maria reached for the pouch at the same time. As their hands touched, there was a warm exchange. Damon thought it strange, but didn't comment He just looked at Maria and shrugged. Maria did the same, not wanting to say more.

Damon kissed Maria on the cheek and headed back to the door and down the stairs.

Maria closed the door behind her.

Chapter 18 A Premonition

Lindsay Ballenger

Captain Jimmy Ennis sat at his desk reviewing folders of suspected arson cases for the last few months. Whenever a fire "was struck" (put out) and the cause was indeterminate, a file was prepared by the lead officer at the fire, and then forwarded to the Inspector's office. Ennis's boss was District Commander O'Keefe. O'Keefe was in the hospital for most of the year suffering from cancer and the associated treatments that were being given to extend his life.

In effect, Jimmy Ennis was in the charge of the office for over a year now. The higher ups were aware of his dedication and ability to search out causes for fires, that others may have missed. In a few words, Captain Ennis was very proficient in his job. He also would give praise to his team and associates Lindsay Ballenger and Ed Sands. Ballenger was a firefighter with eight years experience and a good head on her shoulders. Sands was new to the job, but was a quick study. Both had degrees in chemistry.

Lindsay Ballenger walked by the open door and Captain Ennis called out to her with a greeting. The woman continued past the door and without turning her head, waved back her acknowledgment. The Captain felt this a little unusual, as she would usually bounce in and sit in a chair without invitation and offer a cheery, "What's up boss," to him.

Today, she seemed to want to be out of the way. Jimmy Ennis made a mental note to check with her later as he continued to breeze through the pile of folders on the desk.

"Hey, nice shiner there Lindsay," he heard one of the janitors remark from outside his door. He thought the comment peculiar and decided to find out what was going on with Lindsay Ballenger. He found her making coffee in the tiny closet they used to house a small refrigerator and coffee area. She looked up as he approached and he could see the dark bulge at the corner of her right eye.

"What the heck…" he started, but she waved him off.

"Ran into a door boss," was the quick retort.

"Hmmmm," Jimmy Ennis responded with a questioning look.

"Eddie and I had a little disagreement," she offered honestly, knowing she was not fooling him.

"Mind if I ask what happened?" was Ennis's reply.

"He's cheating on me and I thought I caught him in a lie, so I told him so."

"And he hit you?"

"Yeah, that's the way he likes to end arguments."

"Happened before hasn't it Lindsay?" Ennis asked earnestly.

"Yeah, it has," the woman responded, holding her hand to the bulging skin.

"It's the drugs."

"He's on drugs, Lindsay?"

"Oh yeah! Big time."

"I'd like you to talk with a friend Lindsay."

"Well, I've about had it with this type of treatment; sure I'll talk to someone," she responded dryly.

"I'll set it up Lindsay."

"Thanks boss."

Jimmy Ennis returned to the office and placed a call to Ellie Mulcahey. He was going to have Lindsay Ballenger talk with Ellie's friend Maria.

Ellie picked up the phone.

"Ellie, this is Jimmy."

"Hello tall dark and handsome, what a pleasant surprise"

'Can you get me your friend Maria's number at the Shelter," he asked.

"She's right here Jimmy, hold on."

Ellie smiled at her friend who just stopped by to say hello.

"It's Jimmy Ennis from the fire department," Ellie conveyed to her friend as she handed over the phone.

"Hello Captain," was Maria joyful greeting.

"Hi Maria," Jimmy responded with a somewhat serious tone.

"Could you find time to talk with one of my people?"

"Why sure," came the quick reply,

"Is the person there?"

"Just a sec, thanks"

Jimmy Ennis rose to step out into the corridor.

"Lindsay?" He called loudly.

"Lindsay Ballenger's head popped out from one of the office doorways.

Lindsay saw her boss waving her over.

"This is Maria Esparza from St. Rita's Harmony Shelter, the shelter I told you about?" He handed her the phone.

Jimmy Ennis walked toward the office door and closed it behind him.

Lindsay took the phone and began talking to Maria. Raising her hand to touch the swelling below her eye, she remembered the stark reminder of the reason she was talking to this person. The two women talked and at the end of the conversation, arranged to meet tomorrow at the Shelter.

Putting It Together

Maria sat down at the desk as she hung up the phone. Some things were beginning to make sense to her now. There were no reports of anything unusual from her friends since the meeting. Only Mrs. Leriget, whom Maria had intentionally touched, reported anything since the day of the meeting. She then remembered Ellie's husband, Damon returning for her glasses and the touch. She reminded herself to check that out too. Maria made a few notes on the tablet nearby. Her friends were responsible for a beneficial event for someone else they met. Those events, however, only happened after they had been in physical contact with her.

It seems that there have been multiple incidents. A strange feeling began to invade Maria's senses. She was always the one responsible for something happening. She was a little uneasy at the prospect of certain other resulting situations. Those included the ones that happened to those who seemed to wish harm to another. The local bad kid running into the post chasing the lottery winner's young son and the attacker in the parking garage that Mrs. Leriget told her about came to mind.

The pieces of the puzzling power that she now possessed began to fit in place. Maria's awareness of this awesome responsibility shook her deeply as she began to grasp the power to change the lives of people who met her. One thing was obvious. The one she touched, either was affected or became a transmitter of something good, for a person he or she met. Beyond that was the fact that anyone who tried to intervene or hurt the person to whom that miracle was conveyed, would be in some kind of dire straits if they tried to interfere, or they would be changed for the better somehow. She sat shaking her head at the enormity of the situation.

Maria decided it was time to visit Father Ruby, her friendly pastor of her church in Cicero. She decided it was time to talk further about her situation.

An Unusual Visitor

As she prepared to leave the Shelter, the doorbell rang. Maria pressed the intercom button to the doorway and asked who was there. The response was a very comforting voice that said that Mrs. Leriget sent her and that she wanted to drop off a few things for the Shelter. Maria buzzed the woman in and went to the door to receive her.

As she watched, a middle-aged woman climbed the stairs with a box in her arms, Maria moved down a few steps to offer a hand. The woman's smile was warm and genuine, on a face that gave Maria a sense of comfort. Her head however, seemed to be bleeding from a cut.

"Thank you for seeing me Ms. Esparza," the woman said.

Maria invited her in to sit at the table.

"Let me look at your head my dear. You seem to be bleeding," Maria stated.

"It's nothing," the woman responded. "The sore comes back every now and then."

"You should have it looked at."

"It's okay, it will go away again. I've had it for a long time," the woman said.

"We have a mutual friend," the woman continued.

"Mrs. Leriget finds work for me from time to time.

"I do some cleaning and janitorial jobs when I can fit them into my schedule."

Maria looked at the woman and found her comments to be a little confusing,

The woman took a seat and placed her purse on the table next to her.

"How are you doing Maria?"

Maria felt it a little unusual for a stranger to be asking; yet responded,

"We're doing pretty well thank you. Phones are starting to ring with women who are asking for help and inquiring about the Shelter."

"That's very good to hear," the woman responded. "I know a few things about being a battered woman."

"Do you need help now," Maria asked.

"No, it was a long time ago, but thank you for asking."

Maria felt she wanted to ask the woman's name, but something kept her from doing it. She was surprised at her feelings about the woman and just wanted to listen.

"You are gifted and will be very successful here," the woman said to Maria with a smile. Maria felt such a level of comfort talking with the woman, that she was momentarily mesmerized.

The woman rose after the short conversation and picked up her purse from the table.

"I just wanted to stop by to leave a few things and now I must be going," she said to Maria.

A bit surprised at the suddenness of the pending departure, Maria rose to walk the woman to the door.

"Thank you so much for allowing me to visit," the woman said in a kind tone.

"I must shake your hand the woman said to her," extending her hand.

Maria offered her hand. As she grasped the woman's outstretched hand, she felt the woman's skin to be extremely soft. Unlike that of a person who performed janitorial chores. Maria's own hands had calluses and she was surprised at the softness of the woman's hand. As their hands met, the woman looked to Maria and said in a gentle voice.

"A storm is brewing, because drugs are destroying many of our Deity people's lives. A time of atonement for some is nearing. Trust the man with the dog, continue your belief and do the best you can with what you have. Remember you are loved. Continue what you are doing for others."

The woman gave Maria a troubled look and started down the stairs. At the bottom, she turned to wave.

"Speak with Father Ruby and Richard, Maria," the woman said.

"Who shall I tell Mrs. Leriget called on us," she queried quickly.

"Tell her Rita," the woman said with a smile. "She'll know me."

The woman then opened the door and left.

Maria stood transfixed. She shook her head to make sense of the conversation and its meaning. "Who is Richard?" She thought.

Maria felt a very odd sensation and ran to the window to see the woman again. There was also no mention of Father Ruby during the conversation with the woman. She opened the window and looked out into the street. No one was visible. She looked at the two parked cars in front and both were empty. Surprised, she ran to the door and down the stairs, as quickly as she could.

Opening the door, she ran out onto the sidewalk and looked in all directions. No one was visible anywhere except a short bald-headed man waiting at the bus stop across the street. As she stepped out from the doorway, she noticed the man looking in her direction. She thought of walking over to him, but decided it would seem strange to ask if he had seen anyone. She turned, as her eyes surveyed the area.

The Shelter entrance was located in the middle of the block, so it was well nigh impossible for someone to move that quickly as to be out of sight. She walked to the fronts of the stores on either side of her door. The insides were well lit with no obstructions. In others, the doors were closed and no one was inside any of them.

Chelle Leriget

How very strange she thought to herself. She glanced around again and ran upstairs. Closing the door, she went immediately to the phone and called Chelle Leriget who answered right away. She asked Mrs. Leriget about sending a woman with some things in a box, to the Shelter as she described the woman. Chelle Leriget was in surprise, as she didn't tell anyone to go there and wasn't aware of anyone who wanted to drop anything off.

"She said to tell you her name was Rita."

There was complete silence on the phone.

"What is in the box," Mrs. Leriget asked Maria, avoiding a response to the Rita person.

"Hold on, while I see," Maria responded remembering that she had not even looked.

Maria opened the box. Ice crystals sat in a smaller box, with no evidence of melting. Next to that were some baby toys, some blankets and diapers.

She told Chelle Leriget of the contents.

"How strange," was all Chelle could Muenstat in response. "How very strange."

Maria also felt confused at the visit and the box with the unusual contents.

"Well thanks Chelle, maybe the answers will be forthcoming, but for now confusion reigns."

"Same here Maria, keep me posted will you please?" Chelle Leriget asked.

"You bet'cha, I will," Maria responded with a half laugh into the receiver.

"Bye for now."

"Bye," Chelle responded as she hung up the phone and looked at it with a quizzical eye. She shook her head slightly and turned to the papers on her desk.

Maria stared at the hard ice crystals in the box. She reached in and picked up a few of the crystals for closer inspection. They were cold to the touch and clearly translucent. She carefully replaced the crystals in the box and placed it on the table. The small plastic crib and blankets she removed and placed in a drawer in one of the bedrooms.

She had the uncanny feeling that something would be happening as a result of the woman's visit. Even more unusual was how the woman seemed to disappear upon walking out the door and the fact that Chelle Leriget was mentioned and had no idea of any woman with that description. Looking at her coat, she decided to nix the idea of going over and talking to the priest at the church. Somehow, Maria received all the positive feelings needed from the woman during her brief visit. The way the woman talked and how she mentioned that all would be well provided in time. Maria achieved a level of comfort that made her at ease with everything happening around her.

Somehow, she knew what she would be doing, and how it should be handled. That awareness was now deeply seated within her. Maria heard of people being visited by outsiders or angels. The thought kept running through her head. Is that what had just happened. She would be paying very close attention to the powerful influence she was able to generate. Maria sensed that everything would be all right, just the way the stranger had told her.

As she walked into the front room, she heard a story on the television. Bandits or drug dealers had killed two missionary women, who were working in Colombia. Local residents in the mountainous area outside Bogota had found the women's' bodies. Maria thought sadly, wrong place at the wrong time. The story continued, that the woman were licensed nurses who made annual trips during their vacation to bring medical supplies to help the mountain people and they were doing that on their own with their own money as well as donations from medical facilities. Maria felt a deep saddening at hearing the rest of the story. It set her into a melancholy mood. Maria knew of the heartless mentality of the drug cartel people in South America. Two women, whose only reason for being there was to help, were killed just because someone saw them as a threat. "How terribly sad. This situation with drugs is becoming impossible to do anything about and it is getting worse," she said softy to herself.

Father Ruby

Maria picked up the phone and placed a call to St. Philomena Church. Father Martin Ruby picked up the phone. Maria explained her situation and requested time for a conversation. Martin Ruby thought for a moment and decided that sooner would be better. He had a feeling that this was going to be something important. They agreed to meet later that afternoon.

Understanding and Revelation

Father Ruby greeted Maria at the door. He invited her into his office where Maria immediately began to tell him what was happening. She began by recounting the events leading up to the woman's visit. The longer she talked, the more mesmerized Martin Ruby became.

Maria decided to ask Father Ruby about her visitor; the woman who knew Father Ruby's name without Maria mentioning it. Upon hearing this, Father Ruby sat back in his chair. Surprise became apparent on his face.

Almost all of the happenings Maria voiced to him were verifications. The passing of goodness to another person was actually taking place. The retaliation against evil was something new to him, but understandable. The protection of the healer and the agent against harm he had surmised. He told Maria this but she was already aware of it.

She mentioned the strange comments about "time of atonement for some" and the mention of the dog. Another thing that puzzled her was to see Father Martin Ruby and find out about this fellow Richard. She wondered to herself if they were apocryphal. Father Ruby made no comment other than, "I see, does that trouble you Maria?" She shook her head in the affirmative.

Maria verified some of the things Father Ruby explained before. What was unsettling to the Priest was the purpose of the strange visitor. He wanted to believe it was a good omen, yet doubt sat in his mind about atonement. Who's atonement and for what?" The questions stymied the Priest.

"The woman said another strange thing that I don't understand Father."

Father Ruby waited for Maria to continue.

"She said talk to you and Richard. But I don't know of any Richard."

Father Ruby thought for a moment and then it came to him.

"You have to have faith on this one, Maria."

"If you say so Father." Maria replied.

The Priest then told her of the man in a close by suburb who built a Chapel inside his factory and office building. He told her the man studied the Saints and was very knowledgeable about the Church, Relics and religion in general.

"Perhaps you might want to go and talk to Richard?" Father Ruby asked.

"If you think it will help understand some of this, I certainly will Father."

"Good Maria, I'll get his phone number and address for you."

Maria felt relieved of the burden she was carrying. Knowing now that another person knew and could understand what was happening provided a meaningful sense of relief. At the door of the Rectory, Father Ruby gave Maria the man's address and phone number.

He watched the woman walk down the street in the bright sunlight. In the recesses of his mind, he reflected on his studies on the Cross-of the Crucifixion. This could be the event happening again. Just as it had since the time of Christ. Every three hundred years someone seemingly is chosen to be a catalyst for good. He knew it was happening again. What was happening though? What is it, that is so awesome as to be incomprehensible to human thought?

The Priest walked to his study and retrieved the closed box labeled Thesis. It contained his work on the study of the Crucifixion and the happenings thereafter. He had been so proud of delivering the results of his study in his last year at the seminary. It resulted in some ridicule and much hazing. He thought he would give up, but some force brought him strength through the adversity. The force was his friendship with another seminarian that believed in his research and had agreed with his findings. The seminarian's name was Jimmy Ennis, with whom he had long lost contact. His friend had given up on his studies and joined the Fire Department to retain a legacy his family had created for three generations. His friend was by his side during all the tough times. Martin Ruby told his friend that it was he, who provided the ability to continue.

As the Priest opened the box, he thought of Jimmy and wondered what Jimmy was doing now. He made a mental note to make contact again if he could locate him. Opening the folders Martin Ruby began to review his works of years past, delving into the unknown where he had tried to separate fact from fiction.

He glanced over the papers, noting the similarities between the woman's story and the facts from the past that he was able to unearth and verify through his limited resources and contacts. His eyes glanced through the pages, stopping at a note in the margin of one of the yellowing sheets.

Staring at the note, he wondered aloud.

"An animal was a presence during events where God's goodness and wrath had both been shown."

The note referred to several pages of the work. He quickly skimmed to the noted pages. In each case, there was something of a violent nature where people died in horrible fashion. In each of the happenings, they appeared to be the worst of human elements.

In the instances, there was a note about an animal being involved. In the few situations he was able find, there had been a horse, a monkey, a bird......he continued to skim the notes. In many of historical cases a bull, an eagle or a lion were mentioned. In the more recent centuries, a dog was noted. A large black dog with a bronze muzzle was the description. He found the resemblance in four of the situations dating back to the sixteen hundreds. The description of the animal was the same each time.

He remembered that the bull, eagle and lion were associated with Seraphim Archangels.

The woman mentioned an animal. Could she have been an angel?

His thoughts spun.

What animal?

What did the animal have to do with anything?

How could some animal play any type of role in what happened?

He read again, finding that he had discounted the presence of the animal. Shaking his head, he tried to remember why he hadn't felt it significant. The reason escaped him. He just couldn't remember. He decided to look further in his notes for the instances where an animal was mentioned. A faint memory of comments during the years was there, yet he now wanted to know more of the connection. He began to look through the papers in earnest.

He began to search his notes for the man he had spoken with many years before that had similar circumstances. Maybe he could still be contacted and shed more light on this mysterious series of events.

Chapter 19 The Drug Topic

Shots Fired

Jimmy Ennis walked out of Fire Department Headquarters onto the bustling street. Cars swept by, causing small gusts of wind, which swept papers sitting around curbs into the air. There were times, Jimmy Ennis thought of the street as a racetrack, where pedestrians could be taking their life in their hands, just trying to cross from one side to the other. Today was no exception. Reaching the end of the block, he turned the corner leading to the parking lot behind the building. For some reason, he always liked to walk out the front door. It caused a fast awakening to the sights and sounds of the city much more quickly than the parking lot entrance provided. He exhilarated in the feeling of the hustle and bustle of the streets. A few firefighters passed by offering greetings as they customarily did.

Suddenly, a shot rang out, followed by another and then a burst of gunfire as if in response. Jimmy Ennis and the men who had just passed him all hit the ground with eyes searching for the source. The firing started again, shots coming in quick succession. The men heard bullets ricochet off the metal of the cars around them. None raised their heads to see what was happening. The safest place seemed to be closest to the ground. Silence returned just as suddenly as it had been broken. The men hesitated in rising to their feet fearing another outburst of gunfire that could fill the air at any time now. The silence continued, pierced now by the wailing of approaching police car sirens. The men looked at each other with surprise on their faces.

"What the heck was that all about?" One of them said to no one in particular.

The sound of car brakes directed their attention to the front of the lot. A blue sedan was turning quickly into the lot. As it approached the group of men, the car suddenly stopped and its horn began to echo through the lot. The men could see bullet holes in the windows and in the hood of the car. They raced toward the car.

Inside was a man slumped over the wheel. One of the men, Tommy Kennedy was an EMT and took charge of the situation. Unfortunately, he had no equipment. Another helped remove the man from the driver's side of the car and placed him gently on the ground. He was bleeding from the right shoulder. Tommy quickly looked him over for other wounds and found none. The men turned the man over to see if there was an exit wound. There was an area of blood on the man's back where a bullet had exited his body.

168

Terry Connors came to help from the station, and he reached for his car keys and handed them to the closest firefighter with instructions to grab his medical kit from ambulance car. The firefighter took off immediately to fetch the kit. In the meantime, another of the men raced into the headquarters building to call for help. Connors examined the man's wounds more closely and expressed to Jimmy Ennis, that it didn't look good. He was sure the bullet had punctured a lung and maybe even a major artery of the heart the way he was bleeding. The man returned with the kit and Connors removed some large bandages to cover the wounds. He applied pressure to stem the flow of blood that seemed to lessen somewhat from the man's chest.

People started to gather all around the man and the firefighters. Jimmy Ennis looked up and noticed the red lights from the headquarters ambulance coming toward them. The red truck stopped and the men quickly joined their brother EMT with the man. They lifted him onto the cart and rolled it to the rear door of the ambulance. In a moment, the siren started and they drove by the men for the trip to Rush Presbyterian hospital nearby.

As the ambulance pulled out with its siren wailing, two police cars entered the lot and pulled up to the group of firefighters. They approached the men who gave way leaving a path to Captain Ennis. They all nodded their acknowledgments and conversation began about the incident. The police searched the car and found the man's wallet behind the seat along with other items of interest. Conversations with the firefighters continued.

Sydney and Damon Anderson

Sydney Anderson and her husband Damon were hanging some new pictures they purchased a while back. It was spruce up the place time. Linda Ronstadt's sultry rendition of "What's New" filled the air from the CD player. The O'Keefe prints together with works by Toulouse Lautrec provided a new perspective to the dining room. The couple was having fun measuring and asking each other about alignments and heights. Damon playfully tickled his wife while she held a picture against the wall for his opinion on placement. It was Damon's job to hammer in the nails.

He was not very accomplished with a hammer. Because of this, he found his finger suffering from a missed blow a few times. He yelped each time. Sydney would come over and playfully kiss his finger to "make it better for my baby", stressing the baby. They were happy with the results of their efforts and were having fun.

They were surprised at the sudden volume increase on the television. They figured it was just a commercial at first. Then, looking at each other in surprise, they listened to the words from the newscaster anchorperson. The woman was telling of a band of thunderstorms forming in the Gulf of Mexico and expected to hit land in Louisiana during the evening and move up through the Midwest during the next few days.

Damon, who was something of a weather enthusiast, listened with interest, while Sydney joked about more rain in Louisiana. Damon held up his hand as if to still his wife's comments. She noticed his interest and stopped to focus on the television screen again.

Damon pointed to the screen and put his finger on one of the weather front lines approaching from the Western US. Sydney watched with increasing interest as his hand followed the lines across the screen. She sensed from her husband that he was drawing some conclusions. She loved it when he would develop a scenario about the weather and tell her what he expected to be the outcome. He was usually very accurate too. She watched him with fascination; wondering what he was thinking, as his hand ran over the television screen.

"Hon, this is amazing," was his initial comment.

"I've got to look at this on the Internet," he said as he walked over to the computer.

"Well tell me; what do you see?"

"A convergence of separate storms." he said quickly as his fingers touched the keyboard.

"It's very unusual to have air masses meeting in the way they're showing on the television."

"I'm surprised they haven't realized the possibility of what could develop."

An Exploding Computer Screen

"This is like WOW time Hon," he said with more excitement in his voice.

As Damon looked at the weather forecasting tools available on various sites of the Internet, a picture of a massive buildup of rain coupled with high winds formed in his brain. He pointed this out to Sydney as he clicked from page to page, verifying his findings and drawing his conclusions. A storm of massive proportions was going to take place in the Midwest very soon, he told his wife.

"If this materializes honey, it's going to be the biggest storm conflagration we've ever witnessed."

Sydney looked at her husband with interest, as she patted the back of his neck.

"Hon, there isn't anything you can do about it," was her somewhat resigned remark.

Damon just continued clicking through the pages of weather on the screen. At one point, he patted his wife's hand as it rested on his shoulder. He pointed to the computer screen with his finger to note the gathering weather mass. He touched the screen at the center of the mass. At his touch, Sydney screamed as the computer screen exploded showering pieces all over the desk. Both looked at each other to see if they were ok. They were. Sydney clutched Damon's shoulders in shock. They both stared in a stupor at what was left of the computer screen.

Jimmy and Ellie

Jimmy Ennis parked in front of his house. The afternoon sun was casting shadows from the buildings against the cement of the street. He was thinking of Ellie and decided to stop over to see if she had any plans. Usually, he would call her first, but this time, he simply felt like surprising her. It was not going to be a surprise. Ellie heard the car approaching and was looking out the window as her friend stepped out of his car. She decided to have some fun with his unannounced visit. Running to the bathroom as she pulled off her clothes, she grabbed a towel and wrapped herself. Turning on the shower, she dunked her head under the stream of water and quickly turned it off. Running out, she gathered her clothes and threw them in a heap by her open closet.

The doorbell rang. She slowly walked to the door with the dark green towel draped around her and held snugly in place. Her hand reached out to open the door, and there stood Jimmy Ennis with his handsome smile. Immediately, his face turned a darker shade of red as his eyes viewed the sight of Ellie, dressed only in a long towel answering the door. She leaned over and gave him a peck on the cheek with a quickly thought up, "Hi there dear, was just getting into the shower." Jimmy Ennis stood with embarrassment showing from every pore on his face. Ellie reached for his hand drawing him inside.

"My goodness James, I don't want the neighbors to see me answering the door like this. What would they think?"

171

The firefighter allowed her to yank him into the room as he closed the door.

"Just give me a few minutes.

"Why don't you grab a beer and relax?"

A beer sounded good, as he walked into the kitchen and opened the refrigerator door.

Ellie always had a penchant for the unusual, and today was no different. He glanced at the shelf in the refrigerator. There was a variety of beers sitting there. One that drew his attention was called simply Beer. A white can with Gold letters. He quickly decided to avoid that one and took a Miller Draft Light instead.

Ellie was in a devilishly playful mood. She heard him walk by the bathroom door on the way to the front room. She gauged her timing just right. As he was about to take a seat in the oversized chair, she opened the door calling to him.

"Did you have a good day today?" As she spoke, she exposed most of her right leg while she held the door ajar, so it could be seen. Predictably, she waited until Jimmy came and rounded the corner leading to the bathroom. Looking down, she quickly pulled back her exposed leg with a giggle.

"Oops, sorry," she said jokingly.

Jimmy had seen the nicely formed gams of his woman friend and it brought a smile to his face as she closed the door again and left him with his thoughts.

Manny DeLeon

The police investigator finished a conversation with the doctor in charge. Investigator Manny DeLeon entered the patient's room.

The man was identified as Felix Felix. The name was a little strange, but not surprising. He was resting comfortably sipping water from the straw. The Investigator spoke in Spanish: a tactic he found usually opened doors in the information gathering process. The man asked for safety in trade for providing information about a big drug deal. This was an old ploy, used by many immigrants. Yet, the man seemed to be in earnest and was certainly afraid for some reason. So afraid, he wanted to be taken out of the hospital.

As DeLeon continued his query, the man provided more information that indicated there was something very big in the process and it was going to take place soon. Manny DeLeon excused himself and went to use the phone. He called Lieutenant Brennan, his superior.

He asked him to come down to the hospital for what he felt was a very important situation. Trusting Investigator Deleon's instincts, he reached for his jacket as soon as he hung up the phone.

Lieutenant Brennan arrived at the hospital and proceeded to meet with his investigator and the informant. The story sounded interesting. He took a seat and listened as DeLeon resumed questioning the wounded man.

Wanda and Lori

The mid-sized woman with short blond hair surveyed her office from high atop a downtown building. She was an attorney for the law firm of Stafford and Mayes. Everything about her was understated. The right clothes, yet not the right combinations. A potentially attractive face, yet with not sufficient makeup in the right places to make her look more than average. Gazing out the tall windows, she could see the planes approaching O'Hare field, some twenty miles distant. The day was clear and afternoon sun reflected from the glass of the adjoining buildings. The phone rang and she picked it up immediately. She listened intently to the voice on the phone.

The Chicago police just arrested a drug kingpin. The voice was telling her of the need to get the man released as quickly as possible. She made the customary assurances. The law firm relied heavily on the business with the man and his other companies. Consequently, this focused assignment would be addressed, as quickly as possible. She listened to the instructions for bail money and how to proceed, once the man was released.

Stafford and Mayes was a firm with over a hundred lawyers that dealt mainly with personal injury and small hoodlum cases. They were also known for representing defendants on drug-related crimes. This produced a vital amount of the firm's income. The partners of the firm seemed to close an eye, when it came to representing drug defendants. As the caller was saying good-bye, Wanda Benefice buzzed her secretary to come in. She was a good secretary but an eyesore. Certainly not eye candy, but she seemed to go out of her way to be unattractive. Benefice's firm was instructed to hire her and that is why she was there. Lori Boby came through the door like a freight train through a crossing and pulled up a chair in front of the desk. Wanda gave instructions. Lori wrote them on her pad.

Without further ado, she rose and left to address the necessary bail ritual to which she had become accustomed. There was no love lost between the two, but they were a good team when acting for their clients.

Wanda returned to the papers on her desk, unable to dispel a feeling of dread that suddenly seemed to wash over her. She shook it off at first, but it quickly returned. The feeling made her uneasy. She walked over to the bar and poured an afternoon Clan McGregor single malt scotch, neat.

Meanwhile, no big deal, the secretary thought, as she looked at the name Miguel Domingo, one of the more notorious drug lords in the Midwest. He was arrested for some minor infraction, but that was all the police and State's Attorney needed to create significant frustration for the man and his operation. Miguel Domingo was from Columbia and here on a visa. Lori Boby had her work cut out for her. She would be checking on visa status and other associated Immigration department requirements. Her job was to be sure the firm had adequate information.

Felix Felix
The man in the hospital bed suddenly began to gasp for air. His hands reached out as if trying to find something to hold onto. The alarm went off on the monitoring device with a loud beeping sound. Attending nurses rushed down the hall to the room. A crash cart followed with an orderly at a fast gait. As the nurses reached the room, they witnessed the man collapse back to the bed, his arms falling haphazardly to his side. As the nurses reached the bed, they knew already that the man had gasped his last breath. The finality of the man's life was apparent. The team tried to revive him, but each knew there would be no recovery. The man had died.

The attending nurse called Investigator DeLeon's office and Lieutenant Brennan picked up the phone. He listened to the all too often comment.

"Your victim expired sir."

Brennan had heard it many times before. At least this time, they were able to glean some information; that would prove valuable in obtaining warrants against some notable drug dealers. Time would tell. He pushed the call button to talk with his inspector, to inform him of the patient's demise. There was no response from Detective Deleon's office. Brennan left a voice message and hung up the phone.

Manny DeLeon was on the West Side, following up on a few leads provided by the gunshot victim. It seemed that everyone he spoke with had vile contempt for the drug kingpins in the area. It almost seemed as

174

though the residents were about to take up arms to combat the vicious men who took over their neighborhood and drove everyone to fear. DeLeon received his voice page and checked on the message. He heard his boss's voice informing him of the passing of the gunshot victim. Detective DeLeon decided it was time to stop by the pound to take another look at the car the man was driving. It was just a hint, yet he felt it was something that required follow-up. He got in the police car and headed for the pound, where the victim's car would be waiting. While on the way to the pound, DeLeon turned on the radio and listened to the WMAQ weather report. The weather person was telling listeners of the potential for a substantial summer storm, approaching from the gulf with another potentially dangerous front, moving in from the West. Both would be converging on the Chicago area within the next 24 hours.

Chapter 20 Meetings And Thoughts

The Alley Victim

The woman from the alley rested peacefully in the hospital room. Northwestern Memorial Hospital was near the downtown area, and was the closest available from where she was found. Cuts and abrasions seemed to be the worse part of her condition. Other than being weak from a lack of food, she and the baby seemed to be doing as well as could be expected. She was about a month from delivery and after a little rest; she would be put out on the street again.

Curiously, she remembered the cut on her forehead that was bleeding profusely, when the stranger came. Feeling her forehead, she could not find where the cut had been. She remembered the man touching her, but didn't think anything of it at the time. That now bewildered her.

Frank Bellini

In the lower levels of Wacker drive, Frank Bellini awoke with the dog by his side. It was time to move before the police came and rousted him and those around him. He shook his head to clear the sleep from his brain. The dog was instantly awake and sitting next to him as if waiting for instructions. Strangely, the large black animal took matters over. With a loud "Woof", it rose and began to walk in the direction of the exit from the lower level. Frank Bellini followed. They were walking under the sunlit street above, when a small sandwich vendor truck pulled up alongside. The window rolled down and the driver held out a rolled sandwich. Frank recognized the driver, who occasionally would give him a sandwich and then drive on without waiting for a thank you or anything.

"You look like you could use some food," was the comment from the driver.

Frank and the dog approached the side of the truck. Reaching for the wrapped sandwich, he readily grasped the food and bowed his head to the driver.

"Here, take this too," the driver offered as he held a cup containing a soft drink beverage of some kind, and another small sandwich.

"That's for the dog."

"Thank you," Frank responded.

With that, the driver gunned the engine and pulled away, leaving Frank and the dog with the food.

"Well how about that." He exclaimed with surprise in his voice as he offered part of the sandwich to the hungry dog.

The dog looked up and barked a soft noise into the air taking the offering and inhaling the contents of the breaded meal. It was gone in a flash. Man and animal continued walking toward the sunlit street wondering what the day would bring.

Walking around a corner, Frank instantly froze. He and the dog were interrupting a drug buy. The man and woman, who were exchanging money for a packet of white substance, immediately jumped at the sight of them. The dog growled viciously at the pair. With just a quick look, the couple fled in different direction.

Frank looked at the dog. The dog's eyes seemed to be following the path of the pair continuing to run down the street. The large animal gave a bark and settled back to a calmer state. They began to walk again with no particular destination.

Frank thought about the pregnant woman from the night before. He remembered the ambulance driver mentioning Northwestern Memorial Hospital, on Huron Street. The Hospital was not that far away. As they walked, the dog seemed to be reading his mind, as it began to lead him toward the hospital area. Both seemed used to walking a lot, so the couple of miles to the Hospital were no significant trek for either.

Chaos Brewing

Sydney listened to the weather forecaster on the radio. A smile crossed her lips as she remembered how excited Damon became when noting the convergence potential of the weather fronts as they approached Chicago.

The phone rang. Damon lifted the receiver in the kitchen as Sydney entered the room. It was Maria calling. She was asking about the storm. Damon was happy to provide her with the lurid details, of what could become a major weather event. Sydney pulled up a chair and listened to the conversation until her husband pushed the receiver toward her.

"It's Maria for you Hon," he said playfully, handing his wife the phone. Sydney took the phone and went to the other room to converse with her friend. For some reason, Sydney got the impression from Maria that she was fearful of the coming weather situation. Maria decided to tell Sydney about the mysterious woman that came and seemed to give her a veiled message about what was coming. A feeling of fear suddenly swept through Sydney as their conversation continued. She told Maria about what Damon foresaw about the weather, and the shattered computer screen. That seemed to confirm Maria's thoughts. They agreed to speak with each other later.

Preparations Continue

At the Channel 5 weather station, people gathered to listen to the meteorologist's explanation of what could be the largest storm force to hit Chicago in quite some time. She was telling listeners of the combination of weather forces pushing simultaneously up from the Gulf and from the West. Apparently, they would meet over Chicago at the same time. She continued that the storm could produce major winds and rain in the area. This was no wimp of a storm building, she told her listeners.

Newscasts reported the upcoming weather event and cell phones were ubiquitous as they rang throughout the United States with information about the apprehension of the drug czar and his cohorts in Chicago.

Drug Delivery Plans

Plans were hurriedly put in place that would allow the continuity of numerous drugs available in the area in case of a major storm. New conduits of entry were mapped out from South America, Mexico and Chicago. Chicago was the major staging area. Plane routes were adjusted as were over the road delivery points to maintain a high level of supply. Supply and delivery channels were changed as quickly as information could be produced. At all costs, the locations and drop off points could not be jeopardized within the Midwest.

If local police or Federal Investigators were to find out the enormity of the Chicago operation, there would be consequential trouble for the entire family of drug cartels.

The phone lines of small law firms and individual lawyers who worked on the periphery of the drug scene were lighting up with requests for information about what the police were doing. Lawyers at a few of the more notable law firms were feeling the pressure from drug lords in the area to find and deliver information.

Lawyers at Stafford and Mayes were feeling considerable pressure, especially Ms. Wanda Benefice, who was fielding phone calls from all over the city. Law enforcement officials who relied on funds from the drug dealers were pressured to deliver information about their departments' planning.

On the streets of Chicago and numerous other Midwest cities, the word of change moved quickly. Drug dealers were pressuring everyone for more money. Their futures depended on it as there were always new faces wanting to join the ranks and partake in the substantial profits.

Drug dealers at the middle level prepared new places to warehouse the supply. New chains of delivery were developed to bypass the law officials who were sniffing around like bloodhounds for information.

The Internet was alive with activity from dealers, pushers and others. The flurry of activity did not pass unnoticed by the Federal Authorities, who monitored certain IP addresses, screen names and websites. The Feds were aware that something of critical proportions was underway.

Lindsay Ballenger

She pulled up in front of her apartment building with a feeling of dread. The shiner on her face reminded her of how brutal he could be. She was sickened by the reaction of her boss, Jimmy Ennis, at the sight of her puffed up face and eye. She knew this kind of relationship she suffered with her husband was doomed and it was time to end it. How he would react was the problem that concerned her. His outbursts were always so unpredictable. Nonetheless, it was time to act.

She placed her key in the lock and turned it pushing against the door to open. She placed the key ring back in her pocket. As she entered, she caught the odor of something burning. Walking quickly toward the kitchen, she found the pot on the stove wafting a smoky silhouette into the air. She turned off the burner looking at the mixture of something that appeared to be chili sitting caked together in the bottom of the pot. There was a bottle of vodka sitting on the kitchen table with an empty glass nearby. Not a good sign, she thought as she walked past toward the bathroom. She looked at her face in the mirror. What she saw staring back was in stark contrast, to the pretty skin and eyes, she once exhibited. She looked rough, like someone who hadn't done anything to improve her looks in a while. She thought of applying makeup, then remembered that she left her purse in the car.

As she watched, she caught a glimpse of him out of the corner of her eye.

"What are you looking at?" Came the words of a sarcastic voice.

"My face Billy, my face."

"You look like crap," her husband's voice responded.

Lindsay Ballenger decided to restrain herself from further comment, lest she ignite an argument with her husband. She just looked at him through the angle of the mirror. He started to walk away then stopped in mid stride to return.

I Don't Think So

"You wanna go to a movie or have sex?"

"I'd just like to sit and relax Billy. I'm tired," Lindsay Ballenger replied.

"Well I been sittin' around here all day, baby," he slurred.

She knew more trouble was brewing and she did not want another assault on her face and body from the drunken and drug crazed man leering at her. She reached for the top button of her blouse and began to open it. He approached and without warning, she felt the blouse being ripped from her body. His hands grabbed, pulling her toward him as he forcefully placed his lips on hers, grinding their mouths together. She thought she would be sick. Suddenly she was pulled and half dragged toward the bedroom. He threw her on the bed.

"Get sexy for me babe, I'm gonna do you," was the comment from Billy's drunken mouth. She pulled herself up on the bed and away from him. He sensed her refusal and reached to grab her. She knew the drill on this. He would forcefully take her and when he was done, punch her for not satisfying him again. It was an old record being played again. Only this time, Lindsay Ballenger had enough. It was time to fight back.

She knew she would not be able to hurt him. His six-foot plus frame was muscular and active. She would have one chance and it was time to play her card for that. She raised her leg, pulling it toward her. He climbed onto the bed crawling toward her until he was just a few feet away.

Her foot lashed out to catch him between the legs. With a loud cry, he doubled over in pain. Her athletic ability gave her the edge she was waiting for. With a quick leap, she was over his body and heading to the bedroom door. She slammed the door and raced toward the stairs. Her blouse was in shreds, but she didn't care.

She reached quickly for her coat and raced down the stairs. She groped for the keys to the car. Finding them, she shoved the key into the door and opened it quickly. She jumped into the seat and started the car in quick moves. It took only seconds and the car was fishtailing down the street. She fought for control of the car and her senses. Easing off the gas, the car found a straight line. He had no way to follow her, since their other car wasn't running.

She reached over to her purse. Groping inside, she found the slip of paper with the number of Maria Esparza and the Shelter. She lifted the cell phone and called the number. She made a decision. No more beatings from some slob of a man.

The woman at the other end of the phone answered. Lindsay Ballenger blurted out the need for help. The voice was immediately reassuring and provided just the right amount of confidence Lindsay needed. She asked for the address and immediately made a turn to head for the place. She decided to wait until she calmed down to call Jimmy Ennis, knowing that he would approve of her actions and be on her side.

The Alley Victim

Frank Bellini, with the large dog, maneuvered their way to Northwestern Memorial Hospital on the near Northwest side. As they walked, he become accustomed to the dog responding with a "ruff", to his comments. It was almost as if the animal understood what he was saying.

Upon reaching the hospital, the two walked toward the emergency entrance door. As they neared the entrance, the dog veered off and began a trot in another direction. Soon the large animal was out of sight. Frank Bellini shrugged his shoulders and continued into the waiting room. Deciding to spend a few moments in a bathroom to alter his looks, he noticed the "Mens" sign and entered. He looked in the mirror. He began a short conversation with his alter ego.

"You, my friend are a mess, and you look like a wreck."

His dark hair was off to one side and his unshaven face bespoke a look more of a seaman arriving from the ship at sea than a normal person.

Looking at his surroundings, he noticed a travel pouch resting at one of the sinks. Willing to explore its contents, he opened it. To his surprise, it was a fully supplied travel kit. Shaver, hair trimmer, comb, toothpaste and brush all neatly placed inside.

He looked around for an owner. He was alone. A small smile lit the corners of his mouth as he reached in with grubby looking hands to fondle the contents.

As he turned on the faucet, hot water streamed onto his hands. With the soap dispenser close by, he took advantage of its contents and began to clean off the days of dirt that had settled on him. He thought, at least he might be able to look half way decent to the hospital staff while he searched for the woman from the night before.

Lindsay Ballenger

Tears streamed down her face as she drove. She could hardly see as she turned the car into one of the available parking places in the lot behind St. Rita's Harmony Place Shelter. Turning off the car, she reached for her purse and climbed out of the little red sports car. Following the instructions from Maria Esparza, she saw the long open wood stairway up to the second floor, proceeded to climb the wooden stairs, and rang the bell at the rear entrance to the Shelter.

Maria met her at the door with a smile and an extended arm, inviting Lindsay Ballenger into the sanctuary of the Shelter. She led the woman to a chair and offered a box of Kleenex without saying a word.

"Coffee, Lindsay?"

"Yes, that would be nice."

Maria looked at the woman who resembled a train wreck. Her hair was wildly askew, face red with the burning sensation from so many tears, and in general, the look of a woman who was mentally trashed.

The Ballenger woman looked up.

"Thank you," were the only words spoken to Maria.

Maria replaced the coffee pot on the oven and moved over to place her hand on the woman's shoulder.

"Things will start getting better now," she assured the sobbing woman.

Without thinking, Maria reached her hand to cover the clasped hands of Lindsay Ballenger. Immediately the warm feeling flowed between the two women. Lindsay Ballenger's hands moved slightly at the feeling, as her eyes looked up to fixate on the woman standing by her. Maria grimaced initially, and then relaxed. What will be will be she thought to herself. God is working his own magic here, so who am I to think otherwise. She sat and the women began to chat.

Chapter 21 Coming Together

Frank Bellini

He used almost all of the contents of the travel bag, from trimmer to shampoo. The toothbrush was still wrapped, so he used that too. Nothing was left untouched in the bag. As a gesture of finality, he took the green bottle of Polo after-shave and patted the liquid on his face. He looked at the neatly trimmed beard and felt a lot better.

His thoughts stirred quickly to the time when he had it all as the owner of the Investment Software Company, "Investware". Then how his life crashed in a few short months after the accusations began. He and the company were the fall guys for someone. He just wasn't able to figure out who that person was, so he paid the price, losing wife, property, all the money and so many more intangibles, that his heart hurt at the thought. Worst of all, he could not tell friends from enemies. He shook his head to relieve himself of the memories and placed all the contents back in the travel bag.

One thing he did, before the money dried up and his sources of friendship disappeared was to obtain another identity. Frank Wilson became Frank Bellini. A new person was created at the other end of the alphabet. It took a little getting used to, but within a short time, he acclimated to the new name.

In the process, he also obtained a Social Security Number and other identification, including a credit card and bank account. His resources were extremely limited requiring him to limit spending to the point of absurdity. Yet, he continued to survive in his newly created world.

He thought about taking the bag, but decided against it. It belonged to someone else. Something new had taken over now and he felt himself returning to his world of ethics and honesty. The feeling he remembered was a good one and he liked its return. He left the bag on the sink and proceeded to the door, with a last look in the mirror for approval. As he opened the door, a man came through almost knocking him over. As Frank fought for balance, his hand touched the man's hand that was coming in. Each felt an immediate coldness. Frank Bellini didn't know what to make of it. He saw the cap on the floor that said, *Muenstat Electric Company.* Good naturedly, Frank reached to retrieve the cap and returned it to the man, who responded with an "hmmmp."

Frank Bellini abruptly left the man standing at the doorway to the mensroom. He studied the splinter in his finger thinking, he had to do something about getting it removed.

Monica Mentor

Knowing that the woman would most likely be in the maternity ward, he found the floor and began his unobtrusive search. Peeking into doors as he avoided the nurses scurrying about, he looked for a sign of the woman from the alley. Remembering that the police had mentioned they had a Jane Doe, he wondered how the hospital would track that kind of person. He decided that an outright lie was the best tactic. With that in mind, he approached the nurse's station.

"Hello, I'm looking for my sister," he announced to the nurse on duty.

"Name?" Came the curt reply.

"Monica Mentor," was the reply that popped into his head.

The nurse scanned the record of patients.

"No one here by that name," was the eventual reply.

The nurse took a more appraising look at the man standing in front of her. Frank Bellini, could sense her thoughts.

"I just got in from the airport. My luggage hasn't arrived yet."

The nurse took another look and passed on a further comment.

"She was brought in last night," he replied in a friendly tone.

"No identification with her."

The nurse looked at him questioningly, but his smile was so genuine, she relented.

"We have a Jane Doe, but you'll have to talk to the police before I can let you see her," was her reply.

Unabashed by the comment, he quickly responded.

"Oh, that would be fine. Who do I see?"

The nurse picked up the phone and dialed a number.

She handed the phone to the still smiling man.

"This is Detective Briscoe."

"Hi, Detective, this is Frank Bellini," the man said in a cheery voice.

"I believe my sister was brought in last night as a Jane Doe, because she didn't have any identification, as usual."

The conversation continued for a few moments.

Frank Bellini handed the phone back to the nurse.

After a brief exchange, the nurse looked at him with the smile.

She hung up the phone.

"Have a seat Mr. Bellini; someone will be here to talk with you shortly."

"Thank you," was his reply.

Frank Bellini decided to stick it out. For some inexplicable reason, he needed to meet the woman and make sure that she was all right. A far cry from how he felt earlier in the evening when he intended to have his way with the woman in the parking garage.

He realized how completely his life had changed in just a few short hours. Then he thought about the big dog and wondered about that too.

Detective Fred Briscoe was a cop with a large chip on his shoulder. Being passed over for promotion so many times, he grew weary of the politics and decided to hang in there to his retirement. He didn't like many of his peers and the feeling was mutual. He was a good investigator though; but many times, no one wanted to listen to him.

Frank rose to meet the short stocky figure approaching. The guy looked like a cop. He decided to remain pleasant no matter what took place in the exchange of words that was about to come.

Detective Briscoe was naturally inquisitive, just as he should have been. There were a lot of questions and the man provided realistic and logical responses. The detective finally decided that no harm would be done, if he let the seemingly kind fellow see the woman he claimed to be his sister.

With a motion of his hand, Detective Briscoe said, "follow me."

The two men walked down the hall silently to room #302. They entered with the nurse.

The woman lying in the bed was staring off into space. At the intrusion, her vision shifted to the two men and the nurse entering the room.

The detective spoke first.

"Do you know this guy?" He grumbled to the woman in the bed.

She looked up to the awkwardly handsome face of the man standing there.

She nodded imperceptibly.

She remembered the face from last night in the alley. It looked much more clean and alive than the night before, but she was sure it was the man.

Before she could utter another sound, the man spoke.

"Monica, I'm so glad you are all right."

"How are you feeling?"

"Is the baby ok?"

The questions were blurted, as if held in and then suddenly to escape.

The Monica person thought, "who the hell is Monica?"

Then her mind wondered again.

"Who the hell am I?"

The question lingered, clouding her thought process.

The man sat at the side of the bed and gently passed his hand over her forehead, moving her hair from her face. The hand was warm as she felt a slight tingle and it felt refreshing against her skin. She allowed a look of comfort to appear on her face.

The detective was beginning to feel like an intruder.

"I'll check back in a little while," he said to the couple looking into each other's eyes at the bed. He turned and left the room.

"Who are you?" The woman asked.

"Name is Frank Bellini."

"So who is Frank Bellini?"

"I'm just a guy who found you in an alley last night. You were in pretty bad shape too."

"Yeah, well I got beat up and thrown out of a car last night," was the retort. The guy I was living with told me he did not want to care for any eight-month pregnant woman and didn't want to have another mouth to feed, so as we were driving in his friend's car, he got mad and he threw me out.

"At least you're ok now, that's the important thing."

"Oh sure, feeling just dandy being eight months pregnant, nowhere to live and lying in a hospital bed I can't pay for."

"You bet I'm ok," was the capricious comment.

"Things have a way of working out," the stranger sitting on the bed reminded her.

"We'll see about that when I get out of here."

"Yeah, we will," he said to the woman looking into her eyes.

"I'll let you get your rest and check back with you later today."

"Yeah sure you will," was the questioning reply from the woman.

"I will, you'll see."

With that, the man rose and started for the door.

"What'd you say your name was?"

"Frank Bellini, at your service," the man responded with a tip of his hand to his brow.

"I'm using the name Frank Bellini for now. My past is a little shady according to some."

"I have no idea what my name is, Frank," she suddenly blurted.

"Be Monica for now," was the swift reply.

"If you come back, my name's Monica," the woman said rolling her eyes.

"If you don't, my name is garbage."

"I like Monica better. See you later Monica."

"Yeah okay, Frank Bellini or whatever your name is."

The woman turned her head to look out the window. When she looked back to the doorway, he was gone. A grimace covered her face.

Drugs and Drugs

The cell phones were lighting up all over the city and suburbs. Lawyers, pimps, dealers, cops and anyone who had knowledge of something happening with drugs in the city were looking for ways to benefit. Even some of the staffs at hospitals and clinics were in on the information highway.

At Stafford and Mayes, pressure was building from the pending charges against Wanda Benefice's new client, Miguel Dominga of the Dominican Republic and some of his lesser-named cartel members.

Ms. Wanda Benefice decided to recruit a few of the junior members of the firm to help with the communications and research for the drug czar. She felt like she was in the middle of a storm. Little did she know at the time, how accurate that feeling would portray itself to be in reality.

Signs

A number of police officers who were on a street beat became aware of the upcoming situation. Snitches were talking in the hope of being granted some leeway and freedom to get involved for their own profit. Money began changing hands in a grand style. Quite a few people that already were receiving protection money were becoming richer by the hour and the day. Plans were actually drawn to create anonymity for pushers and dealers. The streets of Chicago and its suburbs were teeming with potential customers and everyone involved in illegal drugs was going to make a few bucks on the upcoming events.

Mob leaders, who were hiding silently behind the scenes, had their lieutenants and block bosses out digging for information. Everyone who was known to participate in the drug industry was being tapped for alliances or protection.

In Oak Lawn, a well-dressed man walked into the Fast Signs store and sauntered over to the sign shop section. An employee greeted the man warmly. The customer presented a sign layout that would be used on panel vans that his company, *Muenstat Electric Company* owned. He requested a quote. The employee walked over to one of the computers and input some information. Returning to the customer, the employee smiled and informed the customer that the signs would cost $550.00 per vehicle. True to form, the employee also offered the customer an application for commercial credit at the store. The customer reviewed the quote and decided to have second thoughts about the order. He told the employee that he would review the quote and get back to him in a day or so. The customer took the quote, the commercial application, thanked the employee and left the store.

Upon reaching his car, the customer dialed a number on the cell phone and told the person who answered that he wanted to meet with him right away. There was no way they were going to order signs from some major company that wanted an application for credit to be filled out. The situation would create too much suspicion if the order were placed without submitting the application. The application also required too much vital information about the company. Another venue would have to be found for the signs.

As he was driving on Joliet Road, his eyes glanced upon a small sign company by the name of Signs by Black. He parked the car and walked into the store. The owner greeted him with a smile as he presented the layout and asked for a quote. The older, yet very pretty woman owner looked over the requirements and offered the man a figure of $600.00 per vehicle installed. The man thought for a moment and decided to ask for the price as "ready to install", as he had a man who would do the installation. The woman was non-plussed and offered a price similar to the quote the man received from Fast Signs. He wished he had time to spend with the woman who was so attractive and nice. The man ordered five sets of signs and reached into his pocket.

He placed $2,000 on the counter and the woman owner cheerfully took the money and went to the computer to prepare a receipt. She informed the man that the signs would be ready by 5:00PM, which satisfied the man's timetable. As she was preparing the receipt, the woman stopped and walked back to the counter with a color chart. She offered the man a selection of colors for the signs. The man looked at the chart and selected a PMS color in green for the signs. The woman wrote the color on the order invoice and thanked the man for the order.

The man stopped at a few other small sign shops on the way back and placed similar orders. All of the signs would be ready today. This would fit nicely with the plan. All he needed was a couple guys to install the signs on the trucks. No big problem.

Preparations Continue

Gangs in the black and Hispanic neighborhoods were already formulating plans for receiving deliveries and providing distribution citywide. Gold chains were visible in every section of the city along with the Cadillac Escalade, driven by the kingpins. The tell tale sounds of the cell phone calls were going off in every venue from hotel lobbies to basement apartments.

The Internet was a swarm of activity with plans for delivery and distribution of significant sized shipments of white dust and a veritable plethora of pills that would be saturated with chemicals for the masses of users.

Websites and private chats were plentiful, as the contacts were hot and heavy with everyone trying to vie for a place in the pecking order of supply and demand.

Federal agents were scooping some of the sites. Information gathered was being forwarded to local taskforces for analysis and planning. The Feds learned about a plan to use delivery vans with some unknown business name. Hopefully, they would turn up the name of the business in time to foil some of the transfers.

Many of the small airports dotting the landscape within a hundred miles of the city were becoming active with small planes taking off and landing with greater regularity than usual.

Limousine services were being called on for hourly rental of drivers with their stretch models. Meetings were taking place inside the limos during long drives to the country and surrounding suburbs. Black suited drivers were seen standing around the vehicles in hotel parking lots and home driveways. The limo services were calling in every available driver to cover the demand for rentals.

On Lake Michigan and the inland waterways, boats bustled about in their usual manner. Parties took place daily on many of the pleasure craft. A few of the large boats belonged to people in the drug trade. Plans were continuing for the use of the boats to transport copious quantities of the incoming drugs to other locations across the lake in Michigan and Indiana. The boats would make a great cover for the shipments as they were often seen traveling across the lake with many partygoers on board, thus reducing suspicion from police and coast guard. The police received a tip from a reliable informant about the *Muenstat Electric Company* van signs.

Chapter 22 Discerning Revelations

Doctor Pedroza

Dr. Pedroza opened the car door and Maria easily slid into the front seat, reaching over and planting a gentle kiss on the Doctor's cheek.

"How did the day go," she asked smiling.

"Not too well."

"Oh, what happened?"

Doctor Pedroza told Maria about the hazing and the actions and words from the other doctors. He said it made him feel very uncomfortable. Maria sensed his feelings and understood how he could be made to feel that way. She thought about what to say in response. For the time being, she exchanged in small talk and silence to his place.

When they reached his house, he pulled the car into the driveway and waited as the garage door opened for them to enter. Once inside, he let the door close and proceeded to unlock the door to the house as they entered. Inside, he turned to the woman and took her in his arms, placing kisses on her lips and sides of her face in a sign of affection that she loved.

Maria knew that this wonderful man was going to have trouble with what she was about to tell him, so she asked for some wine and told him that it would be good for them to talk about the day's events. He, at first waved his hand as if to dismiss the thought, then acquiesced and invited her to sit at the table with him.

Maria decided to tell it as she thought it to be and quietly explained the uncomfortable position in which she was placing him. She refrained however, from telling him about the stranger's visit. That was going to be a secret she shared with Chelle Leriget for some unexplained reason and decided that there was no need to tell anyone else for the moment. As it was, the Doctor was going to be absorbing quite enough from what she was going to tell him.

Dr. Pedroza looked at her with a disbelieving face when she told him about the effect of her touching people with the gift that she carried. As she continued, he listened with interest and began to understand how some of the events could have been possible from the way she explained the situation. He was still not yet willing to believe the amazing power that existed.

At one point in the conversation, he stopped Maria in mid sentence.

"If what you are saying is true, Maria, Then I could possess the power of life and death over patients because of my association with you. That is something that is really hard to believe and even understand how it would be possible."

"You are absolutely correct Doctor," she responded without hesitation.

"Just because we are together, you may be able to have that power."

He sat back in the chair with a stunned look on his face, as he grasped the unmistakable potential.

"I can't do that," he finally blurted.

"I know, Doctor," Maria responded.

"It would be extremely difficult for you to carry the decision of life or death for your patients."

"How could anyone possibly carry that weight?"

"Tell me what you understand about this power," the doctor asked.

"Can you explain what you understand?"

He sat staring into her eyes. For a long moment, there was silence. Maria placed her hands, palm down on the table.

"I don't know everything, but here is what I have been able to piece together," she said in a calm tone.

"It has to do with this sliver in my finger. Remember when you tried to extract it?"

"Yes of course," the Doctor replied.

Maria continued. "Since then, some unusual things have happened. I can't find any other explanation to the events other than to attribute them to contact with me."

Maria recounted events to him: the car fire in Jerusalem, the patient at the hospital, Ellie and the accident victim, Chelle Leriget and Lori Boby, the fire and the terrorists, the woman with the lottery ticket, the accident victim and now even the Shelter. I know about these ones. There may be others."

"So you feel you have this unbelievable power that you didn't ask for, but have been granted, to do good things for people?"

"Yes," Maria responded.

"This is crazy," He responded.

"Then you explain it Doctor."

He sat shaking his head. "I just can't believe this Maria."

"It's way too far out to be believable."

"Yes, I know," was her simple reply.

The doctor rose and began to pace around the room.

"Do you realize what this means?"

"Oh yeah, I realize it Doctor. You bet I realize it"

"What I don't understand is why."

"I have no idea why I have been selected or chosen or whatever."

Doctor Pedroza stood shaking his head with his hand on his cheek.

"So if what you say is true, I can just touch your hand anytime I feel the need and can go out and save some patient."

"It's not supposed to work that way Doctor, Maria shot back."

"Well how does it work then?"

"I can't be responsible for it and I can't allow someone to just take advantage of it. No one can just take the power." she exclaimed.

"In fact, it seems that anyone who comes in contact with me is given an opportunity for something good to happen or to pass it on to someone else. I have no control over the outcome nor does the other person. It just happens. At times, it invokes detrimental aspects to the person. I just never know what lies in their heart."

"I'm not even sure, I'm able to just give it to someone either."

"The possibility also exists that someone trying to receive this so called power cannot get it because they want it. In fact, dire consequences could happen to someone who might think they would control it, and touches me just for that reason.

"I've touched people and nothing happened one way or the other as far as I have been able to tell.

"There seems to be something with the good or bad within a person that creates an opportunity or a detriment to themselves, or others they come in contact with."

"So, if I understand you accurately, you can touch me all day long and there would be nothing that I might receive or be able to pass on to someone else." The Doctor asked.

"Something like that, yes," Maria said with a frown of resignation on her face.

"I will not be able to save someone's life just because I associate with you then, is that correct?"

"I think that is right, Doctor," Maria responded.

"Well believe it or not my dear that is a great relief to me." The Doctor said with a smile.

"A great relief," he reiterated.

"On the other hand, when we touch, you will receive the gift at times I believe."

"What you need to understand however: is that you will not be able to control it nor decide what benefit anyone may get from it. You are just a messenger or agent. Can you grasp that part Doctor?"

"Yes Maria, I think I do understand that now.

Dr. Pedroza rose and looked down at the woman who was becoming close to his heart.

"I think we should keep some space between us until I can digest this situation," he added.

"I'm not really sure if I can handle this, if what you believe is true."

Maria looked back at the handsome Doctor with an anguished look on her face.

"I understand how you can feel Alhandro, I really do."

"I'll abide by your choice and keep some distance between us."

"I'm sorry Maria," the Doctor responded, placing his hand on her cheek.

Instinctively, she reached to touch his hand. The inevitable warmth was felt by both.

"Darn it, I'm sorry," she said to him rising.

"I'll be careful with this gift Maria. I promise."

With that, he walked toward the door and waved as he closed the door behind him.

Meeting with Richard

Maria called the number that Father Ruby gave her. Richard seemed like a nice man and agreed to meet with Maria. He would also show her the Chapel in the building that housed his factory and display building.

Richard met Maria at the front door. Unlocking the door, he led her into the showroom. The door was locked because at times, no one was in the front to see someone enter the building.

They exchanged small talk, as Richard guided Maria to St. Joseph's Chapel on the other side of the showroom. Maria looked into the room and became mesmerized by the number of statues, artifacts and the general look of the Chapel. She had never seen anything like this before.

Recovering from her initial reaction, she told Richard about her discussion with Father Martin Ruby. Richard explained that he knew Father Ruby well and that every once in a while, Father Ruby would say Mass at the Chapel. Maria told him about the conversation that took place with the visiting woman and that the woman did not seem to be who she portrayed herself to be. Richard listened intently. The conversation was very one sided as Maria told him of the visit and the conversation with the woman.

When she mentioned that the woman seemed to be bleeding from a wound on her forehead, Richard's eyes became larger and he leaned closer to Maria. Maria also told him about the "atonement" statement that she failed to understand. Richard thought for a few moments.

Richard turned and led her to a corner of the Chapel in which rested a statue and picture of Saint Rita, who is known as the "Patron Saint of the Impossible". Richard related the story of her life and Maria stood transfixed as the life of the Saint was told.

"Perhaps the woman was telling you something about your defense of the helpless, that the Shelter is doing daily, and giving those the feeling that they are loved and trusted to be good people. I'm sure many of those women feel they are suffering calamities from which there is no hope of return. St. Rita is one who can make a difference for those in helpless situations. Maybe God is getting upset at the use of drugs and their effect on innocent people and preparing all of us for some serious actions that might be coming."

Maria stared at the man and was speechless at what she just heard.

"Richard?" Maria questioned, to get his attention.

"Yes Maria." The woman said her name was Rita. I forgot to mention this to Father Ruby.

This woman said she knew Ms. Leriget, but when I asked her, she changed the subject.

"It sounds pretty interesting to me, Maria. "You may want to talk to Ms. Leriget again and learn more.

Maria nodded her head.

"Do you really think something drastic might happen to people and the woman's visit was a warning?"

Richard responded with a shake of his head indicating he did not have an answer.

She was especially interested when Richard explained the wound in her forehead. Recounting the conversation with the woman, she vividly remembered the wound and was surprised to learn why the Saint bore the wound until her death. Maria also understood the significance of the Saint's wish to suffer in place of her husband and children.

He told her of the exhumation of St. Rita's body. It was perfectly preserved. She also sat up and opened her eyes when the casket was opened.

Maria was unable to put all the facts of the visit together, yet she found a peace that she could take with her after her discussion with Richard.

Richard escorted Maria to the door. As they walked, he told her that St. Rita was also known as the "Advocate of the Hopeless" and "Saint of the Impossible". With an invitation to call or visit whenever she felt the need or want, he opened the door. As Maria looked at him, he said to her.

"There's one more thing about St. Rita you should know. She is also known as the Patron Saint of Battered Women."

Maria reached up and kissed Richard on the cheek, smiled and left him standing at the door.

Chapter 23 Good Or Bad Fortune

Samantha and Randy Marsten

The couple planned a short getaway to Mexico. It was Pacey Creighton's gift to Samantha for ruining her dress, while saving the woman in the lake, on the night of the gala. They arrived at the airport, the obligatory 2 hours before the flight and everything proceeded as planned.

Is It All Worth It for Two Crooked Cops

The police car was moving slowly as the two police officers scanned the street for unusual activity. The sun was bright on this windy afternoon. The two made quite a mutt and Jeff pair. One was tall and skinny, while the other carried a front porch that gave new meaning to the word overlay. The plain white envelope rested between them on the front seat. The contents represented their weekly "gift" from the drug pushers who thrived on the narrow streets of the neighborhood. The driver glanced at the envelope and smiled. The police officer in the passenger seat opened it to reveal a small stack of $100 dollar bills. Ten of them.

The exchange between the two officers was quiet and simple.

"Not bad for spending money huh?"

"You got that right man."

"Easiest money I ever made."

"Let's say a little retirement savings."

"Yeah."

"Got me a condo down in Phoenix with this already," said the driver with a smile.

"Yeah, I have to get something like that," replied the passenger with a smirk.

They both laughed and looked back out the windows at the faded neighborhood.

The passenger picked up the envelope in his manicured hands. He took five of the bills and handed the rest to the driver who slipped the money into the pocket of his uniform pants.

Streetwalkers frequented the area, in order to pick up their johns almost at random during the late afternoon. Today the street seemed quiet with very few people in view. Next week they'd get another envelope from a couple pimps. That's just the way it worked when you were lucky, thought the police officer behind the wheel.

The car turned the corner toward the L tracks that ran overhead and met with the tracks coming from the West on their way to the downtown "loop" area of Chicago. Vagrants, bums and street people frequented the area under the tracks as it provided a shelter from the day's sun and the night's activities. Few wise people would venture into this area for fear of the unknown. On this day, the two police officers looked for signs of life. Ahead to the left, they noticed a solitary figure sitting against one of the steel L supports apparently reading a book. Alongside was a large black dog, that ran away as the patrol car approached. The car rolled to a stop.

Frank Bellini and Webster

"What're you doing here," growled the gruff voice of the police officer in the passenger seat.

"Just relaxing and trying to get in some quiet reading," was the laconic reply.

"You live around here," asked the police officer.

"Just killing time between visits to the hospital," the figure replied looking up at the officer.

"You sick or something?"

"No, just waiting for 4:00 o'clock to visit a friend."

"What's your name?"

"Frank Wilson."

"What's your friend's name?" "Monica Mentor," he replied.

"Let me see some ID," the driver interrupted.

The man sitting against the steel began to rise as the police driver got out of the car.

Frank knew the routine; he had been through it many times before. The police were just trying to hassle him and get him out of the area.

"Here," he said, giving the policemen his State ID. The cop pushed him against the steel support, forcing his hands up above his head. There was a strong sting, then coldness, when Frank's skin met the police officer's. The police officer noticed it immediately and removed his hand. He shook it a few times and stared at the bum. At the same time, the dog returned and growled at the police officer.

He offered no resistance as the other police officer got out from the passenger side of the vehicle.

The first police officer frisked him. Emptying his pockets, he found a few crumpled dollar bills and threw them to the ground along with a small pencil and scraps of paper.

"I don't have any weapons," Bellini said quietly.

"We'll just make sure of that," the cop shot back gruffly.

"The policeman unbuckled Frank's belt. He continued to stand with his hands remaining above his head against the cold steel. His pants fell to the ground in a heap. He had no underwear so his bare ass was openly visible.

Frank uttered "Geez."

The cop, who was frisking him, grumbled with disgust in his voice. Bellini continued to offer no resistance.

He felt a hand at his shirt pocket and felt something being inserted.

Suddenly without warning, the second police officer spun him around.

He moved up to Frank Bellini's face.

The sharing of breath odors made each feel queasy.

The police officer put his hand on Frank's throat and squeezed slightly, using just enough pressure to get his attention. He got every bit of it.

"What's this?" The cop's tone had turned mean.

"What?" Frank replied.

The police officer reached into the shirt pocket and pulled out a small bag of white powder.

"This!" The cop yelled, holding the bag in front of Frank Bellini's face.

Frank knew it was just planted.

"We're taking you in on possession," the cop screamed in his face.

The other police officer came up and whispered something in his partner's ear.

Frank heard part of the comment.

"Don't waste the stuff on a bum," was what he heard.

The cop looked at Frank Bellini again.

"You better get out of here buddy, before something unfortunate happens to you.

"Alright," Frank replied.

The cop released his grip.

Not wanting any trouble with the two police officers, Frank began to bend down to retrieve his pants. As he did, he felt a foot against his rear end and before he could steady himself, was hurtling through the air from the police officer's shove. He landed in a crumpled mass. As he did, he felt a kick in his side, from the cop's foot. It sent stars through Frank's system as the pain burst in his brain. The cop was about to kick

199

him again when he heard the loud growl. It was the Black Lab that seemed to have appeared from nowhere.

With just a short leap, the massive animal's wide jaws grabbed the foot of the police officer in mid air. With a tug of the canine's large head, the police officer went reeling into the air, landing hard. Immediately, the dog turned to the other police officer who already began to reach for his gun. The dog stared at the man, its eyes penetrating and threatening, as if to warn the cop of his understanding of the gun. The cop's hand continued slowly to the holster strapped to his belt.

His hand never felt the gun, as the dog leaped, covering the man's hand with its mouth. The large animal dug its teeth into the flesh, to hold the hand in place. The cop froze looking to where his fellow officer lay crumpled and trying to get up. The dog seemed to be in command of the situation. The animal looked up into the eyes of the frightened cop who was well aware that his hand could be torn from his arm at any moment. The fear paralyzed the officer into stillness. The other officer finally rose. As he noticed what was happening, he began to reach for his gun.

The huge dog's teeth tightened their grip on the police officer's hand. With a shout, he warned his partner.

"Don't pull your gun or this dog is gonna eat my hand off."

"I think the dog wants you to drop your gun on the ground, Frank said while pulling up his pants the rest of the way. The police officer looked at the dog and deftly placed his hand on his gun and lowered it to the ground.

The second cop stopped his arm's movement toward the holster. His face was tormented. He wanted revenge for what the animal had done to him and he was going to get it. He would just have to wait for the appropriate moment to take out the dog and maybe even the stranger who was standing by the steel support with a sickly smile on his face.

The second police officer began to walk toward the car. The dog turned his potential victim so that his eyes could follow the cop's footsteps. The car door opened, and the police officer sat behind the wheel watching to see what would happen next.

The jaws of the dog relaxed on the other police officer's hand. Quickly, that police officer moved toward the passenger side of the car and jumped in without ceremony. The car started and pulled away, spraying dirt from the spinning wheels.

Frank looked at the animal. Watching it, as its eyes followed the police car through the haze of dust. The dog sensed something and moved over to stand in front of him. Frank watched curiously, as he saw the police car turn around and head back toward them. The dog ran forward a few steps and stopped with its eyes focused on the moving police car.

"I'm gonna take care of that guy and that damned dog in my own way now," the driver roared.

"I think we ought to just get away from here," the other officer responded.

"We will, as soon as I take care of that bum and his dog."

With that, the driver buried the gas pedal against the floorboard as the car's rear end swayed back and forth with the wheels spinning up a cloud of dust. As the wheels found traction, the car lurched forward moving faster and faster toward the man and the animal.

With a start, Frank realized the police car was picking up speed and heading for them.

He yelled quickly.

"Come on dog, let's get away from here."

The animal remained fixed on four paws watching.

The police car was approaching quickly. There was little time left to run, but Bellini decided that was the only choice. He called back to the dog again, but knew the attempt to get the animal's attention would be futile. Frank stopped running. With disbelief, he watched the car approach the place where the dog stood its ground. He screamed again at the animal to move. It was useless.

"You stay right there you miserable animal," the driver snarled.

"What are you doing?" The other officer screamed.

"I'm gonna finish off that dog and then get that bum too," the driver responded through clenched teeth.

The car was almost upon the animal. The car seemed to pick up speed as the engine roared toward where the animal was standing. The driver had the animal in his sights. He was going to make sure this dog would never put that big mouth on anyone again. He glared at the dog as the car bore down on the defenseless animal. Bellini waited for the sickening sound of the thud, as the car would mash and make mincemeat of the dog's flesh.

The car reached the point of impact and both police officers prepared for the impending contact with the dog. The thud never came. Instead, Bellini watched in amazement, as the dog seemed to vanish in front of the police car and now reappeared a short distance from the car. No other noise but the loud sound of the roaring engine could be heard. His eyes continued to follow the path of the car.

Inside the police car, the driver's foot tried to find the brake pedal. He was too late.

"Look out," the passenger screamed covering his face.

With a loud crash, the police car hit the unrelenting steel L track support column. The car's front end seemed to bend around the support as its rear end lifted from the force of the impact and bounced once to the ground. With a loud whoosh, the car exploded in a fireball of flame and flying debris. Frank Bellini felt the urge to run toward the car, but a second explosion quickly ended his movement toward the vehicle.

He never saw the occupants of the car after the impact. He looked around for the dog. It was not around. He continued to look for the animal, hoping the big dog survived and ran away.

"Better get as far away from this place as I can," he thought quickly.

He ran as his fast as his legs would carry him, toward the other side of the small field, and then headed toward the Hospital. His mind raced at the happening of events. A pang of regret for the dog was his only feeling about the incident. After running for a couple blocks, he slowed to a fast walk, allowing himself to catch his breath. After having once been an all-state champ in the mile run, he was no longer in shape for any kind of distance trek. He finally slowed and bent over to allow air to gather in his aching lungs again.

Frank Bellini was having a difficult time trying to assess the importance of becoming friends with the pregnant woman he found in the alley. Nothing made any sense; other than he felt very different about her. Something very unusual was happening. As he raised his head and began to walk again, he noticed the large dog walking toward him. It was the Black Labrador, looking unscathed. It approached and took up a gentle gait at his side. He reached down to pat the dog on the head and was rewarded with a gentle "ruff".

"Hey, if we're going to be around together, you need a name," he said looking at the large canine.

"Let's call you *Webster*, since you're so smart. Yeah, from now on, your name is Webster." They continued down the street toward the glow of orange against the blue sky as the sun began to set in the Western sky.

Monica

Frank Bellini approached the Emergency entrance to the hospital. Webster trotted away from the door as if knowing the fear he would place on people entering or leaving. Inside the elevator, he pressed the button for the third floor and felt the slight surge as the doors closed and the elevator began to ascend.

Inside her room, the woman sat staring at the setting sun. Her mind was trying to grasp something of a memory string as to who she was and what had happened to her. She drew a complete blank. The doctors examined her thoroughly, and proclaimed both the baby in her womb and she to be in reasonably decent condition.

Only one big problem remained. She still had no idea who she was. It was as if she had just been born in an alley. No past, no friends, no nothing.

She heard a noise at the door and saw the rugged features of the man from the alley, who called himself Frank Bellini, or Bellini or whatever.

"Hi there."

"Hi yourself."

"Told you I'd come back."

"And you did."

"When are you getting out?"

"Day or so, the doctor says. They want to observe how the baby's doing."

"Why, are you wanting to take care of me?" She asked with a sense of frightened laughter.

"Me?" The voice asked.

"Yeah, you," was the woman's response.

"Well, yeah, sure if you'd like."

The woman laughed aloud.

"You're sicker than I am," she retorted in an accusing voice.

"Yeah, probably," Frank Bellini responded.

"You're probably right."

"What time tomorrow?"

"Eleven or so"

"Ok. I'll be here to get you then."

"Fine, that's great."

"Ok, see you then. Bye for now."

"Yeah, sure. Bye."

The weird conversation between the two strangers ended and Frank Bellini headed back for the elevators.

The woman lay in the bed wondering if what she just witnessed had really happened.

She pulled the sheet over her head and decided to sleep. Closing her eyes, she regretted that there wasn't much she could do at present.

Frank Bellini stepped out into the evening air and began to walk down the street with no particular destination in mind. As he walked, he heard the noise behind him. He looked back and sure enough, there was Webster lazily following. He patted his hip and the dog leaped forward to be by his side. He patted the dog on the head. They continued down the street.

As the strange pair reached the corner, the sound of screeching tires filled the air. The man and the dog barely had time to step back away from the curb, as a red 72 Oldsmobile cutlass, convertible bounced on the curb and around the corner at full speed. Sirens of a police car immediately began to fill the air as the convertible passed. As he looked, he saw the police squad with its blue, red and white strobes, coming quickly toward the corner. He looked again at the convertible. As he watched, a bag flew out of the car onto the sidewalk ahead. The police car reached the corner and turned with its tires squealing in hot pursuit. The police car sped by the bag chasing after the car.

Deciding to investigate the bag sitting near the sidewalk ahead, Frank Bellini moved quickly toward the object, while Webster bounded ahead. Two boys ran toward the bag from the porch of a house. They also saw the cars pass by and the bag flying from the convertible. It was no race however as the boys spotted the large dog at full gallop toward them. They quickly ran back between the buildings from where they came.

Webster reached the bag. In a single motion, he took the bag in his mouth and spun around to return to Frank Bellini's side. Not wanting to be seen around the area, Bellini quickly changed direction and crossed the street on the run with the dog beside him. They disappeared around a corner and continued to run for another two blocks before changing direction again.

As he rounded another corner, Frank Bellini found himself looking across the field at the wrecked police car. The area was filled with squad cars and fire department equipment. They skirted the scene and quickly walked down another block before continuing toward downtown. He reached to take the bag from Webster's mouth, and the dog snarled loudly. He decided to let Webster carry the bag.

In his mind, he was thinking himself crazy. Frank Bellini promised to help the woman in room #302 at the hospital find a place to stay. He didn't even know the woman and she was really pregnant to boot. What was happening to him? In addition, why is the dog hanging around? It was as if the dog insisted on being with him. There was no way he felt he could get rid of Webster now. When wondering of the dog as his companion, he looked down and petted Webster's head and the dog gave a quick "ruff".

They reached Grant Park on the lakeside of downtown Chicago. There were people playing ball and kids running around all over the place. He and the dog would blend in without being noticed for a while, at least until dark.

Webster suddenly stopped walking and "ruffed" as it sat down with the bag still in its mouth. Frank had forgotten about the contents of the bag as his thought meandered to his strange circumstances. He watched Webster as the dog dropped the bag at his feet. Not sure whether it was all right to reach for it, he slowly lowered his hand to the bag. Webster watched with his tail wagging. As he placed his hand on the bag, Webster looked up into his eyes. Frank would learn that this was a gesture of approval from the large animal.

Frank Bellini lifted the bag, unrolling the top to look inside. As his eyes met the contents, he almost dropped the bag. Inside, all he could see was dozens of hundreds, fifties, and twenty-dollar bills. He reached for a white slip of paper. It was a list of names. He dropped it back into the bag not knowing if it might be useful later. He could feel something heavy at the bottom. He reached his hand inside and grasped a plastic object. Lifting it, he saw it was a cell phone. Laughter came quickly as he looked at the small fortune in cash and the phone. He walked over to a clump of bushes and sat down. Webster followed and before Frank reached the ground, the dog was lying there panting with its tongue hanging out. Frank felt almost as if the dog was showing he was happy. An absurd thought but real just the same.

He lifted the cell phone and punched in a phone number. The female voice answered in a pleasant tone.

"Hi Katherine, don't say anything."

"Is that you Fr..." the voice stopped in mid word.

"I need a little help, just listen ok."

"Sure, go ahead."

"I need a place to take a pregnant woman who's lost her memory."

"Huh?" The voice responded.

"You heard me."

"Hold on."

"Call this number," the voice came back in a business like vein.

Frank Bellini repeated the number and committed it to memory.

"Thanks Katherine, will talk again soon."

"Bye."

Katherine Battersby stared at the phone as she cradled the receiver. Her thoughts drifted to her brother Frank and she wondered what he was doing. She knew he was on the lam so the short conversation was understandable. Still, she worried and wondered about the once powerful Frank Bellini. Shaking her head, she reached for her purse and made a note to check with Maria Esparza in a day or too. Maybe she might find what was happening.

He pressed the end button on the phone.

He lifted the phone again and pressed in the number his sister had given him.

Maria Esparza answered.

They exchanged a few words of introduction. Frank Bellini gave Maria a short narrative of the pregnant woman. Maria gave the Shelter's address and they agreed on an appointed time for a meeting tomorrow.

As he hung up the phone, he expressed a sigh of relief. The hot breath of the dog covered his hand as the mushy tongue gave his hand a hot bath. He laughed and breathed a silent prayer; something he had not done in many months. His mind kept asking why he was so intent on helping this pregnant woman. Shrugging his shoulders, he looked out to the setting sun. His hand reached for Webster's head as he gently patted the huge animal that lay beside him.

Frank Bellini reached into the bag and began to sort the large number of bills that were inside. He placed hundred dollar bills in his inside jacket pocket, fifties in his left pants pocket and twenties in his other pants pocket. The pockets were filled and there was still a substantial sum of money in the bag. He curled the bag and stuffed it into his jacket pocket. With that, he began to walk across the park toward the lagoon where the boats were moored. He figured to pay a few dollars to Harry the boat keeper guard, to let him sleep on one of the boats, that wouldn't have owners coming down tonight.

Chapter 24 Preparations Galore

Lindsay Ballenger

Lindsay Ballenger was recovering in a quiet room at the shelter. Maria also gave her a phone, which she usually did not do for those who sought help at the shelter. She feared them calling their abuser; out of fear, to report where they were. She did not think that Lindsay Ballenger would do that after their conversation. The Ballenger woman also had a responsibility to the department for which she worked.

True to form, she reached for the phone and began to dial. Jimmy Ennis lifted the receiver at the other end.

"Hi boss."

"Hello Lindsay, how are you?"

"I'm gonna be fine sir, found a wonderful new friend in Maria here."

"Maria at the Shelter?"

"Yep, I finally took the step and she's a big help."

"That's great."

"I'll need you in as soon as you can get back Lindsay."

"I know sir, and I'll get back as soon as my face stops scaring people. I got pretty beat up again, sir, and it really hurts right now."

"Well you just keep in touch Lindsay; we'll all get you through this."

"Just don't contact that jerk again, please."

"You got that right sir. No way am I going to contact him."

"Good Lindsay. Keep in touch ok."

"Will do sir, and thanks so much again for your help and understanding."

"You bet Lindsay. You just get yourself back together, I need you here."

"Thanks sir. Goodbye."

"Goodbye Lindsay."

Lindsay Ballenger put down the phone and lay back in the bed staring at the ceiling. The shadows danced above her head as she allowed her weary eyes to close peacefully for the first time in days.

Damon Mulcahey

Ellie came into the room wearing a smile from ear to ear. She just finished hanging pictures in the bedroom and was extremely satisfied with the results. Her husband Damon was finishing a conversation with a fellow wannabe meteorologist. He smiled back at his wife as he hung up the receiver.

"Just spoke with Teddy Dunn," he mentioned casually to his wife.

"About the weather I suppose," she responded with a laugh.

"Yes, about the weather."

"I've been invited to visit the Marseilles, IL weather station and I'm leaving in about an hour."

"Good for you."

"Isn't that about an hour south of us, honey?" Ellie coyly commented as if she didn't know.

"Yeah, you remember the place where all the radar tracking is done for Illinois and much of the Midwest."

"Sure I remember, maybe you can share some of that knowledge you've been storing with those guys out there."

"Don't be condescending, honey," he responded.

"Not doing that honey."

"I just know how wrapped up you are about this unusual weather front."

Damon kissed his wife and headed to the bedroom to change for the hour-long drive to Marseilles.

Ellie picked up the phone to call her friend Maria at the Shelter. It was Friday and she wanted to verify that their usual get together was on for this evening. Maria answered at the other end and confirmed the gathering for the evening at Sparky's Bar and Grill.

The drive to Marseilles was effortless on the clear sunny day. Damon arrived at the weather station after the long drive on Highway 80. He was greeted at the parking lot by a guard who recognized him from previous visits. Still, he was asked for identification, which he quickly provided.

Upon entering the building, he was escorted to the room with the large screen arrays of digital weather maps on the walls.

Blaine Discher greeted him warmly as he led Damon over to one of the computer screens. Pointing to the two divergent fronts approaching the area, they both watched the screen as Blaine Discher tapped on the computer keys to show the expected effects of the approaching fronts. Damon let out a low whistle as the fronts merged on the screen. For a moment, both men stood motionless without sound.

Damon Mulcahey looked at Discher. Discher nodded his head in quiet assent to the unspoken question.

"It's gonna be a hum dinger, unlike anything we've seen before. Another unusual aspect of this is the air in the Jet stream up above. It's already acting unusual and unpredictable. Several airline pilots have reported extreme changes during flights in the last few hours. At one moment the wind would be pushing the aircraft at a high rate of speed, in a short time, they would be bucking headwinds with the same velocity and speed. Something very unusual was going on in the upper air as well as with the ground level movement and pressures," Blaine Discher commented.

Discher told Damon Mulcahey that he had already been in touch with the National Weather Service who confirmed unusual air mass build ups and wind velocity. All were in doubt as to the cause. They were also very concerned about the effect of the changing air masses. The single point of agreement was that there was a storm brewing of monumental proportions that would include thunder, rain and with the changing pressures within the air masses a potential for a significant pounding of damaging hail.

They were already considering grounding aircraft and not allowing flights into or out of the Midwest airports ranging from Minneapolis to St. Louis and through Illinois to Lake Michigan and Elkhart, Indiana. The FAA responded that they would consider the report and asked that they be kept abreast of the advancement of the potential storm. Representatives from the FAA did not seem alarmed in the least. They lacked concern for any real danger. The two men continued to look at projections of the storms while eliciting a number of remarks about the potential for damage and impact on the areas. The storms have picked up speed. They agreed the big blast would hit within eighteen hours with lesser storms before and after.

At the offices of Central Midwest Airlines, phones were ringing off the hook. The airline's operator was busy making reservations for regular customer as well as a completely new group who were making reservations for the first time. A majority of the reservations were for flights between small Midwestern City airports rather than the major airports. Officials thought the increase unusual, but welcomed the additional business. Arrangements were being made to lease a few additional planes to accommodate the additional traffic.

Cell phone systems were alive with traffic created by additional communications between drug dealers, suppliers and customers. All were hearing of pending shipments and wanted to make sure they were included in the distributions that might become available.

Police informants were reporting a high degree of additional information about pending drug deals. Detectives were assessing the reports and trying to determine a plan of action to deal with the situation. Those police on the inside who were associated with the drug kingpins were freely disseminating information about police plans.

At Marseilles, Damon Mulcahey was intently listening to the hastily set up conference between the National Weather Service and the Federal Aviation Administration. He was shocked at the lack of serious intent to act by the FAA administrators. It seemed to be a matter of "all right, you've done your job." The impression around the weather station was that the FAA was going to do nothing. Flustered by the lack of interest, some of the officials at the weather station took it upon themselves to call the major airlines and inform them with information that the FAA didn't seem to feel was important. As expected, airline officials commented about taking the warning under advisement.

A number of abandoned warehouses on the West and South sides of the City were readied for deliver and storage. Plans were in place for the deliveries, acceptance, packaging and distribution to the Chicagoland area as well as shipment to other cities. In all the operation was taking on huge proportions.

Monica

The morning air was damp from the light rainfall. Frank Bellini started the motor on the small boat as Webster also jumped onto the craft. Together they watched, as the shore loomed closer while the boat made its way to the pier. He tied the borrowed boat to the pier. The two companions, walked to the shack where "Salty" stayed. He was the watchman for the boats in the harbor.

He slipped a hundred-dollar bill into Salty's rugged hand as he asked to use the phone. With a gleeful smile, the old mariner waved an introduction to the phone on the desk. Lifting the receiver, Frank Bellini called the limo service he had used quite often in his previous life. The dispatcher listened and explained the rates. Frank Bellini didn't care as he told the dispatcher he would be paying cash and wanted the car and chauffeur for 6 hours.

The sleek limo pulled up within fifteen minutes and Frank directed the driver to a barbershop on the near West Side. While the limo waited, Frank ran in and told the barber to give him a quick trim. With the way Frank looked, it took a little more than a quick trim to get him looking presentable again. The task was accomplished in fifteen minutes and he was out the door. The next stop was Northwestern Memorial Hospital. There was a bit of hesitancy on the part of the chauffeur at being alone with a mean looking dog in the car. A fifty-dollar bill quieted any further comment from the chauffer. Within a few quick turns, they were on their way to pick up the woman at the hospital.

As they reached the hospital the clock on the building showed 10:00. Frank used the cell phone again to call the woman's room. Upon recognizing the voice on the other end of the line, the woman known as Monica was in disbelief. It took a few minutes for Frank Bellini to ease the tension, but he was well practiced in the art of selling and did a very nice job of convincing the woman that he was acting in her best interest.

He explained Harmony Shelter and the appointment for her there. She could stay until the baby was born and he told her of a few other facts that made the woman feel more at ease. The Monica woman looked at the phone as Frank hung up and wondered how all this good fortune had decided to shine on her. Considering she had very few alternatives, she agreed to leave the hospital with him and go to the Shelter as he described.

The wheelchair driver took her to the exit where she looked through the window and noticed the large limousine sitting in the driveway. Frank joined her at the door and helped her to the car.

As she looked inside, she was immediately fearful of the large animal sitting with its tongue hanging out. Frank did his best to assure her that Webster was friendly. She looked at the dog and did get the feeling that it was not going to harm her. She hoped that was true. She climbed into the comfortable seat as the driver closed the door behind her. Frank joined her from the other side.

The driver pulled away from the hospital and headed toward the address Frank provided earlier. He and the woman exchanged small talk as she continued to wonder what was going on. She figured she could be in a worse situations than this and settled back to enjoy the ride to her new temporary home.

As they pulled into the back alley of the building, Monica's suspicions immediately sharpened. The driver opened the door and Frank helped her out of the car. Webster remained in the car, which made her feel a little more comfortable. She heard a pleasant voice from the upper porch.

"Hello there, welcome."

It was Maria Esparza, the Shelter Director.

Immediately, all her fears subsided as she walked slowly up the wooden porch steps to the smiling face watching her.

"Hi there, I'm Maria Esparza," please take your time. We don't have an elevator yet."

"Hello Maria, my name for now is Monica."

Maria laughed.

"I know dear, Frank explained everything to me."

"Come in and let's get you situated."

With a smile and a shake of her hand, she admonished Frank to leave.

Maria also shook Frank Bellini's hand and the comforting warm feeling again was felt by both.

"Bye for now," was his retort as he turned to retrace his steps down to the waiting car.

"Frank?" Monica exclaimed quickly.

"Yes?"

"Thank you for what you've done for me."

"No sweat," Frank responded.

"I'll call later to check on you."

"I'd like that Frank."

"Bye!"

"Bye!"

Maria led the woman inside to one of the neatly made-up rooms. As the woman had no baggage or clothing, Maria opened a box and presented a number of necessities to the woman. Comb, hairbrush, toothpaste, toothbrush, bath towel, and washcloth, as well as a few other feminine necessities, were included.

"Why don't you freshen up and take a shower. Then we'll sit and talk for a bit."

"That would be wonderful," the woman responded.

"I could use a clean up," she added.

"Go ahead; let me know if you require any assistance."

"Thank you Maria, you are so very kind."

With that, Maria left the woman and went to the kitchen to prepare some food.

Frank returned to the limousine and directed the driver to take him to an address on the South side of the city. He again counted the money. Webster looked on as if genuinely interested in how much money there was. Maybe he thought that part of it was his, since he grabbed the bag in the first place.

212

He decided there was enough to make a few small investments that could reap considerable returns. After all, he had always been able to make money. Making money was his specialty. His specialty was Options at the Midwest Exchange. He was going to take advantage of what he knew now. The next few days were going to be fun playing the market again. The limousine pulled up in front of the address and Frank told the driver to grab some lunch. He'd be back in a half-hour. With that, he handed the driver $20.00 and entered the building. Webster stayed in the limo.

Maria and Monica

The two women were chatting amicably when the doorbell rang. The Monica woman immediately jumped at the sound of the buzzer. Maria quickly placed her hand on the woman's arm. Both women, at the touch, felt the warm charge pass between them. Maria's mind raced as she felt the electricity between them. Darn it she thought. She did not mean that to happen.

"I think it's the Doctor," she said quickly, trying to ease the obvious anxiety of the woman."

"One of my friends is a Doctor, and he asked a friend to stop by to check up on you. It's also a requirement of the Shelter for any new arrival to have a Doctor's exam."

With that, the woman began to relax.

Maria opened the door and greeted Doctor Milano. She had known him from the hospital and he was a very highly respected Pediatrician.

The Doctor joined the women and sat with them. He asked the Monica a few questions and the three continued their conversation.

It wasn't five minutes, before Monica made a loud exclamation of pain.

"Oh my God," she exclaimed suddenly.

"It's coming, I can feel it."

"My water just broke. Oh I'm scared, help me."

Doctor Milano was on his feet immediately.

With Maria's help, they walked the woman to the bedroom and the bed.

Dr.Milano began to examine her as Maria went to prepare, what would be needed for the birth. They both knew there was no time for an ambulance.

Maria called one of the on-call nurses that were at the Shelter and the nursee came right over.

The birth was unbelievably swift. No more than a half-hour passed and the baby was breathing for the first time outside the womb. Doctor Milano examined the baby and pronounced the newborn boy healthy.

Maria wanted Monica to visit the hospital with the baby, but she would have none of it. No way was she going to a hospital again. She had no insurance and the baby was already born. She saw no need to complicate things by going to a hospital again just after she left one. Doctor Milano conferred with Maria and they decided to leave Monica in the capable hands of the nurse.

The Shelter was well prepared for birthing, with all the necessities at hand. Doctor Milano had even helped with the selection and purchase of the items required. In addition, the stranger had left the mysterious gifts of the baby crib and blankets almost as if knowing what was going to happen. As Maria opened the box, she lifted the crib and blankets. The ice crystals were still there. She reached in to touch them. They remained as cold as could be. They hadn't melted. She left them in the box and returned to the room, with the crib and blankets. She told Monica she could remain at the shelter provided she was examined daily, for the next couple of days. Monica gratefully agreed.

One of the nurse psychologists would be coming in for her shift in a short time. She was going to see Lindsey Ballenger and then could look in on Monica. Maria relaxed at the thought. Everything was going to be all right. Monica's memory loss bothered both Maria and Doctor Milano. They agreed to ask one of the professionals on call to stop by to determine the severity of the memory loss.

Chapter 25 Building Perils

Watching with Interest

Planes, cars and boats were being directed to specific locations at certain times, to prepare for the upcoming events. All was done on a need to know basis to avoid excess knowledge from being conveyed to authorities.

The upcoming weather change was watched with interest, as it would provide cover for the operation, limiting the ability of authorities to move and see the intended plan coordination.

Damon Mulcahey

Damon and his friends were watching the approaching storms with intrigue and interest. They had developed prognostications as to the location and path of the pending winds and rain. All involved believed that this would be a potentially damaging event. It would affect the City of Chicago, as well as many cities in surrounding areas of Illinois and Indiana.

Major news stations were also aware of the approaching weather phenomenon. They were announcing the uniqueness of the situation to listeners on television and radio news. Officials and Community Leaders in Chicago and the suburbs developed emergency plans to deal with injuries or damage that might develop from the anticipated storm. The width and breadth of damage that could occur was mind blowing.

A Seiche?

Some forecasters were even telling listeners of the potential for a seiche on Lake Michigan. A seiche is a long wave motion in a lake, bay, or a similarly enclosed body of water. Thus, the water level will begin to fall on the left side and—at the same time—begin to rise on the right side. As the water reaches its highest level on the right side, it will reverse direction, moving toward the left side. The water level will then fall on the right side and rise on the left.

The last time one hit Chicago was on June 26, 1954. Those atmospheric ingredients resulted in a deadly tragedy killing a number of people. Some of the local residents were becoming quite alarmed and were deciding to vacate the area near the Lake. The exodus wasn't massive, but it was noticeable.

Lieutenant Brennan and the Chicago police brass were listening to the snitch tales, trying to sort fact from fiction. The high command wanted to know as much as possible about what was going on and had high-ranking officers meeting with patrol officers at district stations all over the city. They were planning a coup to present to the Mayor regarding a major drug bust and the round up of major dealers and contractors in the drug business. Phones were extremely active in the precincts as well as at headquarters at 11th and State. The DEA, FBI and Chicago Police all had boats plying the Lakeshore searching and waiting for suspicious craft to appear. The plan was to board any craft that they thought might be suspect. Communications equipment was active and the airways were filled with constant check-ins to headquarter locations. Even the boats of the Chicago Fire Department had officials from the DEA on board under an agreement with the Mayor and City Officials.

Cops on the take were also listening hard to what was being sifted through the police department planners. A hefty bonus could be expected for providing information that would protect their payoff sources from arrest. They actively sought information about planned busts and stakeouts. All types of information and data were passed. Some true, while much was simply fabrication to look good.

Terry Shuman and Arnie Boman were cops on the beat. They regularly collected their payoffs from the street pushers for looking the other way during trafficking of drugs on side streets and small shops on their beat. Today their awareness of other officers was paramount. They listened intently to the conversations of other officers; hoping to find some information regarding moves by the police, to use as a tip off, that would fatten their wallets. Because shootouts with druggies were rare, they salved their consciences about giving the drug people information about the moves the police would be taking. No one would be hurt, and consequently, they really wouldn't be hurting their fellow officers. That was their reasoning anyway.

On the Waterways

At some of the ports on the inland rivers, small boats were loading with boxes and packages. The contents weren't visible, but could be known or figured out if anyone cared to give it a thought. The packages were placed below decks and in hidden places. The weather was going to be a wonderful cover for the transport operation.

An old, yet beautifully redone Boston Whaler reversed its diesel engines as it backed away from the pier. The name "Lazy Daize" was painted tastefully on the aft board. Its teakwood and dark mahogany chart house presented a feast for the eyes of boaters. Many watched in awe as the boat plowed its way slowly toward Lake Michigan and back.

Boston Whalers possessed significant power from their dual diesels, to travel just about anywhere in the Great Lakes region. They were built to take a hard pounding from the seas off the East Coast of the United States. Their stamina was the best for the Midwest lakes. The "Whaler" would be ideal for the job at hand. That would be, moving drugs to the shores of Indiana's Far Eastern shore, waiting to move the valuable cargo to other distribution points. The same type of scene was being re-enacted on many of the connecting waterways in Illinois. Boats of all shapes and sizes were taking part in the disbursement as small delivery trucks arrived and left after depositing their cargo. All was going according to plan.

Small planes began arriving at little airports in the far suburbs from Union to Pontiac in Illinois. They landed and unloaded their cargoes into vans and trucks. At the Union airport, the airport director was somewhat surprised at the increased number of landings. Three times as many small planes were visiting the airport than usually used the small airfield sixty miles northwest of Chicago. The trucks that were being loaded from the small planes all had small business decals from heating suppliers to construction companies. All of this transport seemed common. This was one of the ways; small companies received supplies and equipment in the outlying areas.

At small out of the way offices and warehouses throughout the city, men and women were preparing for the arrival of distributor cars and trucks to be loaded with the hoards of boxes and bags that were lying in stacks inside. The Chicago police had learned long ago that drug dealers plied their trade in multiple locations and settings throughout the city. The supply of drugs always seemed endless too.

Drivers of cars and trucks were given small slips of paper with a time written for them to be at a specific location. In many cases, the location was simply a place for further contact. Drivers were given further instructions. Secrecy was paramount.

The Chicago police and FBI were very active. They already began to make arrests in the hope of finding out more information about the deliveries and drop offs that were being planned. In some cases, the accused had turned informant and provided information about the plans that were in place. Elaborate plans were developed for intercepting shipments and following drivers to their appointed locations.

The Boston Whaler plowed slowly through the ugly green waters of the Illinois River toward Lake Michigan. Many other boats that came from various locales were also in the water, wending their way to open water ahead, for a day of pleasure on the lake. The Whaler's hold contained a number of five-foot rolls of vinyl pipe, capped at each end. The term "deck rails" was stamped prominently on the white painted surface of the canisters. Inside the twenty rolls, bags of white cocaine lay crammed into the opening with packaging at each end indicating "top" on one end and "bottom" at the other. It was a common method of transport and highly lucrative for the owners.

On this trip, the valuable cargo was estimated to be $1 million. The Whaler made the trip to the far side of Indiana on a weekly basis. The captain and crew were well known as suppliers of quality materials for expensive crafts. The cover worked beautifully, as the captain often exhibited high quality brass accoutrements for boat owners throughout the Great Lakes. When the craft reached the open waters of Lake Michigan, there would be meetings with a couple other craft to transfer a few of the canisters.

Small business vans and delivery vehicles crisscrossed the city. Many businesses and warehouses anticipated deliveries. Although slightly overcast, the sun continued to shine, basking the city in light and warmth, during the early hours of the afternoon. The approaching storm seemed to have stalled south and west of Illinois. A light rain fell on parts of far southern Illinois, and to the west in Iowa and Missouri. It was nothing of the proportion that was predicted. Weather forecasters were scratching their heads at the phenomenon. The storm should have been rushing to the area inundating everything with rain and strong winds. Many of the boaters laughed as they looked at the lightly clouded sky and the shining sun. Looking to the West, the sky also appeared clear as they prepared for a day of fun on the Lake.

At the Marseilles weather station, the first warning of the storm front moving appeared on the radar screens. A stunned look appeared on the face of the Station manager as one of the women at the screen let out a small scream as she watched the picture on her screen. The storm front seemed to jump without warning and was moving at alarming speed through Southern Illinois. Within seconds, it had traveled a hundred miles and its speed seemed to be increasing.

Within minutes of the surprised happening on the weather screen at Marseilles, rain began to fall on the Illinois River. The skipper of the sturdy Boston Whaler on Lake Michigan looked up at the sky as cloud cover increased. The boat just cleared the river locks as it steered East on Lake Michigan with many other small craft in the water spurting plumes of spray as they dashed about joyfully. It was only a few minutes since he last glanced skyward to feel the warm rays of the sun shining through a partly cloudy sky. Now the sky was turning dark with amazing speed.

Chapter 26 Danger In The Air

Flying High Flying Low

A Cessna banked and began to descend, as instructed for its approach, to the small airport in Union, IL. The flight controller's voice was familiar, as the pilot followed instructions for landing the small plane. The pilot was anxious to unload his precious cargo of drugs and pills that would be turned into fortunes for the dealers. He could see the waiting van parked below. A light rain began to fall, but it wasn't causing a problem for the small plane. The pilot knew he would be on the ground in just minutes, far ahead of any serious weather. The landing was routine as the pilot backed off the throttle and taxied to a quiet area of the airport. The pilot called the small tower with a request for a fuel truck. The tower operator acknowledged the request and picked up the phone to call the fuel truck driver.

"Cessna requests fuel," the tower operator said dryly.

"I'll tell Jake when he gets back," the voice responded.

"Okay, make sure you tell him."

The helper hung up and went out to the fuel truck, got in and started up the truck. He started the vehicle moving forward then stopped after a short distance and thought better of doing a refueling on his own. He got out and went back to continue working on his car in the garage.

The pilot headed for a pit stop at the small deli to get a sandwich and use the restroom. He saw the fuel truck driver get into the truck and start toward his plane as he hastened his walk.

When he returned to his plane at the field, he watched as a white Muenstat Electric Company truck approached from the side road.

They arrived at the same time. After a short exchange of pleasantries, the driver of the van unloaded the boxes from the plane, placing them gingerly in the back of the van. The driver reached into his pocket and presented an envelope to the pilot. The pilot opened the envelope and surveyed the money inside. Satisfied, they shook hands receiving a sudden icy feeling, they quickly pulled their hands away. Neither mentioned the incident. They waved good-bye and Cessna pilot opened the cockpit door, placing the envelope in his travel bag. He climbed in and pulled the door shut. The pilot picked up the cell phone to call his girlfriend.

"Hey, hi," she answered.

"Hi to you," he said. "Where would you like to go tonight, I'm in a mood to celebrate."

"Can I dress up and we can go to an expensive restaurant?"

"Oh yeah," he responded.

"Oh, that will be great. When will you be home?"

"I'm taking off now and should be at Pewaukee airport in an hour."

"Good, I'll jump in the shower now."

"Okay, see you soon."

A large smile shone on the pilot's face as he turned the key to start the engine. He reached down to pat the envelope again before pushing the throttle of the small plane forward.

The tower operator finished filling out the supplies request form and reached for the phone.

"Did you refuel that Cessna?"

"I didn't know the Cessna wanted fuel, the fuel operator replied.

"I told that helper of yours," the tower operator replied.

"Didn't get the message and I don't see him around.

"Well he does need fuel and seems to be in a hurry. Can you get over there right away?"

"Will do," was the quick response.

The driver replaced the receiver and lit a cigarette as he walked over toward the fuel truck. Stopping well short of the truck, he turned and looked up as the sky. The phone rang again. He quickly retraced his steps and jogged to get the call at the hanger.

As he picked up the phone, his wife reminded him of their shortage of money. The man stood listening to the common complaint. As he listened, the seething began as it usually did, at listening to the constant complaint, about not having enough money. He took a couple deep drags on the cigarette and flung it away.

"OK honey, I know."

"I'm working on it, yes."

"We'll talk more tonight," he said

"OK, bye for now."

The man turned and began walking toward the fuel truck. He thought a moment, and decided to head for the restroom.

A Fateful Flight

At the tower, an argument ignited between the field owner and the tower operator. The discussion became heated, as the two men argued with each other. The radio receiver in the small tower buzzed. The operator lifted the receiver to take the call. It was the Cessna pilot.

"Requesting wind speed and direction"

"South to Southwest at 10," came the reply.

"Permission to taxi for takeoff?"

"You got it Cessna 22X17."

"Take off at your pleasure."

"Roger tower."

The small plane moved toward the end of the runway. As the pilot turned, he pushed the throttle forward to begin his takeoff. The small plane jumped forward as the pilot pushed the throttle to its limit of travel.

The fuel truck driver finished his business and jumped into his truck. He drove toward the fueling area. He looked twice as the small Cessna turned at the runway and began its takeoff. Surprise took over as the driver watched the small plane begin to accelerate down the runway. His hand began to reach for the truck phone but slowed as he watched the small plane gather speed for takeoff. Must not have needed the fuel he thought as he began to turn the truck around at the end of the fueling area. He continued to watch the plane.

As the plane began to pick up speed, the pilot smiled silently to himself. A few thousand dollars was a nice little sum, for flying a few hundred miles to make a delivery. He was enjoying every moment. His eyes focused on the runway, as the plane approached take off speed. He began to raise the yoke as the indicator told him he was moving fast enough to take off.

As the front wheel lifted from the solid surface of the runway, the engine sputtered. The pilot looked quickly at the gauges. "Holy…" The frightening thought struck him like a load of concrete. He had forgotten to check the fuel before taking off. He fought for control as the small plane lost altitude with its engine missing.

The pilot thought quickly. If he could gain more altitude, he could do a quick turn around and land again. His thoughts told him that would not be possible as he heard the engine sputtering. He fought the urge to push the yoke down to land again, as he was too far down the runway to stop before running into the traffic on the busy highway in front of him. He decided for the fly around and pulled back gently on the wheel as if to coax the plane up higher into the air. The effort proved futile as the nose began to dip toward the ground.

He said a silent prayer as he watched a large truck coming down the highway, their paths converging. Watching helplessly, his hands gripped the wheel tightly as the impact approached.

He closed his eyes, as the load of lumber appeared to close on him with alarming quickness. The impact impaled his body onto the wheel as he felt the push against his chest. His head was thrust forward as it smashed into the windshield. The pain lasted only a second as the rest of the plane compressed his already lifeless body into pulp.

The impact of the Cessna had little effect on the trailer. As the driver hit the brakes, the trailer continued its sideways travel as the wheels locked. The long trailer spun around toward the front of the truck. It came to a halt in the reverse position from where it started. The cab of the truck and trailer stopped facing the oncoming lane of traffic in a perfect U-turn. As the driver looked out the window, there was no traffic coming toward him on the road. Not knowing what had truly happened to the small plane other than the collision, the driver hurriedly got out of the truck to investigate. He grabbed flares to set up on the road in front and behind of the vehicle.

Not far away was a State Police Highway station. As the accident was taking place, a couple of the State Police officers watched in amazement from the nearby rest stop, as the small plane disintegrated into the side of the trailer.

The remnant of the plane was barely visible. It had buried itself into the pile of wood. The panel van with Muenstat Electric Company's sign on the side, reached the highway from the airport drive. The driver saw the impact just up the road. He turned the steering wheel and decided to turn east for his trip back to the city. He failed to see the semi coming off the tollway. The panel van pulled out into the path of the truck. The semi driver applied the brakes too late to avoid the collision. The crash killed the van driver. The semi driver was extremely upset, but unhurt.

Muenstat Electric

As the afternoon sun passed to the West, drug trafficking activity continued to increase. The vans of Muenstat Electric crossed the city with their valuable cargoes. People were getting richer by the moment as delivery after delivery was made. Some of the drugs were being warehoused, while others were transported to other locations for further movement in and out of the City.

The police and FBI were active. Many of the snitches were being threatened into telling what they knew about what was going on. Police were actively making arrests throughout the city on the tips they received.

Lawyers' phones had begun ringing with calls from busted drug pushers and dealers needing legal help. Bail bondsmen were having a field day.

Wanda Benefice's office was a chaotic scene, thriving with activity. Junior lawyers were scurrying about, looking for records of defendants that the firm was being called to represent. Upstairs in the head offices, some of the Partners in the firm were becoming a little jittery at the number of cases developing that the firm would have to represent. After all, the firm had a name that might become tarnished or even targeted if the Government and law officials felt they had a selective interest in representing people associated with drugs.

Many law firms wanted some of this business; because it was so lucrative. Each also needed to be careful, that they didn't become known in profile, as representing large numbers of people tied to the drug industry. Independent lawyers were also thriving on the potential, as the number of arrests mounted.

Wanda Benefice absent-mindedly stated, "This is a grand day for the lawyer profession." Lori Boby, her assistant, struggled with the unending stream of phone calls, as she scribbled notes for later delivery to her boss.

Although the police department arrest focus was in high gear, there remained some police loyal to the payoffs of the drug industry. They continued to look the other way and in many cases began to grab small time pushers and users who were in most cases unknown on the streets. This allowed those police to show they were doing their job.

Frank Bellini

Breaking his train of thought, Frank Bellini reached into his pocket for the cell phone. To his surprise it still worked. It would be his last call though, as the possibility of tracking was becoming much too dangerous. He called The Shelter and Maria Esparza answered on the other end.

"Hi Maria, how is Monica doing?"

"Pretty well thanks to you Frank," was the thoughtful reply.

"Can I speak with her please?"

"Frank, I told you we don't like our people to talk with outsiders. After making the statement, she thought for a moment. But since she's special you should know something."

"Her baby was born this morning."

"She and the baby are doing fine and will be staying here for the time being."

Frank Bellini was surprised and exhibited the excitement in his tone.

"That's wonderful, he responded quickly."

"Monica asked about you Frank."

"Ahuh," was the only reply he could make.

"Why don't you come by tomorrow morning and plan a short visit with her. I think it will do her good."

"I'll do that Maria, thank you."

"OK then, see you tomorrow Frank, but please call first."

"Will do, and thanks again."

Maria hung up the phone and put her finger to her cheek wondering what was going to happen to the woman and her baby.

Frank Bellini walked down the street. He deleted the phone numbers in the call logs and deftly dropped the phone in one of the huge waste containers at the corner. He decided to visit his investment agent and hailed a passing cab for the trip to the offices. By his calculations, he should have a tidy sum built from his investment selections.

The cab pulled up in front of the office and Frank paid the driver a handsome tip as he exited the cab and pulled open the door to the building. Inside, he made a beeline for his investment advisor, who noticed him coming and quickly rose to meet him. The investment person was gushing with the good news, which Frank had already been able to determine. They talked for a while and Frank left more instructions for additional investments. He also asked for a check for $25,000.00. The investment person was ecstatic shaking Frank's hand until his arm became strained when he gave him the check. Frank Bellini smiled and left the investment company offices.

Frank's Friend Norah

The homeless woman ambled slowly down the street; her breathing more labored than ever. Her heart was giving out from fighting the increasing buildup of liquid in her chest and she knew it. There would only a matter of time before her tired heart would give out.

She heard the squeak of brakes and looked toward the street. A car pulled up alongside. She instinctively moved away from the curb as it stopped. The window rolled down as she saw the clean nicely contoured face of Frank Bellini looking out and calling to her. She was able to stifle a laugh at the sight of her street friend. She had never seen him shaven before, but the look in his eyes was rare and unmistakable. "Come on Norah, get in."

"Are you crazy Frank Bellini?" She asked.

"Nope. You need some help, and we're going to get it."

"Oh sure, got a few grand there Frank?"

"Whatever you're gonna need, I've got, Norah. Get in."

With a small laugh, she shrugged her shoulders.

"What the hell Frank Bellini, where are you taking me?" She joined him in the car.

Norah was no raving beauty, yet she shone from within. Frank Bellini learned firsthand that the woman's heart was golden. When he first arrived on the streets, in a state of total confusion and despair, she befriended him. Under her tutelage, he quickly learned how to survive. He owed her a large debt of gratitude.

He also knew how she would always find a way to help someone in need. When a friend needed some money, she would scour the alleys and streets with a bag lady mentality to find objects of value. She would give, sell or trade these to help friends. She was relentless in her quest, to make things better for her people, as she referred to her friends. Frank knew that she would be rewarded some day and he wanted today to be one that she would remember. A friend would give her something back for the good she did for him.

They drove to Northwestern Memorial Hospital. It wasn't very far away, and walked into the emergency room. Frank Bellini took charge. Before anyone knew it, the Heart Specialist on duty was examining Norah. A few hours later after a number of tests, the diagnosis was congestive heart failure. The doctor recommended some X-rays and more blood tests. Frank Bellini gave the billing clerk a Cashier's Check for $25,000 dollars with the comment that.

"If you need more, I have it."

"Are you employed sir?"

"Well, I'm self employed," Frank responded.

"I'll need a certified financial statement then"

"Just happen to have one with me," Frank said.

Reaching into his pocket, he produced the financial statement of his holdings from the recent investments. The balance was sizable to say the least. It was certainly enough to satisfy the clerk. The statement was certified, as a "True Copy", by an official of the Investment firm.

"Will you sign a guarantee of payment for the patient sir?"

"Of course."

The clerk reached for the keyboard completed a few lines on the computer and the printer whirred.

Frank Bellini scanned the form, signed it and handed the form back to the clerk.

The clerk issued a receipt and Norah was admitted to the hospital for treatment.

Lindsay Ballenger

Lindsey stepped from her room and walked down the hallway toward the kitchen. She stopped by the open door of a woman known as Monica. She sneaked a peek at the newborn baby resting peacefully in the small, crib by the woman's bed. It brought a smile to her face, as she nodded and continued down the hallway.

Looking into the refrigerator, Lindsay lifted the container of orange juice and poured a glass for herself. She noticed the weathercaster on the television. The woman was tracing the path of an approaching storm and her words were expressing caution about being outside, when the storm approached. She thought of calling her boss, Jimmy Ennis, but decided she was in no shape to be of any help.

The Storm

Winds increased in speed as temperatures began a quick descent on the thermometer. Clouds rushed toward the city as the storm seemed to magnify quickly all around the city. Over the lake, the winds were swirling too.

At the weather observation posts, it appeared as though two storms were converging on Chicago. The situation appeared quickly and bulletins were sent to all media outlets; informing them to alert the public, to the imminent danger.

Flight 238

On its approach to O'Hare airport, the lumbering 747 jet was gently gliding towards runway 27L, (the left runway of the two west facing runways at O'Hare Field). Only a thousand feet of altitude and three miles of distance separated it from a smooth touchdown and the end of a long flight.

Without warning, the wind at 900 feet above the ground suddenly shifted from a quartering headwind to a very strong tailwind. Airspeed was bleeding off rapidly and ground speed was dramatically increasing as the tailwind pushed the giant jet from behind as if it were a feather. The red "STALL" lights on the glare shield above the instrument panels lit immediately and the computerized voice from the cockpit speakers could be heard all the way back in the upper deck gallery shouting, "STALL STALL," followed by a few seconds of silence then "STALL

STALL", could be heard for the second time. The situation was not good. The loudspeaker changed its warning to "WINDSHEAR WINDSHEAR" Both pilots were aware of the dire situation and trained for this in the simulator, but never this close to the ground.

As the Captain reached for the throttles, he disconnected the autopilot at the same time. He thought to himself,

"Lord help us, as heavy as she is, I don't know if we can save her from this altitude."

Samantha and Randy Marsten were on the plane returning from their short vacation. They became immediately aware of the change in flight speed. They sensed danger and grabbed each other's hands with a knowing look. Samantha remembered shaking hands with the pilot when he greeted the passengers coming aboard. She remembered the gentle warm flow between hers and the pilot's hands at the time.

Captain Newman pushed the throttles all the way up to the mechanical stops and the engines roared to full power. He rotated the nose to 15 degrees, nose up attitude on the artificial horizon and tried to hold it there. The *stick shaker*, (the warning for an impending stall, that starts a small device attached to the bottom of the control yoke, to physically vibrate the control column), started immediately, it's *"rada, rada, rada"* noise and vibration. When this happened, Captain Newman gently eased the yoke forward and dropped the nose to 10 degrees. "Dalton 238 O'Hare" the voice from the tower droned, "midfield winds are showing easterly 090 degrees at 50 knots". (Knots is short for nautical miles per hour)

"Roger", the copilot called back.

"We are experiencing a strong windshear at this time, we'll call you back."

The controllers knew what to do with the daunting information and immediately broadcast, "ALL FLIGHTS ON THIS FREQUENCY, WINDSHEAR HAS BEEN REPORTED ON APPROACH TO RUNWAY 27L, HOLD AT YOUR PRESENT POSITION AND ALTITUDE AND CALL APPROACH ON 119.87"

Airspeed was coming back, but at a very slow pace and they were still descending at an alarming rate..."800 feet"...."700 feet"..."600 feet" the copilot was shouting out, as he was trained, "airspeed 110 and increasing,"..."we are descending at 1000 feet per minute." The nose was now at 10 degrees and the *stick shaker* stopped. At a thousand feet per minute Captain Newman figured he had 30 seconds to stop the rate of descent or hit the ground hard and well short of the runway. He raised the nose again to 15 degrees to stop the downward rush of the Jumbo Jet. In a few seconds, the stick shaker activated with the *"rada", rada, rada, rada"* and he eased forward on the yoke again this time to 12 degrees, where the noise and vibrating stopped.

"500 feet"…."450 feet"…."400 feet..speed 125," the copilot called out.

He added. "and descent rate is now 200 feet a minute."

They were now one-quarter mile from the end of the runway and still in the windshear. O'Hare tower called, "Dalton 238 advise your intentions when able".

"Forget him," shouted the Captain, "I need your eyes glued to that instrument panel and just keep calling out airspeed and sink rate."

"Roger," shot back the copilot as he continued to scan the instrument panel.

"Speed 127 and sink 100", the copilot exclaimed…..speed 135, sink zero."

At the mention of "sink zero" Captain Newman shot a quick look out the window. They were only 150 feet from the end of the runway and the altimeter was showing only 100 feet above the ground, which meant that the main landing gear was only 50 feet above the approach lights.

Just as they passed over the end of the runway, the windshear strengthened and they dropped hard on the runway, slightly left of the centerline. As the wheels began to spin up, the spoilers on both wings were automatically commanded to full deployment. The Captain yanked hard on the thrust reverse levers and all four engines immediately responded with full reverse thrust. The nose came down hard onto the runway and luckily, they didn't blow out either nose tire. A few of the main gear tires blew on impact with the runway, but that would only affect the amount of braking they could apply. The Captain could see that they were eating up runway faster than he had ever seen and jumped on the brakes and commanded the copilot, "get on these brakes with me and see if you can't help me slow her down before we run off the end!" The copilot did as he was told and it seemed to help, as the plane started to slow. More tires blew as the heat from the brakes melted the fuse plugs in some of them, but it was working and it continued to slow.

"Make sure they called out the equipment and tell them to shoot these tires with foam as soon as we stop," The copilot picked up the microphone and started barking orders to the controller.

The huge plane came to a stop just 800 feet from the end of the runway and with the engines at idle, they let off the brakes while Captain Newman turned the nose wheels to 90 degrees to keep the jet from rolling any further forward. He did not want to set the brakes because the heat would have been so intense that a brake fire could occur. The copilot started the auxiliary power unit, put it on line and the Captain proceeded to shut down all four engines.

Samantha and Randy Marsten looked at each other, held hands and kissed. Randy commented.

"Well that landing was interesting." Samantha countered. "That was scary as all get out. We have to thank that pilot"

Captain Newman looked over at his copilot.

"You really did a great job. Thanks."

"Would you advise the airport of our situation and tell them we won't be using emergency evacuation procedures. Get the airport to send us stairways."

Before the Captain was finished, the copilot was on the phone with the controller updating Flight 238's condition and requesting assistance.

The Captain came out from the pilot's cabin and picked up the loudspeaker in the forward cabin.

"This is Captain Newman. I'm sure you're aware of another reason for wearing seat belts and I apologize for any discomfort during our landing. There is no need for an emergency evacuation. The airport will be sending us an airstair, which is a mobile stairway to exit the plane. We experienced what is known as windshear. This is a sudden phenomenon where strong winds suddenly develop without warning. We experienced a very unusual and sudden change of high wind direction and velocity, but we were able to land safely. I think we have a few flats, so we don't want to travel too far on the remaining tires. Our brakes are still pretty hot and that's why we'll be waiting for airstairs to disembark."

Samantha reached for her cell phone as soon as the plane landed. Her first call was to her dad to make sure everything was okay. Everything with him was fine, and they agreed to meet the following week. Her next call was to Harmony Place and Maria's private line. Maria answered as if nothing was happening with the weather. In fact, she was not aware of the approaching storm. Samantha guessed Maria had other things on her mind, like caring for over 20 women who required assistance. Maria asked Samantha to stop by and help her pick out a few necessities. Samantha agreed to stop by tomorrow.

Midway Airport

Two small planes left the commercial area of the airport. One of the pilots was curious about the situation, yet he didn't know what to make of it. One was a twin jet sabreliner and the other a twenty passenger, prop type aircraft. Both, had just been filled with deliveries from Muenstat Electronic and had no passengers, save the crew onboard. The pilots knew what their cargo was, and were wearing big smiles. The jet was headed for Canada, by way of Wisconsin and the other would be traveling to the Pocono area of Pennsylvania. Both hoped to get into the air before the approaching storm reached the airport area. With the precious drug cargoes, the owner pilots figured to have a very nice payday at the ends of their trips. Neither knew it, but that was not going to happen.

A 757, the largest aircraft the airport could handle, taxied toward the takeoff area. The pilot was in conversation with the tower controller. The 757 received permission to take off and reported a wall of water approaching the airport from the South. The plane took off without mishap.

The airport controller allowed the two small planes to approach the runway with the intent to take off immediately. They approached leading to the runway in tandem, as the air temperature began to drop precipitously lower. A light rain began to fall. The pilots were accustomed to this, and neither was bothered by the minor annoyance of the rain.

As the pilot of the sabreliner jet looked out the cockpit window, he noticed what appeared to be a wall of water approaching from the West. He looked up into the sky and continued to see nothing but the approaching wall of water. It was approaching quickly.

Both pilots tried to contact the tower controller without success. The airwaves were static.

The pilot of the prop aircraft noticed the strange phenomenon at the same time. The wall approached quickly as the light rain began to turn into pinging balls of hail. Both pilots watched out the cockpit windows. Each heard through the static, the airport controller tell them to stand by because of a weather front. They sat with engines running and nowhere to go as the hail began to increase in size at the end of the runway where they sat. Each watched the hail begin to pound the wings of their aircraft. The balls of hail also continued to increase in size.

Fear began to replace complacency as each of the pilots felt their aircraft shudder under the pounding. It grew more intense. Dents began

231

to appear in the wings of each aircraft and the hail continued to increase in size and fall with greater intensity. The wings began to wither under the heavy assault from the skies. The pilots were trapped at the end of the runway. There was no place to escape the intense assault from the hail. It grew louder and more intense.

In horror, the jet plane's pilot watched as pieces began to fall off the disintegrating wings. He could only imagine what impact the heavy balls of ice, was having on the rest of the aircraft. In another few seconds, the damage would be significant. He looked out the cockpit window as cracks began to appear. The pounding became so intense; the cockpit windows began to cave in under the unrelenting pressure. In the prop aircraft, the ceiling of the cockpit began to cave in over the pilot. The hail was pounding both aircraft.

The pilot in the jet looked up to the ceiling of the cockpit. He began to speak but the words became trapped in his mouth forever, as the ceiling crushed him under the relentless pounding of the large balls of hail. The aircraft became heavier than the wheels could hold as they exploded under the extreme weight boring down on the plane.

The prop plane was faring no better. The cockpit's protective covering disintegrated as the balls of stinging hail cut and gashed through the body of the pilot. In seconds, life ended. The wheels exploded as the plane slowly caved in toward the waiting ground. The pounding continued at the end of the runway. Both aircraft were being literally flattened, by the pounding of the icy onslaught. They crumpled into barely recognizable masses on the airport cement.

The controller's calls from the tower fell on deaf ears. No one could see what was happening at the end of the runway until the explosions. What was left of both planes exploded at the same time. The explosion was subdued by the amount of ice covering the remains of the aircraft.

As suddenly as it began, the hail stopped. The wall of water disappeared quickly. The controllers in the tower, had issued a warning to approaching aircraft, and ordered them to circle in dangerously close proximity to the airport. There had been no time to prepare for the emergency.

The controllers, who thought there would be two small aircraft at the end of the runway, looked and saw the runway clear. They began to allow the approaching aircraft to land, thus avoiding the dangerous condition that existed with the circling planes.

The controller who was guiding the two small aircraft looked bewildered toward the end of the runway and saw no aircraft. He called each of the pilots and received no response. Calling the chief controller over, he explained the situation that was taking place just before the strange storm hit.

The chief controller picked up the phone and called the airport firefighting unit to check out the end of the runway. When the fire department SUV reached the end of the runway, the radio cracked with an excited disbelieving voice.

"Ah, Unit 6 calling tower."

"Go ahead Unit 6."

"Ah, there are two small aircraft out here," was the tense response.

"OK, thanks," the controller replied.

"Ah, you don't understand sir," the voice replied.

"What's that?"

"Ah well sir, the two planes are crushed right down smack on the approach apron."

"What?" The tower chief asked.

"You have to see this to believe it sir."

"They are flat against the cement sir. Engines and all. Completely flat."

"What the…" the chief controller responded.

"Please get someone out here sir."

"Alright Unit 6, remain on station until a supervisor arrives."

"Yes sir."

The conversation ended as the two firefighters alighted from the vehicle to get a closer look at what was left of the two planes. Neither could believe what they saw. The rest of the airport personnel wouldn't believe it either. No one could imagine this type of destruction to an aircraft on the ground. No one.

The strange phenomenon also took place at a few of the outlying airports. Aircraft simply crushed to unrecognizable proportions while other planes remained unscathed. Such a selective destructive force was beyond the comprehension of those who witnessed the results. For the moment, flights were allowed to land, but no takeoffs were allowed at the airport, until some sense of the situation was made.

St. Rita's Harmony Place

Maria and the others were listening to the weather forecasts with concern. The wind was blowing and hail was coming down all around the shelter. Strangely, the Shelter was remaining unscathed by the storm. All of the women came together to watch the events on the television and some listened on the radio as well.

The newscasts were telling of situations about planes destroyed and trucks being smashed to unrecognizable forms. All knew that something drastic was happening. They remained scared at what might happen to their own safety

Sydney and Damon

Damon called for the fifth time in an hour, begging Sydney to come down to join him at the Marseilles weather station. She finally agreed and went down to the car. It began to rain as she exited the parking garage and continued through her entire trip to Marseilles. Upon arrival, she was greeted warmly, by all the employees. Damon gave his wife a big kiss in front of everyone, after which Sydney turned a lighter shade of pale. It dawned on her, why the tumultuous greeting. Of course, she was the only woman there. She laughed at recognizing the reason for the cheerful outburst from the men.

Ellie and Jimmy Ennis

The two became quite the pair. Everywhere they went; they were greeted warmly and made to feel perfectly welcome. They were invited to a soiree at the top of the John Hancock building restaurant. It was an invitation only affair and Ellie felt proud to be invited, along with the handsome fire captain.

Chapter 27 Atonement And Retribution

The Last Martini

The classy female stockbroker slid into the Classic 70 Red Mustang convertible. Her long trim legs were catching the attention of anyone who saw her today.

She wore a pleated celery skirt and matching jacket accented by a yellow, silk, button down blouse. With her yellow heels, the woman looked like a Vogue model.

She had been through a grueling day at the office and needed something to get her into a better frame of mind. Although clouds were overhead, she lowered the top, gunned the engine and headed for the Near North restaurant parking lot where she and many like her stopped on Fridays to pick up their supply of "coke" for the weekend.

The woman satisfied her habit a few times a week, always stopping for her martini and her "lift". She was looking forward to another mind-blowing experience at her fave night spot, after the effect of the drugs took over.

Pulling into the parking lot, she eyed the attendant with a nod and proceeded to the special parking space right near the door. The attendant nodded at the lithesome woman with wishful eyes. She laughed to herself at the look from the impetuous young man.

"No way mister," she said to herself, "you wouldn't even have a chance on my worst day". She tossed the attendant the keys and motioned for him to put the top up. He nodded and opened the car to satisfy her wish. On the way to the door, she jumped back as a large dog that seemed to come from nowhere, crossed her path. She stopped to catch her breath as the animal's eyes met hers and it sidled up against her for the briefest moment. The dog quickly continued down the street.

Inside, she walked straight to the bar and nodded to the bartender. Within a few seconds, a very dry, Bombay martini with a red pimento olive was in front of her, with a glass of Perrier water for accompaniment.

She took a sip and glanced around the room. It was beginning to fill with patrons. Some she knew and nodded in recognition. Others she eyed and toyed with as she displayed her legs, letting her skirt ride high enough to garner the men's interest. She loved doing the "don't you wish" act on the men who cast lustful glances her way. She found she could keep their attention to the point of distraction and it made her feel very much in charge.

Her need for the night's rush became more prevalent. Recognizing it, the woman took a few more sips of the Bombay martini and dropped a twenty-dollar bill on the bar. With a quick slide from the stool, a few quick steps brought her to the door. She walked out into the damp night air feeling the significant drop in temperature since she arrived. She shivered and walked toward her car as the parking attendant approached. He opened the door and she slipped easily into the front seat providing another notable display of her legs to the attendant.

The attendant handed her a small pouch. She took the pouch as she put a hundred-dollar bill into his waiting hand. He smiled, she winked. The woman started the car and easily backed out of the parking place near the door. As she shifted the red convertible into a forward gear, she noticed the small yet hard balls that suddenly began to fall with increasing intensity. As she watched, the front window suddenly disintegrated. She felt the stinging little balls pounding against her shoulders, arms and legs. She looked out the side to see the attendant falling to his knees under the impact of hail that seemed to increase in size, reaching critical damage stage. A few of his regular customers were also feeling the impact of the hail as they tried to scurry inside.

The hail increased in intensity as she saw the hood of the car dented repeatedly by the impact. She felt helpless and tried to climb into the back seat for protection. The downpour of hail changed direction and followed through the open front window pounding her relentlessly. She tried to cover herself in vain. Her legs were bleeding and she reached up her arms and hands to cover her face. Nothing protected her from the relentless pounding. She saw the attendant crumple and remain still. His body absorbed the full impact of the large hail falling in a wall around them. The car's convertible canvas gave way, opening the interior and her to the pounding. She lost consciousness as the hail folded the car in its center, filling the interior with large icy crystals. The bag of "coke" remained in her lap.

The roof of the restaurant began to buckle under the sheer volume of ice that was falling from the sky. Customers scattered in every direction. The owner stood in total confusion as he watched the chaos. Many of the customers took home dessert in the form of a small pouch when they left, leaving a generous "tip" for their additional "services."

As a group waiting to pick up their "desserts" looked up toward the ceiling, the last sight was the roof coming down, as the walls buckled outward. As it fell, life left the bodies buried under tons of timber and metal from the falling roof. The patrons tried crawling under tables for safety to no avail. All protection gave way as the remaining portions of the room and supporting columns crashed down on them. Some of the patrons appeared from under the rubble dazed, but alive and able to move. They must have been the lucky ones. Outside, the hail continued in baseball size as it buried everything it covered. Selective cars on the street were also leveled. Some cars had passengers cowering inside. The hail relentlessly pounded the buildings as huge chunks of brick and cement fell to the street. Friday night pot and coke parties were being disrupted throughout the area as the hail continued its onslaught on the neighborhood. In a short time, everything looked like a disaster area with demolished buildings, automobiles and bodies strewn throughout.

Across the street, and a block away, stood a hospital. The building was unscathed. To the casual observer, it might seem as though something very selective was taking place. The news events to come, would display the unexplained catastrophe. Some would explain it as a God event. Others would simply shake their heads in disbelief.

The Storage Warehouse

The cavernous warehouse stood in the midst of an old area of factories. It blended perfectly into the surrounding scene. Inside were trucks and SUVS of every variety. Some were being loaded, while others were depositing their contents into stacks of boxes, in various sections of the huge storage area. Numerous vans with the Muenstat Electric Company signs were evident.

The rain's pitter-patter sound began innocently. Inside, few listened as the noise began to increase in volume. Suddenly, windows began to blow in from the assault of hail as the rain turned to ice. The old roof structure quickly began to sag under the weight of the ice buildup. Those inside looked to each other with surprise looks on their faces. Some started to walk with quick strides toward their vehicles and the roar increased in volume. The roof continued to sag inward as engines started. Dealers were yelling to remain calm as trucks began to drive around seeking an exit. The heavy overhead doors remained closed as the walls began to bulge from the weight. Unable to open the doors, the trucks circled looking for a way out. There was none.

Suddenly the sound of the roaring wind reached the ears of those inside. The roof that was bent downward was lifted and blown away like a piece of straw. In its place, the relentless onslaught of large hail chunks began pounding the vehicles and people inside. Trucks began to crumple under the beating. The intense cascade of ice crystals struck men, who were scattering in all directions. They fell first to their knees then simply lay there unable to protect themselves. The continuing wall of hail began to fill the cavernous warehouse. It was pouring out the ten-foot high windows, burying everything in a casket of ice within the building.

Wherever the drug dealers converged, buildings and vehicles were being destroyed beyond recognition. Men and women who were working with the deliveries and drop offs were also paying the ultimate price.

Torreo Has a Close Call

Maria's brother Torreo went to the place where the young teen was pushing drugs near the school. Torreo had a previous discussion with the police, who decided not to pursue the drug pusher. He then had talked to the drug supplier, asking him to avoid the kids at the school. The conversations were of no help. The young drug seller in the alley, was a few blocks from the school and up to his daily routine. This time his supplier, whom Torreo didn't care for at all, was also there. They stood in the shadow of the stairway waiting for the kids from school to come by. Torreo and a few of his friends saw the two and began to walk toward him.

The hail began as a slight rain and continued to increase in intensity. Torreo and his friends took shelter under the stairway to avoid being struck as the rain turned to balls of hail. As they watched the size of the hail increased. Soon it was the size of golf balls. He and his friends stepped further back into the shadows. A door opened suddenly behind him, as one of the residents threw a bag of trash out the door toward the garbage can. The drug pushing boy and man jumped quickly to avoid being hit by the large bag. In doing so, they jumped out into the storm of hail. It pelted them painfully as he young boy tried to return to shelter. He never made it. As destruction took its toll around them, Torreo and his friends stood in disbelief. They stood untouched by the surrounding pounding of the hail. Even though they were out in the open, the deadly downfall of ice seemed directed away from them. The hail beat relentlessly on the young drug pusher and his supplier, as they crumpled to the ground. In a few moments, their bodies no longer felt the sting or the cold. They were entombed in a cube of ice. The last look on the young man's face was one of shock and pain. Life was over for them.

Someone Is in Trouble

Similar scenes were taking place all over the City and Suburbs. It seemed that drug dealers were absolute targets of the hail and rain. Escape was impossible, as bodies became solidified within blocks of ice. The drugs sealed with the bodies.

As events unfolded, a large canine was observed watching, as people and buildings were being destroyed. With each event, the large animal would turn and trot on further down the street as if selecting the next place, to be hit by the driving hail and ice.

Police were on the lookout for the Muenstat Electric Company vans. In Chicago and the suburbs, officers were stopping the vans and confiscating the cargoes of illicit drugs by the ton. Heroin, cocaine, marijuana and pills of every shape and color were being confiscated. Shock was the norm for most of the suburban police departments, who never saw such a haul of drugs in their departments' history.

In Chicago, the FBI worked in tandem with the police. They were rewarded for their effort. The number of arrests mounted throughout the day and night, minimized only by the toll taken by the unusual storm raging selectively through the area.

Those police who were cooperating in the drug trade, found themselves isolated in the pounding storm of hail. Many of their lives were extinguished, as if by some Divine will to exterminate the people supporting the drug trade.

Terry Shuman and Arnie Boman, the beat cops who were enjoying the favors of the dealers met a sudden end as their car was riddled with bullets in an alley. A couple of drug dealers had spread the word that the cops were feeding info to their senior officers. Nothing could have been further from the truth, but in the drug world, there were few second chances offered, if you became suspect. Crack houses, that weren't destroyed, were raided by police.

Stafford and Mayes

In the law office of Wanda Benefice, phones were ringing off the hook. Lori Boby was at her wit's end fielding the calls. Chelle Leriget never prepared her for this type of situation. If she had, no amount of money would have made her take the temporary position. She would be sure to tell her that at the first opportunity.

The volume of potential clients quickly exceeded her ability to maintain or memorize the names. Wanda Benefice was all over Lori. At one point, she pointed at Lori.

"You are a total incompetent."

That was about all that Lori Boby had to hear. She knew that the Benefice woman was cutthroat and had an ominous feeling, her job would quickly become unnecessary, when the day's events were over. She also believed she had sufficient information to put the law firm in court for years and out of business too if she chose to use it. She decided she would leave that decision to a later time and decided it was time to leave.

Waving to Wanda Benefice when she was able to catch her eye, she picked up her purse and started for the exit. Pointing to herself, she made the motion that was clearly understandable to the lawyer by taking her finger across her throat from side to side. She was leaving. Wanda Benefice saw the gesture and made a beeline for the secretary. Lori saw the woman approaching and continued her walk toward the office doors. As she reached the door, she felt the attorney grab her arm and forcefully twist her around to face her. Lori Boby felt a strange coldness on her skin. Wanda Benefice jerked her hand away quickly, after having felt the same thing.

"Where the hell are you going?" The lawyer exclaimed

"I'm going home. This place is way out of line with its policies, or there is definitely something the matter with the ethics of this law firm. In either case, I'm outta here."

"You get back to your desk and phone or you're fired," was the vehement reply from Wanda Benefice.

"Why would you want an incompetent working for you?" Lori Boby replied, not waiting for a response.

A bald headed man walked toward the two women, edging the secretary closer to the door, yet remaining between them.

"I'm outta here."

Lori Boby pulled on the door and walked out, much to the astonishment and surprise of the lawyer who was her boss.

The man turned and made a beeline for the elevators.

Lori entered and the doors closed as the elevator began its descent.

You Wouldn't Want to Be There

Wanda Benefice stood frozen in amazement. She didn't need to stand that way very long. As she turned, livid with rage at the secretary, the first of many twelve-foot high glass windows blew in showering glass over desks and everyone inside. Then, sounds of the wind began howling at tremendous intensity, sending papers flying and people scurrying for cover.

Other windows began to implode under the intense gusts of wind. Hail invaded the offices through the openings with intense volume and size. Everyone tried to find shelter.

The wind increased as desks, partitions and people began to fly out the open windows. Screams filled the air over the howling wind. The entire office was exposed to the elements and the result was disastrous.

Wanda Benefice jumped into a nearby office and opened the door to a closet. A place she would never be caught dead in otherwise. It was probably her undoing although there weren't many people left in the offices at the law firm. Most had already met their demise falling out of windows. A few survived by remaining in inside offices under desks.

As she stood crouched in the closet, the door was suddenly torn from its hinges by the howling wind's force. She was pelted relentlessly by large chunks of hail, as she tried to cover herself with the mops and a bucket used by the janitors. The last thing her eyes viewed was the onrushing wall of ice. It quickly encased her almost lifeless body in a cold tomb.

As Lori Boby left the elevator and walked toward the exit, she saw a torrential downpour of hail beating the concrete and surrounding buildings. The fire alarm was squawking also. Unbeknownst to her, the L tracks above hid the carnage that was erupting from the offices she had just left. The tracks were filled with office equipment and some of the bodies that were blown out of the now open areas of the 37th floor. Facades were quickly becoming frayed or swept away by the gusts of wind that blew the hail with critical force. She decided to wait until the storms intensity lessened. She quickly walked down the stairs of the Banker's building on Adams Street. She remembered the lounge and felt she could use a drink. Joe Rubenstein greeted her at the doorway, with a

"What's going on up there?"

"I think something happened up near the top of the building. We can't get out because of the storm, so here I am." Walking past the owner, she took a stool at the bar and ordered a dry martini with two olives. If it was her turn, she was going to go with two olives. She never had two olives before and thought of what she would say to Chelle tomorrow. At least the assignment was over.

Across the street in the shelter of a doorway, a large dog stood motionless. At another law office, a few blocks away, a similar situation was developing. The firm also made a lot of revenue defending drug-associated crimes. Winds and hail tore through that building just as it had the offices of Stafford and Mayes.

Numerous other law offices that served the drug industry were being destroyed throughout the city. In some cases, entire houses had been demolished, as the fury of the winds and hail seemed to find selected targets. Many of the targeted firms belonged to individual attorneys or small partnerships. It seemed that anyone in the law profession, associated with drugs, was paying a high price for their representation.

Lindsay Ballenger's druggie husband was with a friend in a back room bar on the near West Side. As they sat drinking and sniffing, a deafening noise filled the air. Patrons looked around to see the source of the disturbing sound. Before any had a chance to move, the front windows blew in with tremendous force and a wall of biting hail followed. The wall of hail angled obliquely, driven by the wind and acted as shrapnel, cutting through walls and bodies alike. The hail froze creating a disturbing scene of encased bodies in every state of movement. As the Ballenger man looked up, his body was cut to pieces by the force of the icy invasion.

Wherever groups of drug users gathered, the storm found them. The forces at work were unforgiving and gave no quarter. Cars were crushed and buildings literally pelted apart by the driving forces of wind and hail. In parts of the city, people with drugs were turned to statues of ice.

Lake Michigan
It was Friday on Lake Michigan and many boaters were out enjoying the last days of summer. The sky turned black as the temperature dipped 40 degrees without warning. What began as rain, turned quickly to a driving hail.

"Lazy Daize", the beautifully restored Boston Whaler was heading toward the Far Eastern shores of the lake to make its delivery. A few other smaller craft had teamed up with the boat as Captains waved in acknowledgement. As the smaller craft huddled around the boat, the crew began to extract tubes from the hold.

As the first boat moored alongside, a satchel filled with money, was handed to the crewmember. Payment for the goods delivered would make the captain and crew rich for a while. Each boat would do the same as they had many times before.

Suddenly, they felt the air filled with chilling cold. The sky that had been sunny just a half-hour before now consisted of towering dark cumulous clouds. Rain began to fall.

Soon, the rain turned to ice as small pebble sized pellets began to shower the boat decks. The captains were becoming concerned with the sudden change in weather. Some looked to the sky with worry, desiring to get their shipments and head for the safety of shore. The hail continued falling with increasing intensity. Soon, the icy balls that fell were becoming larger, landing with more devastating impact. Splinters began to shower from the teak deck of the Lazy Daize. The other boats felt the impact on their fiberglass hulls from the assault of hail. Soon the deckhands were scurrying for shelter. The captain of one of the larger cruisers turned about toward shore, hoping to avoid further damage to the large expensive craft.

As the cruiser turned, the wind increased dramatically, blowing it almost 30 degrees in a list to port. The captain fought to retain his grip on the wheel as the large boat leaned precipitously on its side. The listing increased as the unrelenting wind continued to push the top structure toward the water. Crewmembers jumped overboard in a vain effort to escape the inevitable capsizing to no avail.

Shock registered on the faces of the other boat captains. Whether large or small, there was no escape. The hail continued to pound the hulls of the boats and the crews operating them. The smaller boats began to come apart as the blood of the crewmembers that were being pelted senseless washed on the deck.

The hail continued to increase in size. Holes punctured the decks of the boats. One fiberglass craft disappeared as it was weighted down with tons of ice forming from the downpour. Other boats began to sink in the same fashion. The captain of the Boston Whaler watched in horror as his ship began to splinter apart under the torrent of ice driving from the sky. The Plexiglas windows shattered as shards drove themselves into the captain's face and chest. He expired before his body reached the deck. The other crewmembers were sharing the same fate. Some were becoming statues of ice while others sank to the deck senseless from the onslaught of hail.

A Coast Guard boat received distress calls from a number of boats on the lake. As the boat approached, the Guardsmen watched helplessly as the boats were pounded by the incessant torrent of hail and wind. The sturdy craft powered its way through the rising waves as its crew watched the destruction of the entire group of boats around the once proud Boston Whaler.

As the patrol boat neared the scene, the hail stopped and winds subsided. The captain and crew surveyed the area, as small pieces of flotsam littered the water. There were no signs of life. No life preservers or humans could be found. It was as if the boats and crews were dissolved into the water.

Closer to the shore, some of the party boats were enjoying their cruises. Alcohol and cocaine along with a variety of other drugs were freely distributed and consumed. As if directed by some unknown force, these craft seemed to become targets for scattered intense hailstorms. The devastating force of nature was so selective in nature that some boats right alongside some of the party boats were spared as some of the party boats were ripped apart and sank, or were destroyed.

The City

Throughout the city, fire alarms were sounding and frantic 911 calls were filling the telephone lines. As the fire department responded to each call, they expected to find houses ablaze from electrical and gas fires. To their surprise, there were no fires; just ice forms that included buildings, people and vehicles.

Stafford and Mayes

As firefighters entered the 37th floor offices of Stafford and Mayes, they witnessed carnage rarely observed before. People were frozen and encapsulated in ice and an uncanny silence that sounded thunderously tacit to the ear overwhelmed the area. The air was totally still. Nothing moved and none of the workers was alive on the 37th floor. Without warning, the sound of breaking glass was heard. Each of the firefighters looked around waiting for something unforeseen to happen.

As they watched in awe, a janitor walked out from one of the offices. His eyes were as large as saucers as he took in the strange scene. He was babbling something unintelligible and shaking. One of the firefighters quickly took off his heavy coat and draped it around the man. The man could only babble and stare with his eyes straight ahead. The firefighter took the man by the arm and sat him down on one of the few remaining desks. That seemed to calm the man somewhat. The staring eyes focused on the firefighter.

"What happened here?" The firefighter asked the still shaking man.

"You won't believe it, but I'll tell you anyway."

The man recounted the events to the inquiring group of firefighters. All remained silent listening to the man's description of events.

The West Side

The storm subsided as quickly as it had begun. Weather stations watched and announced disbelief as storm clouds dissipated from their screens. Temperatures quickly rose back to the normalcy just before the sudden storm.

Residents began to exit their houses to observe the results of the storm. Incredulously, there were people frozen in mid stride as well as standing still. Some revealed nothing. The placidity was eerie. Photographers scurried about capturing the scenes. Pictures could not tell the entire story, just the aftermath. In some places, children looked at their frozen parents in disbelief. They escaped the wrath in some unusual way.

Icy figures presented stilled testament to something incredible. Although the temperature was far above freezing, the figures remained concealed in their icy tombs. Nothing was melting. The picture throughout the Chicagoland area was surreal. Ice figures remained frozen in spite of the temperature. A child ran up to one of the frozen figures in the street. Curiosity rampant, the child touched the icy figure, as his mother shouted no. The figure exploded into a shower of powder at the child's touch. The mother stood transfixed and horrified. The child ran to the next figure with hand extended. The mother ran toward the child, screaming for him to get away. The child's hand touched the figure with the same result as the first one. As the mother reached the curious child, she pulled him away from the figures still standing in the street in their icy state. In shock, the boy's mother led him away from the horrible scene.

The question on everyone's mind was "what just happened?" The only answer that prevailed was "something awesome was at work." The final question on many minds however remained. "Is this God's work?"

Father Martin Ruby sat on the overstuffed gray couch observing the devastation wrought throughout the area on the television. The news was breaking into scheduled programming, as the enormity of the storm effect was realized. Eyewitness reports were beginning to pour in as excited newscasters were grasping for explanations and reactions. He wondered. Was this was the event that Maria was told about by the mysterious visitor?

Chelle Leriget was watching the events happening on the television. Thinking of Harmony Place, Chelle reached for the phone to make a call. Maria answered and Chelle expressed a sigh of relief. They agreed to get together later in the week. Chelle hung up the phone and smiled.

Maria earlier in the day, called all of her friends for a little impromptu celebration that she planned that afternoon.

Frank Bellini's cab approached Harmony Place where he planned to visit his friend Monica. A large dog suddenly loomed in front of the vehicle. It was Webster. The driver screeched to a halt avoiding damage to his car and the animal. In the back seat, Frank laughed with a cackle. He reached over to open the door and the large Black Lab jumped into the back seat. The driver looked back at the size of the animal and peed his pants. Frank and Webster's eyes met with keen understanding. A knowing, shared look expressed the future of fascinating adventures and accepted reliance on each other. Bellini patted Webster's head as it settled on the seat next to him.

The cab driver thought about telling his passenger that no pets were allowing in the vehicle, but looking at the large canine, thought better of saying anything.

Maria sat at the second floor window looking out upon the street below. She watched as her finger throbbed gently. The sliver was pulsing. Across the street, she witnessed a large dog climbing into a waiting car across the street. A smile broadened over the driver's face as he looked up at Maria.

Ellie Mulcahey, Jimmy Ennis, who was off duty, Sydney Anderson, Samantha and Randy Marsten stood at the next window witnessing the scene before them. They all looked at each other with doubt in their eyes as to what was happening.

Monica began to shake as her mind cleared. Her name wasn't Monica. It was Kelly Auxier, and she was a computer programmer, who designed programs and knew programming very well. She still didn't remember getting pregnant, who the father was, her family, and many other things. But her memory was returning.

She smiled as she entered the room carrying a sopping wet cardboard box. Silently, with a perplexed look, she held it out to Maria. Maria studied the inside of the box. The ice crystals had dissolved.

The television screen showed the magnitude of the damage, with the announcers offering the question, "Why?"

THE END

Made in the USA
Lexington, KY
11 April 2014